CHURCH
OF
MARVELS

CHURCH

OF

MARVELS

LESLIE PARRY

ecco

An Imprint of HarperCollins*Publishers*

CHURCH OF MARVELS. Copyright © 2015 by Leslie Parry. All rights reserved. Printed in the United States of America. No part of this book may be used or reproduced in any manner whatsoever without written permission except in the case of brief quotations embodied in critical articles and reviews. For information address HarperCollins Publishers, 195 Broadway, New York, NY 10007.

HarperCollins books may be purchased for educational, business, or sales promotional use. For information please e-mail the Special Markets Department at SPsales@harpercollins.com.

FIRST EDITION

Designed by Suet Yee Chong

Library of Congress Cataloging-in-Publication Data has been applied for.

ISBN 978-0-06-236755-6

15 16 17 18 19   OV/RRD   10 9 8 7 6 5 4 3 2 1

For my sister

In what distant deeps or skies
Burnt the fire of thine eyes?
On what wings dare he aspire?
What the hand, dare seize the fire?

—"The Tyger," William Blake

ACKNOWLEDGMENTS

Claudia Ballard, you are the hero of this tale. Thank you for believing so ardently in this book, and for your wisdom, insight, patience, and humor. Thank you to the team at Ecco, especially Megan Lynch, Lee Boudreaux, and Dan Halpern. I couldn't have asked for more incisive, clear-eyed, sensitive editors. Thanks to Elizabeth Sheinkman, Tracy Fisher, and the dedicated folks at WME; Jane Warren and Iris Tupholme at HarperCollins Canada; Lisa Highton and Federico Andornino at Two Roads. (And *grazie*, Federico, for helping me with the Italian phrases.) To everyone at the Iowa Writers' Workshop— my teachers, my peers, the staff—profound thanks. This book would not exist without you.

  This is a work of fiction, but I found inspiration in the writings of Nellie Bly, Herbert Asbury, and Earl Lind. I'm grateful to institutions like the New York Public Library, the New-York Historical Society, the Brooklyn Historical Society, and the Tenement Museum for further stoking my imagination. Thanks to Yaddo, the Vermont Studio Center, and the Kerouac Project—welcome shores on stormy seas.

Thank you to Adam Farabee, Melelani Satsuma, Zachary Mann, Sharon Smith, Dan Gomez, Jan Wesley, Virginia Parry, and Cris Capen for supporting this undertaking (and its roving author) at many vital turns. To my parents, Dai and Susie Parry, who were always ready with a word of encouragement, or a sing-along around the player piano. To my first reader, my sister Peanut: French martinis on me. To Florence Parry Heide and Suzanne Vidor Parry, who spent years listening to my stories, and regaling me with theirs: I wish you could hear this one. And to Joe Gerdeman, who was so certain for so many years: thank you for giving me a place to come home to.

PROLOGUE

I HAVEN'T BEEN ABLE TO SPEAK SINCE I WAS SEVENTEEN YEARS old. Some people believed that because of this I'd be able to keep a secret. They believed I could hear all manner of tales and confessions and repeat nothing. Perhaps they believe that if I cannot speak, I cannot listen or remember or even think for myself—that I am, in essence, invisible. That I will stay silent forever.

I'm afraid they are mistaken.

People who don't know any better assume I'm a casualty of the stage life I was born into: a stunt gone awry beneath the sideshow's gilded proscenium—mauled by a tiger, perhaps, or butchered by a sword that plunged so far down my throat I could kiss the hilt. But it's a bit more complicated than that. No sword I've ever swallowed has been sharp enough to cut. At worst, those blades (blunted by pumice stones in my dressing room after hours) tickle like a piece of straw.

When I first came to Mrs. Bloodworth's I knew nothing beyond the home I had left. I'd never been to the city before. I believed I had already seen the worst of the world, but of course I was wrong. I was just a scrappy tomboy from the seashore, my voice a blend of Mother's airy lilt and the peanut-cracking babel of the boardwalk. My mother was fearsome and beautiful, the impresario of the sideshow; she brought me and my sister up on sawdust, greasepaint, and applause. Her name—known throughout the music halls and traveling tent shows of America—was Friendship Willingbird Church. She was born to a clan of miners in Punxsutawney, Pennsylvania, but ran away from home when her older brother was killed at Antietam. She cut off her hair, joined the infantry, and saw her first battle at the age of fourteen. In the tent at night, she buried her face in the gunnysack pillow and wept bitterly thinking of him, hungry for revenge. A month later she was wounded. In the leaking hospital tent, a nurse cut open her uniform and discovered her secret. Before the surgeon could return, however, the nurse—not much older than Friendship herself—dug out the bullet, sewed up her thigh with a fiddle string, and sent her back to Punxsutawney in the dead of night.

But Friendship never made it home. Instead she traveled out to the great cities of the Middle West. She joined a troupe of actors and journeyed on to New York. She played town halls and hog fairs, bawdy houses, nickel parlors. She built her own theater at Coney Island—the Church of Marvels—and made a life for herself in a sideshow by the sea. It was the water she loved most, far away from the hills of Punxsutawney, from the black dust that fell like snow twelve months of the year. But she couldn't shake the coal mines entirely: she prized industriousness and made us work.

All great shows, she told me when I was little (and still learning to flex the tiny muscles in my esophagus), depend on the most ordinary objects. We can be a weary, cynical lot—we grow old and see only what suits us, and what is marvelous can often pass us by. A kitchen knife. A bulb of glass. A human body. That something so common should be so surprising—why, we forget it. We take it for granted. We assume that our sight is reliable, that our deeds are straightforward, that our words have one meaning. But life is uncommon and strange; it is full of intricacies and odd, confounding turns. So onstage we remind them just how extraordinary the ordinary can be. This, she said, is the tiger in the grass. It's the wonder that hides in plain sight, the secret life that flourishes just beyond the screen. For you are not showing them a hoax or a trick, just a new way of seeing what's already in front of them. *This,* she told me, *is your mark on the world. This is the story that you tell.*

But I was young. I mistook my talent for worldliness, my vanity for a more profound sensibility. It was only when I arrived in Manhattan that I saw myself as coarse and strange, a Brooklyn savage with a bag of swords and ill-suited for any other life. I had come to seek the help of Mrs. Bloodworth, and in her care I tried to forget my old life, the troubles that had ended a naïve and happy childhood.

But the real troubles had yet to begin.

I would stand beside her in that smoky, sepulchral office, the curtains drawn against the hot glare of July. I wore a benign smile on my face while other young women, pale and nervous, sat before her desk. They cried into handkerchiefs, fiddled with abalone combs nested in their hair, drew fans to their faces when they felt sick or faint. Mrs. Bloodworth kicked her heels up on the desk and sighed out smoke. She nodded her head and closed her eyes in sympathetic meditation while the young girls sang of their sorrows. Before I lost my voice I sat there too, sick with the smell of blooming flowers, listening to my secrets echo off the mahogany walls.

Many think now that I've disappeared for good. They might even believe I have died. I can see them huddled in their grim houses, ruffle-breasted and thin-lipped, rattling dice over a backgammon board, kissing their pretty children good night. They believe they are safe. They believe that all is past and that I'll hold my tongue. Sometimes I want to laugh and say, "Oh but I have!" I've stared at it in my own cupped hands, stiff and bloody and fuzzed with white, gruesomely curled as if around a scream.

At seventeen I crossed the river alone. I didn't know, when I departed, that in a few short months I would see the islands of New York—from Coney Island to Manhattan Island to the Island I shudder to name. Like the girls who came to Mrs. Bloodworth's, I believed my decision was singular and private; I didn't know that it would determine the fate of people I'd never met. The girls were frightened and alone, in need of a confessor. With a name such as mine, they believed me to be some sort of saint. But how could they know, as they trembled there at the desk, just how cruel the world could be, and I a willing part of it?

Let me say, this life is not the one I envisioned for myself. I remember the long-ago days when my mother would come up to me after a show, when I was tired and sweaty and sliding my swords into the rack. She'd pull me close and say, "My girl—how proud I am," and I would hug her and smell the hair oil melting down her neck, her gabardine coat trailing the musk of the tiger cage. There are times when I long to feel just something of that old life—the crunch of sand beneath my feet, the beads of salt in my hair, the sight of Brighton Beach at dusk. I think of my sister, who is still there. I always believed we'd be together—the two of us living in our house by the sea, playing duets on the old piano, ringing in the new century as fireworks showered from the sky. (1900—how far away it seemed to me then! and now only a breath away.) And thinking of this, of her alone, of what I have never been able to tell her—this is something I cannot bear.

But this story, in truth, is not about me. I am only a small part of it. I could try to forget it, perhaps. I could try to put it behind me. But sometimes I dream that I'll still return to the pageantry of the sideshow, hide myself beneath costumes and powder and paint, grow

willingly deaf amid the opiating roar of the audience and the bel-
low of the old brass band. It will be like the old days—when Mother
was ferocious and alive, before the Church of Marvels burned to the
sand. But how can I return now, having seen what I have seen? For
I've found that here in this city, the lights burn ever brighter, but they
cast the darkest shadows I know.

ONE

NEW YORK CITY, 1895

S YLVAN FOUND THE BABY ON A BALMY SUMMER NIGHT, WHEN
he was digging out the privies behind a tenement on Broome
Street. All night long the damp air had clung to his skin like a
fever, and now, with only a few blocks left before his shift ended, he
was huddled halfway inside a buckling stall, his vision blurring and
his arms growing numb. Beside him the other night-soilers, slope
backed and sweating in the privy doorways, bent and pushed and
hoisted and slung. They kept up a rhythm—shovels scraping at the
bricks, waste slapping in the buckets, mud sucking at their boots.

Sylvan was hunched over the pit, sifting through the mire, when
his shovel came up under something solid and heavy. He stopped and
squinted, but it was too dark to see anything. He gripped the handle
and watched the shovel head quiver up into the lamplight. Five pink
toes pearled above the falling slop, then a foot, then an ankle. Leaning in closer, he saw a small face, still as a mask, floating in the dark.

He drew up the shovel and shouted. He dropped to his knees,
closed his hands around the slick body, and, trembling, fell back on

his haunches. The head was limp and slippery in his palm, the hair like moss under his fingers.

The night-soiler next to him, a gaunt and graying man the others called No Bones, leaned his shovel against the open door of his privy and lifted his lantern. "What's it this time?" he asked. "Good one? Piece of china? What happened to that pitcher from last week—you keep it?"

Sylvan didn't answer. In his arms the baby was slack and still, lighter than the bucket he hauled across the yard and emptied into the barrels of the slop wagon. He unknotted the kerchief at his throat. In the dark he mopped the baby's lips and cheeks and the blue bulbs of its closed eyes.

No Bones took a small, curious step forward. The heady smell of kerosene and lime powder and sweat emanating from his clothes made Sylvan's nose sting and head pinch; he could taste it, burning, in the back of his throat.

"Lemme see there," the old man muttered, raising the lamp over his head. "Let's see what you brung up now."

Light fell across Sylvan's lap. For a moment neither man moved or breathed. The only sound that passed between them was the steady creak of the lantern.

"What is it? What'd he find?" came voices from across the yard.

No Bones turned his head and whispered hoarsely, "It's a baby—a white baby. Girl."

Sylvan stared at her. She was pale, with a small nose and a dimpled chin like a pat of butter someone had stuck their thumb in. Whorls of dark hair were greased against her scalp. Slowly and gently he drew her up to his chest.

The other night-soilers dropped their shovels and crowded around him. Their faces were grim and green in the swinging light of their lanterns.

"Looks like a Polack," someone said.

"No, a Scot—see the way the ears point up? That's a kelpie."

No Bones whispered, "Is it dead?"

Sylvan tried to nod but only managed to drop his chin. He had unearthed all sorts of things in the privies: coins, buttons, bottles of hair dye and bourbon, a set of grinning false teeth. But nothing even close to this. Night-soiling was summer work—he and the crew collected waste from the slums and delivered it to a fertilizer factory on the river, always hoping for a small treasure of their own. Back in his cellar on Ludlow Street, the walls were lined with things he'd smuggled home in the dark—loot all the way from Essex Street to Centre, from Canal up to Delancey. He knew it was foolish, but he kept hoping he might discover a gold watch chain, or an heirloom stone slipped from its tarnished, Old World bezel, some small fortune that would allow him to leave Ludlow Street forever. A ticket away from the sickness and noise, the nostrums hocked on street corners, the heavy-lidded undertakers who haunted the halls with their burlap and twine.

But now this. He hadn't held a child since Frankie.

Suddenly the baby's chest rose and shook. She mewled weakly. Sylvan's hand jumped back and hovered above her in the lantern light, his shadow whipping over her skin like smoke. He watched as she took a breath and opened her eyes. They were a dark, watery green.

The foreman pushed his way to the front. "Back to work," he ordered somberly. "To your posts—now."

The group of men disbanded, pulling at their beards, crushing their hats between their hands. The light disappeared with them, and Sylvan was left squatting alone by the privy with the baby breathing weakly in his arms.

Beside him Mr. Everjohn scraped the ground with his boot and sighed. "Let's see it."

Sylvan stood, wiping away the remaining dirt with his handkerchief.

Everjohn leaned in closer. A slug of tobacco jumped from one cheek to the other. "Christ," he whispered. "You see anything? Anyone here when you come up?"

Sylvan shook his head. "No, sir."

"Anyone seen you—or this"—he tilted his head toward the baby—"since?"

"Just the others."

The foreman pushed his hands into his pockets. He glanced warily around the yard, to the offal-stained gangway of the butcher shop, then up to the darkened windows of the tenement. "Goddammit," he hissed.

Sylvan took a deep breath. "There's the mission over on Hester," he said. "Convent runs an orphanage, too, over on Mulberry."

Mr. Everjohn turned back to him, grinding the tobacco between his teeth. "You know I can't keep it on my watch," he said. "Someone'll find it by dawn—take it there themselves." He slurped and spit. "Best for all of us if we leave it where it laid."

"She might need a nurse—"

"We've got the Bloody Gutter beat tonight—you know we can't be bringing a child through those streets."

"It's just another few blocks," Sylvan said, but he saw the look on the foreman's face and knew he should retreat before his shovel and bucket were taken from him and he was turned out into the street without the week's wages. At nineteen Sylvan was youngest on the crew, strong-limbed and quiet. Mr. Everjohn liked him well enough, but the other men were clannish and wary. Under their breaths they called him Dogboy. He'd been puzzled over and picked apart all his life—*the skin of a Gypsy, the hair of a Negro, the build of a German, the nose of a Jew*. He didn't belong to anyone. They stared at him with a kind of terrified wonder, as though he were a curiosity in a dime museum. One of his eyes was brown, so dark it nearly swallowed the pupil, and the other a pale, aqueous blue.

Sylvan looked down at the baby. He thought of the drunkards and gang boys, roosting in alleys and doorways from Mulberry clear out to the river, waiting in the warm night for someone, anyone, to cross them. And the night-soilers, a piecemeal crew of blacks and Irish, Slavs and Chinese, near-cripples and convicts and rye-pickled drifters, were a mark. He'd heard a story last summer about a night-soiler who tried to help two children find their way home. A gang of neighborhood men, believing he meant to kidnap them, clobbered him to the ground and tied him to the back of a wagon. Sylvan wondered if the children were there to see it, if they saw him die in the street, if they screamed because they couldn't understand why the man who'd taken their hands and helped them home was now being dragged through the dirt with his mouth open and eyes bulging like two boiled eggs from their sockets.

The foreman's tongue flicked up into his moustache, tobacco juice wetting the ends. "I'm not putting the boys in danger—not for some whore-trash's baby."

He put out his hand and rested it on the baby's head. Then, pulling away, he cleared his throat and said, "At least you dug it out. But we've just got one job to do—and you keep doing it, right?" He clanged his shovel against the ground and disappeared across the yard, down the narrow gangway to the street. "Gather up, gather up!"

Sylvan knelt down and placed the baby on the ground, far away from the butcher's barrels, which were filled with feathers and bones. He stroked her forehead to soothe her, then stood up and jammed his fists into his pockets. He willed his legs to move but they felt like wood. He watched as the folds of the knapsack sagged around her, exposing her naked body to the night air. He bent down and tucked her in again. When she pushed out her tiny fists and batted down the sides, he found the clasps and buckled the sack tightly across her chest. Her body arched and trembled. She opened her mouth and began to cry.

Sylvan felt his throat close and his nose prickle. He took his kerchief from his pocket and dropped it over her face, then grabbed his bucket and shovel and staggered down the gangway to the street, where the slop-wagon was waiting. The other soilers were resting on the curbside among ash heaps and garbage piles, their knapsacks open in their laps. They took draws from water canteens and shared slices of bread, chatted in loud whispers, but Sylvan could still hear the faint cry, raw and tuneless, coming from the yard.

He emptied his bucket over a barrel in the back of the wagon. There was nothing he could do, he told himself. Mr. Everjohn was right. By morning she'd be sleeping alongside a dozen other found-lings in the troughlike crib of the orphanage, nursing Tammany milk. Or some family from the tenement might take her in, raise her as their own. Or perhaps the person who'd left her behind would still come back for her.

Sylvan rubbed his eyes as if trying to make the image stick. Even through the stench of the slop-wagon, he could smell the blood and viscera from the butcher shop. He raised his eyes to the win-dows above. There could be fifty people living in that building, maybe a hundred. Who would have done such a thing? The baby wasn't just abandoned to the whims of the city streets—she hadn't been entrusted to another's care, or left in a well-traveled place to be discovered and rescued. Sylvan shivered though the night was hot and still. The baby, he knew, was meant to die.

"Broome to Orchard!" the foreman called from down the street, clanking his shovel head against the walk. "Orchard and Broome—step in, hey!"

The other men got to their feet, gathered and readied them-selves. Sylvan felt nauseous and light without the sack on his shoul-der, without the loot clinking and knocking against his hip. From the yard the wail seemed to come louder. Quietly he slipped out of the stretching, laughing knot of men and ran back down the gangway and into the yard. He stared, breathless, at the small bundle beneath him in the shadows. He knelt down and picked the kerchief off her face. The crying stopped. The baby stared up at him, her eyes glimmering in the darkness.

"Moving out, moving out," the foreman cried down the road.

Sylvan fell into the back of the line and marched down the street with the others, their caps shoved tight on their heads, their clothes black with grime. They began to sing, as they did every night when they felt their limbs tiring and eyelids pulsing. They moved together like one giant shadow, their bodies low-bent and taut, their shovels striking out a beat in the moonlit dust. The baby slept soundly against Sylvan's chest, rocking with each long stride. When the band turned on to the main thoroughfare, she kept so quiet that Sylvan thought no one could know she was hidden there among them, except for the brief moment she flashed into view, like a cap of foam on a dark wave, as they rolled through a nimbus of streetlight.

AT THE CORNER he slipped away. He fell back behind the others, hid the baby in his coat. He made his way blindly down the alley— stumbling past wheelbarrows and rabbit hutches, blinking back the drizzle in his eyes. They wouldn't notice he was gone, not right away—maybe not until they returned to the stable, where the men heeled off their overshoes and scrubbed themselves clean. It was near the end of the shift, he reminded himself. When he reported for work the next evening, he'd say he'd been jumped—maybe by a tough he'd once trounced in an underground match, a fellow fighter hungry for revenge. Would they believe him? Would they even be surprised? *Dogboy's a wild one. He has no people. He's got no tribe.*

He reached his home on Ludlow Street just before dawn. In the yard he placed the baby on a crate and peeled off his sticky shirt. Ducking his head under the spigot of water, he rubbed at his

curls and lathered his arms and face with a bar of soap. He gazed
at the girl through the falling water and realized he was shaking.
Perhaps he could put on Mr. Scarlatta's brown suit and take her to
the convent himself, where blind Sister Margaret taught orphans to
make shoelaces.

He filled a bucket with water and carried it down the steps to the
cellar door, cradling the baby in his arm. Inside they were greeted by
loot from the privies—the rusted door keys and clay pipes, the saucers
and belt buckles and green glass bottles—and the few things he'd foraged from the Scarlattas' glove shop upstairs: a good pair of mittens
for winter work, and the dummy hands that now lined the shelves like
drowning men reaching for air.

He warmed the water on the stove and poured it into an old
washtub. He set the tub, sloshing, on the floor and knelt down beside it. Other than the throaty purr of flies, the room was silent. As
he bathed the baby, he saw the red lattice of veins beneath her blu-
ing skin, the tiny claws of her fingernails. She was skinnier than he
thought she'd be, with puffed-up eyes and a trail of fuzz down her
back, like a wolf pup.

When she was dry, he fashioned a diaper from a rag, then
swaddled her in an old tablecloth. From the shelf he retrieved a glass
bottle with a rubber hose attached. It had been Frankie's. He'd been
born just over two years ago, heir to the glorious emporium his father
dreamed of building: Scarlatta and Son's Fine Gloves and Handwear.
Frankie, with his hammy legs pedaling through the air as if he were
riding an invisible bicycle. "An athlete, maybe!" his father cried,
tossing him up. "A strongman!"

Sylvan filled the bottle with milk, which he kept cool in a hole
in the floor. He pushed the nipple, gnawed and misshapen at the end
of the hose, between the baby's lips. She ate slowly, sluggishly, her
skin growing warm against his.

He tried to envision a woman creeping outside to the privy,

shaking out the folds of her skirt and watching the baby turn over into the shadows. He tried to picture her posture, the set of her face, the way her moist and terrified eyes would have widened in the dark. But as hard as he tried, the only person he could imagine standing there, stooped over the hole and feeling the bloodstained skirts fall back around her ankles, was a tall woman with wet cheeks and a white kerchief tied around her head. He didn't know if this woman was a dream or a memory, but it was an image that had been flickering in his mind for as long as he could remember. She was leaning against a wall, crying into her hands. Her shoulders were bunched and heaving, her cheeks half-shadowed and wet. He tried to recall what had happened, who she was—his mother; his nurse? Had she died? Had he wandered away from her in the street? Had she looked up from the fly-spotted flanks of meat at the butcher's and realized he was no longer at her knee? Or had she, for whatever reason, set him down in front of a Punch and Judy show in the market square, turned on her heel, and walked away?

He didn't remember much before the age of four or five, when he came to the Scarlattas'—just strange fragments of a life on the street, which clicked through his mind like the framed photographs in a Mutoscope machine. A few months ago he'd gone to a Mutoscope parlor up on the Bowery. He waded through the cavernous room amid a crush of eager, queuing people. It was so crowded he only had the chance to see one strip. He balanced himself on a rickety stool and pressed his face to the cool, slick metal of the eyepiece. He wound the crank slowly at first, so that the pages creaked forward. Each photograph was a little different from the next. Then he spun it so rapidly the pictures whizzed by and turned into a single movement: a boxer knocking out his opponent with a bloodthirsty windmill punch. Slow, then fast. Slow and fast. Separate photographs, then a living story. The boxer's arm poised behind him, his lips pulled back over his teeth. Then, a few flips later: the opponent's chin thrust in the air, the muscles in his neck twisting, a spray of saliva fanned against the black. Sylvan stood there, alternating between still life and moving image, until his nickel was up and the screen snapped to black.

His early life, he thought, was like the slow flip of photographs: the images were too sparse and sporadic to make any sense together, but each was so vivid that whenever one flickered to his mind, he was startled by its intensity. How could certain visions like these remain so luminous, and yet he had no recollection at all of what had come before or after? A whip-scarred pony, neighing in a leaky stable. A band of red-haired children chasing him down the riverbank, pelting him with rocks. Sleeping in a pile of damp, foul hay. Sleeping in a cedar box on the waterfront. The wood of that box, unpainted and cotton-soft under his cheek, and the sticky sap that dripped from it like a wound. (Mrs. Scarlatta later told him those were the paupers' coffins, waiting to be filled and taken over the river.) And then this, perhaps the most vivid of all: a square of white cotton blowing down a frosted alleyway. The shape of a hand had been cut out of it. It flapped in the breeze, the missing fingers waving him forward. It tumbled down a set of cellar stairs and landed at a door. He tried the latch, and it opened.

The day Mr. Scarlatta found him hiding in the Ludlow Street cellar, he brought him upstairs to the family's apartment and crowed, "Look, a stowaway!" Sylvan had heard Mr. Scarlatta recount the story over countless suppers, damp eyes alight with wonder as if seeing it for the first time: "I'd gone down, you see," he'd begin, rolling his hands in the air as if to coax the story into motion. "A cold, cold morning. There was nothing down there, just a little room of things nobody wanted anymore, not even robbers!" He was proud of the fact he could afford to own things he didn't use. Some things had come with him and Mrs. Scarlatta from across the sea, and now they had the dignity of occupying their own quarters, too, rather than being turned into firewood for beggars and vagrants. "What I was even looking for that morning—how can I remember?" he'd chuckle, tugging at his whiskers. "But what I should come upon! I go inside—and! Like a little elf had been there. Everything was nice on the shelves! The floor was swept. And this little boy, he was rolled up in a yard of cotton, fast asleep. I was astonished. This little elf"—he lowered his hand to his waist—"just this high, and how did he do all of it?"

Sylvan had been sick and delirious when the Scarlattas found him. For days he slept on a makeshift bed in their apartment—three uneven chairs pushed together—next to a pair of sewing machines. He lay wrapped in that same yard of cotton, shivering and hot, while the treadles tamped out a rhythm beside him, while knitting needles *tsk*ed from unseen hands. Once in a while he'd open his eyes and see the flash of scissors, hear the whish of a skirt. Sometimes a hand would slide under his neck and roll his head forward, bringing a saucer of broth to his lips.

As he grew stronger, Mrs. Scarlatta asked him where his mother might be. Sylvan had answered quite plainly that he didn't have one. *She's dead then?* No. *She's left you?* No. *You've run off then, haven't you?* Sylvan, confused, said no once again. When he was able to sit up and move about, she gave him a pair of old shoes, a mended coat, and a polished penny. If he went up the street and bought himself a new set of laces from the convent, she said, he could have a sweet roll when he returned. But the prospect of being out on the snowy street again paralyzed him; he only stared at the penny, red as a burn in his palm. When Mrs. Scarlatta nudged him toward the door, he tried to carry the stained yard of cotton with him, whimpering and clinging, getting tangled up in its train. Finally she took a pair of scissors and cut away the corner. She tucked the square in his pocket, next to the penny. *There—just if you get scared—but you won't, will you?*

The cotton, which he had found in a scrap heap in the cellar, had come from a mill in Connecticut. *Sylvan & Threadgill,* Mr. Scarlatta explained as he rubbed his fingers against the grain—*it makes for good church gloves, see?* And so this was how Sylvan Threadgill—collective son of the East Side winter, a glove's carefully scissored outline, and an unlatched basement door—came to Ludlow Street.

After this, the images in Sylvan's memory came quicker and easier; they joined together in a smooth, whirring story, one he recognized. Mr. Scarlatta kept him clothed and fed in return for daily chores: mopping the stairs, replacing cones of newspaper in the privies, shoveling out the effluent that flooded the yard from the street, washing soot from the windows with a cold wadded rag. He hauled buckets of water up to the tenants, plugged cracks in the walls and floors, brushed ice from the walk in the winters, polished the banister until it gleamed. He made a room for himself in the cellar: sewing his own pillow and stuffing it with newspaper, teaching himself to read those same newspapers, stacked in the corner for kindling; shoveling coal and fixing the stove, boiling his own coffee in a small tin can.

Now the sunlight crept into the cellar, gilding the grime on the high, narrow panes. The baby coughed wetly, rolled her head away. He tried to picture her in the convent's home for girls: marching in single file under the milky eyes of Sister Margaret, breaking the stale bread that had been donated by parishioners. A life of answering to a false name like Agnes or Claire, pretending to be some other girl in an ill-fitting dress, waiting to emerge from the gloomy, floating world that separated the child she was born as and the free woman she'd become.

Her eyes fluttered open, staring wetly at nothing. *A dogboy brought you in when you were no more than a babe,* one of the sisters would say. *And that's all I can tell you.*

Sylvan knew he would never be able to pass the clapboard wing of the convent, where the orphaned and abandoned girls lived, without craning his neck and imagining what had become of her. He couldn't see those girls marching down the street—with their powdery complexions and nunlike pinafores and modestly parted hair—without wondering which of them she was. And so she, too, looking for a bearded man in a wrinkled brown suit, would turn her head as they passed on the street. It would be a moment of frightened curiosity when their eyes met: a tremor of recognition, an ache so hollow and lonely in their stomachs that it made them feel faint. They'd find themselves unable to speak, and later, when they turned to look back into the crowd, the apparition would be gone and they'd wonder if they had even seen each other at all.

TWO

WHENEVER SHE WAS SPINNING ON THE WHEEL OF DEATH, Odile tried to focus on one simple and particular thing, like the smell of spun sugar, or the melancholy wheeze of a boardwalk accordion. If her eyes were open, she trained them on Mack's glinting watch fob while the colors of Coney Island whirled around her. It was a weird calm, when the clamor of the crowd seemed to dull to a whisper and she felt completely still, as if she and the fob were fixed in space, and it was the world that spun madly around them. But today she was having trouble. Her eyes darted through the crowd; her arms strained against their strappings. She felt dizzy and sick. With each revolution of the Wheel, the blood rushed to her head, and so did thoughts of her sister's letter.

Belle had left home three months ago, in the spring, not long after their mother died. Friendship Willingbird Church, the grand dame of Coney Island, the fabled Tiger Queen of the sideshow, a woman who had survived so much (a Rebel's bullet, falls from a trapeze, animal bites, and sword slashes) that to have her die so close to home—in a fire, in the very theater that she built—remained unthinkable. Odile still expected to see her in the crowd, swinging her fist to the beat of the cornet, gesturing for her daughter to *keep that chin up*. She still expected to see Belle every time she walked home after a show—sitting there on the porch railing, smoking a cigarette, her mane of hair loose and wild in the twilight. But Belle was gone now to Manhattan, without explanation or apology. After ten weeks of waiting for a letter, a word—nearly three months of fury and despair—Odile had begun to think the worst. But that morning the postman had left an envelope on the front porch, next to the brass elephant she rubbed for luck every day before the show began. Odile had torn it open as she hurried down to the boardwalk.

> *Odile, I hardly know what to say. I'm sorry for everything. Please don't be angry with me—I know you must be, and it breaks my heart. I have started this letter so many times, and yet I still cannot summon the words I need. I think of you every minute of the day, and of Mother. I wonder where she is—heaven, yes, but where is that? The sky itself? The ether and stars? Sometimes I imagine it looks like the Church of Marvels, with painted clouds lowered down from the rafters, and glitter fizzing in the air. Sometimes I imagine it is quieter, an undersea cave. I picture her there sometimes, a floating mermaid with a seaweed harp, and the tigers have fins. Then I realize I've been sitting too long in the hothouse, staring at the flowers, and the rain is coming down heavy on the glass.*
>
> *It is hard for me to sleep—sometimes I don't know what is real and what is imagined. I'm writing this sometime in the night. Who guides my hand across this page, I wonder? Is it I, alert and sound? Is it my dreaming self, compelled to find you in the dark? Is it another spirit? I cannot say. You, dear sister, have always been the brave one, the good one, the strongest of all. Not I. And yet you are me and I am you, and I believe that courage must reside in me, too, though I have yet to find it.*

I'm sorry if I was ever short with you, or impatient, or didn't listen when you tried to confide in me. If for some reason this is the last letter I should write to you, please know that I love you. And you must believe, no matter what, that you are where you belong.

Your Sister

The crowd shrieked and gasped as blades zinged through the air and lodged, humming, next to her ears and above her shoulders. They protested gleefully as Mack snapped on his sequined blindfold and turned his back.

Odile squeezed her eyes shut. The routine was unbearable today. Each thud of the blade, each beery pant of the crowd made her tense. Her fists curled against the leather cuffs. Even the knives seemed to be coming slower. They didn't sound right when they struck. Loose, sloppy, they rattled in their grooves. Usually they were thrown so powerfully, so precisely, that they sank into the wood as if it were a wedge of butter. She opened her eyes and watched the ash-blue proscenium flip over. A sea of gaping mouths rose into the air. She felt her insides slosh from one side of her body to the other. A blade plunged into the wheel half an inch above her head, pinning her back by the hair. Somewhere in the front row a woman screamed and fainted.

"Watch the pretty lady go 'round and 'round, 'round and 'round!" shouted the dwarf in the otterskin hat.

Odile swallowed the bile rising in her throat. If Belle were still at home, she'd be headlining. She'd be the draw. Isabelle Church, the Coney Island Shape Shifter—her twin sister and their mother's protégée. At seventeen, Belle could swallow longer swords than most men. She could twist her body into impossible shapes. She could stand on top of a piano, bend over backward, and play a ragtime melody upside down. She was daring and mysterious and utterly unafraid—the audience loved her.

At first glance the twins looked alike—they were both freckled and hazel-eyed, with thick blond hair and the snub nose of a second-rate chorus girl. But that was where the similarities ended. Unlike Belle, with her lithe and pliant acrobat's body, Odile had a permanent crook in her neck and a slight curve to her spine. As a girl she'd been made to wear a brace, a horrible thing like a metal corset, with a tin collar that trumpeted up her neck and flared beneath her chin. She looked like some kind of Elizabethan monster, clanking down the boardwalk in the ocean fog. *Croc!* the other children teased as she herky-jerked her way down the street. *Croc-Croc-Croc-Odile!* At night she would cry as her mother unbuckled the brace and put it away, as she rubbed eucalyptus cream over the bruises and welts left behind. Her body looked as though it had been gone over with a pie crimper. Why was she different?

It's just the way you were born, their mother said. It's the same thing she said about the marks on their scalps. Odile and Belle each had a bald spot, a crescent of shimmery white skin behind her ear—Belle's was on the left side of her head; Odile's was on the right. *They're birthmarks,* her mother would say. *You're unique.* Unique! Mother said the same thing about Georgette, the dancer born with four legs. Or *singular,* which is how she described Aldovar, the show's half-man-half-woman, who had died that day in the fire, too.

For most of her life Odile had watched the show from beyond the footlights. As a child her posture had made contorting and sword swallowing impossible to master. Her lopsided lungs kept her from much exercise at all. (The only thing she had ever been allowed to practice—between shows, in the alleyway behind the theater—was knife throwing. The doctor had thought it might help to stretch her muscles, relieve her back. So occasionally Mack would carry out a corkboard and a quiver of his favorite knives and try to teach her. But her aim was terrible, always off—she keeled too far to the left, and before long the side of the theater was flecked with pits and grooves.) When the brace came off for good last year—thrown with no small bit of ceremony into the ocean—Odile was given a small role at last: the angel in Belle's Daring Devil routine. There, high on a trapeze above the Church of Marvels—a theater-in-the-round, with a floor of sand—Odile's sweaty hands grappled the rope. Her heart struggled against her powdered chest. She descended from the cool rafters into the stinging light, wearing a halo and a pair of paper wings. Beneath her, Belle, in horns and a red silk dress, danced and leaped and twisted her body into knots. Odile's job was to hurl three heavenly thunderbolts, all of which Belle caught between her toes and promptly dipped down her throat. Afterward Odile was cranked back up to the rafters, where she watched the rest of the show beside the noosed sandbags, which swung around her head like the great weights of a clock.

Now the knives were hitting so close to her skin she could feel cold air shaking off the metal. Above the cries of the audience she heard Mack lurch and grunt. His feet didn't seem to land right— the floorboards, which usually echoed his steps so musically, now groaned, overstressed. Odile drew a breath and tried to concentrate. *You're making him nervous!* she scolded herself. In the crowd she saw a white hat rolling above the dirty, black-felted bowlers. It belonged to Mr. Guilfoyle, who had taken over the sideshow after the Church of Marvels burned. He'd come off the traveling circuit, but unlike Mother he spent most of the time in his office, eating nougat candies and sweating over pamphlets, writing letters to showpeople he'd known out west and cajoling them to come to Coney Island. Why, of all days, did he have to be here?

"Step up and see her survive the Blind Man's Bluff!" hollered the dwarf. "Eleven knives and not a drop of blood!"

Whenever Odile got nervous, her fingers would creep up into her hair and rub at the smooth, silky mark, as if it were a charm or a rune. But now her hands were trapped, her ankles cuffed. She felt her whole body shiver and buck. The letter sounded so melancholy and despairing—not like her sister at all. *If for some reason this is the last letter I should write to you*—what did that even mean? Was she feverish? Ill? A hothouse, of all things—isn't that where consumptives lay on wheeled chaises, languishing under ferns?

She thought of how restless and aloof her sister had been in the weeks after Mother died, when all Odile had wanted was someone to cry with, even as she rose early and set to work at the kitchen table, writing letters and settling accounts. Belle had stayed up late into the night in their mother's room, leafing through her things, even after Odile had snuffed the candles and gone to bed. One morning there was simply a note left on the kitchen table: *I need a change for a while—you understand, my dear—so I've gone to Manhattan. Perhaps I will find some fortune there. I promise to write.* When Odile asked Mr. Aggis at the post office if Belle had sent or received any letters recently, he recalled only one to Manhattan—an address someplace on Doyers Street. He assumed it was a response to one of the many letters the girls had received—sympathy and prayers for their mother from all over the country.

Afterward Odile had searched through Belle's wardrobe and dresser, hoping for something more, an explanation. But the drawers were jumbled with everyday litter—paper valentines and trolley tokens, lozenges of beeswax and throat balm. Odile was outraged and bereft—she couldn't begin to grieve another, especially when there was so much left to be done. So she threw herself into a mania of arithmetic: tending to Mother's outstanding affairs, calculating expenses and balancing the books, practicing with Mack for Mr. Guilfoyle's show. When her sister didn't write, Odile convinced herself it was because Belle was busy—she must have found a role on

the vaudeville stages of Manhattan. Still, Odile kept the house ready
for her, listened for the creak of floorboards in the night. When she
couldn't sleep, she turned and faced the empty bed beside her. She
gazed at the faded quilt Mother had made for them when they were
young: a dozen tiger faces stitched from scraps of felt, with yarn
whiskers and button eyes. She thought of how, as little girls, she and
Belle would sit by the fireplace at night, each with a sleeping cub
in their laps, and listen to Mother recite poems from an old book:
Tyger! Tyger! burning bright . . . In the forests of the night. She remembered, after the shows, putting her hands through the bars of
the cage and feeling their great rough tongues roll between her fingers. But these days, when the sun dimmed outside and the arbor
of white lights crackled on, the quilted faces seemed to leer at her
savagely, their green button eyes shining in the electric wonder of
Surf Avenue.

Then—it happened so fast that at first she didn't think it happened at all. It was like coming up from underwater: the noise of the
crowd roaring over her, her body arching against the wheel as she
gasped for breath. A pain shot through her knee, icy and stinging.
She didn't wince, or wiggle, or throw herself back against the boards.
If she reacted, the crowd would, too. So she continued to spin, her
body rigid against the wheel, the accident undetected, the blade bur-
rowing deeper into the gash with each rotation.

There were cries of relief and crescendoing applause as Mack
brought the Wheel to a stop. Odile lowered her eyes as discreetly as
possible. She hadn't been stabbed, just sliced. The knife had come
in at an angle, grazed her right above the knee. Mack unstrapped her
ankles and wrists and helped her down from the wheel, his smile
growing hard and terrified when he saw the carved skin. As she
stepped forward, her stocking ripped, and hot blood started to dribble down her calf. Still, she hobbled to the edge of the stage and took
two quick bows while smiling assuredly at the audience. Everyone

looked deformed, as if she were seeing them through the bottom of a drinking glass. "Ladies and gentlemen," roared the dwarf in the otterskin hat, "the amazing Mr. Mackintosh and his lovely assistant, Miss Odile-on-the-Wheel!"

Another bow, and as the whispers started up in the front row, patrons leaning in and pointing, she hurried off the stage, limping and grasping Mack's arm for support. She collapsed in the wings. A stagehand rushed up with a fresh strip of linen and a flask of rum. While he washed and bandaged the wound, she took a few nips and looked around for Mack. She wanted to run after him, tell him it had been a mistake, an accident, she wasn't concentrating the way she should have been. But all she could do was sit there, weak and shaky, with a single line running around in her head.

You are me and I am you.

BELLE COULD BE HOTHEADED at times, too sensitive. She was painfully meticulous about each stunt in her act—she punished herself when she didn't master them, and yet refused to believe others when they told her she had. How many times had Odile cleaned up flung powder or a smashed bottle of ginger beer in the dressing room afterward, or lain awake at night while her sister brooded in the bed beside her? *Your sister is prone to flights of passion,* Mother explained, as if it were some kind of cross for them to nobly bear. *But sometimes I feel that way too!* Odile wanted to say. But she knew that in herself, any show of emotion would be viewed as something sickly, inferior—self-pity, perhaps; the mark of a weak constitution. But in Belle it wasn't shameful, or even a flaw. It was some kind of artistic right.

One day when they were girls they snuck off to the beach with Aldovar and Georgette. They were only ten or eleven years old at the time, and Belle had just started her sword-swallowing lessons. They were supposed to be at the theater, helping Mother strike the set, but it was too beautiful out, and they were giddy and restless in the heat. Odile sat alone on the beach while the others ran down to the surf. She watched as Belle and Georgette galloped through the waves, tottering under seaweed headdresses, rolling their bloomers to their thighs. Georgette, who had four legs, wore two sets of bloomers that Mother had stitched together for her. She ran on her outer legs, while the inner ones dangled between, shrunken and spindly, kicking up spray from the surface of the water like the paddles of a steamboat wheel. Aldovar, half-girl and half-boy, waded through the shallows, pausing now and again to pick up a pebble, or jot something down in a small diary. Odile suspected him of being a poet. Onstage his costume was a wedding gown stitched to a tuxedo, but away from the lights, down at the shore, he always wore a gray shirt and plain tailored slacks, nothing fussy. His hair, which he kept long on one side, was braided and coiled beneath a houndstooth derby cap. Without his stage makeup—rouge on one side, a penciled moustache on the other—his face was heart-shaped and fine-boned, like a pretty boy's or a dapper girl's. *I am lucky to have two spirits,* he always said. *Most in this life only have one.*

Odile sat alone under a yellow umbrella, guarding the lunchpails, the boots, Belle's dagger in its leather sheath. She was drinking a bottle of sarsaparilla and humming an old show tune when a shadow fell over her—someone stood above her, hissing and snickering, blotting out the sun. She couldn't see his face, just the sunlight glowing through his grimy ears. *Croc!* he laughed—a terrible, wheezy sound, like a balloon losing air. *Croc, Croc!* he said again. He was barefoot, smelling faintly of boiled wash and chicken dumplings. With a snicker, he reeled back and kicked sand in her face. She felt it clump in her mouth, burn her eyes. She coughed, spit, blinked frantically, cried something in a voice she didn't recognize. And then she saw through her tears—just beyond the boy's shoulders—her sister, charging up out of the water. As he reeled back again, Belle jumped on top of him and wrestled him down to the ground. Aldovar and Georgette followed her—they held down the boy's arms and legs while Belle grabbed the dagger from its sheath. Her eyes glittered as she stood there above him, as she lifted the blade high above her head. She brought it down suddenly, with a whoop. The boy thrashed and screamed. Odile saw his little toe roll away in the sand.

Then, just as quickly as they'd pinned him down, Belle and the others let him go. He scrambled away down the beach, tripping and falling, too scared to look back.

The toe lay between them, in the frilled shadow of the umbrella. For a moment the sisters regarded it solemnly, as if they were supposed to eulogize it somehow. Then Belle picked it up and flung it like a peanut into the waves.

It was then that Odile caught sight of their mother marching across the beach, resplendent in her face paint, her heels sinking into the sand. She wanted to turn around and escape, but there was no way; she couldn't run fast enough in her brace. Belle just stood there with her back to the sea, sand caked into her knuckles and hair, and faced their mother, waiting.

Then Mother was standing over them, pointing to the blood on the dagger: *What is that? What did you do?*

She was radiant with anger. She'd only come to find them because they were late for supper—they hadn't met her at the stage door like they'd promised. She'd had to close up the theater and scrub down the tiger pens by herself. And now here was her daughter, slick with seawater and blood, holding the dagger in her tiny fist. Mother sent Aldovar and Georgette back to the boardinghouse, then dragged the girls home by the hands as if they were babies. Belle was left out on the porch to eat alone—too filthy and savage to step inside, Mother said; why, she'd sooner let the tigers say grace at their table. Belle began to cry, but Mother shut the door and latched it anyway. Later, after a silent meal with no dessert, Odile pressed her head to the darkened window and saw her sister out on the steps with a plate on her knees, crying and crying, while the waves crashed against the shore.

Belle could be that way, too. Provoked, she lashed out, and abandoned, she broke.

BACKSTAGE IT WAS STICKY-HOT and crowded, all elbows and chatter and sweat. Odile pushed her way down the hall, hopping on one leg toward the dressing-room door. This theater was nothing like her mother's—it was narrow and shambling, a former sauerkraut house still reeking of grease, which Mr. Guilfoyle had won in a card game after plying the diminutive, frog-eyed owner with a few rounds of Irish punch. Every day Odile had to do battle with the other players in the dressing room—grubby fingers digging into jars of cold cream, costumes getting shed and trampled underfoot. Today, thankfully, it was too hot for anyone to linger, so she sat down at the mirror alone and lifted the tray of her makeup box.

Belle's letter was tucked inside—just a single sheet of paper, so delicate it was nearly translucent. There was no return address, no letterhead, no mention of her life in Manhattan. No Doyers Street, no theater name—nothing that gave a clue as to where she might be. Why had she waited so long to write? And why, if she were so downhearted, wouldn't she simply come home, where she was loved and safe? Odile pressed her nose to the paper but couldn't smell anything beyond the briny musk of the dressing room. *You are me and I am you.* When they were girls they used to hold their index fingers, hooked like crescent moons, up in the air and try to divine each other's thoughts. After a while—when they were scared or upset, when they were banished to opposite ends of the room for misbehaving, when they saw each other on the boardwalk from a distance too far to speak—it became their own private signal, a flash of alliance and sympathy. Sometimes at night Odile would still reach out toward the empty bed, her finger curled in the dark, and wonder if somewhere her sister could read her mind.

"A little heads-up," came a voice over her shoulder. Quickly she folded up the letter and slid it back into the box.

Leland the dwarf stood behind her, blotting his face with a handkerchief. "Guilfoyle's got a bug up his britches," he said. "How's the boo-boo?"

"Pretty ugly." She turned her knee to the light. The bandage was already rusty with blood.

Georgette, still damp from the stage lights, trailed in and sat down beside her, crossing both pairs of legs. "What happened, pet?" she whispered. Her hand, soft and slender as a little girl's, fluttered up Odile's neck and leafed gently through her hair. "Is it your back again?"

"No!" Odile said, a little too sharply. "I'm fine. Really—it's practically a paper cut."

She was grateful that Georgette laughed and began gossiping about something else—the woman in the audience who'd screamed and fainted, and who was now crying into her handkerchief outside the theater, proclaiming this entire place *the devil's playground*. The Daring Devil's, Odile thought.

She slipped behind the screen and peeled off her beaded costume. Half of her wanted to tell Leland and Georgette about the letter, but she didn't know quite what to say. She hadn't talked to anyone about Mother or Belle, not in months. After the fire Belle had grown so quiet and withdrawn. Everyone must have been whispering about it all along: what poor work Odile was doing, looking after her! When Belle left, Odile began to notice that people lowered their eyes—they turned their heads from her and looked bashfully away. If they saw her coming down the boardwalk, they pretended to study their pocket watch, the menu at the frankfurter stand, a tangle of kites in the sky. When she came home at night, there would be food on her porch—gravies and aspics in stained crockery, soaking under damp squares of cheesecloth—but no one was there to welcome her or share her table. She dumped the food over the railing in the back. Bone-thin dogs, no longer scared away by the scent of tigers, waited for her in the wide sandy alleyway, wagging their tails and howling.

She knew people felt nervous, unsure of what to say to her, but it seemed as if they feared contagion. She wouldn't be surprised if they choked into their handkerchiefs as they passed her on the street—as if her bad luck, a pungent curse, steamed from her body like a vapor. Whenever she caught them looking at her sideways, she knew what they must be thinking: the last of the Coney Island Churches, Belle's sister and Friendly's child, the reedy echo of a thunderous sideshow song. It puzzled them all, perhaps, to see her standing alone on the porch of the house on Surf Avenue—seventeen years old, an orphan, wearing a faded fur coat and flexing a tiger switch in her hands.

But now. *Odile-on-the-Wheel.*

She straightened her shirtwaist and buttoned up her skirt. When she emerged from behind the screen, she saw Mack sitting at the mirror, slouched over in his slacks and undershirt. Birdie the glass eater stood behind him, massaging his shoulders and neck with camphor oil. Mack's own hands lay motionless beside him, sheathed in gloves filled with hot cream. He looked up at Odile, his face mottled pink with anguish.

Before she could say anything, however, there was a knock on the door and Guilfoyle blew in, his white cape flapping behind him, powder lifting from his sculpted beard. He glowered at Georgette, who sat painting the toenails on her shrunken feet. (He never had the chance to badger Aldovar, who had run into the burning theater after their mother, and who had died, they were told, from the smoke. *And for what?* Odile thought. *So this huckster could make a few extra pennies? So my mother's good name could be smeared?)* Aldovar and Georgette had been orphaned and raised by the sideshow, where their exotic bodies drew hundreds of awe-struck men and fainting women every week. Her mother had always looked after them, but Guilfoyle didn't like the idea of freaks lark-ing about onstage, where people couldn't get a good look at their grotesqueries. He wanted them up close, in pens and cages, close enough to spit on. Most of his money had been made off barnyard shows out west, where he charged people fifteen cents to see what he promised was a real satyr captured from the verdant stretches of Shangri-La. Then he pulled back the curtain to reveal a strongman wearing furry trousers that had been stitched to the cheap effigy of a goat's body. Before anyone could squint for a better look, Guil-foyle would whisk the curtain back and announce in the wise, sor-rowful voice of a doctor delivering bad news, that the satyr, should he set sight on a human for more than a few seconds, would likely turn them to stone.

Now he glared at them. "What the hell was that?"

Mack lifted his eyes to the ceiling and bit his bottom lip. His cheeks were quivering. "I've never missed," he said, his voice filled with a tremendous awe. "Not once. Not even in rehearsal, with the wax dummies."

Guilfoyle turned to Odile. "What were you doing, wriggling around like a worm up there?"

"Take it easy," Georgette said, fanning her toes with a newspa-per. "She was a champ."

"My knee's fine, actually," Odile said. "Thank you for your concern—"

But even as she said it, she could see Guilfoyle's lids begin to flutter and close. He had a habit of squinching his eyes shut in con-versation, as if it any voice but his own put him instantly to sleep.

"What if it had been your gut?" he interrupted. "Or your face? The show'd be over for good! We can't have something like that, you understand me? Not after the fire."

She stammered for a moment, hot-faced and flabbergasted, unable to think of a coherent reply. She couldn't believe he used the word *we,* as if he'd been there that day to see the sky grow black, to smell the burning wood. As if the loss of Friendship Willingbird Church—and the life that she'd built here—had somehow been his.

"Why don't we do another knife bit?" he said. "Not throwing, which ain't so new anymore. Last year I saw a real lulu in Virginia City. The girl gets into a box and the fella brings out these big Oriental swords, right?" He drew an imaginary weapon and sliced the air in front of him. "He cuts off her arms and legs—"

"You mean it's fake," Odile said. She couldn't imagine Mack fumbling with a set of tin replicas, driving them into mirrored slots while she lay sweating in a box, a look of exaggerated consternation on her face. "Nothing was ever fake at the Church of Marvels, Mr. Guilfoyle. My mother always made that very clear. In fact, I wager she'd be the first to say that there's nothing like a little blood to whet an audience's appetite. It lets them know it's real." *The tiger in the grass.* As much as the audience might speculate or accuse, there was nothing false about Georgette's legs, or the way Belle had contorted her body and swallowed a sword, or how Birdie bit into a bulb of glass as if it were an apple. That was what her mother wanted: no satyrs or mermaids or peepshow shams, but everything genuine and exotic, a catalogue of real human marvels.

Guilfoyle tugged at the fringe on his gloves. "I've told you before—"

"And I've told *you*: if the danger's not real, the audience knows. Who wants to watch something so safe? There's no suspense in it! I assure you, Mr. Guilfoyle, if *I* were sitting in the audience—"

"The suspense is in the *presentation*." He drew the word out slowly, rolling it around on his tongue. "Good lord, all you have to do is hold still and smile pretty! How hard can that be?"

Odile felt her face turning red. "If they want to see a magic show or a stupid mime act, they can go to Mr. Mephisto's tent for a nickel."

"Don't tell me how to do my job, all right?" Guilfoyle blew air up into his moustache, sending a cloud of powder through the air. "Of course they want to see danger—*of course* they want a little blood. But what, I ask you, is more grisly then seeing a girl get her head lopped off? Sure they know it's fake—but it's the thrill they're in for, real or not. All they care about is *how'd-they-do-that*. And what I'm talking about here's a good spectacle, one that'll keep them guessing—and one where nobody gets hurt."

Odile looked over at Mack. He lifted his head and gazed at her with rheumy, stricken eyes. Mother had recruited him nearly thirty years ago, when he was a bucktoothed boy straight out of the Union Army.

"It's just sounds so—" She paused, trying to summon the harshest word she could think of. "So *amateur*."

"Amateur!" Guilfoyle threw up his hands. "This from a gimp not even gimpy enough to make a dime from!"

Odile's knee trembled; her back twitched. They loved her on the Wheel of Death—enough to fear for her life. What could matter more than that? She looked at the troupe gathered around her, at their bad skin and puffy eyes, their numb gaze following Guilfoyle, who seethed around the room in a flurry of white. It was the world that she knew, only now everyone seemed tawdry and misshapen, as if she were staring at their five-cent reflection in the Mirror Maze. Here was Mack, but his face was bloated from too much drink; Georgette, sloppy-mouthed and sunburned, having flings with every two-bit boy from Manhattan; Leland gambling away everything he had on the horses. *You must remember,* her sister had written, *you are where you belong.* But she was wrong, Odile thought—they belonged together.

She heard Guilfoyle calling after her, but she didn't turn around, just stumbled out of the theater and into the dusty, sunlit alley. Her face was hot; the tips of her ears stung. She blinked the sand crumbs from her eyes and kept walking, over the trolley tracks and down to the beach. Her mother's locket knocked against her chest. How hot the metal must have gotten the day of the fire, how it must have burned its leafy pattern into her skin, right above her heart.

She came to a stop beneath the pier. The foam wrapped around her ankles and held there, as if afraid of being sucked back into the sea. She'd hidden here for hours the day of the fire. At one point someone had called her name but she was too scared to call back. The tigers were the first living things she saw. They were galloping down toward the shore, their great legs springing through the sand, cloaks of flame rising from their backs. She waited for them to howl, but they were silent. She didn't even hear the sound of waves breaking over their bodies as they thrashed blindly into the sea.

THREE

HER SECOND MORNING ON THE ISLAND, ALPHIE WAS WOKEN early for exercise. *Promenading,* the nurses called it—as if she were a debutante out for a stroll in the park. In the parched light of dawn, she and the other women, pilloried and aching with sleeplessness, were marched down the path to the river. Leather collars had been fastened around their necks; a long cable yoked them together like mules. Her blue flannel dress, with its coarse, unfamiliar stitching, was stiff with mildew and smelled like turpentine. Her head throbbed; her ears crackled and hummed as if they were full of water. She stared again at her hands. There was a pale, puckering groove around her finger where her wedding band used to be.

She kept smelling odd things in the air: raw and sour meat; moldering lemons; the persistent, sulfurous twitch of a match. She tried to turn her head, to look west over the water toward Manhattan, but the collar pinched at her throat. She could only see as far as the overgrown riverbank, where gulls pecked at the rot in the rushes and scum eddied between the stones. In the horse-drawn cart ahead of them, a nurse with foggy spectacles beat a pie pan with a kitchen mallet, urging them to move. Another nurse sang old Irish drinking songs between spits of tobacco, which sometimes missed the roadside and sprayed Alphie on the cheek. Alphie tucked her head down, juice dripping from her face and the ends of her hair, while insects whirred, curious and tickling, at her lip. Through the ache in her head, she remembered that tobacco was a good base for makeup; it hid the bruises and bee stings on darker complexions. Anthony, though, had been so fair she'd had to grind up chalk with a pestle, mix in some flour and cream. *Anthony.* Even as the women moaned around her, trudging in the grass to the clap of tin, she could still hear the boat horns braying on the river, the flaring hiss of their wakes. Her husband would find out what happened, and he would come for her.

The harness bells clinked as they moved ahead. Alphie struggled to keep up through the lashing, itchy weeds, tripping in her slippers, which were too small and beginning to tear at the skin on her heels. She wouldn't be here much longer, though—she *couldn't* be. She'd been missing for a full day already—Anthony would be looking for her, savage with panic. She pictured him coming home in the evening, only to find her gone and the Signora alone in the parlor, perched at her backgammon table and picking at a dish of licorice drops. Once he learned what his mother had done, he'd be sick and furious, racing to catch the first ferry over. But what if he couldn't find her? What lies would the Signora have told him? Alphie began to tremble. She wanted to scream across the water, to wherever the Signora sat in her oyster-gray dress with its fringed bib of beads. Even now she could hear the beads swaying and ticking from that famously sculpted bosom, see the prisms of light thrown, taunting, back in her eye. She wanted to scream as loud as these other women, but she'd gone hoarse from wailing in the night, partly from the pain in her head, partly from the panic. *Signora.* Even when she said the name, it sounded as if she were trying to shake a wad of phlegm from her gullet.

As they came up through the trees and rounded the bend, the octagonal dome of the madhouse glowed white in the sun. At the sight of it, the woman in front of Alphie—a young half-bald girl named DeValle—started to whimper. "Shut your mouth!" the nurse shouted. Alphie closed her eyes, feeling the collar jerk at her neck, the heat tighten her skin. One of her teeth had come loose in the night—she squeaked it back and forth with her tongue until her jaw ached and she tasted a thin trickle of blood.

Hurry, she prayed. Hurry.

A MONSTER, THE SIGNORA had called her. When Anthony spoke, his voice was as dulcet as a melodeon, but the Signora's was flinty, coarse, two rocks clapped together: *Il mostro, il mostro!* All she recalled of that night were a few scattered images. Each time a memory emerged, jagged and glinting in her mind, she felt nauseous and nervous and faint, and just as quickly it sank away. She remembered a spill, dark and oily smelling, on her bedroom rug. A crushed red flower beside her, the Signora's splattered boots. At some point Alphie had gasped for air and called weakly for Anthony. The Signora, disgusted, tried to yank her up, but Alphie flailed in terror and bit her hand like an animal. The Signora yelped and pulled back. Blood oozed down her wrist and into the sleeve of her dress. Then a pain exploded in the back of Alphie's head—like a firecracker zizzing and popping, over and over again, until she couldn't see anything but light. Everything that followed had the pure and tetherless quality of a dream. She remembered being lifted into the air like a child. She remembered floating in the dark. She remembered lying on the tacky floor of a carriage, the streetlamps passing outside the window like dull yellow moons. Lost in a spidery mass of hair (her own? another's?), she smelled the rusty breaths from a body beside her, tasted sawdust on her tongue, and was aware of the strange lightness at her stomach.

She woke sometime later that night to find herself still clothed in her old boots and filthy frock, the pain in her head like an animal raging to hatch. There was movement around her, but her eyes were weak, swimming in mucus. She stared blindly at the stripes of moonlight across her feet. *Am I in prison?* she thought. *Will I be punished?*

She was sitting on an unfamiliar bench, her stockings wet through her boots. She listed sideways and back. *Wake up!* she commanded herself. *Stay awake!* Then she realized she was rocking—she heard the slap and shush of water, the creak of wood. A boat. Alarmed, she tried to stand, but couldn't—she'd been collared and chained to the bench like an animal. She slipped and fell backward, hitting her tailbone on the edge.

When she opened her eyes, someone was pushing something between her teeth—a wooden dipper. Then came a warm dribble of water. A woman was standing over her with a bucket. Alphie swallowed the mouthful of water, tasted something gritty like silt. "Where's Anthony?" she whispered. "What's happened?"

"I couldn't tell you, miss," the woman said and moved on, dunking the ladle back in the pail.

Miss. Alphie lifted her head. They didn't know who she was? A half-dozen other women were chained beside her, huddled like toads along the bench, black-eyed and stuporous. She stared ahead. There, beyond the bow, was the phantom slug of an island, the lighthouse she used to see from her old room on the shipyard. The moon skipped, the spume chattered; her head felt like a stone.

It was pitch-black by the time they arrived at the gates, darker still by the time the women were herded into a hall and shut in a pen to be processed, like dirty fowl in an abattoir. The Matron walked slowly over to the pen, a blue-burning lamp in her hand. She swung her whistle like a policeman's billy club. The pen, iron bars on three sides and set against the wall, was barely big enough to hold them. As the lamp made its way down the line of blinded women, Alphie saw the wall come to life behind them, pulsing and shivering. It must have been white once, like the rest of the room, but now she stared in horror at the chaos of fingernail-scratches, teethmarks, and stains. There were urgent prayers and lovers' names, carved into the soft plaster or written in body fluids—many in tongues she couldn't read. They were all scribbled on top of each other, hysterical and illegible, the women's last messages to the outside world. Pressed in together, the new women, still sick from the boat and muddled by drugs, wept or screamed.

One by one they were taken away down the hall. When it was her turn, Alphie was led into an airless examination room. She stood there pickling in sweat, blinking against the light as yellow as vomitus. The nurses tried to touch her but she jumped, quivering, clutching at the folds of her dress. Her bladder ached, but she didn't want to use the chamber pot—she couldn't squat there in the corner of a room and lift her skirts while everyone gawped—so she relieved herself, hot and then cold, down her stocking and over her knees, until the runnels dried and itched.

The doctor was a toothy man with cold fingers and an unevenly clipped moustache. He took Alphie's pulse, pressed her tongue down with a spoon, asked her questions that she felt were designed to trick her into something. She didn't meet his gaze, just looked down and away, fixing on spots on the floor.

"Is that blood on your dress? In your hair?"

Alphie, startled, looked down at her hands, fisted and holding tight to her frock. She saw the stains on her skirt, but she had no memory of anything violent other than biting the Signora's hand. She'd been surprised at the salty bubbles of blood, but that was just a puncture, surely—nothing that would have led to this.

"Do you know who you are?" the doctor said testily. "Where you're from?"

She felt confused and tired, but she spelled out her name anyway, tears filling her eyes. "This is a plot, don't you see? She's always hated me! I'm a good girl. Please, please. He'll be looking for me. He'll call the police when he finds out! You have to let me go!"

"Did you do someone harm?"

"I didn't mean to! It was just a little gnash—I wasn't myself—"

"A gnash? Is that what you call it?"

"What did she tell you about me? It's a lie, I swear it!"

The doctor didn't answer, just scribbled something down in his notes. Then he lifted his stethoscope and moved his hand toward her chest, but she slapped him away. "Leave me alone—I didn't do anything! Please!"

He raised his hand and beckoned, expressionless, to someone behind her. Two nurses hooked Alphie under the arms and dragged her, thrashing and slipping in her own piss, down into the bathing hall. They chained her by her ankles to a chair against the wall, then left her there to wait. Alphie could see the filthy tub in the lamplight, and the bath nurse bent over it, red-cheeked and sweating—there was a wadded rag in her fist, a nude flicker in the water beneath her. She grunted and whistled and scrubbed a crying woman clean. For a moment Alphie had the strange sensation that she was looking out at her own slippery body—the red-raw flesh in the greening water, the pink beady nipples, the panicked eyes.

She turned away from the light, touching the sticky hair at the back of her head. Anthony would be here soon. She was sure of it—but how would she survive until then? How could she keep herself safe? She heard the slosh of water, the burbling sniffs, doors opening and closing, then footsteps drawing near. She looked up and saw the bath nurse approaching—the shine of her cheap-greased hair; those buggy, lashless eyes. Alphie tried to turn away, but the nurse took hold of her and pulled her up by the wrists.

Quickly she turned out Alphie's pockets—all empty—then shook the ribbon from her hair and ordered off her boots. Alphie cried at the crawl of curious hands over her body, at the foreign blisters and chewed-up nails. "Please don't take my clothes," she begged, hunched over and holding her stomach. "Don't make me get in the water. I . . . I don't know how to swim!"

"That's nonsense. All women must bathe, and all women must wear a uniform dress."

Alphie slumped forward, struggling for breath. Above her the nurse flicked through a sheaf of papers. Alphie heard the dutiful scratch of a pencil, a belch that smelled like lime soda, an exhausted sigh. She felt the end of the pencil flick through her hair, lift the hem of her skirt. "One pair boots, one pair stockings, hair ribbon, wedding band—"

"Don't write that one down."

The nurse looked up from her papers. She was stringy as a lizard, all muscle and knobs. She was tired, Alphie could tell—dyspeptic and sore after working through the night. She probably looked forward to her bed—wherever that was; a little dormitory apart with a tea tray and a lady's magazine—the kind the Signora always forbade Alphie to read—with illustrations of girls riding sidesaddle by the sea, or smoking Turkish cigarettes on the shore of a lagoon.

Alphie twisted her wedding ring off her finger. "Please—don't make me get in that water."

"You stink of piss. You'd rather have your piss than your gold?"

Alphie didn't answer, just held out the ring. What good would it do her in here? "They don't have to know."

The nurse hesitated for a moment, then took it. She rolled it around between her thumb and her forefinger. "I'm good at my job," she said.

"I believe you."

She tested the ring with her teeth, then stuffed it into her apron and handed Alphie a blue flannel dress. "If there's any trouble from you again, you'll be locked away with the Violents until you rot. I'm good, you see, but I'm not kind." She unchained Alphie, then pointed to a pile of clothes on the floor—"Leave your things there."

As she stalked back to the bathtub and wrung out the rags, Alphie made a show of sliding off her stockings and folding them neatly next to her boots. The nurse came back and damped down Alphie's hair, rubbing it coarsely with a rag that smelled like turpentine—"Just to out the blood." Alphie flinched at the pain in her head. Her stomach cramped. When the nurse stepped into the hall and hollered something to the room beyond (a garbled back-and-forth, the peevish shuffling of papers), Alphie quickly changed against the wall. There was blood on her legs, she saw. Her groin ached; her head spun. *I am kind,* she thought, *but I'm not good.* The nurse returned and led her away in the dark. They left behind a room of shed dresses and empty boots, as if the women's bodies had all dissolved into air.

The Matron was waiting for her in the last room. Alphie cowered in the light of the lamp, the blue dress scratching against her skin. She saw a table in the corner, fitted with leather straps and a stained sheet. Beside it sat a grandmotherly nurse in a bonnet. There was a device strapped to her hand, connected by a wire to a box on the table, which buzzed with some kind of electric current. The nurse stepped experimentally on a pedal, and the whole thing kicked and whirred.

"Number seven, Volpe," the Matron said.

Nurse Volpe didn't say anything, just stirred a bowl of thick black ink.

"What's this?" Alphie said hoarsely.

The Matron dragged Alphie onto the table, cinching her down at the ankles and wrists. They forced a draught of mead down her throat, which burned up into her nostrils and made her cough.

The Matron muttered something to Volpe, who nodded without expression and leaned over Alphie, tracing the skin above her collar. Alphie thrashed and screamed, but the Matron just stuffed a rag into her mouth and tightened the straps. Then the room went dark—a swath of linen was tied around her head, covering her eyes. She could feel the sticky press of Volpe's hand on her clavicle; an elbow pressed on her nipple through the dress. Alphie shrieked and kicked at her restraints, spit flying from the corners of her mouth, until Volpe rose—she heard the stool scrape back and topple over—and planted her hand firmly against Alphie's heart. With a click of the pedal, the motor began to whir. And then the needle set into her, carving a line of tremulous, saw-pitched music into the skin below her throat. Alphie could smell the smoke, feel something trickle and pool in the hollow of her collarbone. The loop and drag of Volpe's hand, the percussive tooth of the needle, the rattling box—all of it made the pain in her head unbearable. She tried to scream but choked. And then, just as abruptly, the motor was cut and Alphie was patted over with a wet sponge. When the blindfold and rag were removed, she could see Volpe's hand was smudged with black and red.

Volpe perched her glasses on top of her bonnet and sniffed, studying her handiwork. Alphie, in her delirium, thought she heard the words, *Did I spell it right?*

Beside her the Matron nodded, her features slack and nonplussed. *That's the name she gave us.*

That night they slept ten to a room on cots fitted with oilcloths and moldy wool blankets. Two women had to be tied to their beds to keep them still. Alphie curled up and covered her face with her hair, then cried her voice away. She couldn't bear it; she'd come so far from her days as a girl on the street, a bony runaway with shoes made from paper, waiting there on the corner with her paint stand and jars. And here she was, through some cruel reversal, sent back to the anonymous hive, trapped in a room full of women who were not missed and not wanted, who would wear the same dress every day until it disintegrated on their hungry frames—a dress she wore, too, formless and smelling of some previous disease, stamped with the words *Ward 5, Lunatic Asylum, Blackwell's Island.*

MANHATTAN WAS SO CLOSE: she watched it shimmer beyond the coal scows on the river; she could see the arched windows of the factories articulated through the fog like the humps of a sea monster. As the promenade ended, a bell clanged near the old boathouse—gulls flapped and scattered, cutting the sky. The day's ferry, Alphie realized, was approaching the island. Maybe Anthony would be onboard—he would be coming, at last, to fetch her.

She tried to turn again toward the water, but the women were jerked away by the cart, sweating up the path toward the asylum. They waded through the kitchen garden, between knots of culm and trees crippled with brown fruit. Alphie could feel her scalp starting to burn. She smelled the piss of the cart nag and the stink of their bodies. She knew it was horrible to be vain, but she missed her silver brush and fine haircombs, the pretty pots of cream on her dressing table, her aquamarine earrings and gardenia perfume. She couldn't help but hope, when Anthony arrived—despite her ruddy, sleepless face, the dress with its crusting bits of tobacco, the strange tattoo—he still found something beautiful. She cursed herself for giving up her wedding band, but he would understand, wouldn't he? She'd been so frightened.

As they were herded into the courtyard, the gate rattled open and the Matron's wooden heels clacked across the stones. Alphie stood there, wavering in the light. Finally, the boat had arrived. Anthony would be coming, at last, to take her home. As the women were unhitched from the cart—as the rope zipped free from the rings on their collars; as the nurses made their way down the row, unbuckling collars and hanging them on a yardstick—she looked anxiously back. The Matron was waiting for the wagon at the turn, scowling and breathless, rolling up her sleeves with irritable, pronounced little flicks. The sound of hooves and wheels drew nearer—it was a sound Alphie had heard, without thinking, every day of her life: the banal song of the icemen and junk-pickers, the crush of hansom cabs on the Bowery. But now it meant something. As the wagon turned into the yard, Alphie craned her neck. The groundsman was at the reins, an elderly man with muttonchops and coveralls. She tried to look around him for the brim of Anthony's hat. But as the horse clipped to a halt, Alphie saw that the wagon only brought the day's deliveries: a paltry sack of mail that the groundsman slung over his shoulder, and a teenaged boy hefting a small trunk of soap. The boy stared back at her with yellow eyes that matched his hair and his teeth. She grimaced. Certainly nothing like Anthony, who, despite his steamed suit and dark coiffure, kept his lips bitten in to hide the pipe burns, and would absently roll his fingers around his cuff links, dislodging the tar under his nails.

The first time she'd paid him a call—a proper call in the middle of the day; not like the nights when he'd stumble out of a tavern and pay her two pennies to clean his face up with a scud of cotton—she'd glimpsed him through a half-open door.

He had dressed Mrs. Miller's baby that week. He showed her the photographs on his desk. A set of twins: one born living and the other dead. They took photographs of him next to his sister, both dressed in their pearl and satin christening gowns and propped against a pillow. The little girl's eyes were wide and shining, her lips wet with drool. One restless hand had dissolved into a smoky plume beside her face. But the boy's head hung forward, until his chin rested on his collar. His legs were stretched straight out in front of him, in a way she'd never seen a baby sit, and his hands were spread in an eerie and unnatural fashion over them, like an old man trying to push himself out of a chair. As she peered closer, she could just see the white crescents glowing beneath his almost-shut lids. She turned away, gasping and sick, and there were Anthony's hands, ripe with the fetor of embalming fluid, offering her smelling salts and a tumbler of strawberry cordial.

Now she watched the soap-boy open his trunk—three feet by two of hand-thumped hogsfat patties, wrapped in newspaper. Not the dyed, scented lozenges at the Signora's house, which Alphie turned to slivers in the bath. The boy unloaded the soap into a wheelbarrow while the Matron flicked through an account book. Alphie saw the newspaper ink on his palms and knuckles, mackled headlines run in reverse. While the Matron turned away to consult with the grounds-man, the boy looked over and caught her staring. Alphie stepped back, but he just sneered and tugged his balls and licked at the gap in his teeth. "They must have locked you away for being so ugly," he said, then tittered and snapped up his case.

Alphie was stunned, then mortified. She wanted to lunge at him, pound his freckles back through the bones of his cheek. But he just turned away and leaned over the ledger with the Matron, scowl-ing as she ran her finger down the columns. "You owe me another five pounds of the Navy soap," she was saying. "Do you know how many floors we have to scrub here? Perhaps you'd care for a tour with this nice group of ladies, just to show you how filthy it can be?"

The boy dug a cigarette from behind his ear and lit it. "I'll bring the difference next week." He had a voice that was naturally high and nasal, one he'd clearly tried to deepen by smoking.

"It will be tomorrow," the Matron said, snapping the ledger closed. "The morning ferry. And it will be correct—or we'll take our business elsewhere. Understand? I won't be cheated." Then she turned to the line of women and yelled, "Breakfast!"

Jallow, the squat nurse with the eyeglasses, drove them all, sore and meek, up into the dining hall, while black-mouthed Bradigan dug another chaw of tobacco from her apron and ordered them to be quiet.

Alphie sat down at one of the long tables. Her stomach growled and ached, even though the room smelled like boiled gristle. When she'd arrived at Anthony's, the air had been so clean—smelling of wood polish and licorice, fruit and cake and mourning wreaths—that it had made her sick. She'd spent her first afternoon there hunched over a chamber pot, watching her vomit splatter against the porcelain. When she blew her nose, she was alarmed to see a clot of translucent mucus glistening in the folds of her handkerchief. When she tried to explain to the Signora that she must be sick—that it was colorless as a ghost, not speckled and gray-brown—she was only met with an arched, disdainful brow.

Anthony had rescued her once before, from a life of few comforts and little promise. The Signora never thought Alphie was good enough for her son—there was always something she found lacking in Alphie's manners, speech, intelligence, style—but Anthony had loved her and made her his wife, much to the bafflement and furious injury of his mother, who was used to controlling everything that went in and out of the house. When they were first married, the Signora even asked to examine Alphie's monthly napkins—she would sit there in the parlor with a lorgnette held up to her eyes, reading the bloodstains like tea leaves, looking for any sign of excitability, wantonness, or infirmity. *Are you reading those romantic novels? Or wearing your corset too tight?* Alphie could only shift impatiently on the parquet during these interviews, unsure how to answer.

Sitting on the hard bench, waiting for her breakfast of beef tea and bread, Alphie dreamt of the smells from the Signora's kitchen larder, the steaming dishes at the dining table: burrata melting over poached egg and asparagus, crinkles of pancetta in sweet potato soup. She loved going down to Mr. Moro's olive cart on Saturday afternoons and staring at the vats, smelling the sardines and vinegar. Mr. Moro would ladle the olives into a jar, and even though she was supposed to return home and leave them on the draining board to be made into paste, an old fear gripped her as she weaved through the crowded marketplace. Sometimes she ducked into an alley behind barrels of trash and gobbled them all—skinning the olives to their pits, drinking the juice, sucking the salt from under her fingernails—hiding there where no one could see her with her hand wedged wrist-deep in the jar, licking the syrup off her fingers like a dog. Afterward she simply told the Signora that her purse had been snatched and the grocery money was gone. The Signora sucked in her cheeks, pale with indignation, but Anthony took out his billfold and counted out the money again.

Next to her at the dining table, ignoring her food, was the jittery young woman named DeValle. She read aloud from a yellow square of newspaper. The women in the asylum weren't allowed paper of any sort, even for letter writing, but yesterday Miss De-Valle had dug this scrap from a rotting pillar in the hall. When the nurses had tried to pry it away from her, she'd wailed and thrashed about, then snapped her own hair out by the roots. Frightened that the girl's father, a congressman from New Jersey, would arrive for his weekly visit to find her balding and despondent, the nurses pressed the paper back into her hand and looked the other way. Now, in quiet moments like these, DeValle took the folded square out from her slipper and recited the advertisement over and over again. She wet and re-wet her lips, her voice frantic and catching: "Malvina Cream! The one reliable beautifier—blemishes, sunburn, ringworm, wrinkles! One tin, fifty cents. Oh, look, fifty cents!" She glanced at Alphie and smiled.

Alphie smiled back. Gently she reached over and brushed back what remained of her hair. There, inked in harried script across the girl's skin, just beneath her throat, was a single word. Her name: *De-Valle*. From across the table another woman glared at them. She was old and ornery-looking, with a bitterly bunched mouth, and as Alphie watched, she lifted her chin and pointed to her own tattoo. But it had been slashed over and over again, as if with a blade, so there was nothing left but a hash of purple scabs.

Alphie touched her chest, which was crusted over and raw-itchy with pain. They'd all been inked—most, like DeValle, with a surname. But some women were brought in and didn't know who they were, or didn't speak English; sometimes they didn't speak at all. Their names became the places they were found, landmarks and street corners and gambling halls: Union Square South, Delancey Suffolk, Brooklyn Bridge. Alphie couldn't see Volpe's handiwork on her own skin, but at least she knew who she was; she knew precisely who she was, even though there were some who believed that she didn't.

She ate her tea and bread slowly, her tooth aching. Across the room, a woman with tangled blond hair slumped over her breakfast and cried. One of the nurses tried to lift the bowl to her lips, help her to eat, but the woman couldn't swallow—the tea spilled right out of her mouth, all over the front of her dress. A string of spit oozed from her chin. Her eyes fluttered for a moment, then set on Alphie's.

There was something about her stare—lucid and snake-green, too familiar—that made Alphie's pulse tick. Quickly she looked back at her bowl, feeling sick to her stomach. She was saving it all up to tell Anthony, everything she saw and heard. She would confess that when the nurse had come to check on them during the night, Alphie had mistaken the ring of keys on her belt for the hand of a skeleton. She would talk about the Polish woman down the hall, who believed a piece of lint was her baby, and the girl from the East Side who sat at the window as if it were a sewing machine, passing invisible sheets of cotton over the sill. There were so many stories—she didn't know how to keep them all in her head; she had to continue reciting them to herself, tending to them, water-ing them like the plants in her conservatory, or else they'd wither and die, colorless husks. The longer she was there at the asylum, the more crowded her garden became, and the more exhausted she grew trying to cultivate it.

I will see to it, she remembered Anthony saying. What a strange thing to conjure up—the fragment of an old conversation, a euphonious refrain. What was it they'd been talking about? She could hear his shy and gentle voice, its rippling catch—*I will see to it.* She imagined him whispering it from across the water—*I will see to it. I will see to it, dear heart.*

The women were all given hot, sweet thimbles of mead, then marched up the great spiraling staircase to their wards. She wanted more than anything to just *go home* but didn't quite know, now, where that would be. She lay back on her bed, staring at the tin ceiling with its incongruous patterns of pheasants and scrolls, and put a hand on her stomach.

Il mostro!

Around her, the nurses scowled and hummed while they tucked in the bedsheets, changed the bloodied rolls of flax between the legs of cycling women, brushed their hair or sponged their necks if they were too weak or delirious. It was as if they were anchored at sea, this white barge of women, gazing out at the corniced cliffs of the city and waiting to be rescued.

FOUR

SYLVAN TRIED TO SLEEP, BUT HE KEPT HEARING FOOTSTEPS on the stairs above, whispers through the walls. Hour after hour, his eyes startled open. He reached over to the baby in the bed beside him. He felt the heat of her small body through the table-cloth, the feeble lift of her lungs. Was she feverish, he wondered, or was it just the swelter in the room?

He rose and pulled on his shirt and his trousers, scrabbled for the last of the milk. He tried to get her to eat, but she wouldn't. She began to cry, her whole mouth turned down—a high-pitched, roostery wail. He rocked her, tried to soothe her, took endless turns around the cellar while she coughed and cried. He found himself fall-ing asleep on his feet, leaning against the wall, grit pinging through the open window as barrows rumbled by.

When he heard a knock on the door, he waited for a moment, unsure if it was real. But then it came again, this time louder. He heard a man's voice, hoarse: "Pup, Pup!"

Sylvan tucked the baby back in the bed and crept across the room. He braced himself, then cracked the door. It was No Bones, leaning against the jamb, still sweating in his work clothes.

"What is it?" Sylvan whispered. "Did I lose my post?"

"No, no. The fight at St. Elmo's—an hour. You ready?"

He'd almost forgotten. He had to go—he needed the money, and the purse this morning was close to ten dollars. Already he'd added the figures in his head: rent, food, a new coat, a horsehair brush to clean his boots, enough left over for beer and the morning newspaper. But now he might need some goods for the baby—fresh milk and diaper cloths, maybe a bottle of Bergoon's cure-all.

"Your name's on the board." No Bones wet the corner of his mouth. "You sure you're all right?"

"Fine." Sylvan tensed. "I'm fine."

No Bones hesitated, folding his hat between his hands. "Just wanted to make sure you didn't fall into some kind of trouble."

Sylvan felt a prickly coolness on his neck and arms. "No." He shook his head. "No trouble here."

"You sure about that?"

There was a whimper from inside. No Bones tried to peer over his shoulder, but Sylvan just said, "I'll be ready," and shut the door.

Back inside he lingered by the bed, breathing in the hot, dusty air that had grown faintly sour with milk. He reached out and touched the baby's cheek. She was warm and listless. A familiar dread took root in his chest. He tried to imagine her here night after night, staring at these walls striated with mildew and candle smoke, listening to the pneumatic hiss and grind coming from the building next door, where a printer set and inked his anarchist dailies. How could he be the person to give such a life to another, when all he wanted himself was to run?

He'd have to take her somewhere else, at least until the fight was over—leave her with someone he trusted. The only person he could think of was Ellen Izzo, the weaver on Cherry Street. She bought the better pieces of loot he gathered from the privies—the brooches and pocket watches, stray baubles and cigarette cases. She'd lived and worked above the oyster house for as long as he could remember, fashioning mementos for the bereaved from their loved ones' hair. And she liked Sylvan—she invited him in for tea when she was lonesome, trusted him to read her letters as her eyes grew weak. She'd had a baby at one time herself, a son now grown and gone—Chester, whom an infection had left with only two fingers (making him the fastest shucker in the oyster house), and whom Sylvan had beat up over a pear one day when they were just boys (he hated to think of it now).

A trickle of sweat moved down his forehead and panicked at the tip of his nose. All around him he felt it, the sickness moaning and reeking from the tenements, the stink of waste and the heat of fever. He remembered following the carts down the street in the winter. Frankie's bag, the smallest of all, was chucked up on top of the wagon by those soot-dusted boys in black. He had watched the bag wobble as the cart turned a corner and disappeared, but all he could feel, when the rumble of the wheels had faded, was how relieved he was for it all to be over.

When the Scarlattas died, Sylvan thought he might send Frankie to live with one of Mrs. Scarlatta's cousins across town. They had children of their own, he knew. But Frankie was too sick, too weak to be moved. So Sylvan stayed with him in the apartment upstairs, made a little bed for him by the stove. Frankie, two years old, his hair wet with sweat and standing up on his head—how to explain what it meant, that his parents weren't coming home? That crosses had been painted on all the doors? Such a faint little voice: *Sylvan, I'm thirsty.* Sylvan found he couldn't sleep at night with the sound of that wracking cough. How could a tiny body, he wondered, make such terrible noise?

For two weeks, while Frankie lay sick on a pile of gloves, Sylvan had broken into the apartments of other families who'd died from consumption, where even as his breaths crystallized in front of him, he could still smell the blood, warm and acrid, in the wallpaper. The families had long since been carried away on the shoulders of neighbors, but their homes, interrupted, still held a patient vigil: dishes in the sink, blankets mussed, food parched and shriveled on the cutting board. He'd say to himself, *Take the bread, check the floorboards,* but instead he found himself at the table, folding the napkins and righting the spoons, as if everyone were expected back for supper.

But soon he grew desperate. He ate everything in the Scarlattas' cupboard, sold off what remained. He stole the apples left scattered after the market had cleared; he took the coat off a drunk sleeping in a doorway, and this Sylvan felt sorriest for, robbing a thin man of his warmth on a winter night. But he thought of Frankie lying in the corner by the stove, sweating even as snow drifted in through chinks in the wall. There were times when he'd lean over the bed as Frankie blubbered and moaned and will him to just *close his eyes.* He was tired of stealing for him, tired of staying in the freezing apartment because he couldn't be moved, tired of waking and worrying, of being so fretful that he threw up his breakfast and was hungry all over again. But mostly he was tired of waiting. For two weeks he watched Frankie get sicker and sicker, and there was nothing he could do. He couldn't be saved. The sooner it happened, the sooner Sylvan would be on a streetcar, and away.

And so one morning, Sylvan had just walked out the door as Frankie's lungs took on a grim, familiar rattle—he walked the snowy streets with his hands in his pockets, shivering in his stolen coat. He couldn't bear to watch. Being there meant that he would let it happen, that he was somehow in league with death, its lame and silent partner. He couldn't do it—he couldn't sit by and watch. If he left, it was in God's hands.

There had been a ghost in the house ever since.

Now, with the baby in his arms, he closed and locked the door, then worked his way through the yard, with its smell of lard and pipe smoke and iron-burned laundry. Undergarments flapped wildly on the fire escapes above, soiled with sweat and blood: private stains, flying high over the city like crests on the flags of a ship. He walked out to Ludlow Street, his eyes aching in the early sun. There were streets named Mulberry and Orchard and Cherry, streets bright and tart, streets with a color and a taste. But Ludlow sounded heavy and numb, like a mouth with a bitten tongue.

It was only a few blocks to Ellen Izzo's, but now in daylight, with the baby in his arms, it might as well have been a mile. He hurried as fast as he could, trying to keep her quiet. She clung to him, nuzzling his coat and leaving a trail of milky spit along the front. *What if we should pass her mother right here on the street?* he wondered. Someone who recognized the dimpled chin and dark hair and green eyes? How would he explain it? When he raised his head—wondering if people were gaping as he passed, or whispering to each other conspiratorially—he saw that they only looked through him, as if he weren't even there.

Your curiosity, Mrs. Scarlatta had once said, *is a dangerous thing. We all need to know our place, or how else would the world go on turning?*

But even then, only a child, sitting on the stairs after a rumble and holding a frozen hog's foot to his cheek, Sylvan wondered, *How does anyone even know what their place ought to be?* He fought for the money now, he always said—and he did; he needed whatever came his way—but the truth was that he liked it. He started when he was nine or ten, because he had to—he needed to fend off the lookouts and guttersnipes, the other boys who tried to bully him and rob him of what little he had. And the feeling afterward—walking the streets like a golden hum—he couldn't give it up. He was good at it—it was the only thing he'd ever felt good at in his life, and the way he looked somehow helped him. It made the men he faced do a double take. *Look,* his eyes seemed to dare them. *Look at me.*

Now he turned down the alley by the oyster house, past the old pear tree that stood dead in the ground. Even though it was hot out, his teeth chattered and his head pulsed. In his arms the baby's eyes fluttered open. Did she know him? he wondered. And would she know when he was gone?

He took the stairs two at a time to Mrs. Izzo's door. She'd be up at this hour, he knew. She lived alone now and had trouble sleeping. Last year Chester had left for work in San Francisco—he'd locomoted all the way across the country, even seen a herd of buffalo running alongside the train. For a while he'd written home every week and sent back a little money. Sylvan—who had learned to read simple lines of English over the years, studying everything from timetables to signboards to newspaper fish-wrap—would read the letters aloud as he sat at Mrs. Izzo's table, drinking blackberry tea. He would linger over each sentence, inventing what he couldn't decipher, eliding what he couldn't explain. Then he'd write a letter for her in return, taking dictation while she licked at her thumbs and polished some brooches and braided a dead woman's hair. He tidied up her sentences, or used different words when he didn't know how to spell hers, and secretly embroidered the banal block gossip. He knew it wasn't fair, but he wanted Chester, wherever he was, to be jealous. He wanted New York to seem exclusive—a potent, faraway thrill. It ate at him. How had Chester Izzo, with his weedy pallor and glutinous, nearsighted eyes, been the one to get out?

And he hated how much he loved Chester's letters—he hated picturing Chester fat and happy, smoking a cigar in the lobby of a gold-rush hotel, gazing down at rickshaws and pelicans and strands of orange lights. He hated how his own voice sounded when he asked Mrs. Izzo if she'd had word from him, how pitched and needy, and how pleased Mrs. Izzo looked when she answered him. But then the letters stopped coming. *He's very busy, I'm sure,* Mrs. Izzo would say. *He's getting himself rich.* But eventually Chester Izzo didn't write anymore, he didn't send money, and her lies grew more fanciful and elaborate.

Sylvan stood there in the heat, smelling the steam that drifted up from the windows of the oyster house. He knocked on Mrs. Izzo's door—a quick rap—and heard footsteps on the other side. The door cracked open, just an inch, and Mrs. Izzo peered out. If the weather had a face, he thought, it would be hers—a stormy mass of graying hair, veins forking down her temples, and a calm, round visage, the color of burnished gold.

"Sylvan!" She beamed. "Good loot this week?"

"I need your help." He leaned in, so close he could smell the glue and silver polish on her skin, and told her what had happened. Without a word she swung open the door and ushered him inside.

In the ancient waterfront house, with its salt-cracked shingles and smoky parlor, Mrs. Izzo set quickly to work. She cleared off a table, set water to boil, and took the baby into her arms. Sylvan sat down at her workbench, sore. He stared at the hanks of hair that hung from the rafters, at her easel with its bobbins and weights and its elegant, half-finished braid. Under a bell jar was the likeness of a seahorse, woven in colors of rust and straw—even the fins were articulated in strands of gossamer blond. It was for a widowed sailor, Mrs. Izzo had told him. He ran a hand through his own sweaty hair, pulling and twisting as the baby cried louder.

Mrs. Izzo checked the heat of the baby's skin and dabbed the mucus from her eyes. She put an ear to her chest and listened to her heart and her lungs. The baby kicked and began to wail.

"What is it?" Sylvan asked.

"Fever." Mrs. Izzo stuck her finger into a liquor jug and let the baby suckle it, then told him to fetch some things from the kitchen: "Cinnamon—ground up—a rag and a bit of oil."

He rummaged through the cabinets while Mrs. Izzo laid the baby on the table and peeled away the wet cloth. She swaddled her in a fresh rag-diaper and cotton blanket, then mixed the ointment.

Sylvan heard pots clanging in the rooms below, the sandy crack of shells. Steam began to drift up between the floorboards, and the parlor soon smelled like lemon and brine. He watched as Mrs. Izzo swabbed the baby's ears with cinnamon oil, as she bundled her up and sat back, shushing, in an overstuffed chair. It was the chair where Chester used to sit on summer afternoons like this one, all the windows open, bedeviled by asthma. Sometimes, late at night while he shoveled out the privies, Sylvan felt a sadness come over him: Chester, for all his scrawniness and whining, his fear of birds and dogs and horses, his goopy, dripping eyes, had meant something to somebody. Footsteps on the stairs, the squeak of the corroded letter box—everyday sounds that he barely heard anymore—these were the things that Mrs. Izzo listened for. Every time someone knocked on her door—as he had just now, a little guiltily—part of her would wonder.

As the baby quieted and yawned, he told Mrs. Izzo about the match. He promised he'd be back that afternoon, with money and milk. "And something else for your trouble"—he said, although he wasn't sure what yet. "But—she'll be all right, won't she?"

"It's bound to happen with them so young. But she's a little bear." Mrs. Izzo smiled. "She'll fight."

Sylvan brushed the baby's cheek. Sometimes it astonished him to think how easily he could have died—should have died, any number of times—and yet, improbably, he was still alive. *Why?* He wanted to tell people, to show them somehow, but he didn't know how to say it. He didn't have a family, or a gang, or a corner club to welcome him home. He had no allegiance to anyone except himself. When he was in front of a howling, chanting crowd, in spite of the pandemonium, things became very clear—he had a purpose, a responsibility. He had a name, and it was all that he needed. It belonged to no one else but him.

Mrs. Izzo began to sing a meandering song—about brier and moonlight, fireflies and fishermen. Sylvan looked at the baby with her elfin ears, asleep in the woman's arms. She's strong, he reminded himself. She hadn't died out there in the privy, even if someone had hoped otherwise. She'd lived through the night. She had food in her belly and air in her lungs.

The lullaby followed him down the stairs and into the street. Sometimes at a match, the crowd would gather around the ring before a fight began. They'd sing an old ballad about the feats of ordinary men—stone-breakers and quarrymen, threshers and blacksmiths. One day, Sylvan liked to think, he might be remembered as well. *Here Dogboy sparred, the unknown son!* And perhaps one day the little girl, older, would be taking in a show with her friends at the hippodrome, or passing by a bandshell in the gardens uptown. She'd hear it and smile. *It's all true,* she would say. *Why, I knew him. He's the one that saved me.*

FIVE

ODILE'S BODY STILL ACHED FROM THE WHEEL—HER SHOUL-
ders were stiff and her limbs were throbbing—but as the ferry
met the morning light along the harbor, the pain began to feel
almost invigorating. Blood beat behind her eyes. There was a burn
in her knee and a crick in her neck. She felt a bruise beneath her
ribs where her costume had chafed; her ankles were strangled by
bootlaces pulled too tight. The hurt drummed through her as she
stared ahead. It made her feel tenderly, thunderously alive. For the
first time, she was seeing Manhattan.

The buildings and smokestacks were gilded in the light; they
seemed to rise from the water like the masts of a sunken ship. As the
ferry pitched and rolled, she gazed at the schooners on the waterfront, the islands in the haze. The city loomed silent and magnificent
beyond. She thought of Belle hidden somewhere deep in its berths,
frightened and alone. She could be sweating away in the brown
gloom of a boardinghouse bedroom, while chorines and seamstresses
gathered outside the door and whispered. It was like a scene out of an
opera—*La Bohème* or something. Belle might lift her head from the
pillow and stare at the faces bunched above the banister or floating

behind the jamb, but none of them, not one, would be Odile. She could be holding on like this, waiting, while one hour leaned into the next and the city moved on, resplendent and oblivious, around her. *I'm so close,* Odile wanted to call across the water. Her whole body tensed and trembled—as if, just by unsettling the air around her, she might send some ripple out toward the city, where it would break over Belle, wherever she lay, like a wave. Glancing around to make sure nobody was watching, she crooked her finger and held it out in front of her. *So close—just wait.*

Without willing it, she pictured the pier on the morning after the fire. Bodies had been lined up along the planks, hidden beneath fronds of burnt wallpaper and the tasseled remains of a curtain. While Belle stayed home, silent and prostrate under her tiger quilt, Odile had stood alone on the boardwalk, tasting smoke in the air, scratching the water from her eyes. She'd stepped gingerly among the dead, coughing back ash and sand, lifting the edge of each makeshift pall just far enough to see what lay beneath. A man's workboots. The brown apron string of a pastry vendor. And then: the single tail of Aldovar's tuxedo, the burned ruffle of his wedding gown. The sight of it made Odile's breath catch in her throat. She remembered seeing the train of his dress disappear into the crowd, toward the burning theater.

And there next to Aldovar, beneath the theater curtain, she spied a long singed braid, tied with a navy ribbon. The breeze made it stir like a living thing. She tried to swallow, but her throat closed. She'd picked out that ribbon for her mother earlier that day, when they were sitting together in the dressing room, waiting for the show to begin. She'd braided the braid with her own fingers, felt the thick, slippery hair twist around her knuckles.

She had to be the one to find Belle and tell her what had happened. The only thing worse than seeing it for herself was saying it aloud. For once it was shared—once she sat down by her sister on a cold, wet bench overlooking the shore; once the words were let loose in the air—it all became true. Just a single breath, an exhalation. That was all it took to undo them. Belle turned away from her and gazed at the wind-whipped sea. Whatever had bound them together began to unravel, and as the days went on Belle drifted farther and farther away, like a kite running off from its spool, until she disappeared altogether. And even if Odile could no longer see her or speak to her, she could feel what remained—a faint pluck in her chest, a shiver in her heart, something that drew her on, even when she tried to ignore it, even when she stood alone on the beach and looked at the gathering clouds and wanted to blame Belle, and her flights of passion, for everything.

WHEN THE FERRY ARRIVED at the pier in Manhattan, she scuttled down the gangplank, hugging her valise to her chest. All she had to guide her was an old map of her mother's and her sister's letter. For weeks she'd gone through the theater papers—alone at the kitchen table with a scrambled egg dinner, listening to a mouse cheep in the grate—running her finger down the columns and hoping for a mention of Belle's name. But nothing had turned up. There were hundreds of stages in Manhattan, she supposed, playing thousands of shows a year—her sister could have found work at any one of them. Still, last night she'd gone through her mother's directory and made a list of the big Bowery halls, the famous vaudeville houses, and a few dime museums. She didn't know where to begin—she had no sense of the city at all—so she decided to start on the small stretch of Doyers Street, where her sister had written someone months ago. Perhaps Odile could find whoever it was—maybe they'd had contact with her sister since she arrived. At the very least, if they'd been an acquaintance or admirer of their mother's as the postman supposed, they might be able to tell her which sort of theaters to inquire at.

She waited in line at the curbside, then climbed into a rickety cab. Trying to muster the confidence and breezy nonchalance of a native girl, she told the driver to take her to Doyers Street, hoping he wouldn't ask any questions. He didn't, and she settled back in the seat.

The cab jostled out into traffic. It was drawn by a rawboned horse the color of curdled milk, who seemed to have all the time in the world. She watched as the wharves gave way to dim, crooked passageways. She smelled corn and fish pies cooking from carts on the corner, and acrid char drifting down from factory smokestacks. Men with wet cleavers sat smoking on the stoops of their butcher shops, purple and yellow flanks swinging above them, guts spilled out on the stained brick beneath. Each time the cab stalled for pedestrians, or slowed to a stop on a crowded street, Odile felt her body stiffen. She leaned forward in her seat, straining to read the street signs farther down the block.

Over the years she'd heard names bandied about the dressing room: *the Battery, Hell's Kitchen, the Tenderloin.* They all sounded so seedy and carnal—places full of hot steam and painted mouths; men and women pawing at each other in the back of a packing house, kissing between slabs of fat-bubbled meat. But now she stared at street signs in Yiddish and German and Chinese, uncertain what to think. Along the streets she saw pushcarts and stands—mounds of sweet potatoes and squash, buttons, clothespins, eyeglasses glittering like the scales of a fish. Mothers pulled their children down the sidewalks, past piles of trash alive with bees. Was Belle living here, like this, or had she made her fortune as she intended—but couldn't, for whatever reason, let go of her grief? (*Just not dead—dear God, not dead.*) As girls they used to read all the lurid pamphlets that reformists passed out in front of the theater: stories of kidnapping and depravity, innocent young women forced into slavery. They'd stashed them away in their room, screaming and howling as they reenacted them at night. Fainting maidens who somersaulted off beds! Captors with wiggling moustaches and bicorne hats, locking the maids in an armoire, forcing them to eat crackers through the door! Now Odile thought of the older women on the boardwalk at night—the real ones, hard and hungry, who lingered outside taverns and bathhouses and beat their parasols against the rails, thumping out messages in code—how they had frightened Belle, with their sinister *swish-swack* from the shadows, when she and Odile took the shortcut home from the stage.

After a series of lurches and turns, the cab came to a halt on a street so congested that another horse pushed his head through the window and snuffled Odile's sleeve. They'd reached the Bowery, a name she'd always conflated with the Growlery, her father's workshop. The Growlery sounded like a place where the tigers might live, but in fact it was just a little room in the very back of the theater, where Mr. Church would sit between shows, drinking his port and reading his copy of Dickens. He wasn't a sword swallower or a stuntman. He wasn't a performer at all. He'd been the show's sign painter, an artist who'd gone back to England when the girls were small, and whom their mother rarely talked about. But Odile could still hear the patient turn of those blue-thumbed pages, the spotty glass meeting the table with regular thumps, a sentimental sigh ruffling her father's beard. That was the only real memory she had of him: seeing him alone among his paint cans, reading in a shaft of light. Had he loved her, she wondered? Or had he been ashamed of her, hunched and rasping at his knee?

She rapped on the roof and yelled up to the driver. "Are we close?"

He looked down from the box. "You said Doyers, am I right? Just down there a bit."

"I'll walk." She got out and paid her fare, then stood alone on the sidewalk. All around her she heard scraping hooves and lurching wheels, the thunder of sewing machines from windows above. She shuffled down the street between umbrella menders and pencil carvers, all putting on a show for the crowd. A current of black hats bobbed between the carts. This is where their weekend visitors arrived from—those blushing couples in line for the Hee-Haw and the Jolly Octopus, the straw-hatted men who marveled at her aloft on the Wheel. She passed a medicine show—a huckster in a suit parading around a shock-haired, dope-eyed girl, claiming he'd cured her after she'd been hit by lightning. Immediately Odile thought of Guilfoyle, and her stomach turned.

Just past the huckster and his bait, Odile saw the sign for Doyers Street. She paused at the corner. At first it looked like a dead end—a thin black seam in the great rock of the city—but as she walked ahead, she saw it was crooked like an elbow. She glanced into each fogged and lowly storefront, at the lettering on every door. She began to worry—nothing looked obvious or familiar. All she saw were rows of silent, sepulchral houses, a shuttered Mandarin tea parlor, two gray goats gnawing at the weeds between the bricks. A few older men sat out on the steps, reading their newspapers, eyeing her briefly and then looking away.

A cloud passed in front of the sun, and then she saw it—there, on the roof of the building at the hook in the road—a glass room, a glowing fog that hovered just above the eaves.

Then I realize I've been sitting too long in the hothouse, staring at the flowers, and the rain is coming down heavy on the glass.

The blood flickered in her ears. She waited for a cart to pass, then hurried over, the valise thumping against her sore knee. On the first floor was an apothecary shop. She studied the stenciled sign in sham goldleaf—*Bloodworth's*—and the pair of oversized spectacles drawn on the window glass, next to advertisements for headache pills and hair restoratives. But the shop was still shuttered, the windows dark. There was only a pair of pigeons roosting on the ledge, and rats chasing each other through the ivy. Perhaps Belle had written someone here for a special order—there were various throat tonics and lozenges her mother preferred. Even Odile's eucalyptus cream had arrived by train from Chicago.

She tilted her head back. The building was simple and plain, three stories high. Perhaps the hothouse belonged to someone who lived in the rooms above, or the apothecary himself. The building, she saw, had two doors: the green shop door, sashed and locked, and a yellow door farther off to the side, set back from the street and half obscured by ivy.

Odile walked up to the yellow door and knocked. She heard footsteps approach on the other side. A small panel in the door slid open, squeaking on its track. Eyes and a nose appeared, but not the hazel eyes and small, freckled nose of her sister. Instead, it was the face of a young red-cheeked girl, out of breath and chewing nervously on a pipe stem. She stared at Odile and blinked. Odile blinked back, the words stuck in her throat.

"Good morning," she stammered. "I don't know if I'm at the right address, but . . ." She stared at the crumbling, fluted jambs and blisters of paint on the door. She cleared her throat and looked at the girl again, forcing a brave, polite smile. The girl took an uneasy drag from her pipe and blinked her eyes, waiting.

"I'm looking for Isabelle Church."

The girl blew out a line of smoke. "You must have the wrong house," she said. The panel in the door shut.

Odile stood on the stoop for a moment, her heart thudding. "Excuse me!" she shouted. "Wait a moment!" She banged harder this time, using the heel of her fist.

The panel opened. Now the girl lowered her voice; some of the hardness was gone from it. "I don't know who you are or what you're after, but you've got the wrong idea," she whispered.

"I've come all the way from Coney Island, and I'm looking for my sister, Isabelle Church," Odile said again. "I've only just received a letter. I'm afraid it's rather urgent. Has she been here? Do you know who she is?"

The girl crinkled her eyebrows. "Did she say she was here?"

"Not to me, no . . ." Odile hesitated. She wasn't sure what Belle had been hiding from her, or why. "She might have corresponded with someone here," she said carefully. "Is there anyone I can speak to? Anyone who might have been acquainted with the Churches of Coney Island?"

"I couldn't say," the girl answered. "I'm only the help."

Odile didn't like the indifferent lift of her shoulders, or the odd, nervous clucking sound she made as she sucked in her cheeks. "I'm not leaving," Odile said, leaning against the door, "until I talk to someone who knows."

The panel shut again, but this time Odile heard bolts slide and latches lift. The door opened, and the girl stepped out into the light, *tuck-tuck*ing on her pipe. She was younger than Odile, maybe twelve or thirteen—bowlegged and weevily, with a whiskery fuzz on her upper lip and a housedress already stained from the morning's chores. Odile could easily have mistaken her for a Coney Island scrub-girl, save for the dagger hilt that flashed briefly above her bootstrap as she shook out her skirt. The girl tapped the hilt, perhaps unconsciously, with the toe of her boot and squinted at Odile through the smoke. "Who are you, exactly?" she said.

"My name's Odile Church." Odile held out her hand. The girl eyed it suspiciously, then leaned forward and shook it.

"I don't have a mind to take up your morning," she continued. "If someone can tell me what business my sister had here, I'll be grateful for the knowledge and quick on my way." She cleared her throat and hurried on, before the words *almshouse* and *sickhouse* and *cemetery* could be suckled from the pipe stem and set loose on a cloud of reeking smoke. "Isabelle, or Belle, as she likes it. Five feet tall, an acrobat of sorts. She might have found work in a theater nearby. They called her the Shape Shifter, if that sounds at all—"

The girl raked the nib across her teeth. "Why don't you come inside, Miss Church?" She leaned against the door, propping her foot up on the wood behind her. "You can wait in the parlor while I ask."

"Why, *thank* you." Odile crossed the threshold into a dimly lit foyer, her heels clicking on the tile. She peered up the shadowed stairwell, then down the corridor, past a pile of blankets and hot water jugs, but saw no one.

Behind her, the girl shut and latched the door. "I was just making a pot of coffee," she said, beckoning Odile down the hallway, opening the double doors to the drawing room. "I'll bring you a cup if y'like."

Odile's stomach burned. She hadn't had anything to eat or drink since early that morning, when she forced down some weak tea and a hardboiled egg. "Yes, please, very black." She nodded at the girl, who studied Odile's flimsy hat and sweat-stained collar, the stickered valise with its glue-plugged corners and layer of sand. The girl lifted her chin, her nostrils flaring with something that was half pride and half menace, curtsied and said, "Make yourself comfortable, miss. I'll be back in a moment."

When she was left alone, Odile scanned the parlor, hoping something would look familiar to her—something small that she might recognize as her sister's. The room was dark and humid and musty smelling, but it was still reasonably well kept—certainly no poorhouse. Odile glanced at the wooden faces carved into the scrollwork above her head, at the footworn carpets and high-backed sofa. There was even an upright piano. But no easy chairs or coffee-stained afghans or sheet music trampled underfoot, no orange, windblown fur floating in through the door. Everything was somber and spare, far from their home on Surf Avenue.

She thought again of the women with their umbrellas, the leaky harem over on Mermaid Avenue. She looked around at the empty ashtrays and burgundy curtains. There was no trace in the air of cologne or sweat or primly held cherry cigarettes. No sound of beds creaking upstairs or men rising from their messed sheets with a yawn, of boots falling tired and haphazard on the stairs, of barefoot girls tiptoeing through the yard to scrub the musk off their bodies in the cool, quiet gloom of the privies. Still, the quiet unnerved her. She didn't even hear murmurs on the stairs, or the clink of cups and saucers. It looked like a stage set after the theater lights had been snuffed.

When the girl returned with the coffee tray, Odile held up her mother's locket, opened to a photograph of Belle. "This is who I'm looking for."

The girl slid the tray onto the table and lifted her eyes, expressionless. "I don't recognize her."

"Can you take a better look?"

The girl picked a shrivel of tobacco off her tongue. "Like I say, I'm only the help. Here." She handed Odile a cup of coffee. "Seems like you need this."

Odile took the coffee and sipped it. The girl didn't meet her eyes, just set the pot back on the table and tucked a stray hair behind her ear. Odile snuck a glance at her ankle, where the boot-skin had worn white around the dagger blade. Five inches and single-edged, by the look of it. It probably had never seen an oiled handkerchief or a square of sanding paper—had up to three burrs, she guessed, along the tongue.

The girl noticed her looking, and she straightened up a bit, a smile gliding out toward the corners of her mouth. "I dare say you've come a long way," she said. "It's not quite like back home, is it?"

Odile bristled. What did this girl take her for? Scared of the streets of Manhattan, trembling at the sight of a knife! As if she were no more than a naïve little sand hopper, alighting in the city with a dead-end letter and a cheap, sentimental necklace. "No, it's not," she enunciated. Certainly she'd heard stories about the wickedness and debauchery of New York, but these were nothing compared to the stories New Yorkers had heard about the perversions at Coney Island. She poured herself another cup of coffee. The muscles in her back were tensing—it was the same pain she felt when Mack threw a knife particularly hard, so hard that the Wheel quaked under her hips and shoulders. Now she was seized with the urge to pull the knife from the girl's boot and fling it magnificently through the air— to slice her pipe in half where it stuck out from her mouth at an angle. The blade would plunge into the wall behind her with a tremulous hum, and Odile would stare the girl down until her smirk disappeared and the sheared pipe nib drooped on her lips.

Instead, she shook her head and said, "We're quite the act back at Coney Island." Her throat seemed even drier now. She sucked a drop of coffee from the rim of the cup. "Maybe you've heard of the Church sisters—taming real tigers from Java?" She pulled up her skirt and pointed to the bandage on her knee. "One took a bite right out of me yesterday. Blood wouldn't even come out of its fur. I had to dress it up quickly to catch the ferry in time. Like I said, I'm here to find my sister, and I'm not leaving until I do." She smoothed her skirt back over her lap and smiled.

The scrub-girl smiled back, her face devoid of expression. "You're welcome to wait."

She stepped out into the hall, closing the door behind her.

Odile felt a cold sweat break across her hairline; her tongue prickled in her mouth. She looked over her shoulder. Something was different—a tang to the air, a ripple in the atmosphere. She stood and took a turn around the room, glancing behind the sofa, between the curtains, but no one was there.

She paused at the piano and ran her hands over the keys. She used to play, though she hadn't in years. For a little while their

mother had hired a man with a cane—a half-deaf, faunlike émigré—
to come to the house and give them lessons. Odile hated running
scales, hated the plucky pastoral études and grim sonatinas, hated
counting out the measures to the ornery clap of his hands. *But it's
good for your posture,* her mother insisted. Belle had loved dance-hall
music the most—syncopated, percussive, a little bit brash. At night
while their mother cooked dinner, they crowded each other on the
piano bench, playing sloppy duets together, hollering nonsense in
fake opera voices.

She pressed down on middle C. It twanged and stuck, out of
tune. She played a quick trill, part of Belle's old routine, hoping
someone through the walls would hear it and know. She missed hearing Belle talk about "glisses" and "quarter tones," seeing sheet music
litter the floor of the parlor. She missed coming home and finding
Belle at the piano with a pencil in her mouth, getting down a tricky
refrain. She remembered how Aldovar had harmonized beautifully
when they all sang together in the wings after an exceptionally good
(or bad) show. She missed hearing the audience gasp as Belle played
her ragtime upside down, all sweat and bluster, her body arched beneath the lights. She even missed her mother's old songs—learned
long ago from a circuit rider in the hills—the lyrics a blend of bonny
Scotch-Irish and Pennsylvania Dutch—and which she only sang
when she thought nobody was listening, pinning the clothes to the
line on Sunday mornings.

Odile heard a creak behind her and turned around. Someone
was standing there by the door, now open—a little girl in a sleeveless
cotton shift, carrying a lantern in her hand. She was no more than
eight or nine years old, with wide, wary eyes and thick brown hair
chopped short like a boy's.

"I'm sorry," Odile started, looking to the piano and back. "I was
just playing a song we used to . . ." Her voice died in her throat. The
girl, she saw, was missing her right arm. In its place was a wooden

one, jointed at the elbow and wrist. An iron socket cupped her shoulder; a leather strap buckled under her armpit. As she leaned in closer, Odile saw that the wooden fingers were long and delicate, individually whittled. The forefinger and baby finger were raised, the thumb slightly curled—as if they were about to flutter down to the piano and play a chord.

The girl whispered, "Don't drink the coffee."

Odile blinked, lifting her eyes to the girl's face. "I beg your pardon?"

"I've seen it before," the girl continued. She wore a purse around her neck, a burlap pouch on a length of twine, but Odile couldn't tell what was inside. "They put something in your drink to make you sleepy and when you wake up, you've got no money or shoes."

Odile clicked her tongue against the roof of her mouth, trying to draw up saliva. This would be quite an elaborate setup, wouldn't it, for something with such a small payoff? If the scrub-girl had simply wanted her pocket change and necklace, why hadn't she just threatened her with the dagger? "They can pick me over all they want," she said, "but I'm afraid they won't find anything worth stealing." She mustered a laugh and dabbed weakly at her temples.

The little girl was quiet for a moment. "You said a tiger bit you. But I thought the tigers died."

At first Odile didn't know if she'd just imagined it or if the girl had actually spoken. "What?"

"The tigers—I thought they were buried right next to her mother in the graveyard. They had their own coffins, she said, with little dwarf pearballers."

"P-pallbearers."

"So how could one bite you yesterday? Did you get more?"

The blood rushed to her head. She had the sensation that she was on the Wheel again—the room started to turn around her—(But where was the hot breeze? The smell of rotting seaweed and beer?) She studied a circle of light on the runner, trying to spot herself, but it swung left and right, left and right, like the tongue of a tolling bell. She put a hand on the piano to steady herself. "Where is she?"

The little girl shook her head. "She's gone."

"Is she in trouble? Is she hurt?"

"No one knows what happened to her." The girl hung the lantern on her wooden arm as if it were a coat peg. "But she left something. Maybe you want to see it?"

For a moment Odile didn't know who to believe—the surly scrub-girl with a boot knife and moustache, or this tiny girl with a wooden arm. "What is it?"

The girl said, "I'm not supposed to open it."

"Then show me—now."

She led Odile into the hall, to a little door behind the stairs. When she opened it, no light or sound came from below, just a soothingly cold draft and the raw clay smell of earth.

The light swung out in front of them, illuminating a set of dirt stairs that spiraled down into the darkness. Odile followed the girl down. The corner of her valise dragged against the wall—she could hear the sound of it catching and scraping, feeling its way along the curve. As they wound deeper and deeper into the black lung of earth, Odile stared at the lantern, trying to see beyond the shadow, but her vision began doubling and tripling until it seemed there were a dozen lanterns dancing about her head, brilliant as the electric canopy at Coney Island.

This, she thought briefly, might be Belle's greatest act. Perhaps by now she had transcended herself entirely. Perhaps she had shifted into something else—not a shape anymore, not even a body. Perhaps she had turned into the light itself.

SIX

BEFORE ALPHIE WAS MARRIED TO ANTHONY, SHE'D BEEN A penny Rembrandt. Her earliest turf was on the Bowery, just south of Delancey, where nights were busy and raucous, and where she was able to earn enough money to pay for a room in the back of a Chinese boardinghouse. But after a while she found herself working closer to the ports, where the gentlemen slummed with the rabble, where she made even more money cleaning up wastrels after long, boozy nights at the dance halls, before they returned home to their parents and wives. She'd sit under a string of lights, powdering over ring-stamped cheeks and blackened eyes, coloring in bites left by a whore. Every night as it grew dark, she carried her stool, her folding table, and her box of paints down to Water Street and waited for men to spill out of the saloons. On occasion, to bide the time, she'd clean up a few scrapping boys for a penny, so they wouldn't get in trouble when they returned home for supper. They lay there whimpering and dazed, chunks of ice melting against their jaws, while Alphie, mixing paint in a coffee can, proudly cooed over their split knuckles and swelling eyes. But when it grew dark and the gentlemen started to slink in among the sailors, jittery in their faun coats and grosgrain ties, doffing their top hats with satin petershams, she shooed the children away and readied her brushes. For a little extra, she also offered lemon drops to sweeten the breath, a spritz of cologne, and clean handkerchiefs she'd stitched herself.

This was how she met Anthony—on a chilly autumn night, stationed outside an unmarked saloon called the Shingle and Plank. He had staggered out alone, his lip sliced and his eye a fiery, bruised pink, the color of a mashed plum. He had crossed the wrong man, he said. She dabbed at the cut and painted the skin beneath his watery, upturned lashes. "You're lucky he didn't bury you," she told him. He only laughed grimly and said death to him was as constant as the moonrise at night. Then he lifted his head and kissed the inside of her wrist. He had a very particular scent, she noticed, something like ether and orange peel.

Alphie found herself waiting for him, week after week, choosing the clubs she knew he frequented. The sight of him sent a charge through her—the black armband he wore on his coat, his sensitive, thoughtfully pursed lips. By that hour of the night, his face was always stubbled, his clothes messed. He drank too much, offended too many men, then retreated to the opium dens beneath the city to forget himself. It awoke something in her, to see someone so kind and giving, so full-hearted, and yet so lost, so wretchedly bent on his own destruction. She had left home, ashamed of herself and the fury she'd caused, but now the prospect of love didn't seem like such a dangerous thing at all.

He visited her stand regularly—mostly when he needed to, sometimes when he didn't. One night he lingered for a while in his nice black suit, telling her stories from Italian operas (which she'd never heard of or seen before, although she didn't want to admit it). She was fascinated by the tale of Violetta, a Parisian courtesan in love with a gentleman. "But she dies, of course," said Anthony offhandedly. "For love." He gave a blithe little laugh. "Don't they all?" (*Do they?* Alphie wondered.) Even the word *opera*—it sounded so sophisticated to her, so continental, so very far from the soot and fog of the waterfront. Meanwhile Anthony bought one of her handkerchiefs and tucked it in his breast pocket. He wore cream-colored gloves, she noticed, and freshly polished shoes. He was meeting someone, perhaps—a girl—but she didn't ask. She only tried to sing along with him, her voice thin and scratchy beneath his warm, vibrant tenor: *Sempre libera, Sempre libera.* Another man stumbled by and glared at them, hollering something unintelligible. He swayed on his feet, drunk and reeking, sweat prickling on the florid dome of his head. He repeated whatever it was—a threat?— but she only looked away as if she hadn't heard him. And then he was on her, calling her names, yanking her back by the hair, kicking over her stand. She screamed—it was a man with church-wine breath, just like her father, and giant tuberous fists pink from factory dye. He kneed her in the gut, tried to punch her between the legs. Anthony lunged forward, wedging himself in front of her, but the man, drooling, just knocked him back. *Fuck off, faggot.* Then something in Anthony snapped. He took the jar of brushes and smashed it against the man's head. He kicked him where he lay, over and over again—in the ribs, the face—until the man sputtered and went limp. Alphie stared at the body, face-up in the street. Was he dead? She couldn't be sure. *He doesn't look very good, does he?* Anthony said. He crouched down and left thumbprints of rouge on the man's cheeks, painted his lips a ghastly pink. Then he picked up the scattered brushes, one by one, folded up the stand and took Alphie, shaking, back to her room at the boardinghouse. He left his shoes by the door and threw his gloves, now ruined, in the stove. He helped her wash her face, brush her hair. *Shh, shh.* As she leaned over, crying into her hands, she felt the bristles tug and scratch against her scalp. He smoothed her hair behind her ears, kissed her neck, her cheeks, her lips. And when he left the next morning, ambling down the dark lane in his rumpled suit, she looked at him with a kind of wonder. He'd saved her. Later that day, when she walked by the corner where her stand had been, still smelling Anthony on her skin, she saw that the drunk man was gone. Whether he'd left on his own two feet or in the bed of a bodywagon she wasn't sure. But she never saw him again.

After a while Anthony started spending the afternoons with her. He stopped in on his way between funerals and brought her flowers, which no man had ever done, and even if she suspected they were swiped from the lid of a dead man's box, she arranged them sunnily in an old paint jar on her windowsill. They would eat kidney and quail pies at one of the quieter alehouses, farther afoot from the thoroughfares, then return to her room at the boarding-house, where they drowsed in bed for hour after hour, as a square of tensile light waxed across the walls. Even though she wanted the life he had promised her—a house with a sitting room, the peace of routine—Alphie would come to think of those days, those long and secret hours before he had to return home for supper, as being some of the happiest of her life. She would lie naked beside him and listen as he talked in his scattered, searching way, smoking a cigarette and stroking the blond fuzz on her arms. Meanwhile, the landlord's canaries trilled just outside the door, and somewhere across the yard an old man played a war song on a fiddle.

Anthony told her that he lived behind his mother's home, in the quarters of the old carriage house. He worked as an undertaker—a trade he learned from his late stepfather, a quiet, heavyset man, who said little, smiled less, and hobbled through the rooms on swollen, gouty feet. He had taken Anthony on his routes during the day, traveling the neighborhood with his box of fluids, swabs, and needles; guiding the carriage to the cemetery and back. In each dark apartment Anthony learned the secrets of bodies—their contours and shades, their flaws and their beauties. There was nothing under heaven that disgusted him.

Where others had branded Alphie common and vulgar, he considered her elegant. Her curiosity had provoked her parents to call her "unreasonable," but he told her she was quick and clever. Never had she believed that in her circumstances she would find such sympathy and trust, especially in someone so unlikely: a man who dressed the bodies of the dead, who pumped their veins full of dye and plugged their wounds with cotton batting, who brushed their skin with wax and lard until they glowed ethereal.

Anthony talked often about his beautiful, temperamental mother: sometimes as if he longed to impress her, as if he craved her approval and admired her taste. But other times he'd arrive at Alphie's in a state, his eyes gone black with fury, and for the rest of the night he'd sulk so devotedly that there seemed to be no way Alphie could break the spell.

What the Signora could never know was that the first time Anthony had been with Alphie—the night after the fight, after he'd escorted her back to the boardinghouse—he'd paid her. Alphie had to do a little bit on the side—everyone did—but only when she really needed it. The memory of those earliest months made her sick—the gangrenous, popeyed drunks lurching for little children in the alleyway, the smell of those narrow closet-rooms behind the shipyard. For a time, just out of her father's house and alone, she'd worked at the worst of those places, where they were all made to wear matching blond wigs. The men on the waterfront called them the Widows. Sometimes the Widows huddled together on the mildewed terrace overlooking the yard, but usually they were kept inside, in that rickety little building as dark as a coal mine. Some strain of shoe-black liquor was served at the saloon downstairs, and by the time the johns pulled themselves up to the second story, they had become beasts. And the more ashamed they were, the worse it was for the Widows.

One night a man knocked out two of Alphie's teeth. Another beat her with his cleated shoe, leaving a permanent lump on the crown of her head. For a while, lying on the floor and waiting for daylight, she thought about death. She studied every beam in the rafters; she dreamed about the black depths of the river. But in the mornings she fixed her mind elsewhere; she had to. She learned to paint over the others' bruises and scars, draw in eyebrows that had been burned away by a cigar. It was the only comfort she could give. Some of them were just babies: nine or ten years old.

She'd been on the street since she was fourteen, when she was turned out of the house by her father for kissing a boy (Sam, the grandson of old Mrs. Vetz next door), for letting him touch her in the back of the shop behind the feed bins. She and Sam had been friends their whole lives. Still, her father beat her with a garden rake, saying it was all her mother's fault, her slut mother's, who had made her weak and stupid, who had always let her try on perfume and the other tools of the devil, even when she was small. Alphie had waited for her mother to run after her, to comfort her, to curse the temper of her father, who was prone to wild and evangelistic rages. But her mother had done nothing at all, only turned away when Alphie was handed a dollar and driven out into the street.

Growing up in her little town, she had only ever seen two ways to be a woman: tending the hearthfire, as a wife to a man; or waiting in the dark outside the factory saloons. *Plucked harps,* her mother called those women. Alphie believed that her fate had long ago been sealed, that she was ruined for any other life. But here was a man who protected her from what people thought she rightly deserved. Here was a man who was brave in a way that others could never be. So when she saw Anthony's sullenness, his sad and feral eyes, she only wanted to make him happy, with a desire so fierce that it hurt. When he said to her one afternoon, *I couldn't be what I am without you,* and closed her hand in both of his, she felt a rare fulfillment. She had something to give, something another person couldn't live without—she'd never known such a feeling.

Then, one day without warning, Anthony disappeared. He'd promised to take her uptown, to a posh, discreet club near Union Square—they planned to meet in the park at half past ten, then walk the last block together. She's been in a state of excitement all day: scrubbing and re-hemming her best dress, brushing out her blond hair until it crackled, spending more than she could afford on a gardenia corsage. She waited and waited at the corner of the square, but he never arrived. In the pit of night, back on the waterfront, Alphie went from tavern to tavern, asking after him, but no one had seen him in days. At the Shingle and Plank, the bartender gave her a finger of whiskey and a plate of Welsh rarebit. The other patrons flirted with her and bantered with her, but she couldn't bring herself to look at them. The food went uneaten. The corsage withered and died. Enraged, distraught, she haunted the alleys where he was known to stroll; she waited, shivering, on the corners outside his favorite saloons. The only place she wouldn't go was the house at the back of the shipyard. From a distance she could still see the Widows in their blond wigs—waiting in the darkened windows and doorways; milling, drugged, on the terrace.

She cried alone in her room for weeks, feeling stupid and blind. She went back over everything they'd said to each other, wondering what she could have done differently. Sometimes, in the middle of the night, she woke up to a greater fear—what if something had happened to him? What if he'd been robbed? Gutted and left to bleed on the floor of an opium den? She was overcome with the urge to hurt herself—even more than she was already hurting—for it was her fault, after all, wasn't it? She hadn't been enough for him. She was weak and perverted and foolish, and why would a good man like him love a broken bird like her?

As the weeks passed, an older, portlier gentleman from the

Shingle and Plank started frequenting her stand for lemon drops and cologne. He'd been a sailmaker in the British navy and now worked as a clerk for a tea company. He was red-faced and squinty-eyed and had a big, bushy beard, but he was kind and gentle and treated her well. His accent made everything he said sound thoughtful and intelligent, even if pitched at a polite half whisper. If he seemed reserved or quiet, it was only because he was content and didn't require anything, and then Alphie wasn't exactly sure what her role was, how she should behave, what he wanted or needed from her. But he was comforting, and after a while she let herself enjoy his company, although he rarely touched her—he brushed her cheek, maybe, or her hand, but he seemed shy, which was unusual for the sort of man who spent his nights scouring the waterfront for dice games.

One afternoon they went to see a vaudeville show on the Bowery. As they emerged onto the street afterward, she glimpsed something through the swarm of people: the flash of a familiar coat, the shimmer of a black armband. The sailmaker steered her by the elbow against the crowd, offering his opinions of the show, asking her where she'd like to eat, but she didn't hear anything he said. She kept looking back over her shoulder through the crush of revelers, wondering if she'd imagined it.

The next morning Anthony showed up at the boardinghouse, hysterical and drunk. *How could you?* he shouted, pounding on her door. She lay in bed, silent under the sheets, wondering if she should just wait for him to disappear. But the neighbors began to yell at him, and he yelled back, so she pulled on her dressing gown and tiptoed to the door and let him in. His shirttails were loose and his overcoat gone. He'd been crying so hard his eyes were almost swollen shut. She bolted the door and turned to him, relieved and thrilled and frightened.

That fat man? he seethed. *I saw you with him. I saw you holding hands—I* know *what you're doing.*

Her heart was pounding, but she kept calm. She rolled herself a cigarette and tightened the sash at her waist. *Please,* she said. *I'm not your concubine. You can't just come and go as you please.*

He fell down in the chair with the broken bamboo seat. He stared glumly at the floor, snorting back tears. *Do you love him?* he whispered.

The wounded, boyish break in his voice sent something fluttering inside her. But she just stood there, smoking and staring at him without expression. *I'm a real person, Anthony.*

He shook his head. *Mother wants me to marry. And this woman—she's perfectly nice, but I can't.* He grabbed Alphie's wrist and pulled her toward him and brought her roughly down in his lap. The edge crept back in his voice, firm and venomous. *You're mine.*

What could she do then? She'd never felt like she belonged to anybody anywhere. She couldn't go back home, not ever, not to the people who created her and then reviled what they'd created, who punished her for being the person they had once claimed to love. And why would the Signora force on Anthony a woman he didn't care for, when she, Alphie, loved him so desperately? She knew the risks, but they didn't matter. This was a chance to live a life she'd dreamed of: a real, loved woman, a wife better to Anthony than anyone could ever be.

Why would she let anyone take that away?

Perhaps she thought, for a moment, that the Signora would be like a mother to her, too. Anthony worked so tirelessly—he cared for others in their grief; he looked after the house and supported himself and his mother both. But what Alphie knew—and what the Signora did not—was that his secret life at night would be his undoing. She wanted, more than anything, to give him a safe place. A sense of warmth and predictability—not just the unending days of dead bodies, the hollow debauchery of the night. All Anthony longed for, she saw, was what other men recoiled from, worried it would turn them into eunuchs, ghosts, or dullards—domesticity. He wanted so much to be normal. So when she first climbed the steps of his mother's house, when the door opened and she was led into the sitting room, she was convinced, somehow, that the Signora would approve.

But the Signora, all talcum and licorice, only stared at her with eyes as blunt and lusterless as nailheads, her freckled breasts heaving, her coiffure pinned up with an ostrich plume. She had been a great beauty in her youth, Anthony had said, and Alphie saw she still had the powder-soft skin and calculating mouth of a young girl. She wasn't yet forty years old.

The Signora began to address Alphie in Italian, but Alphie couldn't understand it. She looked to Anthony to translate, but he only turned his eyes shamefully, pleadingly to his mother and said, *Mamma, per favore . . .*

The Signora studied Alphie a moment longer, then murmured, *Nessuno.*

That was one word—from her years on the street, from the Italian johns who'd exposed their cocks to her in raging shame and hunger, who'd beaten her up in the little back room when she spit out their come, who'd wept openly and with disgust when she got off her knees and held out her hand for the money—that was a word she did know.

Nobody.

BUT HE MARRIED HER. He defied his mother and made Alphie his wife. They moved into the old servants' quarters above the carriage house. The doorways were narrow and untrue, and the switchback stairs always squeaked underfoot. Still, there was something she loved about the place—navigating its corners and nooks like the galleys of her own little ship. They had privacy there, a little aerie away from everyone else, even though the yard was flanked by tenements, and the stench from the privies crept in through the windows. Years ago, as a fifteen-year-old chambermaid, the Signora had lived there with her first husband, Anthony's father, the horse-groom. When he died, she married their employer—the gouty undertaker—and moved into the main house. She refused to make her way across the yard anymore, to visit the carriage house or climb the stairs. She'd fallen down those stairs once before, Alphie had learned. Her first husband pushed her while she was nursing Anthony. Her arm hadn't hung right since.

Alphie didn't know much about Anthony's blood father, other than that he'd been kicked in the head by a horse and was never quite right again. He believed that people were hunting him (shadowy figures from the old country who had followed him faceless across the sea), that they were unscrewing his skull in the middle of the night and looking at the secrets in his brain. Some nights he'd even attacked the young Signora, bitten her all over her body. Alphie had seen the marks on occasion—the purple circles on her arms, the cleft in her ear.

Sometimes, when they all sat together in the parlor of the main house after supper, drinking coffee and eating cake, Alphie would see Signora's face go slack. Her eyes would fix upon a spot on the wall, and she'd hold her cup suspended, trembling in front of her, as Anthony played the accordion. Alphie wondered what it must have been like, to be sold off to a drunkard as a fifteen-year-old girl because your own father couldn't pay his debts, to bear a sickly child at sixteen, and then, at seventeen, to watch your husband die in front of you. She had seen him thrown from a horse and trampled in the street.

All Anthony remembered about the incident was that his mother had asked that the horse be spared—she put out her hand as they lifted the gun.

Once, in a fit of warmth brought on by a glass of anise liquor,

Alphie told the Signora that it was nice to have a mother again, that she hadn't seen hers in such a long time. She wanted to add, *My father got rid of me when I was a child, too—I know what it is to be hurt—but look what we've made of ourselves.* The Signora had smiled, even reached across the table to pat Alphie's hand. *Cara!* she murmured. Then, over breakfast a few days later—Anthony's birthday—Alphie presented him with a black armband that she'd knitted herself. *I worked on it nearly every morning, before you woke!* Anthony loved it: he pulled it on over his sleeve and kissed her—fully, on the mouth, right there at the table in front of his mother. The Signora refused to look at her for the rest of the day, and later that night, when Alphie knocked on the kitchen door to return the knitting needles she borrowed, she began to wonder if she'd misspoken, if her Italian wasn't coming along as well as she thought. The Signora was busy preparing the birthday supper, quartering a bulb of garlic, coaxing the jellied marrow from a calf bone. A pot of stew simmered on the range. When Alphie handed her the needles, the Signora only sniffed, *Every morning! Why, I thought you did your best work at night.*

Alphie had retreated, numb, to the carriage house. She sat by the window and looked down at the yard next door, at the children playing with the wash—making costumes out of blankets, swaddling a cat in underwear. She thought inexplicably of Sam Vetz, wherever he was—older now, riddled with carbuncles, maybe a foreman at the factory and diddling cotton threaders in the cloakroom, opening and closing his clamshell watch as the trains sang by, rutting some wife: silent and anemic, with the complexion of a broken egg. When her father found them by the feed bins, Sam had said it was Alphie's doing—she had *attacked* him; he hadn't wanted it, and her father—her own father—believed him. Sam Vetz, somewhere upriver and fat as a carp, skulking down the lines of a factory, past the young girls bent over their work, pausing now and again to trace the ridge of a reddened nape, or to feed roughage to the silkworms. Did he wonder what had become of her? Did he ever feel sorry for what he'd done? Some nights she dreamed about finding him. Hunting him down, tying him up, making him watch while she pleasured herself, ferocious. *This is what you wanted. This is what you've made me. This is the woman I've become.*

THE INMATES OF THE ASYLUM were turned out, weary, into the kitchen garden to pick radishes and beans. There used to be an old military building on the island, but all that remained of it now were a dozen weathered stones strewn throughout the grass. The women turned in circles in the sun, petting the stones as if they were children who needed to be soothed. Alphie recognized DeValle in the bean rows, digging through the dirt almost tearfully, and the woman with the mutilated tattoo squatting beside her.

The nurses sat farther away, against the wall of the stable. Jallow sorted through baskets of grubby lettuce heads and potatoes, squinting behind her spectacles; Bradigan snipped up radish greens with a pair of scissors. They passed a cigarette back and forth, gossiping, and even though Alphie couldn't hear what they were saying, she saw that their bullish personas had dropped for a moment, that they were almost relieved to be rid of the burden of their work and revert to their ordinary selves. She saw, when they thought no one was watching, how they laughed with each other, how Bradigan listened to Jallow with focused eyes and pursed lips, how she nodded with compassion as Jallow knuckled a bead of snot from her nose and gestured in the light.

Alphie moved slowly down the rows, a basket on her hip. Through her slippers she felt the slick, dewy grass, the easy give of mud. The wind picked up, and she heard the mournful bray of a boat horn somewhere in the distance, then the slap of water as it chugged to rest. The asylum wall glared in the white heat of noon, the stones worn smooth by the ardor of passing hands. She didn't know how much longer she could wait—every time she crouched and stood, every time she reached out her hand to touch something squarely in front of her, the world seemed to quiver and spin. She felt faint. The smells came sharper now: mildew, smoke, wet bandages. Her vision blurred as she dug her nails into the dirt, as the shadow of the octagon shimmered across the grass.

She wondered if anyone had ever escaped. Even if she managed to scale the walls, or slip through the gates and steal away to the bank, she'd have to swim across the river, with its rough current and charging ships. The shore of Manhattan wasn't far (a quarter-mile at the very most, she guessed), but patrol boats still circled the island (keeping watch over the asylum and prison, the poorhouse and hospitals). She'd seen them during the promenade, just west of the lighthouse. Even if she succeeded in evading those, even if she jumped into the river and swam swiftly, unseen, she would still be weak from whatever they put in the water and food, still muddled from the pain in her head.

The coal scows passed on the river, sending black clouds drifting in the air. Dust settled in her hair, in the baskets. The asylum ferry brought sundries in the morning, and women in the dead of night. Anthony had to come for her, rescue her; there was no other way out. She tried hard to remember the last words they'd spoken to each other—if only she had that much to live by!—but all she remembered was him kissing her on the forehead as she slept. He was gone that night, wasn't he? That's right—he was getting on a train. The four o'clock to Poughkeepsie. He was taking his mother on holiday, she remembered. She had studied the timetables over and over again, late at night in the carriage house.

A young nurse came by with a water pail and dipper. Alphie took a sip without protest, then spit the water into the weeds when the nurse had passed. She was thirsty, but she had to stay vigilant.

She was sure they kept the women here drugged and stupid so they weren't able to run or plot or threaten each other, so they were too weak to fight back. She just had to wait a little longer, she told herself. Anthony would find her.

She made her way through the rows, waving away gnats, squatting down to twist vegetables from the dirt. The sun sat heavy on her shoulders. Her knees began to ache; the skin around her tattoo stretched and burned. As she shook the grit from a snarl of onion bulbs, she heard DeValle, nearby, start to whimper.

Alphie looked over. She saw DeValle drop her basket and slump down into the radish-bed, twitching and kicking, biting anxiously at the weeds. Her eyes rolled back in her head; her mouth began to foam.

The nurses looked up from their scrubbed potatoes. Another woman began to point and cry. Bradigan bolted up, letting the radishes tumble from her lap. She lifted a bridle from a peg on the shed, then marched through the rows with Jallow waddling at her heels. They stood over the young girl, smiling and sucking their teeth.

"What's wrong?" Bradigan jeered. "Feeling frisky, pony?"

She threw the bridle over DeValle's face, fitting the bit in her mouth and yanking it back between her teeth. They forced her down, their knees at the small of her back. Jallow straddled her, bucking and swinging an invisible lasso. Alphie stared at the girl, the foam rolling back in her ears and hair, the mud trickling down her neck. Some of the other women started whimpering too, wringing their hands.

"Faster, ugly!" Jallow heeled her in the side. "Giddyup!"

Alphie saw a trickle of blood at DeValle's mouth, her tongue lolling and clicking against the bit, spit snailing down her chin and onto the ground. She felt a rage she hadn't known since she was a child—something she'd tried to hold back, something not herself.

She dropped her basket and lunged at them. She shoved Jallow off DeValle and threw her hard against the ground. "Get away from her, you cunt!" she screamed.

To her own ears, her voice sounded strained and hoarse. For a moment Jallow just looked at her, stricken, her glasses swinging from her ear.

Alphie coughed and wiped her mouth with the back of her wrist. Jallow tried to scuttle away, but only slipped and fell backward, twisting her ankle in the mud. Then Bradigan hit Alphie in the small of her back, brought her to her knees. Suddenly another girl—a girl with a mane of ratty blond hair, the same green-eyed girl who'd spit out her tea at breakfast—jumped between them, pushing Bradigan away. And then, whistles across the yard—other nurses were on them, wrenching their elbows back, kicking at their knees.

"She's hysterical," one said, grappling Alphie. "She's having a spell!"

"They're hurting her!" Alphie cried. "She's a young girl, for God's sake!"

While another nurse helped Jallow to her feet, Bradigan yanked Alphie back by the hair and pressed the scissors to her throat. "You're so strong, you're so tough. Is that it?"

Alphie didn't know what to say: her head began to spin. The nurses dragged her and the blond woman back through the yard and into the kitchen, past the range and the chopping block and the cankers of soap on the ledge of the sink. She saw one of the scullery girls drop her rag and scurry to the ice room with a pick as big as a tent stake. Bradigan and Jallow wrenched them through a doorway, down a dark hall to a chamber that smelled like piss, then, working in tandem like a swift machine, they bound each woman's hands with rope. Alphie trembled as the knots were cinched tight around her wrists, as the nurses grunted pink-faced over her hands, as the scullery girl came in and shook a bucket of ice into a tub filled with gray, scabby-looking water. Too stricken to speak, she stared at the tiles on the floor, at the black mildew stains on the wall. The blond girl thrashed and clawed as the nurses dragged her toward the tub, as they forced her to her knees and yanked her back by the hair.

She made a sound then, but not a word, just a rolling, toneless cry.

They pushed her face-first into the water. She writhed, her feet kicking and slipping along the tiles. Still they held her under, their sleeves drenched to their elbows. Alphie heard a terrible noise coming from under the water—a scream. The girl's breath rose to the surface in frenzied bubbles. Then the nurses whipped her back, her lash of hair flinging water across the room—a great silver arc that landed with a slap on the floor, splattering Alphie where she huddled, sick, trying to wriggle her hands from the cuffs. Three, four, five more times they pushed her under, all the while chanting, "Mother's Milk! Mother's Milk!"

The girl wailed and went limp. Then, as they turned her over and dropped her to the floor, as she coughed up water and cried, they reached out their wet hands to Alphie.

Alphie howled as they grabbed her by a chunk of hair and dragged her over to the tub. *Should I just let it happen?* she wondered. *Should I just give myself up?* They wrenched her back by her collar, choking her, and slammed her face into the water. The ice burned against her skin. She screamed and gagged, twisting around, her knees slipping and bruising against the tiles. They pulled her out and then plunged her in again, grunting: "Mother's Milk! Mother's Milk!"

She tasted turpentine, hair, the oil from other women. Her lungs rattled; her eyes stung, hot and raw. When at last they pulled her out and dropped her on the floor, her hands still tied behind her, she could only roll onto her stomach and retch up the water.

"Hand me those scissors," said one to the other.

"There ain't no scissors."

"I thought I put them on the table?"

"I said they ain't *here*."

The nurses scanned the room, while Alphie lay with her cheek in a puddle of sick, trying to keep from crying. Bells clanged in the kitchen, then out in the yard.

"Fine." Bradigan sighed. "They can catch their deaths for all I care."

They stepped over Alphie and kicked her hard in the tailbone. She watched them march out of the room, their heels smacking up water, laces loose and slithering behind them. As they turned into the hall, she heard Jallow whisper, ashamed, "I really was frightened for my life!"

"They can't hurt you," Bradigan said, soothing. "They're really nothing but babies."

Alphie rolled to her side, her legs locked together, belching cold water through her teeth and nose. Her wet clothes clung to her skin. As the nurses' footsteps disappeared down the hall, she smelled the nip of a match, the flowery smoke from their cigarettes. They'd be returning to the yard, she knew, to herd the women inside for their drams of mead.

Desperately she tried to squeeze her hands out of their cuffs, but the soggy rope only grew tighter. She ran her tongue along her penny-tasting gums, worrying her loose tooth, wondering if they would strip her and beat her, send her up to the Violents for good. She looked over to where the other girl knelt cowering in the shadows. A strange sound came from her throat.

What Alphie saw next made her weak. Something was sprouting from the girl's mouth. It grew and grew, pushing upward and out, the muscles rippling in her throat. Her lips kept moving as if she were saying *now!* over and over again. *Now, now, now, now!* Then she gagged and spit. A pair of scissors went clattering across the floor, pulling a long, clotted thread of mucus behind them.

Alphie stared. "What did you do?"

The girl only coughed and gasped for air.

Alphie leaned forward. The girl's tattoo had scabbed over and was beginning to peel, but through Volpe's bloody thumbprints, Alphie could still read the name. *Orchard Broome.*

SEVEN

I N THE CELLAR BENEATH DOYERS STREET, THE LITTLE GIRL
pushed open a door and led Odile into a tunnel. It was dark and
cool, redolent with the smells of wood-rot and loam. The cut in
her knee throbbed, but she followed the flame of the lantern, trying
to stay calm. In the light the walls seemed to quiver, as if they were
on the verge of buckling, collapsing, burying her alive. Gazing up at
the archway of rough-hewn brick, Odile couldn't help but imagine
her mother in her grave.

The day of the fire, just after the twelve o'clock show, Odile
had been eating lunch at the beer garden alone. All morning her sister had been tense and moody, refusing to do contortions, paring
her routine back to a few easy stunts. She even cut the Daring Devil
routine—no matter that Odile was already up in the rafters, waiting
in her halo and wings. The audience, mostly families with fidgety
children and a few bleary sand-bums, clapped tepidly or fell asleep.
Meanwhile Mother fumed and paced, her brows drawn together, her
eyes hot and black as bits of coal. Afterward Odile didn't stop to
ask what was wrong—she just shrugged a coat over her costume and
hurried down the hall. As she passed the dressing room, Mother

opened the door and called to her: *Come in for a moment, will you?*
But Odile had just waved her off and continued out of the theater
and down the boardwalk. The last thing she wanted to do was sit
around and watch them argue. Belle was most likely doing this to
antagonize their mother, and Mother would respond in kind with
a scene of self-righteous ire. Even when they fought, it seemed they
were only trying to outperform each other.

At the beer garden she tried to put it out of her mind. She read
a newspaper and drank a cold glass of lager. She smelled the smoke,
but she didn't think anything was amiss at first—there was always
some kind of mishap or commotion going on, every weekend of
spring. But then she heard people pushing back their chairs and
gathering at the edge of the terrace. Looking up, she saw a black
cloud billowing into the sky. The crowds on the boardwalk were
drawn, mothlike, toward what was burning—she couldn't see it
from where she sat—and then the volunteer fire brigade was clanging down the street. *It's that building,* someone yelled, *the one that
looks like a cake.* Odile stood up, spilled her beer. She started running. She didn't think of her mother at first—robust, resourceful,
quick-witted Mother—but of her sister, gloomy and aloof, slower
than usual. *Don't let it be my theater. Don't let it be Belle.* But then
she turned the corner and saw the Church of Marvels burning,
black and illuminated, like the negative of a photograph. She saw
Aldovar, too, running down the street. She grabbed his arm—what
was it she said to him? Something frantic, babbling, a string of
words: *In there—she's in there!* Around them a crowd had gathered,
awed and gawking, as if it were all part of the show. Odile watched
as flames jumped from the roof of the theater and chased down the
spokes of the Ferris wheel. She saw people trapped in their car-
riages at the very top, rocking back and forth, shouting for help. A
few climbed out of the windows and onto the beams, their clothes
flapping in the smoke. She couldn't watch. The heat was terrible,

the smoke explosive. She couldn't get any closer—*coward!*—so she ran toward the open air, the beach, and hid gagging and half-blind under the pier.

She hated herself for it now.

Ahead of her the girl with the wooden arm swung out the lantern. Somewhere a pair of rats chittered, scrabbling in the dark. Noises began to echo back to her—laughter in wheezy peals; the trickle and splash of water. The tunnel widened, and soon she began to see rooms branching off to the side—golden burrows filled with smoke. She heard the clink of glasses, the rattle of beads, voices low and sibilant. A woman sang a song somewhere in the darkness, in a language she didn't know. As they drew closer, Odile peered through the doorways—men were hunched over fan-tan tables and poker games. Under the white lamps the smoke was so thick that she couldn't see their faces, only roiling clouds where their heads ought to be.

"What is this place?" she whispered.

The girl looked back over her shoulder. "The Frog and Toe."

Odile knew gambling parlors had sprouted along the Coney Island boardwalk, too—behind the candy store where the floor was sticky with marshmallow paste; under the beer hall where the cops filled their bellies and stuffed their pockets and looked the other way—but Belle had never seemed to take an interest in any of it. She'd been too busy with her swords, her piano. She was so disciplined onstage—her energy focused, her body refined. But sometimes afterward, freed from the theater, away from the constraints of her costumes and paint, she ran a bit wild—like a whip drawn taut and then traveling to crack. Once she and Aldovar had gotten drunk on an empty trolley in the station yard, and Pipkin the beach cop had to bring Belle, singing and listing, around to the house. Mother had just shaken her head and put her to bed. But that was as much as Odile could recall.

Beside her the little girl whispered, "Can you do the hot sandwich?"

Odile looked down at her, startled. "How do know about that?"

"She showed us once. Four swords *and* she smoked her cigarette the whole time!"

The hot sandwich had been the blow-off to Belle's show: the grand finale. Odile wasn't sure if the girl was trying to trick her into something, so she just said, "Why don't you tell me about the tigers?"

"Oh! Their names were Ulysses and George, and they were very big and strong and had magic shapes."

Odile swallowed hard against the burn in her throat. "Shape shifters, you mean."

"They could swim underwater," the girl went on. "In the ocean they grew fins like fishes. They could fight octopuses and whales."

"Yes," Odile said, feeling her eyes sting. "That's very true."

She craned her neck as they passed the half-lit rooms, listening to dominoes shuffle and click. Hands floated over the tables, drawing croupiers' wands or fanning cards, but they all belonged to men: knotted and woody, rimed with dirt. She followed the girl around a bend, drawing the valise closer to her chest. How could she be certain someone wasn't lying in wait to rob her in these tunnels? How would she find her way out to the street if she met with any trouble?

She needed to get Belle home. Soon the season would be over—summer would burn into autumn; autumn would wash away into snow. Winter was the time their mother had toured, or devised new acts for the spring debut, when the beer stands and music halls were shuttered against the cold. Together, Odile thought, she and Belle could sit by the fire with cups of jasmine tea, sketching costumes, graphing stunts, choosing fabrics and bunting. They would build it up again, side by side. *The Church of Marvels: A Living Museum! Human Wonders, Sincere Sensation!*

"What was my sister doing here?" she whispered.

"Sometimes she came down from the shop to visit us. She couldn't sleep a lot. But like I said, she's gone now."

"And she didn't tell you why she's left? Or where she's headed?"

The girl shook her head. "People come and go. It's always that way."

Odile tried to think back to the letter, tease apart anything that might have hinted at an underground warren, or a girl with a wooden arm. Why wouldn't Belle have mentioned something so unusual? Of all the letters she'd claimed to start—all those seconds, hours, days spent thinking about home—why hadn't she at least written about this? Even something as simple as, *I've found work as a shopgirl*—or would that be too humiliating for someone like the Shape Shifter to admit?

"What's your name?"

The girl looked back over her shoulder. "Pigeon."

"And where are your parents, Pigeon?"

She cocked her head, as if no one had ever asked her such a thing. "I don't have any."

"Isn't that funny?" Odile swallowed. "Neither do I."

This was the question she found herself returning to over and over, late at night while the empty house settled around her, while mutts in the yard licked the crockery clean and snuffled crabs from under the porch. If she had done just one thing differently that day (turned into the dressing room instead of forging stubbornly ahead—a mere step), would she even be alive? Would she and Mother be dead together in the ground? Or would something else have happened? Maybe if she'd walked through the dressing-room door, just as her mother had asked, she might have saved her. She might have rescued her from the fire instead of crying to Aldovar and hiding on the beach. Her mother would be alive, her sister safely at home: three pairs of boots left to dry on the porch after a morning walk by the sea.

If anything, Odile thought, their mother's death ought to have inspired Belle to stay, to continue the Church family legacy. Everyone knew Mother was crafting Belle in her image. And everyone adored her. Why hadn't that been enough?

The girl lifted the lantern higher. "You look like her, you know, just funnier."

Odile gritted her teeth. She never understood why people insisted on saying that, as if she weren't reminded of it every time she and her sister had brushed out their hair in the mirror at night. Everyone knew that Belle, with her lithe body and cut-glass jaw, was striking, if not beautiful. Next to her Odile, even with the same features, felt shrunken and warped, as plain as a teaspoon bent in the heat.

"Your hairs are different," Pigeon explained. "Yours is smaller."

Self-consciously Odile touched the coil at the nape of her neck—Belle never wore hers so tight.

"And you're littler," Pigeon continued. "The littler sister."

"I'm her twin sister," she said.

"But you're like this—" She tilted her body at the hip.

"Yes, I know," Odile replied, pressing at the bandage on her knee. She felt suddenly small and hobbled, no bigger than the rats scuttling in the mud. Around her the tunnels echoed with shouts and trills, a garbled song. Her breath began to feel tighter in her lungs. She thought she heard a heavy, scraping sound in the distance, like a body being dragged.

"Pigeon," she said, trying to keep her breath steady. "How did you lose your arm?"

Pigeon shrugged matter-of-factly, the metal socket creaking at her shoulder. "That's the way I was born."

"And what is it, exactly, that my sister has left down here?"

"It's a surprise for you!"

Odile felt the mark behind her ear begin to burn. "Listen," she said, taking the girl by the elbow and crouching down in the dirt. "If I find out that you have lied or tricked me—if I find my sister has come to any harm—I will send the tigers after you. Do you understand?" She leaned in. "The new ones are as big as horses. And they can smell a person from a hundred miles away—they're just waiting. And the longer they wait, the hungrier they get. All I have to do is whistle." She brought her fingers to her mouth.

"I'm not a liar," Pigeon said. "I'll really show you."

At the end of the tunnel they passed under an arch, then stepped down into a cavern. Odile heard echoes coming back to her—the whispery chatter of children—and saw Pigeon's lantern pick out tiles along the wall. She paused, letting her eyes adjust to the darkness. Above her the green brick walls had the look of a moldy honeycomb— stippled with alcoves and thrown into relief by dim, smoky lamps. It was an old crypt, she realized, a forgotten vault—maybe one of those churches built on a Frenchman's pasture a century ago, then razed as the city bulged and steamed and ate up everything wild.

But she didn't see any remains—only children, peeking out from the alcoves like bats—a wall of glittering eyes, looking down on her with fearful, bewildered wonder. A few rushed toward her, but Pigeon batted them out of the way. "She's going to see the play!" she told them. "The play!"

Odile's heart beat faster. What was it her sister had left for her to find? In some of the alcoves she saw smaller versions of the Frog and Toe rooms: a makeshift saloon, where roughed-up boys sat with saucers of whiskey on their knees. Another where children squatted over marbles and dice, and a mutt chased after rolls gone astray. One held a kind of trading post, where a boy and a girl organized newspapers, cigarettes, rolls of yarn and twine, walnuts, matchsticks, used candle nubs and spoons. The boy wore five neckties, the girl three petticoats, all different shades of white and edged with mud. The alcoves were stacked five high, joined with a criss-cross of ladders and rope—one boy hoisted a milk-crate up by a pulley, singing a tuneless song to the creak of the wheel.

Odile held tighter to her valise. At the end of the cavern they followed a passage into another room, this one smaller, dark. At one end a low stone platform had been turned into a stage. Above it hung a curtain: a white sheet strung across a bowline. On the walls a few torches—limelights—whickered in their grooves.

A stage.

Pigeon and the other children set to work. They drew the curtain taut and tied the corners down. Odile took a tentative seat on the edge of her valise. The torches hissed and flickered beside her, throwing feverish shadows on the walls. She heard the children bustling behind the curtain—hisses and whispers, the clatter of props, a few injured whines. After a few minutes a hand emerged and gave a signal. Two boys sat down on a box with a fiddle and a horn. Another blew out the lanterns and snuffed the torches. Odile was suddenly in darkness; she couldn't see anything, not even her hands, clenched and sweating in her lap.

Now in the dark of an underground tomb, a light began to glow. It bloomed slowly behind the sheet, rippling out to the edges. As the fiddle larked and dipped, a figure appeared in silhouette—it was a shadow play, Odile realized. The boy, in profile, bowed to an imaginary partner. He brought a monocle drolly to his eye and doffed a top hat. Then he swiveled to face the other direction, and his figure transformed into that of a girl. She fluffed out her skirt, blew a kiss through the air, waved her handkerchief. Odile leaned forward. This was Aldovar's routine.

One by one the shadows emerged, distorted but sure, billowing behind the makeshift screen. A girl lifting what looked like a glass bulb to her lips. A blindfolded boy flinging sticks through the air. Another girl twirling and dancing, four-legged. Odile leaned forward, her breath catching in her throat. Birdie, Mack, Georgette.

The shadows danced and mimed. The fiddle fallumped to a finish; the horn keened. Odile clapped, alone in the hush of the chamber. The sound of one person's hands coming together, without answer, seemed unusually sad.

Then, as the fiddle started up again, a taut shimmer in a minor key, another figure stepped out from the wings. The sheet rippled; the lantern hissed. Odile recognized the silhouette of Pigeon's arm as she fluttered sideways into view. On her head were two horns, in her fist a bouquet of lightning bolts. She was dancing a simple jig. Odile felt the tears start to well in the back of her throat. The Daring Devil. She watched, breathless, as Pigeon drew a bolt through the air with a flourish, as she tipped back her head and opened her mouth, as the bolt magically disappeared down her throat like a gulped worm. But there was no angel here, no Odile swinging down from the rafters. The devil was onstage, alone.

The fiddle played faster and faster. The silhouette danced. All of Belle's rhythms, in shadow, in miniature. But when the silhouette turned to the side, something looked different. Wrong. At first Odile thought it was just a trick of the light, the way the sheet snapped and swayed. She leaned in closer. The devil, ghoulish and merry, lifted another bolt in the air. A flame popped in the lantern; Odile jumped. She stared, dizzy, at the sight in front of her, her mouth dry, her skin tight. The silhouette's belly was swollen, plump. The devil dancing, and with child.

EIGHT

T HE FIGHTS WERE NEVER ADVERTISED. BILLS WEREN'T PLAS-
tered to fences or hung in tavern windows. There was no
swaggering talk from street-corner barkers (who ballyhooed,
for a fee, anything from a politician to a whorehouse to a two-bit
revue). The matches were hasty, ramshackle, fought in any place
that happened to be empty and unpatrolled. The dead cornfield on
Henry Street. The burned-out shell of an old gin distillery. It was
for the toughs to earn some money and the drunkards to smell some
blood. Today the turf was the floating church, St. Elmo of the River,
which was docked in the shadows just north of the bridge.

Sylvan walked there alone, past the dumps along the waterfront,
trying to focus, to keep himself calm. He stared at the ragpickers who
foraged through the heaps, dragging their sacks over tin-scrap and
bones. Once a grand pier had stood there, a marvel of industry. Its
glass pavilion had shone and rippled above the water: a ghostly, fiery
schooner of light. It was almost like being inside an aquarium, they
said—ladies floating through the motes in their muffs and pearls,
gentlemen basking in the exotic shadows of fronds and gullwings.
But the pavilion had since sunk to the bottom of the river, and now

only the dome, or at least its skeleton, could be seen anymore, battered by wrack and plumed with birds, its mossy iron skull cresting above the dull and lusterless water.

Sylvan walked farther along the wharf, staring up at the masts. From the rolling gurneys and crates he could smell spices and bilgewater, the ripe rot of fish. He took a deep breath, feeling the blood beat in his jaw. He'd never been in the water before. Even as a child he hadn't jumped from the dome the way the others had, not even on a scorching summer afternoon. He'd seen them all out there together, laughing in the wake of freights, splashing away rats. He hated their dumb loyalty, the way they showed off for each other, clambering up the rungs of the old pavilion and leaping off, hollering and wheeling their arms.

Sometimes he thought that if he'd grown up with another life— in that room with the crying woman in the white kerchief—he might have learned how to swim. He might have been a man who dove beneath the slick, baked water of the river, down to the coldest depths, to the black ravaged bed and nests of hoggleweed. He might have glided through mazes of fallen cargo, prizing open crates, turning out the pockets of drowned men and scavenging shipwrecks for loot. He imagined swimming through the sunken pavilion with turtles and eels, twisting glass baubles from old chandeliers, wresting caviar spoons from the river shrubs. But instead the sight of the river— sucking at the rust on the hulls, foaming and whipping in the morning wind, tossing flotsam on its way to the sea—only made him sick.

St. Elmo was a small ship, moored between a creaking, tar-breasted bordello and a clipper that had once been a Union hospital off the coast of Virginia. (Ex-soldiers still convened there, seeking morphine in the rotting cabinets and chests, lying drugged on the floor in the darkness.) He drew himself up and crossed the bowed gangplank, keeping his eyes fixed on the steerage cabin ahead.

When he dropped down into the berth, he saw that men had

already started to gather. There was a rawness in the air, an ache particular to the morning. The numbness and blunder of nighttime had worn off, but there were many who couldn't stand to see it end—they huddled there under the swinging lanterns, hiding from the sunrise, anxious for a fight, some blood, anything to keep them rolling. The preacher passed around a jug of crabapple liquor. Three potbellied brothers played a game of faro with girls from the bordello. One of the girls, the youngest one, sat by herself in the corner, running her finger along a prayer card and trying to read the words under her breath.

Sylvan had barely slept; his back was aching and his eyes were dry. He looked around in the dark, trying not to stare at any one person too long. He felt like an animal out of its shell, a scooped oyster. He'd made it a point not to make friends here—he was a mystery to them, and it served him better that way. As a dogboy he always found matches to fight—he could be an adversary for just about anyone. And the crowds were bigger now that word had passed among the privileged circles: *See a gentleman coxswain fight a lowly night-soiler! See a Moscow brute battle a New York rogue!* Some fighters came in signature regalia, trailed by a gang of bootlickers, all in their banner colors. In the crowd Sylvan could already see ribbons of purple and blue. He rolled back his shoulders, ruffed out his beard. When the preacher blew the whistle, he stepped into the ring.

Over the years he'd witnessed every sort of unusual bout—he'd seen a man with no arms fight a man with no legs. He'd seen a Bowery Boy, victorious, draw an American flag on the chest of an Irish tinker with the man's own blood. He'd seen another fellow's eyeball pop out mid-fight and loll against his cheekbone, still rooted to the socket. Gasping, the man had cupped the jellied eye in his palm and stumbled around the room, until one of the whores laid him down on the floor and sank it back into his skull with the aid of a matchstick.

This morning's round he was paired against an older Englishman named Banto Qualms, who sported a purple waistcoat and blue top hat, which he shed with genteel ceremony as he entered the ring. He worked as a stevedore on the western docks, Sylvan knew, but still carried himself like some kind of swell. He was pale and pudgy and top-heavy, with broad shoulders that narrowed down to spindly ankles. Blue veins cauliflowered in the crooks of his elbows, on the backs of his knees.

They circled each other under the lanterns, rocking on the unsteady floor. Sylvan felt a turn in his gut, a primal thing like hunger or dread. He wasn't a brutal man, or a thief by nature; he didn't like to bring on trouble—but still, he'd grown familiar with this feeling. A poisonous, antic adrenaline, an inability to be still or feel safe. He studied the way Banto lurched back and forth with the sway of the ship: his arms were oversized and apelike, his gut sagged tremendously beneath his shirt, but his knees looked brittle and jittery, an old man's joints.

The preacher raised his hand and blew the whistle. Banto lunged at Sylvan, throwing his arms around his waist and bringing him fast to the ground. They grappled on the floor, flipping like two hooked fish, the dust rising around them. Over the shouts of the crowd, Sylvan could hear a baby shrieking. He moved to jam his fist into the divot behind Banto's knee, but Banto rolled away and hoisted himself to his feet. Sylvan jumped, swinging his fists, slamming Banto in his lip as he tried to duck. Banto grunted and threw back his head.

Sylvan swiveled around, trying get an elbow to his kidneys, but Banto knocked him to the floor with one shoulder, pinning him down by the neck. "You got a tail, Dogboy?" he said. "You shit-licking piece of trash?"

His fingers wriggled over the top of Sylvan's trousers, gouging his skin, digging into his tailbone. Sylvan thrashed and kicked. With a whinny, Banto pulled his pants down to his knees. Sylvan flopped on the ground, his ass exposed to the air. The crowd began to bark and howl.

Sylvan tried to twist around, to get a blow to Banto's ankles, but Banto knocked him back with a quick pop to the jaw. Sylvan's teeth cracked together, ringing; his head slammed against the floor. He felt the blood bubble up under his tongue and run down the back of his throat. He opened his eyes but couldn't focus on anything; the dust was wet against his cheek, his beard sticky with spat wine. He saw people, riled and shifting, just beyond the ring of light. A few clapping hands. The slick glint of teeth. Above him Banto stood with his legs stoutly apart, his arms raised in victory. Then Sylvan's muscles twitched. Quickly he hooked his feet around Banto's ankles and launched himself forward, springing up in the air. Banto, up-ended, fell flat on his back. Sylvan went tumbling over him, his pants still loose around his waist. He got his balance and crushed his knee to the man's sternum, then started pummeling. Despite the blisters from the slop shovel and the sting of his skinned knuckles, his fists were tight. He got a few good slugs to Banto's chin, a haymaker to his cheek. The tremor of contact traveled up through his arms and shoulders and spine, then exploded in his brain, an electric white light.

Banto jabbed him in the groin with the points of his fingers—hard enough for Sylvan to flinch and buckle forward—then came a one-two punch to the left cheek, the throat. Sylvan toppled to the floor, struggling for air. He tried to lift his head, draw a full breath, but Banto was already standing over him, a green heel pressed against his windpipe. He cracked Sylvan once more, on the side of the head, and it was over. Sylvan lay still on the ground, unable to breathe.

The whistle shrieked. The preacher pulled Banto to the middle of the ring and held up his arm. Sylvan rolled to his side, panting. There were hoots and taunts, a smear of sound, nothing he could really understand. In the swinging light, clusters of faces flickered around him, like a wormy knot of coral. The preacher handed over the purse and Banto, thumbing up his suspenders, thanked him and counted out the dollars. Everything seemed false: a pantomime, a shadow of life. In the crowd money flicked, exchanging hands. No Bones stood against the wall and stared at Sylvan with tired, jaundiced eyes, wine dripping from his beard.

Sylvan pushed himself to his feet, left the ring without a word. He was conscious of the sweat shaking off of him, the sappiness on his knuckles. He poured water from a canteen over his head and shivered as it ran down his face, through his hair and over his chest. He shook it off. *Dogboy.*

He had a strange feeling then—as if he were floating above the room, staring down at his body, sweat-slick and covered in dust. He could see his pants hanging off the yellowing knob of his hipbone, the blood in the grooves of his knuckles, the beads of grit embedded in the skin of his back. He could see everything in St. Elmo's berth, thrown into sharp relief—the sprigs of violet in hatbands and buttonholes, the thumbprints on the porthole glass.

He wrapped a chunk of ice in a rag and pulled himself up to the deck. A few people were cooling themselves between rounds, their faces turned into the wind. He could smell the wine drying in his beard, the iron tang of his blood. He felt everything at once—the ache in his kidney, the crack in his jaw, his flummoxed and galloping heart. He stood there for a few minutes, dragging the ice over his ear and his cheek, buttoning up his shirt. A group of men hollered at him, waving their hands. They hoisted a couple of flasks and cheered. Sylvan never knew what he was supposed to do in these situations. He was dying for a drink—he always needed a beer after a fight, a shot of grog to soothe his head—but he just looked awkwardly away, as if he hadn't seen them, and continued up the waterfront, the sun rising higher and burning through the fog, the ice melting against his face and running down his neck.

Sometimes when people did seek out his company, he grew wary and withdrawn, to the point where his aloofness discouraged attention, no matter how desperately at times he craved it. Because he looked so unusual, people assumed that his life was dramatic and full of adventure, that it was as wild and uncanny as he appeared. He could sense their growing disappointment in his ordinariness, in his normal appetites and habits: how, after a fight, he went home and cooked his own meal and practiced reading the newspaper. There was nothing to apologize for, he felt, or to be ashamed of, but he sensed that others—passing friends, women he'd taken home— were surprised by this. Sometimes it seemed they held it against him, although in anyone else those same pleasures might have been wel- come, even comforting. Why, he wondered, did he have to peddle his difference for their amusement, and yet at the same time temper it, suppress it, make it suitably benign? Eventually these people drew away, and afterward Sylvan burned with an indignant satisfaction. Being right had become more important to him than being loved.

He wasn't sure what to do with himself once the Scarlattas were dead and he was suddenly alone. He had no money and no real plan. The glove business had moved elsewhere; there was no longer anyone to give him work, to keep him fed. He stayed on in the cellar, piecing together odd jobs where he could: shoveling snow in the winter, clear- ing trash in the spring. He kept fighting. If you didn't have something to live for, he reasoned, you'd die. Not just to live for, but to live *toward*. He thought for a little while he'd live for someone else—a woman, Francesca. She'd grown up on the other side of town, in Greenwich Village, the daughter of a well-to-do family. Last spring she started coming down to see the fights. Her father owned a glass company, she said, and her mother was Italian—a fact she was quick to point out, as if that were something unique that bound them together. He was excited by her at first—a girl from outside the neighborhood who had chosen him, who had seen him fight, who recognized something in him that was worthy. She wasn't classically beautiful—she had an upturned nose and a downturned mouth, which sometimes gave her

the look of a startled lapdog—but she was spirited, dirty-mouthed,
arch and aggressive in a way that he needed. He felt wanted—for the
first time in as long as he could remember—really *wanted*, and even
if it was for the wrong reasons, it was better than being alone with
his own mind. When they had sex she came quickly, vigorously, with
what he suspected was a bit too much theatricality. Afterward she
put on a mood: she'd shrug him off and order him around and flick
him away when he tried to touch her hair. Still, night after night she'd
come down to the waterfront—he looked for her, always, in the crowd,
straining to catch a glimpse of a watered-silk dress, a mauve hat flit-
ting between the soggy caps and fedoras. He tried his best to scrub
up, look handsome, but she wanted him dirty. She wanted him just
after a fight, when he was sweaty and bruised.

Sylvan knew he wasn't in love with her—he disliked her self-
absorption, her automatic sense of authority—but she was different—
nervy and vital, with an appetite for everything. She laughed easily,
kissed hard. (He knew she had money, and he hated to say it, but he
liked it—he liked fucking a girl whom other gentlemen, refined and
well-bred, were apparently proposing to, still thinking she was pure.)
She wanted (discreetly) for everyone to recognize that she had more
money than they did. She wanted them to envy her (fizzing about in
her French silk and lambskin gloves), but she also wanted them to
admire her for slumming it, for drinking cheap beer in a run-down
saloon.

She played up her Italian blood as if it were part of her lusty,
continental disposition—something that couldn't be *helped*—even
though, like Sylvan, she'd never been out of New York City. She'd
throw around Italian words (usually the wrong ones, although he
hesitated to correct her), and even in her roundabout, airy way, there
was always the suggestion that her Italian-ness was superior to his
(*but I'm not Italian*, he wanted to say, *or if I am I don't know it*). From
what he could discern, Francesca's mother was a quiet, respectable

Catholic woman who spent her days keeping books for the glass company and teaching music lessons. Why should there be any shame in that, he wondered? And where did Francesca tell them she went, the days and nights she spent with Sylvan along the waterfront? *The Ladies' Club,* or *tennis lessons,* or *my cousin's in Chelsea*—she really didn't care if they believed her or not, they were so *bourgeois.* She wanted to make it very clear that she was wild, artistic, free, and bohemian, unlike her small-minded peers. But in the end, Sylvan realized, she didn't seem to do much more than seethe. She was fed not by her passion for experience, but by her fury for others. What would she do without their boring conventions? Where would she be if there was nothing to run from?

The last time he saw her was at a party in Greenwich Village. She'd invited him as her guest—even loaned him a suit, already pressed. Flattered, he'd agreed, but all week he was sick with nervousness—if people on his own block didn't know what to make of him, what would her friends think? That afternoon, when he and Francesca arrived at the brownstone on Barrow Street, it had already begun to rain. Inside there was a large, buzzy, boisterous crowd, all smoking and swilling wine and talking too close. Sylvan stood there in a three-piece suit, drinking a glass of French wine that he couldn't pronounce; his hair, parted and greased just an hour ago, had started to frizz in the humid air. Francesca introduced him to a series of well-heeled gentlemen as her pugilist. *Please meet my pugilist, Mr. Scarlatta*—which wasn't his name, and she knew it, but which he supposed sounded more bloodthirsty and exotic than Threadgill.

My pugilist. Mine.

That's when he realized he wasn't there to keep Francesca company at all—he was only meant to shock. He could see it in her proud smile as she dragged him from group to group, each introduction a little more manic than the last. *Have you met my pugilist from the East Side?* He braced himself, but everyone just smiled and shook Sylvan's hand: *Hello, sir, hello, how do you do. Nice to see you, Mary Frances.* They were all exceedingly polite, which Sylvan hadn't anticipated—he was overcome with relief, even a bit of brotherly warmth—but looking over to Francesca, he realized that wasn't what she wanted at all. She was livid and tense, drained of color. And he could see her now the way the others did—embarrassing herself with social stunts and performances, dramatic bids for attention. But they were all determined to staunch it with cool, unruffled acceptance. No men, he realized, were fighting to marry her—they only gritted their teeth when they saw her approach. And the look in their eyes when they shook his hand was one not of jealousy, but of sympathy. *Good luck, chum.* He would never forget the look on her face—like a girl about to blow out the candles on her birthday cake, only to find that another child had already stuck his fingers in the icing.

She glared at Sylvan, distant but accusing, as if this had all been his fault. Whatever had thrilled her—the danger, the impropriety, the illicitness—was gone. He drank the last of his wine, pulled off his collar, and left. He walked all the way home in his borrowed suit, through the spill of the factories at shift's end, shouldering blindly through a crowd that smelled thick and familiar—rosin and sawdust, wood glue and linseed oil, the liverwurst in their lunch pails, the cheap powdered soap that scrubbed the sap from their hands.

He didn't see Francesca again at the fights, and he was glad for it. Other women followed—he just wanted to feel something else for a little while, something other than the mortal dread that hovered around him (sometimes he'd wake up with a pounding heart, startled to realize that he was, in fact, fully alive, no matter what he might have dreamed)—but the affairs quickly grew tedious, until he was acting more out of habit than any real pleasure. He spent too much time growing dizzy in the taverns, counting the boot scuffs on the rail, dreading the empty apartment that awaited him. He surrounded himself with people—loud, boorish, smugly glazed—but it only made him feel more invisible somehow. To be seen but not known was perhaps the loneliest feeling of all.

He had to live for that loneliness, he decided—for the private life of his mind, for the possibility of flight. There was nothing left to keep him on Ludlow Street except the fact that he knew it well, almost too well. It had made him. But into what?

For months he'd waited for the ghost to show itself. For months he'd listened at the doorway, watched from the stairs. Then he heard it in the cellar, moving in the dark, stumbling through the clutter that remained. He saw it staring back at him, wild and bearded in the glass. The ghost, all along, had been him.

NOW HIS BODY was a golden burn, sparking, loose, zigzagging through the streets. The cold water drying on his face, the sweat stinging his eyes. He'd lost—there was no extra money for Mrs. Izzo or the baby. Back to night-soiling at dusk, with No Bones whispering to the others. Back to the cellar on Ludlow Street; back to the loot. It was a strange sensation—a kind of euphoric fury. Everything around him appeared heightened, almost divine—even the glitter of mopwater tossed in the street; the quarreling birds in the sky—and yet his world had never been narrower. To fall to Banto, of all people—an old speck of gristle, as queeny as a peahen, strutting around with a spray of dyed flowers in his hatband and stinking of cod. How could he have let that happen? What good was he if he couldn't wallop a brittle old man? And the baby—Sylvan's nose began to burn, but he sniffed it away—he couldn't stop thinking of how her eyes had opened in the phosphorous glow of the lanterns.

Around him Broome Street seemed fragmented and unreal. He stepped to the side to let others pass, grumbling. He tried to hold on to one simple thought, something clear and unremarkable. This was the place he'd been the night before. Here was the butcher shop, with its German signs and waxy, headless hogs. Here was where the slop wagon had stood. Over there was the garbage pile where the other night-soilers had rested with their canteens—now swarmed by crab-pink junkmen, picking through scraps in the naked sun. And here, near his feet, was the spot where he'd stood alone, listening to the baby crying in the yard.

He walked back down the gangway, smelling the fresh spill of guts, the lavender blossoming in the yard beyond. He saw the privies standing open in the sun, glimmering like the murky cavities of a paint tray. Laundry flapped on the line above. Everything seemed remarkably, dismally ordinary.

Back on the street he noticed a man in the window of the butcher shop, hanging a row of quails above the hog legs. He was young—an apprentice, most likely—with a ruddy, sideways nose and a wedge of white-blond hair.

Sylvan knocked on the glass and the man came out, mashing a rag around in his hands. He swayed forward in his galoshes, yeasty smelling and maybe a little bit drunk.

"Were you here last night?" Sylvan asked him.

The man scowled, then said in a thick accent, "Why?"

"I'm looking for a woman," Sylvan asked.

The man snorted. "I sell only one kind of meat."

"Maybe lives upstairs? One who was expecting a child? White woman, girl—could have green eyes?" Sylvan went on. "Maybe one who seemed . . . I don't know . . . troubled? Mad, even?" He tapped the side of his head.

The man paled a little. "The witch?"

"The what?"

He lowered his voice. "Aren't our boys scared of that one?" He leaned in closer. A quail egg slipped from his fingers and broke across the ground. "Used to buy blood in a jar."

"What?"

"That's who you mean, right?" The man rubbed the yolk into the ground with his toe. "She don't look right. No . . . she don't *seem* right."

Sylvan stepped back. "You know her name?"

He shrugged. "She ain't been by in a while—but then she come in sometime last week. All swelled up, had a funny way of walking." He paused to take a nip from his flask. "Nervous, I'd say—always looking around. I ask if she wants a drink of the water? No. She needs to go back in yard for the privy? No. Bought a quart this time, not just pint. Lee . . ." he stammered. "Lee and Eddie, I think?"

"Lee and who?"

"That's who you mean, right? Lee and Eddie's woman. She'd stop by on her way to the poppy box." He pointed to the stairs that led from the sidewalk down to the basement.

It took Sylvan a moment to realize what he was talking about— an opium den.

Then the butcher himself sidled out, apron strings tight against his belly, cleaver swinging in his hand. He glared at Sylvan and said pointedly, "You here for quail?"

"Not today," Sylvan said. "Thank you."

The man stared him down—a bullfrog pop of the cheeks, a casual swing of the blade. Sylvan knew that look well, so he turned and walked the other way. He could only imagine what his face looked like: bruised chin, split cheek, a salty crust of blood on his lip. He stood for a moment on the sidewalk, staring at the wooden staircase that buckled down beneath the butcher shop.

He felt the hurt sing through him—his eyes picked out a door in the shadows. A golden bell hung above the jamb. *Aren't our boys scared of that one?* Lee and Eddie's woman. A dragon-chaser. The witch bringing home the blood.

NINE

ALPHIE STARED, SHIVERING, AT THE GIRL IN FRONT OF HER. She read the words again: *Orchard Broome.*

She couldn't breathe at first. Her home was near that very corner—her little nest above the carriage house, with its shambling doorways and canted floors, its rooms smelling of horse sweat and gardenia perfume and Anthony's strawberry cordial.

"Do I know you?"

The girl didn't answer, just stared at Alphie and made a clicking sound in the back of her throat.

Alphie leaned in closer. She tried to recall bits of gossip from the block, anything about a madwoman or an idiot, but the pain crackled through her head again, and she doubled over, sick. There was nothing left in her stomach—she could only gag and gag, throwing up mouthfuls of saliva. She felt a shock of embarrassment—she knew it was unreasonable, but she didn't want someone from her new neighborhood to see her like this.

But the girl only looked at her, pleading. Her eyes were clear and green, and she had a bald patch behind her ear in the shape of a sickle. Alphie stared at it for a moment, blinking away spots of light.

She had seen that mark before—she was sure of it—but she couldn't remember where.

"I know you," she whispered, clearing her throat. Was she one of Anthony's neighbors? Maybe the girl by the print shop, with the red-stained hands? Or the seamstress who peddled needles next to Mr. Moro's cart?

The girl opened her mouth, but no words came out, just a low, weak sound without shape to it.

"Are you deaf? Dumb? Is that why you're here?"

The girl just hung her head. She could be here for any reason at all, Alphie knew—sometimes they sent a woman here when she was out of her mind with fever; when she was too moved by the Holy Spirit or too awkward with company; when she was haunted by something horrible she'd witnessed, or when she couldn't hold a child in her body. Still, the sickle mark was one Alphie had seen before. Hadn't she? Or did she just want to believe as much?

Now her ears popped and drained, and the sounds of the asylum became deafening. She looked at the scissors, which had come to rest in a puddle across the floor. "How did you do that?"

The girl rolled on her stomach and inched her feet over to the puddle, then coaxed the scissors up between her toes. She lifted her legs into the air behind her. She curled them up and over her head, slowly, like a scorpion's tail. She rocked forward, slithery and lithe, until her feet hung just inches from her face. Then she drew the scissors open with her toes and gestured for Alphie to hold out her bound hands.

Alphie did so, astonished. "You must be the maddest of all."

The girl flexed her ankles and brought the scissor blades together. The twine around Alphie's wrists snapped and unraveled. Quickly Alphie shook away the cords and rubbed at the welts they'd left behind.

The girl rolled to her side and dropped the scissors to the floor.

Alphie scrambled after them. How often, in her childhood, had she measured and cut the twine for her father's store? How many times had she snipped the gnarled tail off a beet, or a loose thread from a sleeve? And yet here, the scissors seemed miraculous and providential, an artifact from the outside world.

"Who are you?" She leaned over and cut the rope from the girl's wrists. There were freckles on the bridge of her nose, blood at the corners of her mouth. Alphie had seen her once before—she must have—unless the water had addled her brain, made her believe in things that weren't there. "Do you know me?" she pleaded. "Can you speak?"

A door slammed somewhere down the corridor and footsteps echoed on the stones. Alphie tucked the scissors up her sleeve, then folded herself on the floor, shivering. *Please, God*, she prayed. *Don't let them hurt me. Don't let them find out.*

A pair of nurses entered, women Alphie didn't recognize—one with a dark, prunelike face; the other with bits of skinned vegetables stuck to her skirt. "Get her to bed," one said to the other, nodding at Alphie. "And this one"—pointing to Orchard Broome—"we've got to make her eat, since she can't do it herself no more."

Alphie stumbled to her feet, faint and weak, but allowed herself to be supported by the nurse's thick arms. As she was guided out of the room, she saw the other nurse pull Orchard Broome to her knees and strap a mask around her head—the bottom half of her face was sheathed in metal and something like a trumpet horn bloomed from her mouth. The nurse cracked a raw egg over it—Orchard Broome gargled and screamed. Then Alphie was pulled around the corner and away.

HERE WAS HER HOME now, a room with ten rusted beds; ten mangy, straw-filled pallets. As the nurse returned her, shivering, to bed, she said sternly, almost sorrowfully, "No more trouble, understood? You'll catch your death." Alphie dropped her slippers to the floor, her feet slimy and ice cold. She smelled the pot in the corner overrunning with piss. She crawled under the blanket and touched her body, freezing and shaking, while the nurse plodded away. She pissed herself, not even caring anymore. The heat warmed her.

If anyone here should discover what she'd done, what she'd concealed, she wasn't sure what would happen—she'd be stoned, or hanged, or taken some place even worse, a place as bad as where the Widows walked behind the shipyard. She lay with her hand under her pillow, clutching the pair of scissors. If someone should come near her, touch her, she wouldn't be afraid to use these. She pictured the scissors puncturing the heart of the Matron. What a strange sensation it must be to stab someone, popping through the layers of muscle and flesh, grating against the ribs, until the blade came to a rest in the fat, blubbering sac of the heart, while everything else leaked slowly away. A big red sun sinking into darkness.

She turned to face the wall, away from the white-lipped women who sank further into fever and delirium. She cut two strips from the edge of her blanket and cinched them tight around her thigh, about an inch apart from each other. Then she slid the scissors carefully beneath them, the metal slick against her skin, until the hinge rested firmly on the highest knot. A makeshift scabbard. *Look*—she'd say when she was free at last—*at Blackwell's I saw a girl pull this from her throat!* Anthony would laugh and say perhaps she was mad after all, to dream up such a thing. *And I didn't give them back,* she'd say, *I kept them so I could defend myself, so I could fight. Think what might have happened if you hadn't come!* Then he would look into her eyes, take her by the shoulders with his firm hands, and tell her that *of course* he had come for her. Of course.

Tonight Anthony would go to bed alone. She imagined him undoing his collar and his cuffs, leaving them by the dish on the stand. She imagined him turning sideways into bed, sleeping shirt-less in his old pair of long underwear, from which she'd scrubbed blood and opium tar, tobacco juice and tea. She pictured his dark hair tumbling against his face, his stubbled jaw sinking into the pil-low, his back curled against the still-burning light. Sometimes, in the middle of the night, he would seize up in bed and cry out: a terrible, blood-chilling sound that was half choke and half scream. Immediately she was awake beside him, her heart pounding. She thought he was awake, too, but he was still asleep, gasping for air, falling out of bed and punching the floor, his eyes open but not see-ing. Finally she'd shake him, or press a wet handkerchief to his face until he woke, startled. Afterward he was confused and disoriented, unsure of where he was, with a look in his eyes of someone hunted. He'd be thirsty, ravenous, so in the darkest hour of night Alphie crossed the yard and slipped through the Signora's back door to for-age for something to eat. She loved the smells of the kitchen in the main house: the orecchiette in mushroom sauce, the melting balls of cheese, the béchamel. She'd grab something quietly, careful not to wake the Signora, then steal back to the servants' quarters, her skin still buzzing and her heart hammering in her chest. Anthony would sit up in bed, wolfing down a wedge of cheese wrapped in mortadel-la, glugging a glass of whiskey between deep, agonized breaths. She rubbed his knees, his back, but she was shaking herself, and some-how she was angry that he'd put her through this ordeal, too. But she tried to remember how he spent his days—crowding into un-familiar bedrooms and parlors, laying the dead out on his cooling-board. And when the consumption had swept through last year, there was no time to prepare the bodies—they were carted away while he watched, helpless, from the street.

The thing she never spoke about, not even to Anthony, was the ritual he had with his mother when he returned home. Every time he went out to prepare a body, he brought her back a souvenir.

A tooth. She kept them all in a jewelry box, and once in a while she took them out to arrange them around the darts of the backgammon tray. She lifted her spyglass right up to her eye, as if she were an archaeologist on a field study. They were human teeth, but she indexed them by animal: wolf, hippopotamus, alligator, rat. Anthony never explained this to Alphie, and she was too uncomfortable to ask. *He hunts the animals for me,* the Signora once said, but Alphie couldn't tell if it was a joke or not. *He keeps me safe. There are wolves who live in the dumps by the river—don't go past Essex, especially at night.* Pronged molars, spotty fangs, baby's teeth no bigger than grains of rice. Alphie remembered the marks on the Signora's body, and shivered.

She lay awake now in her little buckled bed, listening to the women sigh and weep around her, sucking at the spot where her own teeth were gone. She wiggled the loose one with her tongue until it squeaked and bled. She tried to imagine what was happening back at home, but she couldn't even be sure what day it was. She thought of Anthony, haunting the halls of a Bowery tenement, shaving the beard off a dead man's face, sewing a child's cold lips together. She pictured his mother, counting out dessert forks for a party, or smoking alone in the parlor, the only sound in the house the clatter of dice on her backgammon board, the teeth rattling in their gilded box.

Months ago, in the spring, after an especially bitter fight with his mother, Anthony had disappeared. Alphie tried to wait him out, the way she'd done before, but after days of the Signora's blistering silence and her own sleepless nights by the door, she'd put on her yellow poplin dress and veiled hat and worked her way down Broome Street—she knew there was an opium den he used to visit, back in the days when she lived alone at the boardinghouse. She lifted her skirts as she stepped down the stairs to the basement. She knew the code at the door; the man recognized her, tipped his hat. When she found Anthony lying there on the ground, his clothes tangled, his thick hair pasted to his skin, his beautiful eyes raw and puffed as a rummy's, he looked suddenly old, a stranger.

Get up, she said.

His gaze lingered somewhere over her shoulder. She took his hands in her own, ignoring the sticky mess they left on her gloves. *I know it's bad,* she said, *but you have me.*

He turned his eyes on her then, and the look on his face was one she'd never seen before—disgust, disbelief, a venomous contempt. *You?* he spat. *You? You're the reason I'm here.*

She let his hand drop back to his chest. She walked, stunned, up the stairs, past the man at the door and out into the rowdy street. The sun blinded her; the smell of eels and spilled milk made her gag. He didn't know what he was saying; he wouldn't remember it tomorrow—he could have meant anything by those words. Yet she knew she was a cause of anguish for him, as much as he loved her. Ever since she'd come to the house, he couldn't relax. He only seemed calm when he was working, when he left for the day with his case of swabs and needles, when he took his hat off its peg and marched out into the street. He was so gentle with the families of the dead, so compassionate. But when he came home to the dinner table, she could tell he was drugged. Leaving the den and crossing over the Bowery, she thought, *I'll just keep walking. I'll walk all the way to the train station, go anywhere else. Then he'll be sorry. Then he'll realize what I am to him, what I've given.* But the thought of him coming home, aching and disoriented, and finding her gone, was too painful. She would be thinking about him the whole time, hoping he would come after her. And what if he didn't? She had nowhere else to go.

Sometimes she understood Anthony's midnight fits, for once in a while her own eyes flew open in the dark and she felt a smothering dread. *What am I doing to myself?* she asked of her pounding heart. *How can I possibly keep this up?*

Now, tossing in her bed, the piss turning to a cold burn on her legs, she felt a fever begin to spike. The pain throbbed in her head; her teeth chattered. No matter how tightly she curled under her blanket, she shivered. It reminded her of something else. Her quiet home at night—humming to herself while she put a hand over her belly, while she turned down the sheets and looked out the window, down into the darkening yard—

"Mother's Milk."

Alphie looked up and saw an older woman sitting at the foot of her bed. "I got it, too," she said, "my first week."

Alphie stared at her. It was the woman with the scars on her chest, her tattoo slashed away.

"My eyesight went," she continued. "I was no good at the factory no more. My boys didn't want a leech, so they had me sent here. I'd rather be blind at the factory, stitching my fingers together, than have to wake up one more day and smell this room."

Alphie stared at the scar beneath her collarbone. "What did they do to you?"

"Nothing. Only gave me the name of a family dead to me." She held up her hand and smiled. Her fingernails were claws—gruesomely long, warped and fuzzed with yellow.

Alphie felt herself begin to shake. Heat flooded her cheeks.

"You must drink some water," the woman said. She reached for the pail, wrapping her fingers carefully around the dipper.

"Please, no more water." The wet spot she was lying in began to prick at her skin. She kept playing it over in her mind: Anthony, returning to their rooms above the carriage house. (Where had he been that night?) She saw him pulling himself up the stairs, reaching for the door, only to find the bed unmade, the rug spoiled, the cradle—

Alphie sat up. "Wait." She pushed the dipper away and stood, swaying on her feet. "Oh God," she muttered. "Oh my God."

She wandered out of the room and down the corridor. Beneath her skirt, the scabbard grew tight around a wave of quickened blood.

What was she looking for? There was music coming from another room, but it sounded off tempo, in the wrong key.

She could feel the heat shivering off her skin, light crackling in her eyes. She looked out the window, down to the courtyard, where the women were taking air in the ashen light. They wandered in circles, their hands trailing and tickling the bricks as if they were blind.

Didn't anyone see her? Didn't anyone know?

She thought she heard something behind her—a wet swishy sound, like a mop being dragged. She turned around, squinting, but the hall seemed to bend and dissolve around her. She wasn't mad, she told herself; it must be whatever they put in the water here—but still, she was sure she saw something down the corridor, something on the floor. She imagined for a moment it was the girl from the bath, bound at her wrists and her ankles, slithering down the hall like a snake, her eyes bright and fiery, the metal horn at her mouth gleaming like a frozen scream. Alphie turned and ran, half-falling, around the curve of the corridor. But whenever she looked back, she was sure the girl was still there, following her—shoulders rolling, hips swishing, trailing a wake of slime behind her.

Alphie burst into the music room, but no one seemed to see her. A nurse was playing an old piano that was missing some keys. The madwomen were dancing around her, exalting like frenzied May Day nymphs. Alphie pushed between them, then grabbed one by the wrists. "Where's my baby?" she cried. But the woman only whirled her around, laughing.

"Where's my baby?" Alphie shouted again as she was flung, stumbling, to the ground. She stared for a moment at the slippered feet jumping around her, at the dust rising from the floorboards in agitated thumps, and there—seeping under the far door—a trickle of water.

She tried to scream, but an old woman yanked her up and pulled her close. "You need to shut up," she whispered in a garbled accent, her breath sour and stinking of leeks. "You make it worse for yourself, you understand?"

Alphie whimpered and pulled away. She went up to the pinched, sun-brown nurse who stood along the wall. She brought her voice down, to a whisper, so no one else could hear. "Where's my baby?"

The nurse frowned. "Don't you know, my dear?" she said sadly. "You have no baby."

Alphie shook her head—*no, no*—and broke away. She heard the swish again, coming closer. She ran back to the hallway and down the stairs to the yard. She stumbled and grabbed for the rail but missed—she skidded down, scraping her ankle and slamming her hip. The tip of the scissors sliced into the skin above her knee. Still she pushed herself up and staggered the rest of the way down. Outside she joined the walk of women, turning endlessly around the courtyard in a nervous, murmuring wheel. She folded herself in between them, hoping to disappear.

Then, a few yards ahead, she saw the Polish woman with the frizzy hair—she was leaning against the wall, holding a piece of lint up to her cheek, whispering to it, clucking. Alphie ran after her, tripping in her slippers. She could hear the words come out of her mouth—part of her knew she didn't make sense; the words were not what she meant—but still, she couldn't stop herself. "I need my baby, please, please." She reached out for the lint—it looked so soft, so sweetly silly there in her hand—

"Mine!" the woman roared. She slapped Alphie's face so hard that Alphie wavered for a moment, stunned. And as they stood there, blinking at each other, the lint lifted out of the woman's hand and flew away. Alphie watched her chase after it, all the way to the far end of the yard, shrieking as it turned and jumped in the wind, as it floated over the stanchion and out toward the river. Then, as it disappeared into the trees, she fell to her knees and wailed. Alphie felt that wail down in her bones—something so deep and true that tears sprung to her eyes. She turned and, weeping, walked the other way.

My baby . . . She reached the front gates, wrapped with heavy chains, the locks as big as horseheads. She could see the smoky glow of Manhattan through the trees. Her nose and eyes were running, her breath was ragged, her cheeks burned. A trickle of blood ran down her leg, beading the soft blond hairs, growing sticky in the heel of her slipper. Everything seemed so quiet. There was only the sound of a magpie, burring in a barren tree.

When the Signora walked into the room that night and saw her undressing—when she saw her remove the pillow that was cinched against her stomach—all Alphie could do was stand there with the sick feeling that nothing would be the same again. She felt her old life shrivel up and die inside her, a flicker in the pit of her stomach. But she didn't throw herself at the Signora's knees or turn away ashamed. She didn't fan her hands over her flat stomach with its pearly navel. She just stood squarely in front of her, naked, and met her gaze. There was nothing, she knew now, that she could say. Part of her strangely relished the sensation, holding the perverse stomach in her hand, with its fraying buttons and splitting wales. She watched the woman's eyes go dark, her lips part, her perfect skin turn a sickly gray.

Il mostro, the Signora had said. *Il mostro.*

TEN

LEE AND EDDIE'S WOMAN. SYLVAN PICKED HIS WAY DOWN THE staircase, to the door beneath the butcher shop. He paused for a moment, staring at the small blue star painted on the frame. If the mother were an opium smoker, she might have no memory of leaving her baby in the privy at all. She might have been overcome with madness—some kind of terrible, intoxicated fit. *She don't seem right,* the butcher's boy had said. She might wake this morning sick with panic and horror, turning restlessly through her rooms, unsure of what she'd done. She might have left her baby behind not out of terror or spite, but because she was living in some kind of feverish whimsy, a topsy-turvy phantasmagoria.

His body still crackled from the fight. He turned the knob and let the door stutter open. He'd never been inside an opium den before, but he'd heard a few of the night-soilers talk about them. He expected to see something exotic—golden dragons, men with silks and queues—but he was only met with a pink-nosed, middle-aged doorman in a blown-out chair. The man, heavyset and red-haired, looked up from a lady's dime novel, alarmed. He stared at Sylvan with eyes as sunken and black as a potato's.

"I'm looking for a woman," Sylvan said, peering toward a darkened hall beyond. "Maybe friendly with a pair calling themselves Lee and Eddie."

The man stood up and leaned into him, so close Sylvan could feel the moist breath on his skin. "What's wrong with your eye?" he said. "You blind?"

"If you're as ugly as you look it must be working fine."

The man grinned. "I know who you are," he said. His glossy nose twitched like a rabbit's. "I seen you fight once. On Henry Street, in the cornfield."

"Did I win?"

The man just squawked with laughter, a sound that was somewhere between a belch and a bark.

Sylvan said again, "Lee and Eddie?"

The man's expression changed. He sniffed and held out his hand. "Fifteen gets you a mat."

Sylvan reached into his pocket. He didn't have much on him, but he counted out the coins anyway—there was still some left over for Mrs. Izzo, at least, a fresh bottle of milk.

The man smiled in spite of himself. "I knew it was you! What was it they was calling you again?"

Sylvan shook his head. "I can't remember."

"When you won they all went mad, didn't they? Like this—" He threw back his head and howled like a dog.

Sylvan tensed. "That's me, all right."

The man set down his book and waved a freckled paw. "This way, then."

He led Sylvan down the hallway, through a series of curtains. The floor was slanted, the ceiling low. Corridors branched out around them, gauzy with faraway light, but Sylvan kept his eyes on the man ahead. The deeper the passage took him, the hotter he felt—he pushed up his sleeves, opened his collar. The walls were painted in hues of red—for a moment Sylvan had the dreamy sensation that he was swimming through the vein of a body, toward a lush, warming heart. Ahead of him the man was lumbering and stout, so large he had to duck beneath the doorframes, but he moved quickly, almost gracefully. The passage seemed to turn and fold back on itself, and then it came to an end. The man pulled aside a blue curtain and beckoned Sylvan inside.

It was the whistling he heard first, nervous and discordant, as if he were standing in a hutch of sick birds. A vapor hung in the air, its sweetness cut with the smell of unwashed skin. Through the fog he saw a row of bunks, brittle with woodworm, and lamplit mats along the floor where people lay curled on their sides. No one looked up as he passed, but Sylvan peered into each crowded bunk, at every flop of rags on the ground. Faces glowed in the puddles of light, but their features were slack and strange and dreamy. He saw blissfully pink-bulbed eyes, smiles of ruined teeth, chins gooey with saliva. No women, though—only men.

The doorman came to a stop in the far corner of the room. He waved Sylvan over, then nodded at the ground.

Sylvan stared down at the mat. It was occupied by a young man in a rumpled suit, a long pipe at his fingertips. Beside him squatted a boy of eight or nine, tinkering over an enameled box. The boy took no notice of Sylvan, just speared an opium pill with a darning needle and lifted it to the pipe. The man shifted a little on the cushion beneath him, then leaned slowly toward the light. The flame flickered beneath a glass cowling, and soon his face came into view: first his lips, meeting the carved mouthpiece of the pipe; then the broad, questioning nose; the high cheeks and hooded brow; the moist, choleric eyes. He was handsome but bedraggled, unshaven, stinking of sweat. He looked as if he'd been lying there for days.

He took a long draw on the pipe, which whistled and clucked. Sylvan smelled something bloom in the air, a scent like anise and lavender. He felt light-headed and suddenly nauseous. His ears were still ringing from the fight, he realized; he could hear a clicking in his jaw. The man fell back on the cushion, his chest expanding, his limbs going slack. He turned his eyes up to Sylvan and smiled.

There had to be some mistake. Sylvan looked over, but the large man was already retreating back through the den, his oaky shoulders rolling in and out of the shadows.

The boy with the box stood up. He wore a cone of newspaper over his nose, like a bird in a child's stage-play. Sylvan stared at the wag of his poorly cut hair, the blackened tips of his fingers. A memory flashed in Sylvan's mind—a foggy waterfront street, a gang of boys pelting him with pebbles and trash as he ran, panting, among the maze of coffins. The same dread filled him now, at nineteen years old—how was it possible to be scared of children?—but still, he was relieved when the boy gathered up his tools and left.

The man lay on his back, staring up at the ceiling. "Is your name Eddie?" Sylvan asked.

The man turned and blinked at him, a dimple flickering in his cheek.

"Lee?"

He just smiled at Sylvan, beatific, uncomprehending. A beetle trundled over his coat, which lay crumpled at his side.

Sylvan knelt down by the lamp. "Do you know who I'm talking about? Lee and Eddie?"

The man kept smiling, but Sylvan couldn't tell if it was because he understood or because he didn't.

"Where's the woman?" Sylvan began to feel a little faint—the floor seemed to rise up, the air began to bend. "The woman with the baby?"

The man just shook his head again, confused.

"The one they call the witch—the one at the butcher's shop, expecting a baby. You know who I mean?"

The man must have found this amusing, because he chuckled deeply and closed his eyes.

"Do you understand me? What happened to her?"

"Jesus," someone moaned nearby. "What do you want with him for? Ain't he been through enough?"

Sylvan reached out and shook the man's shoulder. The bones felt fragile through his shirtsleeves, almost spongy. Still, he gripped him hard. "Do you know where they are?" He gave him another shake. "Listen to me! Lee and Eddie!"

The man frowned, tried to open his eyes. "Don't I know where who are?"

"Lee and Eddie."

"Yes?"

"You do?"

"I do what?"

"Lee and Eddie. What happened to the woman with the baby?"

The man drew his eyebrows together. "There is no baby."

Sylvan's vision skipped; the blood began to pop and tingle in his ears. He felt dizzy, too warm, as if he'd been hit too hard, or had too much to drink. The high of the fight was wearing off, and his body began to burn with pain.

The man took Sylvan's hand in his. "Come," he said. "Lie down. You're hurting, I know."

For a moment Sylvan thought he might throw up. He lay down on the mat and stared up at the loose, crooked coffers on the ceiling. With one hand he reached into his pocket and clutched at the old square of cotton, the one Mrs. Scarlatta had cut for him. Beside him the flame burned low and smoky in its glass.

The man held on to his other hand, gently. "He'll be all right. He'll be all right, won't he?"

"She," Sylvan said, an image of Frankie flicking through his mind. "It's a girl."

"Of course." He laughed breathily. "Of course. I meant that."

Sylvan closed his eyes. Next to him the man sank further into a daze, whispering something he couldn't understand. Sylvan heard the breaths come evenly, felt the cool fingers go slack around his. He breathed deeply, too, waiting for the pain to subside, tasting the floral haze in the air. In the dreamy half state between waking and sleeping he pictured the soilers digging him out of the den, crowding around with their lanterns raised, peering down over the rubbled tin and pillows. *Help!* he wanted to call up to them. *Help, I'm down here!* But they just stared into the pit with terrified eyes, grabbed their buckets and disappeared, and when Sylvan turned to see what it was they'd been frightened by, he realized he had a tail, bushy and thick as a wolf's, wagging away in the dirt.

AFTER A WHILE he opened his eyes—had he been asleep?—and sat up, aching. He glanced over at the man next to him, slack-jawed and puffy-eyed, white crusts of drool at the corners of his mouth. He was no one special, Sylvan realized—probably a spoiled child like Francesca, slumming it in the dens, the kind of person who took pride in unbuilding what his father had given him, when he should have been grateful he'd been given anything at all.

He glanced over at the man's cast-off coat—a handsome toffee brown, with a knitted black band around the arm. He shook it out and tried it on. It was tailored, beautiful—nicer than anything he'd ever owned. He remembered the coat he had stolen from a vagrant in the winter, but this wasn't the same, he told himself. This man could afford it.

He wobbled to his feet and made his way past the languorous forms on the floor, the sputter of lamps. He turned through the doorway, then followed the corridor back, looking for a sign of the heavyset man. Curtain after curtain, the air cool at one turn, warm at another—he couldn't be sure which way he'd come in.

He turned a corner and found himself in a small room. Half a dozen boys were hunched over a table with brushes and knives, chiseling tar from opium pipes that were stacked in the middle like kindling. They scraped the residue into little bowls. At the head of the table sat the boy with the paper-cone nose, molding the dregs into soft, lumpy cakes.

Sylvan had heard stories from the other soilers about a gang of wild children who lived beneath the city, let loose like mice in a maze of tunnels, but he'd never believed it was true. The way the men talked, he imagined a pack of feral animals, starved and vicious, prowling their way through a living grave. In the darkness of the earth, he thought, the only thing visible would be the whites of their tiny eyes, the gnash of their baby teeth. But these children sat quietly here in front of him, working as methodically as tailors, their faces downcast and gray.

The boy with the paper nose turned and looked up at him. "Find what you come for?" He smiled—a weird, teasing smile that Sylvan couldn't quite read.

"No."

There was something cautious and foxlike about the boy's eyes; they glittered nervously over the paper nose, watching as Sylvan reached into his pocket. The other boys worked without stopping. Sylvan took out a penny and slid it across the table.

"Has there been a woman down here?" he asked. He described what little he could about the girl at the butcher shop, but the boy only shrugged.

"Never seen one like that," he answered, breathing shallowly through his mouth. He pulled the penny close to the saucer, where the black cake oozed like a sooty pudding. "Sometimes they come looking for a fellow, but no one stays."

"Anyone here by the name of Lee? Eddie? You know them at all?"

"No names here, not with us. That's the way they like it."

"What about that man—the man you were helping?"

"He's been down here all night—he's so sad. Except when Jacky sucks him off. Then he's all right." He sniggered, and Sylvan felt his stomach turn. He had to leave. He had to go back to Mrs. Izzo's, bring milk for the baby. (And part of him dreaded it—he didn't know what he'd be returning to—he could only pray the fever was gone.) He had to pack his hands in ice, drink a beer and eat some meat and rest his body, which seemed to tremble even in the close, overwarm room.

He glanced down the row at the other boys, bleary and gaunt. They picked the pipes apart, chipping and scratching, char falling over their hands and fluttering up to snag in their lashes. One boy, the smallest, upset a bowl of residue with his elbow, and the whole thing clattered to the floor.

The beaked boy screamed and jumped to his feet. "That could be two bits right there!" he hollered. "Now pick it up, every last one!"

The little boy whimpered, then sank to his knees and crawled around in the dark, trying to pinch up the tiny bits of black from the floor.

The older boy settled back on the bench. He set the first cake aside and began kneading and patting another.

Sylvan shook his head. "It's a hard life you're living," he said.

"When I was born," said the boy, "me mother, she saw I weren't me father's. So she cut me."

He lifted the newspaper away from his face. He had no nose. In its place were two black holes that quavered as he drew a breath. "Everything else," he said, "has been easy."

ELEVEN

THE NIGHT BEFORE THE FIRE THERE HAD BEEN A GYPSY party on the beach. It seemed like a dream: torches lit along the shore, plumed horses trotting through the sand, androgynes in fake silks flying high up on swings. Odile had walked around barefoot with bells chiming from her ankle, eating a cinnamon doughnut and watching bats swoop across the sky. Her mother sat by the fire pit in a splendor of scarves and tea-colored skirts, holding court with a pair of castanets. Odile looked around for her sister— they were supposed to meet at the fortune-teller's caravan and head west to watch the fireworks—but Belle never showed. She waited and waited, scratching at her mosquito bites, lolling on the steps of the caravan as the party swelled around her. Eventually she got restless, so she followed Aldovar and Leland down the beach instead. They got drunk behind the bathhouse, then shimmied up a ladder to watch the fireworks from the roof. If she had known that Aldovar would be dead the next day, that the spangled sights beneath her would be gone, she might have taken more time to appreciate them. She would have lingered over the golden glow of the Church of Marvels, the shy twitch of Aldovar's halved moustache, his shirt parted to reveal a chest like a man's but as smooth as a girl's. They lay back on the roof and watched as the fireworks lit up around them, as they zipped and crackled and fizzed to the sea. When Odile sat up to take a slug of whiskey, she thought she saw—just for a moment—someone in the street gazing up at them (Belle?), but by the next pulse of light, the figure was gone.

When the fireworks were over and the music started up again, Odile said good-bye to Leland and Aldovar—she had to get up early, she explained, and Mother would be waiting for her. They parted ways at the corner. Aldovar had slung Leland, too drunk to stand, over his shoulder. Odile watched them disappear in the mist: Aldovar's blue silks trailing behind him, Leland red-faced and snoring. Then Odile turned and walked home alone, over the bridges and under the lights. The water sparked with fallen fireworks, and the night air smelled like gunpowder and roasted figs. She could still hear drums down at the shore, the merry couplets of laughter.

Back at the house she drank two glasses of cold milk standing up at the kitchen sink, then slipped the chimes from her ankle and went upstairs to bed. The rooms were dark, the hallways hushed. Mother was still down at the party, she guessed, and Belle was most likely with her.

The next morning she rose early, around six, and shuffled downstairs in her nightgown, itchy with sweat, hungry for a pickled egg and a slice of cheese. She went to the pantry behind the kitchen and closed herself in as far as she could between the doors of the larder, the way she had as a child, so that a single band of light trembled over the shelves. She stared at the jars of wax beans—ghost fingers, she used to call them as a girl—and sweet potatoes sliced into floating, blood-pink ears.

While she stood there on her tiptoes, the back door whined open and shut, and footsteps crossed through the pantry. Odile turned around in her little triangle of darkness, squinting through the crack in the larder doors. She saw Belle yanking off her gloves, unpinning her hat. She looked tired and wan. She must have been up early in the yard, working on her new routine.

Odile dipped a clothespin into a jar and pinched out a few wax beans. She slid them through the crack in the door, waving them back and forth, scattering vinegar. "Wooo-*ooo!*" she sang in a ghost-voice.

Belle jumped, then put her hand over her heart. "For God's sake!" she hissed. "How old are you?"

"I speak from the crypt!"

Belle narrowed her eyes. Her voice was low and edged. "Why do you need everybody to pay attention to you all the time? It's not like you're a gimp anymore."

Odile was dumbstruck—she couldn't think of how to answer. Belle took a step forward and, without another word, bit the beans in half—quick and gnashing, like a dog. Then she turned on her heels and walked away, chewing stonily, wiping the juice from her chin.

Odile stood there, numb. Her shock turned to hurt, then flared up into fury—she hadn't done anything wrong! She'd only been kidding around, trying to make her sister laugh. She rolled the leftover bits of bean around in her palm, then mashed them into pulp and let them drip to the floor. *Bitch.*

They arrived at the theater with Mother just after eight. As Belle ran through her new routine on an empty stage, Odile snuck out to the pens where the tigers lolled in the morning heat. She carried in fresh buckets of water and meat. After they ate, she let them groom her hair while she lay sideways on the ground—their tongues scraped up her neck and ears, leaving her hair wet and standing on end, smelling sour and muttony. Her mother found her rolling on the ground, fur matted to her skirts, the bucket spilled and wet footprints running amok on the ground.

"Enough horsing around," she said. "I need you to do my hair."

Odile sat up and pointed to hers. "Like this?"

"*Now,* Odile."

Odile sighed and followed her back to the dressing room. *What's wrong with everybody?* she thought. They must have been exhausted from the party and nervous about the show. She gave her mother's hair a few crisp, crackling strokes with a brush big enough for a horse, then waited for her to wince and scold: *Gentle, gentle!* But Mother didn't seem to notice that Odile was standing there at all. She just stared at the glass-topped table with its clutter of jars and bills, as if it were the only real thing in the universe.

When the navy ribbon was knotted and smoothed, her mother stood up. Odile waited for something else—a thank-you, at least. But her mother just went to the wardrobe and started sorting through the costumes. Odile stood awkwardly at the dressing table with the brush in hand, running the bristles over her fingers, swallowing against the lump in her throat. How miserable it was, to stand there and want so much to be seen. Mother wouldn't even look her way.

Something was wrong that morning, but she never bothered to ask. Her mother's private feelings, she would realize later (with no small amount of shame), were of no real concern to her. She only cared about what her mother gave to her and what she withheld. If she ever thought beyond that—to what the woman really wanted—it was only because it conflicted with what she wanted for herself. And so after the show, when Mother had opened the dressing-room door and asked her to come inside, Odile thought that by saying no, she was standing her ground. She was showing her mother and her sister that she didn't need them, that she had better things to do than sit there like a dutiful handmaiden while they quarreled and keened and tried to upstage each other. She had a life and a will of her own; she could ignore them just as easily as they'd ignored her. But all she proved, in the end, was that she was too naïve to consider that something even bigger was happening. She kept walking, proud and cool, ready for her beer and anxious to be alone. Mother had stood in the doorway and watched her pass. She was backlit—a silhouette—framed in a box of sulfur-yellow light, her expression too obscure to read.

It was the last time Odile saw her alive.

NOW ODILE STOOD UP, the blood rushing to her head. She stared at the shadows flickering in front of her, the devil dancing in a circle of light. Before she could stop herself, she flew over to the stage and pulled down the sheet. The lantern blinded her; the horn sputtered and died. Pigeon ran forward, waving her arm. "You can't come back here!" she shouted at Odile. "No, no! That's not part of the play!"

"What is that?" Odile said, pointing to her stomach.

Pigeon looked down at the ground, the horns wobbling on her head. "What?"

"*That.*" Odile grabbed her by the arm and fished under her dress, tugging at the padding around her stomach. She pulled out something tufted and misshapen—"Just a pillow," Pigeon whispered.

Odile turned it around in her hands. It was flimsy and water-stained, losing its stuffing. She ripped it open—sawdust popped and billowed out around her, catching in her mouth and her hair.

Standing there in the hot light of the lantern, watching the dust flutter and settle to the floor—tasting it, ashy, on her tongue—she felt incredibly, stupidly blind. It wasn't just grief that had rendered Belle silent and reclusive in the days after Mother's death—it wasn't simply the loss that had confined her to the house, made her sickly and pale, forced her to run away without apology or explanation. Nothing of the sort.

She was pregnant.

Odile looked down at her fisted hands, at the sprinkling of dust on her clothes. Around her the children whispered and drifted apart; the sheet came down from the line, the horn and the fiddle echoed away in the cavern. *How could this have happened?* Belle had no sweethearts, no beaux, no men who came to call. She had admirers, of course—she was well-known around the boardwalk—but the girls had shared a dressing room (with their mother, no less). Odile would have known if Belle had invited anyone in after the shows. And she never had. It was always just the three of them, pressing their costumes, pulling pins from their hair, scrubbing greasepaint away with cold cream. Odile only remembered one man with flowers, who came to court their mother—but that was ages ago—and he'd never even crossed the threshold. He'd been too frightened of the tigers.

"Why wouldn't she have told me?" Odile whispered. They'd never had any secrets growing up—they, who had no one else in the world but each other. Did Belle really think that her own sister would turn her away, even after they'd watched the Church of Marvels burn? After all that had followed—the daze of the funerals, the tedious meetings with lawyers and the bank, the reassignments to Guilfoyle's company—did she really believe Odile was so fragile and innocent, her loyalty so easily tested? *You, dear sister, have always been the brave one, the good one, the strongest of all. Not I.* She wished she could grab Belle now and say, *Think of what Mother did for her own brother!* She left home. She risked her life. She saw battle, was wounded, was rescued. Odile didn't think of herself as courageous in that way—not even close—but she would have helped. She'd been there for her sister all along—in the bed across the room, at the kitchen table going through the books, making plates of toast and jam and bringing them upstairs, setting them down wordlessly by the lump under the quilt. But Belle hadn't said a word.

She remembered how Belle had looked in the weeks after Mother's death, of course—puffy and listless, preoccupied by something Odile had always assumed to be grief. She'd left Doyers Street, apparently—but for what? Any number of things might have happened since she'd written that letter. She might have died in childbirth. Alone and ashamed, she could have tried to do herself harm.

She might have taken something—one of those special elixirs, the parsley teas for women's troubles. Or she might have paid one of those doctors who tended to unwed mothers—men who slipped through backdoors with their hooks and bowls, who took the money from etherized girls and left them alone to bleed on the bedroom floor.

If this is the last letter I write.

She turned to the children—most of them had crept away, restless or disappointed, but a few of the girls remained onstage, still in their patchy costumes: Pigeon, in horns made from penny pencils; Georgette, with two doll legs tied clumsily to her waist; Birdie, holding a lumpy pomegranate in lieu of a glass bulb. They stared at Odile openmouthed, as if she were performing all the death throes of Shakespeare. "What happened to Miss Church? You need to tell me—now—where did she go?"

They didn't answer, just sat there among the scattered props, watching her pace.

"You expect me to believe you don't know anything? After what I just saw?" She screamed then—a raw, frustrated, disconsolate scream, until her head ached and her eyes brimmed with water. She kicked her valise through the dirt. She thought of all the pitiful things nestled inside—the neatly folded nightgown, the silly peppermints, the old ivory haircomb—as if she'd find her sister staying in some posh hotel.

"This isn't playacting—I'm asking you truly!" She felt a burn in her nose but rubbed it away. Then she crouched down and unlatched her valise, drew out the pouch of peppermints. "What was she doing at that house on Doyers Street? Did she live there?"

The girls gathered around her, coy and squeaking, reaching out their hands. Odile held the pouch high above her head. Pigeon, the smallest, unbuckled her wooden arm and held it aloft, trying to bat the prize out of Odile's fingers. Odile just grabbed the arm away— "No! No cheating."

"That's my arm!" Pigeon said, terrified. "That's my only arm!"

Odile felt a prickle of guilt but she held the limb in the air above her, hearing the dispirited creak of its joints.

Pigeon began to cry. "Please give it back."

"Not until you tell me about that house."

"It's where the broken legs go. I thought you knew!"

She'd heard the phrase before, but only in hushed, pitying voices. A home for unwed mothers. No wonder the scrub-girl at the door had been careful.

"What do you mean, broken legs?"

She leaned down toward the children, but she heard only the rat-rustle of their bare feet, the swish of their costumes as they shifted in the dirt. They held out their hands to her and waited.

Odile tipped the pouch over her mouth and started gobbling peppermints, grinding them furiously between her teeth. "Tell me!" she said, spraying crumbs.

Pigeon looked over to the others, then took a deep breath. "Girls go there when they've got in trouble. Once I was up there, and I saw something I wasn't supposed to. There was a lady who'd come there to get rid of a baby. I could see the bump in her skirt, just a little one, and she cried and said that someone would kill her if they found out. I didn't hear all of it. But the girls, they want their babies to go away. So they go there for help."

Odile blinked back her tears. So it was more than just a home for unwed mothers—the women went there to get rid of it. She felt sick at the thought of it—she'd heard about the potions used, the terrible things that made you sick: days of retching and bleeding. Some girls didn't make it through at all.

"And how am I to believe you, after all of this?" she whispered. "How do I know you're telling me the truth?"

Pigeon dropped her voice. "She left something here. Something she didn't want anyone to find."

Odile handed back her arm. "What is it?"

Pigeon hopped up on stage. She pointed—"this"—and Odile moved over to look. She recognized it immediately—Belle's carpet-bag, still with their mother's crooked stitching along the seam. She knelt down and prized it open. Inside she found a book by William Blake, inscribed *To F., from V.* Pressed between the pages was an envelope with Belle's handwriting—only a single word, scribbled across the flap: *Mouse.* Inside was a torn scrap of paper, but the lettering was in a different hand: *EDGAR, hair dark, skin fair, 213 W 13—girl.* Odile didn't know what it meant, but she tucked it in her pocket and rifled through the rest—some blank sheets of stationery, an empty bottle of throat tonic, a few wig-pins, and there, rustling at the very bottom, a layer of sand.

She sat back on her heels. There was something else, she felt—something heavier sewn into the side. She took a pin, split the stitching, and reached in. Her fingers brushed the length of something soft and pliant—leather, she guessed—and traveled up to a carved wedge of metal. Carefully she drew it out.

A dagger.

Odile bit into the fingertips of her glove and yanked it off with her teeth, then touched the hilt with her bare hand. She unsheathed the blade and saw there, engraved in the forte, *I.C.* Tears burned at the corners of her eyes. *Isabelle.*

She sat down on the edge of the stage, turning the dagger around in her hands. She'd tried to swallow a sword once before, when she was twelve, but it was too difficult; the taste of her stomach acid coming up on the blade had made her sick. And so she watched as her sister moved on to the arrow, the billiards cue, the chair leg. And when she'd finally mastered the hot sandwich—the most difficult stunt in her routine—Mother had put her at the top of the bill.

But this dagger—this was her first. Her favorite. The same one that had sliced off the boy's toe on the beach and sent it rolling through the sand.

Beside her she heard the rustling of paper, the crack of peppermints between teeth. Tears glided down her cheeks and pooled warmly in her collar. *Oh, Belle! Why didn't you tell me about any of this? Why couldn't I know?*

Belle, missing from the gypsy party on the beach. Belle, sneaking through the pantry in the morning looking harried and worn, refusing to play her usual show. Belle, alone now in the city—there could be any number of hucksters preying on lost girls like her. The thought that she might be hurt, or sick, or worse—

"I'm going to find her." She stood up and turned to the girls, who had spilled out the mints and sat eating them from the dirt. "You might as well tell me everything you know because I'll find out soon enough."

She looked at Pigeon in particular; Pigeon, who was now wearing Odile's very best gloves—pilfered from where they'd fallen on the floor—one on her real hand, and one on the hand made of wood.

"What were you doing up at that house just now?"

Pigeon held up the purse around her neck. "We get the flowers from the shop and take them down to the dragon room. See?"

Odile drew it up to the light. Inside was a handful of pink and orange blossoms, sweet-smelling, crushed. She remembered seeing the dens—the Chinese parlors, they were airily called on the boardwalk—in the narrow lanes behind the harem. They all promised exotic reveries, but Leland had said they were nothing more than flophouses, with no-account fellows and bunks that hopped with roaches, and a few fat-faced bohemians spouting poetry on the floor.

"What did Belle say when she left her bag here?"

"Just to keep it safe."

"Did she ever mention a friend to you, a gentleman? Any name at all?"

Pigeon turned the peppermint over in her mouth. "Just once, when I was up there getting my flowers, I heard her talking to the mean girl, all hissy. They don't talk to flower girls, not up there—but I heard them in the back room, whispering about a fellow."

"Which fellow?"

"Just said he'd worked at the Featherbone?"

"What's that? A theater, a hotel?"

Pigeon shrugged.

"I saw something," one of the girls said now—Georgette. She sat back on her heels, licking a mint in her cupped palm. Her voice was soft and nervous. "There was a man in the dragon room when I took my pouch. Never seen him before, but he was sniffing around for a girl, a fair girl going to have a baby. Seen her in some shop, he says? I didn't think much of it—they're all raving there—but he seemed all goosey and cross, like he needed her right away."

"Can you take me to him?"

"That costs extra."

"Keep whatever's there," Odile said, pointing to the valise. "I've got no use for it here anymore." She felt in her pockets—she had her money, yes—the envelope; her handkerchief; the list she'd made of theaters the night before. The dagger.

Pigeon buckled back her arm. "I'll take you there since I've got to turn in my pouch."

"But be careful," Georgette said, pulling the nightgown over her head and blinking up through the ruffed collar. "He's got a bad face, like a monster."

THE ROOM WAS DARKER than the burrows of the Frog and Toe, the air pungent and flowery. Little boys sat clustered around a table.

Their hands were small and fast; they took apart the opium pipes—bowls, saddles, and stems—with reverence and precision, as if they were tending to the instruments of an orchestra. A boy with a paper mask looked up as Odile and Pigeon walked in. He smiled.

"Sniff!" Pigeon cried. She ran over and nudged him with her shoulder—a squeak of the iron socket, a grin on her face—then lined up her flowers on the table.

"I thought you were my best girl!" said the boy, thumping a sticky-looking cake with his fist. "What took you forever?"

Pigeon pointed to Odile, then leaned in and whispered to him about the man who'd been picking around the mats, but the boy shook his head and said they'd missed him—he'd only just left.

"What does he look like?" Odile said. "Quick."

"Gypsy fellow. Ruffy beard, brownish hat."

"A Gypsy?" She could only picture the actors that night on the beach—men with golden earrings and gossamer scarves—barefoot, moustachioed, dancing through the sand with dulcimers and lutes.

"He gypped the weepy fellow, I saw—took his coat," the boy went on. "The one with the black sash on the sleeve. He's a fighter, you can see. His face!"

"Which way?"

He pointed down the hallway; Odile thanked him and ran. Through the tattered pongee curtains, out to a gloomy foyer, past an empty chair with a dime novel tented on the arm (*A Bride for a Day*—she'd loved that one). She ran out the door, up the stairs, knocking a golden bell as she went. The light was bright on the street—she had to stop for a moment, dizzy in the glare. She could smell the meat from a butcher shop, the vinegar stink from olive barrels across the way. Still, she breathed in the wind, cooler, sweet with the traces of bread flour and thyme. Then farther down she saw it—a felt hat, the color of sand. A man, moving away through the marketplace. She thought of Belle, bringing her little dagger all the way to the city,

Mother's old book of poems. She began weaving through the chicken coops and potato wagons, past the fluttering ivory leaves on a stationer's cart. Just ahead of her—a tall man with dark curls, wearing a band on his jacket sleeve.

He turned down an alleyway, beneath an arrowed sign that read MILK. She paused for a moment by a cobbler's bench, matching her breaths to the easy plink of the hammer. Then she gripped the dagger and followed him around the turn.

He stood in the middle of the alley, alone in a wedge of light, counting out coins in the palm of his hand. She drew the dagger from its sheath, held it low at her side. It had been so long since she'd done anything of the sort—just a girl, standing behind the Church of Marvels, practicing her throws against the corkboard, Mack hemming and clucking as she missed. The knives, bouncing off the yellow wall like grasshoppers, skittering through the sand. Afterward she'd licked her fingers and rubbed at the dimples they left behind in the wood, hoping her mother wouldn't notice.

She heard the scuttle of swallows, the low of a dairy cow. She stepped closer, close enough to see the loose twill on his jacket, the fuzz of the knitted band.

He turned around. His face was bruised, his lip cut, but that's not what made her stare. One of his eyes was as dark as pitch, the other a watering blue.

TWELVE

WHEN ALPHIE WASN'T PREGNANT AFTER THE FIRST FEW months, the Signora began to watch her closely—what she ate (*no peppers or sauces*), what she wore (*loosen the stays*), and what she read (*no ladies' magazines*). Alphie was sure the woman was punishing Anthony behind closed doors: *your gutter mouse has ruined her body. Those matchstick arms! Those narrow hips!* After supper, when they all sat together in the parlor and listened to Anthony play the accordion, she couldn't stand it—the heat, the tension, the little box of teeth: it made her feel faint at times, which the Signora marked as proof of her weak constitution. Whatever explanation Alphie offered up in her studious, broken Italian—*I'm sorry, Mother; it's only a matter of time, surely*—the Signora considered nothing more than ninnyish self-pity. Then, when she started asking to see the monthly blood, Alphie felt like a cornered animal. She hadn't expected to be scrutinized like this, her body an object of curiosity and concern. She thought constantly of the shipyard, the Widows, the men with their boots and their fists, even the good ones who babied her and cuddled her and brought her sweets—she lived in fear that the Signora would discover everything. She had supposed that once they were married and settled into the servants' quarters, she and Anthony would be left alone, to live their lives privately and as they pleased. But that had yet to happen.

Alphie lay awake for nights, curled against her husband. *Why can't we just move away?* she begged. He only smiled, amused, and brushed her hair. Once things were a little more stable, he promised, they would find a place of their own. Mother was just like that sometimes, he said—new things were hard for; she wanted to have a say in them. She had buried two husbands, after all—there was no one else in the world for her but her son. At times she was even scared to leave the house—how would she fare if she were suddenly alone? Alphie tried her best to understand. If Anthony wasn't worried, then she shouldn't be either. So as she drank her coffee in the parlor at night, as she watched him leave with his kit in the mornings, as she powdered her face and brushed kohl on her lashes—not too much, or else the Signora would think she looked like a cheap bat who sauntered hungrily under the elevated track (and that was an image Alphie wanted to leave behind)—she told herself things really would change.

But one day, without telling her, the Signora called a doctor to the house. He arrived with a black case, crammed full of cold metal instruments that prodded and expanded, with wagging rubber bulbs and rusted-looking clamps. Alphie saw him from the parlor window in the main house, wheezing up the steps, gripping the rail with his sweaty, bologna-pink hands. Mortified, she ran and hid in Anthony's workshop, trying not to gag into her handkerchief. She kept her breaths small and her body still as the Signora clucked through the house, opening doors and shouting Alphie's name and making nervous, elaborate apologies to the doctor—who, by the sound of his voice, didn't seemed alarmed, only impatient. *Silly, flighty girls,* he said, then asked the Signora for an almond cookie. Alphie hid there for what seemed like hours, until she was sure he was gone.

A few days later, when Alphie sat down to breakfast and announced that she and Anthony were expecting a child, she couldn't tell if the Signora was pleased or dismayed. Some part of her wanted the woman to break—to weep, to hug her, to laugh, genuine and overjoyed—anything but the polite, noncommittal sigh that was her usual expression of accord. Instead, the Signora bit into her toast with a smile that was meant to look relieved but only looked disappointed. Alphie didn't understand—she'd gotten what she wanted, hadn't she? Why didn't it seem good enough?

When she'd first arrived at the house, shy and baby-faced, she'd thrown herself into the role she'd played so well for years: the polite if impoverished young girl, the healer of others' pain. Alphie wanted to admire the Signora's tenacity and pride—all the things this woman had survived; the young man she'd raised!—but too often her toughness gave way to cruelty and paranoia. Some afternoons, when they were alone in the house, the Signora would take out her gruesome museum and lay everything out with a polish and brush. She'd point to Alphie and snap her fan. So Alphie would sit there in the hot gloom, rubbing each tooth with the tiny brush, squeaking them clean with a handkerchief. She arranged them in rows, by color, until she was dizzy and sore. *Fulvous, graphite, egg.* Eggs made her think of her father's chicken coops—the smell of shit, the feed and feathers everywhere: in her milk, her hair, her underwear. The Signora would just stand inertly by the table, staring over her shoulder, while Alphie kept her head down and prayed to disappear.

But Anthony had stood up to the Signora, defied her. He'd married the woman he wanted. Because of that, because of what he had risked, Alphie knew he must love her. What other explanation could there be? He, who had taken a stand on so little, who had lived under his mother's scrutiny and jealousy, who had been shaken by her bouts of wrathful judgment, had stood up in a Protestant parsonage and married a person he had once paid to fuck. Alphie was not

a Catholic or a virgin; she was not as hale as a well-kept girl—she'd
been disowned by her father and forgotten by her mother—but he
gave her a ring of hammered gold, as if she were the purest, loveliest
thing on earth. Such a sweetly simple day: she wore a dress the color
of honeysuckle, a new set of calfskin gloves. She carried a nosegay
she'd bought from a Widow on the waterfront. The parson was a be-
nevolent man with white gums and a scurvied spine—he'd spent his
orphaned boyhood at sea, he said—and because of this Alphie somehow felt a kinship with him; a sense of good fortune, of brighter days
ahead. When it was done, the Signora kissed Alphie's cheek, then
turned away and dabbed at her tears. Alphie chose to believe they
were tears of happiness.

But still there were nights when Anthony would come upstairs
and collapse in bed, his hands falling over her, holding her too hard,
his calluses rough against her bare skin. He'd fold himself around
her, jerk her awake, pinch her stomach and her thighs. She could
feel his stubble chafe the back of her neck and scrape between her
shoulder blades, his lips drag across her skin. He'd had too much to
drink, maybe, but he was home. They'd fall asleep like that, holding on to each other until they woke—intertwined and filled with a
strange, unknowable dread at daybreak.

THAT NIGHT IN THE ASYLUM, Alphie dreamed that her face was
covered in hair—long hair, thick and silky, heavy as a Widow's wig.
It grew from every pore, pulling at her lips and eyelids and nose,
until she couldn't see or breathe. It grew faster and faster—she tried
to hold it, catch it in her hands; she tried to swim through it for
light and air. It began creeping around her neck, slowly at first, then
cinching tighter and tighter. She tried to grab for the scissors, but
her hands got tangled and trapped. Every time she jerked them forward, the hair pulled, excruciating, at the skin on her cheeks. She

screamed for air but it was no use. She was snared in a web that she'd made for herself.

She woke in the asylum bed, out of breath, an ache beating behind her eyes. She put a hand to her cheek, which felt cool and rough. Under the blanket, the scissors had slid out of their loosened hitch and pricked the skin behind her knee. She licked her palm and rubbed at the dots of blood on the pallet. How could she have been so foolish? How long could she last without being discovered?

Out in the rotunda the night nurse made her rounds, walking the moonlit ring around the dome, peering into each room while the keys slapped against her thigh and her baton beat out a bored rhythm on the walls. There was a wet cough as she drew nearer. Alphie burrowed under her blanket, drawing her knees up to her chin.

The nurse paused just outside the door—it was the pink-eyed, dyspeptic woman who had taken her wedding ring. Alphie could see it now through the bars, glinting on a bone-thin finger. As quietly as she could, Alphie inched the scissors up her sleeve. The nurse scanned the room, slow and perfunctory, the baton twitching in her side. The women lay silent in their beds, as if they were holding their breaths. *You must do this,* Alphie told herself, *you must, you must— there is no way out until Anthony comes.*

The nurse took a swig from her bottle of tonic, belched, and moved on. Alphie listened to her heels snicking away down the hall.

Each floor was locked up at night—there was nowhere to go but in a circle, an endless walk of reeking rooms. Still, Alphie knew there was a private washroom for the nurses on duty—it was set off in a little alcove, just behind the barricaded stairs. With the scissors tucked up her sleeve, she waited for the footsteps to die away. Then she threw off her blanket and crept across the room, between the beds where women slept too soundly—it must be those thimbles of mead, she thought. Or else it was fear that had husked them, shriveled their bodies down to the basest cycles. Breathe, sleep, waste, age. She thought of her dream again and touched her face.

The gate to her room was locked, but she managed to pop the latch with the tip of the scissors and slip out into the hall. The windows, brittle and veined, scattered the moonlight across the ground like seeds. She began walking slowly, matching her steps to ticks from an unseen clock. Just past the stairs—which were closed off by an oak-and-iron door, thrice-bolted—she found the alcove. The washroom door stood ajar.

It was a small room, dark and overwarm. She saw a washstand and a dingy mirror, a wooden rack that glimmered with silverfish, pegs that hung empty on the wall. She began rummaging through the rack, turning up old candles and a soggy box of matches, a shoe-brush and a couple of rags, a bottle of lime soda and a moldering box of tooth powder. She tucked the rags against the seam of the door, then lit a candle. The yellow pulsed against the gray, the color of a bruise. On the washstand the soap—a dirty, curling flint—sat in a puddle of its own scum. She touched her cheeks again: they felt coarse and hot.

Through the ceiling she heard a loud thud, then the sound of a body hurling itself against the wall. "Help!" a voice screamed. "Police! *Help me!*"

Alphie shuddered over the washbowl. She poured water from the pitcher into her cupped hand, then sucked it up like a cat. She hadn't anything to drink at supper—she'd been too wary. Her lungs felt tight, her throat dry. The water tasted tinny and sulfurous, but still cool. She drank another handful, then dabbed her wet hands over her face and neck.

"Police! Oh, God, help!" The ceiling thundered again, shaking down bits of plaster. Alphie brushed the dust from her hair and shoulders. The girls upstairs, she knew, were the wickedest of all— they were the girls who'd thrown themselves down staircases, or made nooses out of their stockings, or chased down their husbands with a pistol. They were all locked away for good. They weren't allowed out, not ever, not even to attend Sunday prayer in the sitting room. The nurses called them the Violents.

Should the scissors be discovered in Alphie's possession, she knew she would be sent up there, too. The nurses might be able to ignore all sorts of things, but no bribe could turn them away from a weapon, especially one that was stolen from them and concealed beneath her flannel dress. After that, there would be no hope for her. She wouldn't last, not up there.

Her whole body began to shake. She poured some water into the washbowl and splashed her face. She paused, the water dripping around her ears, listening for any sound from the hall—a footstep, maybe? A creak? But it would be at least another quarter-hour before the nurse returned this way. Besides, she might have been summoned upstairs to help with whatever confusion had broken out. The scuffle had since quieted—Alphie remembered Mother's Milk, the taste of the bathwater burning in her throat.

She stripped to the waist and scrubbed her face with the cake of soap, the dream still alive in her mind. She thought she could still taste the mustiness of that hair, feel its weight, though when she licked her lips and touched her eyelids, they were smooth, slippery, nude. She remembered the gawping soap-boy, the way he'd leered—tickled and witless, licking his teeth, his inky hand squirming down to tug at his balls: *They must have locked you away for being so ugly.*

She stared at her reflection in the mirror, the lather dripping off her face and running milky down her neck, over the scabbed tattoo. She took out the scissors—they were duller than she'd expected, speckled with rust. Still, she pried them open, held them up to the light. She pressed the blade against her throat, so hard that it rolled with her pulse.

Then, on the other side of the door, she thought she heard a noise. She froze, her ears straining against the silence, the scissors poised against her neck. There it was again—a feathery, high-pitched wheeze, a brambly scratch against the door. She thought of the nurse's crabby baton, the old woman's fingernails. There were rats who lived in the walls, too, who made their nests from human hair and pallet guts. She stood there without moving, breathing shallowly. She waited for whatever it was to pass, but then, after a stretch of silence, the door opened and closed, and someone was in the room with her.

Alphie flew back, startled, flailing to cover up her naked chest. She dropped the scissors, but a hand swooped out and caught them midair. As Alphie tripped and fell, struggling to cover herself, the figure stepped into the circle of light. A muzzle of brass gleamed at her mouth; her eyes burned colorless over the mask. Quickly, almost without a sound, she pushed Alphie to the ground and straddled her, smacking away her hands and holding the scissors above her heart. *She knows! She knows!* Alphie felt the vomit burn and chug up her throat—she turned her head to the side, her whole body contracting as she threw up over the floor, into her hair. She shivered and spit while the girl watched, all the while thinking, *This is it. The end.*

But after a moment the girl dropped the scissors and fell back, breathing hard through the horn on her mask. Alphie lay shivering on the floor, too scared to move or make a sound. This girl—the same one who'd hidden the scissors in her throat, who'd curled her body through the air as if she had no skeleton at all—hadn't been startled or confused when she opened the door. She didn't seem surprised at all.

"What do I have to do?" Alphie begged. "Please, please don't tell. I'll be leaving soon—someone's coming for me. You won't say anything, will you?" When she didn't answer, Alphie only cried, "Please! What do you want?"

The girl stood up and looked around the room. She reached for the burnt match in the candle dish, but as soon as she grabbed it, it turned to powder in her fingers. She grunted, then fished the wet cake of soap out of the bowl and started writing on the mirror.

Alphie sat up and rearranged her dress. Her body was weak, too hot. She rubbed away the lather on her face, the dripping sick in her hair, the dot of blood beading through the hairs on her knee. She watched as the girl stepped back and pointed at the mirror, the soap foaming in her hand. Alphie moved closer, lifting the candle so she could see the letters, dripping and ghostly, written around her face.

WHERE IS SHE

Her skin went cold. She looked over at the girl, who stood gripping the soap, watching her, the horn whistling as she breathed. Alphie took a step forward, bringing the light with her. She stared into the green eyes above the mask. They were filled with tears.

Then she remembered exactly where she'd seen Orchard Broome before. She had been in the room with her that night, too.

THIRTEEN

THE WOMAN STOOD IN FRONT OF SYLVAN, HER KNIFE DRAWN in the dusty light. It wobbled and twitched at her side, but she took another step forward, close enough for Sylvan to see the freckles on her nose. She was young—around his age, with wavy hair coming loose from its pins, her head cocked to the side as if he were too much of a threat to face plainly. "What's your name?" she said.

Sylvan, the dogboy—cornered here in the high light of day, in an alleyway paved with cowpat and swill. And this crooked-looking girl, brandishing a dagger as dull as a stalk of celery. He couldn't think what she wanted from him—he only had a few cents in his hand. This neighborhood teemed with tough women, of course—he'd known a few misfit boxers, burled with old-country muscle; he'd seen little girls rob grown men blind; he'd even watched a shopgirl clobber a thief with a mallet until the man was nothing more than a wet flank of meat, left to sputter on the floor. But nothing like that had ever happened to him, not even close.

He told her his name and smoothed the opium-smoker's jacket against his ribs. It fit better than his own, with birch buttons and tailored cuffs and a hint of cologne. Underneath he could smell traces of tobacco and pomade, a faint spice like Mrs. Izzo's cinnamon oil, and then something else, something stronger and more medicinal. He smelled good, at least. He lifted his chin.

The girl's eyes met his. "I'm looking for Isabelle Church," she said.

"I'm not acquainted with any Miss Church."

"Isabelle Church," she said again. "You know her." She tightened her grip around the dagger. "She looks like me."

"You're mistaken."

"You were just looking for her down in the opium den," she said. "I *know*."

Sylvan's blood quickened. He stared at the tip of the dagger, at the girl's angled face. He tried to remember if he'd seen her before—on the street, at a fight—but he could tell she wasn't from the neighborhood. She didn't seem particularly wheedling or coy, the way girls around here could be. She didn't look weak from work or hunger. She didn't appear to be the kind of woman the butcher-boy had described, someone feebleminded or drugged—or even particularly eccentric, despite the dagger in her hand. He couldn't place her—not a churchgoing daughter or factory waif, not a dragon-chaser, not a runaway. She had a directness about her, a way of staring at him with her head slightly atilt, as if puzzled, and with a frankness that unnerved him.

"For Christ's sake," he said, looking back toward the street, "put that thing down. No one here's going to fight you."

The blade trembled in her hand, but she kept it pointed at him. "You were asking around for her," she said again. "She's my sister, so tell me. Where is she?"

"I don't know."

"Is she your sweetheart?"

"No, no—not at all."

"You worked at a place called the Featherbone?"

"I don't even know what that is. Please"—he looked back to the dairy, where pails clanked and a woman whistled to the barn cats. "I'll help you if you want, but it's not safe to be waving that around. Not here."

The girl dropped her arm and sighed. He could see the color in her cheeks, the glimmer of water in her eyes. The wind blew up a flurry of dust; he smelled fresh milk and wet grain, the sweat from her chambray blouse. Out in the street came the songs of the market: a trilling girl with her basket of gingerbread, a suspender-seller clapping two cymbals together.

"I'll tell you," he began, then faltered. He wasn't sure exactly what she was aware of, or what she suspected. She'd followed him from the poppy box—that much was clear. She knew that he'd been down in the dens, asking around for a woman. But she couldn't possibly know about the baby, could she? The baby, safe at Mrs. Izzo's; the baby, whom he'd found only a few blocks away. She would have said as much already.

"I was looking for a woman, yes," he went on, "but I can't tell you her name because I don't know who she is. Just someone who might have visited the dens. An acquaintance of fellows named Lee and Eddie."

"Lee and Eddie?" she repeated.

His pulse flickered. "Do you know them?"

"I've never heard of them." She began to rub at the skin behind her ear. "Why were you after her? Was she in some kind of trouble?"

Sylvan paused; a muscle twitched in his cheek. She was frustrated, he could tell—crossing her arms, toeing the dirt, biting her cheeks to stave off tears. He wanted to believe that this wasn't an act, that her worry was genuine—that she was just as baffled as he was. But how could he know what she was really after? If her sister was the one he'd been looking for, a woman who'd done something so wicked—left a baby to die, disappeared in the night, maybe bought

blood in a jar and kept company with wastrels in an opium den—
who's to say she wouldn't do the same?

"I've never met her," he said carefully, still eyeing the dagger
at her side. "There was some commotion the other night. I'm . . .
a night watchman of sorts, and I thought a woman fitting her de-
scription might know something." He licked his lips and tasted a
scab, still tender from the fight. "Why would you ask if she was in
trouble?"

"Because I heard you were looking for a woman"—her voice
shook, but she lifted her head—"a woman who was going to have a
baby."

Her face caught the light, and then he could see it: the dimple in
her chin. The gold-green eyes. He wasn't sure what he felt, if it was
exhilaration or dread, but he found himself nodding. "Yes," he said.
"Fair skin and green eyes, I'd guess. A baby any day."

"What kind of commotion?" She was staring at the marks on
his face, the bruises and cuts, which had begun to tighten and itch in
the sun. "Was someone hurt?"

He drew a breath through his teeth. "Nothing troublesome."
He didn't want to scare her; he didn't want to see her scream and
faint. What if he was wrong about all of it? What if she accused
him of kidnapping, or worse? "Only a little riffraff, noise in the
street. I wanted to be sure a woman—a woman in her condition—
wasn't inconvenienced. And nothing came of it. I don't know any
more than you." He felt a bubble of guilt rise in the back of his
throat. Quickly he went on, "Did your sister live nearby—near the
butcher's at all?"

"I don't even know where I am!" She threw up her arms and
looked around the alley, the dimple trembling on her chin. "She left
home a few months ago, and only wrote me once. I feel such—*ugh!*"
She turned away and wiped at her eyes with a handkerchief, then
kicked at a patch in the dirt. He watched as her shoulders lifted and

shook. After a moment she looked back—"You're a night watchman, you said?"

"I know these streets as well as anyone."

"Are you with the police?"

He grimaced. "I have respectable work."

"Yes, I can see that." She handed him the handkerchief. "Your cheek."

Fumbling, he dabbed at the cut, then flinched when he saw the cloth come back with blood. "I—I won a fight this morning," he explained.

"Must have been quite the victory."

He felt embarrassed to give it back, but she reached over and took it anyway, folded it down in her pocket. "And here I thought a watchman only snored away in his chair, while the dogs ran off with the sausages." She eyed him. "My name's Odile Church."

"Where you from, Miss Church?"

She bent to stash the dagger in her boot. "Coney Island."

He'd heard stories about that place—the giant machines that turned you upside down, the animals that were allowed into restaurants and served just like people—dogs sitting at tables with napkins tied around their collars, wolfing crème pie off china plates. And all of that water, eating away at the sand—he'd heard about a wave so big that it swept away an entire street, houses and all—it still floated somewhere out in the Atlantic, neighbors tending their gardens, drinking tea on their porches, tossing biscuits to the whales in their backyards.

"We were in a show there," she went on. "A twin act. No woman down there who might have looked like me?"

"No women at all. It's a stag den, if you know what I mean."

"What about these Lee and Eddie people?"

"A couple of dragon-chasers, I would think. I'm not sure."

"Wait a moment." She pushed her hand into her pocket and

drew out a crumpled envelope. "There is one thing you can help me with. I found this with my sister's things." She unfolded a piece of paper and held it out for him to see. "Can you read?"

"EDGAR," Sylvan declaimed, just loud enough for the birds to scatter. *"Hair dark, skin fair, two-one-three West Thirteen—"*

"All right—Edgar. Does that mean anything to you?" she asked. "What about those numbers—an address?"

"Up in the Village, I should think."

He thought of the rainy afternoon at the party with Francesca, the smell of his borrowed suit, the damp press of the gentlemen's hands against his. He looked at Odile—at her locket on its funny glass chain, her wild hair wavy with sweat. What had she been thinking, coming into the city by herself?

"I can take you," he said. "A good neighborhood, but it's too easy to lose your way."

She looked at him for a moment, considering.

"I have nothing on me, I promise you." He pushed his hands into the pockets of his coat, felt his fingers close around something smooth and stippled, no bigger than a pea.

"Here." He held it out for her to see, turning it up in his palm. "That's all. A tooth."

FOURTEEN

THERE WAS A STORY ODILE REMEMBERED, A STORY THEIR
mother used to tell. Once, long ago, in Punxsutawney before
the war, Friendship's brother had taken her to see a traveling magic show. It was the first time Friendship had seen anything
other than Christmas vespers at the hotel bar, where her uncle,
crippled in a mining accident, poured steins of beer for the traveling
businessmen. She and her brother had run down the hill from the
house; their mother had taken to bed with a spell and their aunties
were busy bundling goose feathers in the kitchen. They snuck in behind the miners and toughs and big German families who spoke no
English, huddled in a town hall that had seen dances and auctions
and even a human dissection by the local doctor. The magician had
come all the way from Pittsburgh. When he stepped out from behind
the curtain—his hair molded, his moustache waxed, his spectacles
gleaming in the footlights—he was holding a large, brilliantly green
reptile. Friendship had never seen anything like it before: the medi-
eval, spiny back, the armored wattle, the pink tongue and wizened
face. *Is that a dragon?* she whispered to her brother. But her brother,
who knew everything, could only stare at the stage in wonder, unable

to answer. Some people in the audience screamed; a few ran for the door. The magician stepped forward and asked for a brave volunteer. Friendship's brother elbowed her hard, shoving her into the aisle. The magician turned, squinting through the motes of light, shielding his eyes with his white-gloved hand. Then he pointed down and said: *Yes. You.* And so Friendship walked slowly, apprehensively down the aisle, heads turning to watch her pass. Everything was silent, except for the wooden steps that squeaked on her way up to the stage. She was embarrassed at first, in her hand-me-down dress that smelled like the noosed, oily goose in the smoke shack. But she wanted to get closer to the dragon—nestled there in the man's arms, claws gripping at his sleeve, the striped, molting tail sticking out like a shoot. Her skin tingled as she stepped under the lights. With a whoosh, the magician spun away from the audience, his back to the spotlight, and instructed Friendship to tug twice at his coattails. She did, baffled and giggling, a little afraid. He hopped up and down, then turned back to the crowd. The animal had transformed in his hands—no longer scaly and serpentine, but orange and furred, yawning in his cupped hands. A kitten. Friendship gasped. The magician took a step forward and held it out to her, but she backed away. *Go on,* he said as the audience laughed. *Tell them it's real.* And so Friendship reached out, trembling, and lifted the kitten into her arms. Folded ears and white whiskers. A pink nose that left cold, itchy dots on her neck. She nodded, stunned. *That's your prize,* said the magician. *Ladies and gentlemen, my lovely assistant!* There was a crackle of applause from the crowd, echoing all the way up to the balcony. Friendship felt a rush, a thrill, a sense of being outside herself and yet utterly whole. The cheers grew louder as she stepped down from the stage and walked back up the aisle to her brother. He hollered louder than the rest, whistling and stomping his feet. Something came over her then, and she jumped up on her rickety seat, holding her kitten aloft for everyone to see. The spotlight found her. The audience roared.

It was the first time she had ever been on stage, in front of all those faces, alit with wonder, and life would never be the same for her again.

AT FOURTEEN YEARS OLD their mother had only left a note on a sheet of foolscap under her parents' inkwell: *I've gone to fight.* Friendship Willingbird Church, younger than Odile was now—not just venturing over the bridge to the city, a scant few miles away, but riding off to avenge her brother's murder, living in disguise, every day running from death and discovery. To have seen battle, to have watched men die beside her—some perhaps by her own bayonet—to have felt a bullet passing through her body (like fire, she'd said). And then, jogged away on a rattling stretcher, smelling the rust and rot in the surgeon's tent, hearing the grind of the bone saws—weak and bleeding but still trying to stop the nurse, barely older than herself, as she cut away her clothes. She had risked everything for her brother's honor. To see it done. To know his name. To bear witness to his sacrifice. And then, on crutches, to be helped into a circuit rider's wagon, to be wheeled away in the dead of night through a Union embattlement—how had she done it?

You, dear sister, have always been the brave one, the good one, the strongest of all. But Odile didn't feel brave, not in any sense, and certainly not like their mother. She moved woozily through the Bowery marketplace, past steaming, lemony pots of clam broth, past stacked cabbages and dusty corn, past baskets of discarded corks that at first looked like severed thumbs. She remembered the boy's toe on the beach—how Belle had lopped it right off without flinching. When she wavered for a moment, stalled at the corner while traffic jittered past, Sylvan reached out to steady her.

"Should we stop?"

She shook her head. "I'm well enough."

He held tightly to her arm. She stared for a moment at the callus on the curve of his thumb, as rough and riddled as a seashell. The sunlight hurt her eyes. "Let's keep on," she said.

They walked on through the crush of wagons. She couldn't shake the shadow-play in the Frog and Toe, or the faces of the flower girls as they gnawed at their peppermints. If only she'd gone after Belle immediately. What had stopped her? Her own grief, she supposed. A sense of responsibility. She was anchored to Coney Island—it was her life. It held the mystery and grandeur of the whole world, there on a narrow spit of land. Sometimes she believed that if she were to leave, even for a short spell, everything she'd lost might return to her—like a faithful dog finding its way home—only she wouldn't be there to let it in.

The elevated train clattered overhead, deafening. All around her people pushed and elbowed and squawked, as if they were fighting for the same small breath of air. She kept walking, breathing in through her mouth and spitting back flies. The heady stench—horse shit and roasting chestnuts and trash barrels pulsing with maggots— was enough to make her retch.

Beside her Sylvan kept talking and pointing, rolling his hands through the air, as if to distract her from the pull of inwardness. He went on about prizefighting, about something he called *the floating eye,* the sensation of leaving his own body and regarding it in wonder from afar, even though he was never more fully alive within it. Shedidn't know if he was trying to threaten her or comfort her, but she recognized it as the same sensation she had on the Wheel, although she didn't say as much. She only stared at her shadow rippling over the cobbles, hunched and blowsy, the shape a shriveled bean pod. How selfish could she have been, staying behind for Guilfoyle's shabby dime-show, instead of following her sister, alone, into the city?

Maybe if she'd reached out in the days after the fire, Belle might have confided in her. She might have told her about a man she was seeing, or someone who'd taken advantage of her, someone who'd made her do something against her will. Odile tried to think of the men who hollered at Belle from the audience. There were only ever two kinds—the old doddering drunks with green gums and fishing-line suspenders, loud and sloppy but always harmless. More menacing were the rich boys out to slum it, boys with horsey laughs and barbered hair who saw her as some kind of kinky prize—a harem-girl they could brag about to their buddies back home. Odile pictured them in libraries with Greek friezes and parquet floors, talking up her sister's limber body as they whinnied and honked and ground their chalk against a billiard cue.

When they arrived at number 213—a large brick building with a portico of limestone—they found a woman on the stoop out front, working over a piece of lace. She was older, with hair so white and thin that it glowed pink from the glare on her scalp. She looped and knotted a length of thread, squinting at Sylvan and Odile as they approached. "Who you here for?"

Odile shielded her eyes from the sun. She wanted to shove past the woman and clamber up the stairs, yell her sister's name, but Sylvan spoke first. "We're looking for someone named Edgar."

"Lil?" the woman answered, snapping the thread against her tooth.

"No—Edgar," Odile said. "Or Eddie."

"*Lill-i-an*," the woman said impatiently, turning the sewing over in her lap. "Lillian Edgar, she's at work—what do you think she does, frowse about here all day like the queen of England?"

"Is that nearby?" Odile asked.

"The theater round the corner."

"The—the—?"

"The-*at*-er!" The woman scowled irritably. "What's wrong with your ears?"

It was like hearing her own name. A theater—of course. Sylvan said something else to the woman, but all she could hear was the rumble of blood in her head, the distant swell of market bells. Her eyes followed the woman's thimbled finger, ahead to where the avenue crossed. *A music hall,* she was saying. Perhaps it was a place Odile would recognize from her mother's directory—a name she'd jotted down herself the night before, on the old Church of Marvels stationery. Perhaps, after whatever she'd been through on Doyers Street, Belle had gone somewhere familiar.

Odile muttered some kind of thanks, then hurried back through the gate. She and Sylvan turned the corner in tense silence, passing by flower stalls and fruit stands, listening to the knight-pips and dragon-squawks from a children's puppet show. She pictured her sister idling here beneath these awnings, turning through cherries and pears, buying daffodils and sprigs of yarrow for her dressing room. Lillian Edgar—the name didn't sound familiar at all—but so far everything in the city had proved to be strange.

Ahead of her was the theater marquee. But it wasn't the Featherbone, as she'd hoped, just a small variety hall of white brick and green trim: The Garden. She scanned the posters out front, all tacky with wheat-paste and faded by the sun. A musical revue was playing: *The Lonely Macaroon,* featuring Freddie "the Fried Egg" Eggleston and Lily Up-Your-Alley. No mention of Belle or the Shape Shifter, or any acts of thrill and sensation. A dusty little farce, by the looks of it—what her mother would have called a *mustard-and-pickle* marquee.

The ticket booth wasn't open yet, so she knocked at the stage door around back. She glanced over at Sylvan, who unknotted the kerchief at his neck and wiped the sweat from his forehead. He had such a particular face—the nose, once broken and now slightly hooked; the red bruise on his cheek; the ink-and-water eyes. She found herself looking back and forth between them, as if they belonged to two different minds, as if they saw two different people standing there beside him. She wondered, fleetingly, if the world appeared to him as if through a stereopticon—two different images that merged into a wondrous, impossible third. It made her shiver for a moment—that he might see a person in her place that she didn't even know herself, a person who had never before existed.

He caught her looking and shook his head. "If for any reason your sister should have done something dishonorable, or even—I don't know—something hard for you to understand—"

"She was prone to flights of passion, Mr. Threadgill. And I'm afraid I understand that better than anyone else alive."

The door was opened by a stubbled stagehand in work gloves and a sleeveless shirt. Odile asked first for Isabelle Church—he only shrugged and shook his head—and then Lillian Edgar. The man eyeballed them for a moment, rolling a sticky wad of chewing gum between his teeth, then pulled back the door and let them in. Odile was suddenly aware of how filthy she must look—boots crusted with dirt, the underarms of her blouse blackened by sweat, hair pasted to her brow. The stagehand pointed them down to Lillian's dressing room. "In the back," he said.

The theater itself was dark—Odile heard only the melody of saws and hammers, the crew singing an old Union song. She and Sylvan slipped between the backdrops, making their way to the other side of the stage. She breathed in the scents of paint and cording and sanded wood, the toasted smell of the lamps. There was something about it that grounded her, made her feel right. Not like Guilfoyle's tin can of a theater, where old kitchen pipes leaked through to the stage. She wanted to believe that Belle had felt at home in a place like this—that in spite of everything, she'd found somewhere safe to return. How many times had Odile climbed into her sister's bed at night and held her as she raged or wept over a single, trifling misstep? How many times had they fallen asleep together, heads pressed into the same pillow? And even though Odile reeked of eucalyptus, Belle had never turned her away.

The dressing-room door stood open. At the mirror sat a young woman in a gray gingham dressing gown, pinning wax lilies in her hair. She coughed wetly into a handkerchief, then took a swig of something—a glass of sudsy water, the color of cement. She leaned forward and turned up the lamp and began to paint her lashes. In the mirror Odile saw that her eyes were very bloodshot, her face a milky blue. She coughed again, her whole body contracting, then reached for a dish of talcum. In the doorway beside her, Odile could feel Sylvan tense.

The woman caught sight of them in the mirror, then turned around on her stool, tucking her handkerchief into the sash of her gown. She wasn't old—not much past thirty—with straw-thin calves in yellow stockings and the short, broad torso of a vaudeville tumbler. She looked at them without any recognition or curiosity, only a polite boredom. With her popping eyes, languorous bulk, and a chin that melted away into her neck, she reminded Odile of a woebegone snail.

"Miss Edgar," Odile began.

"Lil's good enough."

"I was hoping you could tell me about a woman named Isabelle Church."

Lillian drew her eyebrows together. "Who do you mean?"

"She's known as the Shape Shifter onstage—contortions and sword-swallowing. Plays a little music, too, usually upside down."

"I'm afraid I don't know that bit," Lillian said. She took up a talcum puff and began to powder her neck. "Come in and tell me, though."

They stepped inside. Sylvan stood closer to the door, a respectable distance in a lady's room. Odile sat down at the mirror. For the first time since she had arrived in Manhattan, she was met with her own reflection: her mud-flecked hat, her wild tangle of curls, her face flushed from the heat: a swamp-flower blooming in the city steam.

"I'm on the stage as well," she said quickly, licking her fingers and smoothing back her hair. "We had a sister act, actually, back home at Coney Island. I thought Isabelle might have passed through here at one point—maybe found work with you."

"Girls come here for work all the time," Lillian said, drawing a line of color around her lips. "But I don't know any sword-swallowers. We mostly do comic bits, song-and-dance numbers. Once we had a hypnotist cat. But no, no—nothing like that."

Odile pressed a hand to her sore knee—she could feel the bandage growing gummy with sweat. "Maybe you've heard of the Church of Marvels? The great conflagration at Coney Island last spring?"

"Not that I recall." She plucked a stray hair from the corner of her mouth. "I'm really very sorry."

Odile began to wonder if her sister went by another name here, if she'd adopted a different identity altogether. She leaned toward Lil, close enough to smell the fresh talc and salty gingham, and opened her mother's locket. "Perhaps you've seen her. She looks like me? This is an older photograph, I know, but still a good likeness."

Lillian frowned and studied it.

"And whatever you know," Odile said as their heads were bowed together, "you couldn't possibly shock me, so there's no need trying to protect her."

The woman just leaned back and shook her head, baffled, glancing from Odile to Sylvan and back again. "Honestly, I've never seen anyone like that here, and I've been working here near on ten years."

"You live at number two-one-three on West Thirteenth Street, right around the corner?"

"Why, yes." She looked at them suspiciously.

"You'd say your hair is dark and skin is fair?"

"You're looking at me, ain't you?"

"This was with my sister's belongings." Odile drew the envelope from her pocket and smoothed it out on the dressing table. "She was living on Doyers Street, I believe. Now she's missing and yours is the only name she left behind."

Lil gazed at it for a moment, cinching the gown tighter at her waist. She lifted the envelope and slid her finger under the flap, then drew out the scrap of paper. She considered it for a long while, then handed it back to Odile. "That's very odd," she said, hoarse. "I can't possibly see why she had it."

"But what does it mean?" Sylvan asked. He leaned forward and pointed to the word written across the envelope: *Mouse.* "None of this is familiar to you?"

Lil coughed—a tin-pan rattle, deep in her chest. She shook her head again, the lilies swishing in her hair. "If I knew your sister, I would tell you. I'm sorry, I can't help you more than that."

Odile flexed her wrist, prompting her to look again. "Won't you please think back? My sister could be in danger."

"If you don't mind, I'm . . . I'm not well today." And it was true, Odile could see—her skin was pale, the color of whey, and even her legs in their yellow stockings seemed to tremble.

"Perhaps you know someone by the name of Lee?" Sylvan suggested. "Or Eddie? Your name *is* Edgar, am I right?"

"It is indeed, but . . ." Lil stammered and shook her head. "I don't know how I can convince you—your sister isn't here."

Sylvan persisted. "You weren't on Broome Street last night?"

"What business would I have there?"

"It's a rather delicate situation," Odile said quickly, glancing back to Sylvan, "She's not well, and she needs to come home. I'm afraid she might have been expecting a child."

Lil's cheeks were damp, her eyes feverish. She coughed very hard, and suddenly Sylvan looked worried—he poured her a glass from a pitcher nearby. "I'm sorry," he said. "I'm sorry, we should let you rest."

Lil took the water and drank it, then got up to close the door. "I'm only saying it once, and you never heard it from me, you understand?" She sat down again and reached for a matchbook. "It's Mrs. Bloodworth's writing."

Mrs. Bloodworth—the name on the apothecary door. "On Doyers Street, you mean?"

"You know her, then."

"Only the name," Odile said. "Who is she? The shopkeeper?"

Lil was quiet for a moment. "She's a Jennysweeter."

"What is that?" Odile asked, looking to Sylvan and back. "What does that mean?"

"I don't know why my name would be here, but it's her writing." Lil drew a shallow breath. "But I've been so poorly lately, and I ain't getting any better, so why not tell you?"

She brushed her eyes with her fingertips, then pulled open a drawer and fumbled around for a cigarette case. Odile could see the white handkerchiefs crumpled up inside, all spotted with blood, like the doves of a luckless magician's show.

"It's all right," Odile said as calmly as she could, even though her heart was thudding in her chest.

"I made a mistake," Lil said, fingers shaking as she struck the match, "and Mother, she wouldn't let me keep it."

Odile understood then. It was what Pigeon had told her down in the Frog and Toe: *They want their babies to go away—so they go there for help.* "I'm sorry, Miss Edgar. What a harrowing thing to go through."

"She—she *made* me go to Mrs. Bloodworth."

"For a tonic, I know."

"I'm sorry?"

Odile leaned in confidentially. "To get rid of it," she whispered.

Lil's eyes grew wide. She shook her head. "Oh, no, no. My baby didn't die. No—I *gave* her to Mrs. Bloodworth." She coughed again, her eyes watering, blood spotting the back of her hand. "She said she would find her a good home. I didn't want to do it, but my parents made me! And I loved that baby, Miss Church!"

"You simply handed her over?" Sylvan asked. "You didn't do her any harm?"

Lil looked up at him. "Why would I have done such a thing as that?"

Odile didn't know what he was after, but she felt a surge, too, both panic and relief. Belle had meant to have the baby after all; she'd come all this way to give it up. No potions or pills or hooks; no throwing herself down a flight of stairs. But perhaps something worse had happened—Odile had no idea what it was like, living in a home of broken legs. So she began again, gently, "Were you there at the same time as my sister?"

"No, no. This was many years ago—a decade, more—and I was just a girl." Lil looked up in the mirror—at her makeup, now messed. She dragged a brush through a jar of carmine oil and slowly painted back her lips, letting the cigarette turn to ash between her fingers.

Odile gazed around the dressing room, at the musty costumes crowded in their rack, at Lillian's prop tray of macaroons painted pink and green. She tried desperately to organize her thoughts. Mother would have been beside herself, of course. She couldn't possibly have known about Belle's condition—if she had, she never would have made her go through with a new routine. She wouldn't have kept her on the stage at all.

"We should take our leave," Sylvan said. "Thank you, Miss Edgar."

"But you've come," she said, turning to them with wet, curious eyes. "Someone's come after all this time. Isn't that an act of Providence? No one has come about Mrs. Bloodworth, or my baby—not once, in all these years. Not even my own family come looking for me." She paused for a moment, fixing the lilies in her hair. "I loved a man, you see, only he—well, he worked in our house. I had to sneak downstairs, find excuses to be alone with him. But soon they could tell—they could tell the thing I'd done."

"So they sent you away," Odile said. "To Doyers Street."

"For a little while they tried to be Christian about it. Mother said she would pass it off as her own, and I was kept good out of sight. I didn't tell them who the man was, the one who'd done the thing to me. Only the girl was born, and she didn't *look* like me. She looked like *him*."

✎ "And they wouldn't keep her? They wouldn't just turn the man out of the house instead?"

"He was from Siam. She was a half-breed, you see? And anyone would know it. So I left her with Mrs. Bloodworth; I signed her away. But even so, my mother and father wouldn't take me back. It's a sin, what I done. I did everything they asked, and still they wouldn't let me home."

"And what would have happened to my sister's child?"

"Sold to a good family, you can only pray. Though why she'd have my name here, I can't tell you. Only Mrs. Bloodworth would know where I am. She's the one who found me the room at Mrs. Porter's, when my parents wouldn't take me in."

Sold! Even the sound of it—one brisk, austere syllable—struck Odile like the clap of a hammer. "If I were to pay her a visit, might she know where my sister is? Perhaps she found her lodging, too?"

"If she has, she'll never tell you. That's part of the agreement, you understand? Your sister is protected. You'll get no information at all."

"But I'm her family."

"There's nobody more dangerous than family." Lil looked back in the mirror and powdered her face again. "I know that to be true." For a moment she stared at her reflection—the grim, hooded eyes;

the burst vessels in her cheeks. Then, mechanically, she brushed back her hair and righted the pins, slid on a bracelet, wound a scarf around her throat. She bared her teeth in the mirror and practiced her smiles—big, hammy, antic smiles, like a series of souvenir photographs.

Odile stood up to take her leave, but Lillian turned back once more. She lowered her voice as carpenters shuffled down the hallway, just outside the door. "Go into the shop tomorrow, first thing. She will only see girls in the morning. Ask for a cup of tea. At least then you'll get into the back room; you'll see Mrs. Bloodworth for yourself. You might find a trace of your sister. More than you'll find here, I'm afraid."

"You mean pretend I'm there for the same?"

"You said you were on the stage, right?" Footsteps drew closer in the hall. "But be careful—please. She is not a forgiving woman."

There was a knock on the door—the stagehand summoning Lillian for rehearsal.

As she stood, she looked back at the envelope again, still clenched in Odile's hand. "Burn it, will you?"

When she left—a barrage of silks and powder and tinkling gems, carrying her tray of macaroons—Sylvan turned to Odile.

"There's something I need to show you."

THEY TURNED INTO a narrow alley off Cherry Street—Odile saw boys shucking oysters, cats stalking through the weeds. Even though it was hot out, her teeth chattered and her head pulsed. Everything came dizzily to life: the sweat on Sylvan's neck, the jammy cuts on his knuckles, the crinkle of his elbow as he reached for the banister and drew himself up the stairs. And the staircase itself, bleached by the sun—in the light she saw a fine web of filaments around it, glowing like a spun cocoon.

A door opened on the landing above. A woman leaned out. She was kind-eyed and stout; she let them inside, whispered to Sylvan. Odile heard the words *She's sleeping* and then smelled cinnamon in the air. She followed Sylvan into the dark, steamy room, listing as if she were at sea.

He beckoned her. There was something at his feet—a basket, lined with quilts. She heard a rustle from inside. A kitten, she thought. A rabbit.

She drew a breath and looked down. She felt the tears start to well in her throat.

"I'm not a night watchman," Sylvan said. "I'm a night-soiler. And this is what I found in a privy."

A baby. A puffy, pink face; a dimpled chin. A drooling, sleeping, milk-sweet baby, with little bat-ears sticking out beneath her silken tugs of hair. She yawned and opened her eyes, and it took no more than a second for Odile to see that she looked like Belle.

FIFTEEN

ALPHIE DIDN'T KNOW EXACTLY WHAT SHE FELT, IF IT WAS thrill or terror. Memories, though shifty and piecemeal, were starting to come back to her. The night that Anthony and his mother were supposed to have gone to Poughkeepsie—the night that she paced the rooms alone—she remembered a faint rap on the carriage-house door, the darkness of the stairs as she crept down to answer it. Mrs. Bloodworth's girl was waiting for her on the step. She wore a hooded black cloak and a white flower at her breast. Orchard Broome, standing there in the shadows, bearing the basket beside her.

And here she was on the island, flanneled and masked, drinking the raw asylum eggs, unable to speak her own name. What a strange bit of fortune, Alphie thought—together they made a plan, scribbled in soap on the mirror of the nurses' washroom, then washed away with a rag.

After they snuck back down the hall, Alphie paused at the gate to the other ward. It was locked—how had Orchard escaped and followed her? As far as Alphie could tell, she had nothing to open it with, not even a hairpin. Alphie was about to reach for the scissors, but then they heard footsteps circle back down the corridor. Orchard dropped to her stomach and slithered beneath the bottom rung—a space of no more than six inches. Alphie stared at the girl's body, flat and slippery as an eel, undulating under the bar. Her skirt dragged and swished, her legs kicked, and then her slippered feet disappeared—*thwoop!*—fast as a penny flicked across a floor. Alphie stood alone in the hall, wondering if she was hallucinating. But back in her own bed, with the taste of sweat and soap on her upper lip, her heart pounded so hard that it hurt: her heart, as real as anything she knew.

She remembered, as a small child, seeing her father dress a doe by the river. He made Alphie hold the knife, then guided her hand and cut into the animal's flesh—the blood began to spill, the skin peeled away, but there beneath the ribs the heart still beat. Just twice: *flup, flup.*

Flup, flup, then still.

It's what we do, her father had insisted. *It's man's way.* Alphie stared at the organs, pulled out in a glistening snarl around her feet. *But this isn't my way,* she thought, although she knew she couldn't say it out loud. The song of the heart haunted her, all through the winter. She heard it in the burning hearth, in the snowy trees. She fell asleep and heard it in the pillow beneath her head: *flup, flup.* Then gone.

Sometimes, when Alphie had worked on the waterfront—a fourteen-year-old Widow in waxy blond curls—she lay alone in her room at night, scrubbing her limbs with a crusted rag. In that room (barely big enough for a body, no brighter than a coal box) she could hardly see her hand stretched out in front of her. There in the dark with nothing else to guide her, her old senses came alive, and she imagined she was back in the house on the river, the place where she'd been born. In her mind she weaved through the old rooms, up and down the stairs, around the familiar corners—to the linen cabinet where she used to hide as a child with her corncob doll pressed to her breast. To the kitchen hearth where she sat making paper dolls, the same doll over and over, while her mother threw dough against the table and sighed. To the foul, low-lying henhouse, where she used to belly-crawl through the straw, groping for speckled eggs still warm in their nests. To the crooked forest path that ran from their house to the shop, thick with the smell of loam and dead leaves in the rain. In the darkness she could still feel the sting of the river water on her naked limbs, taste a buttery yolk as it slipped whole down her throat. She could see the stars through the wind-bent trees, the crooked steps up to the kitchen door, the raccoon's eyes blinking from the old woodpile, even her mother and father hunched over their dinner plates, the knife edges glinting in the lamplight. Sometimes she wept so hard she threw up, and the Widows' erst-while, goggle-eyed madam beat her for the smell of her room, which she had to clean all over again. So she stopped thinking that way. She shrank back from the edges of her mind and stayed in one gray place. For years she stopped trying to think anything at all.

But now, in the asylum ward, she allowed shapes to come alive in the darkest corners of the room. She saw again the bed she shared with Anthony, the little cradle by the range, the pillows she could never quite clean—marked by the black tally of her eyelashes, the grease from Anthony's hair. She saw the credenza, the bottle of cordial, her old paint kit on the shelf, nothing more than a tackle box tied with a sad bit of ribbon. (But the smell of it when she opened the lid!—the mineral whiff of the creams and pastes, the rusty sweetness of the powder, the tang of lemon drops.) She saw her dresses hanging on the rack, the hats on their lonesome pegs. She saw the girl's white flower where it lay on the rug, crushed beside the broken rattle. The rattle—she'd forgotten! Anthony had made it for her just as summer began. A pretty, painted thing of wood. But that night the Signora—*il mostro!*—had cracked it open on her skull, and as

Alphie fell to the floor she saw raining down around her—not dry beans like she'd imagined—but teeth. Children's teeth. Her hand, confused, had flown up to her mouth, where she was missing two of her own, but those had been punched out years ago, by a drunkard who told her she'd suck better without them.

Now in bed she worried her loose tooth with her tongue. She felt a throb echo through her body, down into her groin. She had wondered if resignation would come to her at Blackwell's, the way it had in that dark room on the waterfront—if she would just shrink away from her grief and dreams, and hope that her body survived while her mind disappeared. But something had changed. Now the only thing that could keep her alive *was* her mind—not her body, waiting to betray her.

Where is she? Orchard Broome had begged, but Alphie couldn't tell her. She didn't remember what happened to the baby at all.

SHE HEARD THE HOUNDS at dawn. They groaned and yipped, scraping across the yard on their chains, gobbling up gristle thrown on the ground. Then came the heavy tread in the hall, the drag of Jallow's baton across the stone. She checked her thigh—scissors, secure—and rose from her bed. The other women were startled awake, too—they fell, groping and mole-blind from their beds, hurrying to ready themselves in the darkness. Alphie shook out her shapeless skirt, bowed her head, and waited for Jallow to herd them downstairs for their promenade. When the nurse came clattering into the room, Alphie snuck a glance her way, trying to see if she looked different today (more aware somehow, or suspicious) but Jallow only blasted a pellet of snot out of her nostril and marched them all downstairs to the courtyard, just as she'd done the day before.

It was still dark, with a golden glow just starting to burn over the water. They shuffled down to the south gate, where they were joined by Bradigan and the shivering women from the other ward. Over the river Alphie heard the first sounds of the city—the grate of metal, the hiss of steam, the horns and bells of the longshoremen. She breathed in the early smell of morning, grass and dew. The crickets were thrupping in the brush. Something about it reminded her of her childhood, tramping through the woods to the water—far away from the glowering townspeople at the shop counter, fussing over their push brooms and fennel seeds—far away from her father, red-faced at the woodpile, beating her with a log because she couldn't lift the ax. All those mornings running to the river through the forest, stripping off her horrible clothes, waiting for the green water to hide her, envelop her. Even then, only a child, she knew she had to pretend to be someone else—for her parents, for their customers, for everyone else in that miserable factory town, dark and ashy with smoke—even if it made her sad. If she ran fast enough on those raw, dark mornings through the woods, she might see the trees and morning stars, merrily alive, scurry back to their rightful places. She might hear the animals whisper and sing. And she would gain something special—a secret knowledge, an awakening. Something no one else could know. But until then she had to pass unnoticed, waiting to be delivered to another world where she belonged.

The horses were already harnessed and hitched to the cart, nosing in their feedbags. Alphie glanced around for Orchard. In the blue huddle beyond, she saw the glint of her mask, a small moon floating in the dark. At the sound of the whistle, the women allowed themselves to be guided by the nurses into a single line. Orchard kept close to the front, Alphie to the back, her head down, trying to look tired and unremarkable despite the charge that coursed through her. When DeValle shuffled in behind her, Alphie grabbed her wrist and squeezed. "Whatever you see, don't you dare make a sound—I'll take your Malvina Cream, every last tin. Understand?"

DeValle whimpered and nodded.

Jallow and Bradigan moved in tandem down the row, collaring the women and hitching them together. Alphie kept her eyes down as they passed the rope through the metal ring on her collar, as they talked to each other over the women's heads. The gates rattled open, and the hounds began to bray.

The nurses climbed stiffly into the wagon. The horses pricked up their ears. The charwomen circled the yard with their snuffers, tamping out the lights.

Jallow whistled, and the horses lurched ahead. The women were pulled down the path to the river. Alphie saw the lighthouse to the north, and to the south the almshouse and the prison. Then, at the curve of the road, they passed the groundsman's wagon, coming up from the landing. The breath caught in her throat, itching like a bug—she saw the sneering soap-boy with his banged-up trunk. He didn't even glance at them, just rubbed his nose and stared dully at his boots. She was terrified, but also sick with relief—she needed it to be him. And here he was, the piggy bastard, ready to greet the Matron, who waited behind as always with her blue lamp and musty book. Alphie looked away, as if it were of no interest to her. The order had been wrong yesterday. He'd come, grudgingly, to fix it.

They plodded forward down the road, under an arbor of barren trees. Bradigan and Jallow rode with their backs to the women, conferring about something in low voices. Jallow seemed upset—it was her fellow, she kept saying; her fellow was untrue. Once in a while Bradigan turned to hock a mouthful of tobacco juice onto the road. Jallow steered the horses, wiping at her face, not even bothering with the pie-pan lying beside her. Alphie tried to keep her feet steady. The rope buzzed and burned against the ring of her collar—she could feel the hemp-dust tickle her nose. They looked like one straggling, accordioned creature, she thought, a giant blue millipede.

She couldn't bear for Anthony to see her this way—her body caked with oil and dander, her hair matted and still reeking of Mother's Milk, the skin at her throat now festering, marked by a name she couldn't read.

For a quarter of an hour the women tramped doggedly ahead, their feet lost in a billow of dust. She heard, echoing through the trees, the song of the convicts breaking stone, the echo of hammers, the patter of patrol boats. Then—there it was: the dull clang of the boathouse bell, summoning the ferry's return. She heard the gulls crying overhead, the hiss and slap of water. Her heart answered, fluttering up in her chest.

They moved around a horseshoe bend, down into a copse of trees—the densest, most wooded portion of the promenade—thick with mayapple and shepherd's purse. How strange, Alphie thought, passing through the bowers, that the farther afield they got from the asylum, the more things flourished, returning to life. As Jallow and Bradigan lifted their lamps in the early light, as the horses snorted their way through the trail of fog, she pulled the scissors from under her dress and prized them open. As the women buckled and swayed ahead, Alphie slid the blades around the rope and started grinding. For a moment it seemed the cords were too tough, the scissors too dull, her fingers slippery and numb. Soon the wagon would emerge onto the trampled, sunlit path by the river. She squeezed harder and harder at the scissors, until her palms were chafed and the blades were jammed with bits of thread.

Dismayed, she looked at the fraying, chewed-up twine in front of her. The women kept winding down the path, listing to the side. She leaned the other direction, putting strain on the rope, feeling the muscles cramp in her neck. Then the cords unraveled, hummed, and snapped. The women in front of her jerked forward. Alphie stopped in the middle of the path. The rope unthreaded, slipping through the hoops of each collar with a pop of dust. The horses trotted faster and faster through the trees, with no weight to hinder them. Jallow and Bradigan yelled, struggled to settle them; they whistled and pulled at the reins. The madwomen fell back, watching the rope snake away through dirt, the nurses' bonnets roll and pitch like two black balloons in the fog. They wavered for a moment in their blue flannel dresses, then looked around at each other, confused. Some began to scatter. DeValle began to laugh. Orchard grabbed Alphie's hand and pulled her away through the trees, past the old cannon with its bird's-nest crown, behind the old military wall overgrown with foxglove. She crouched down and took the scissors from Alphie and cut their collars free.

Then they ran between the wraithlike trees, through thickets of ironweed and possum haw. Orchard was quick, much quicker than Alphie, but Alphie ran until her lungs ached with the force of it, until her feet were cut open and her slippers weren't much more than shreds of fabric swinging from her ankles. Through the grove they heard the echoing panic of the pie tin, the nurses blowing their whistles: *Help!*

They ran along the shore, to the landing and the old boathouse— there, the bell with its half-rotted rope, creaking in the breeze. Through the door Alphie could see the soap-boy with his yellow eyes, chewing the skin around his knuckles. He was done with his delivery and now sat with his feet propped up on the soap-case, waiting for the ferry to make its return.

The Matron's horn sounded up the hill. The dogs, excited, began to bray. The boy spit out a hangnail and rose to his feet, bewildered. Alphie hovered there just outside the door, breathing in the balmy scent of wet wood and soap—then Orchard touched her arm and they shoved their way inside, wrestling him back against the wall. "What the devil is this?" he spat. "I'll kill you bitches dead."

Orchard lunged at him, the open scissors flashing in her hand. But the boy was fast—he raised a hand and struck her upside the head, so hard she stumbled to the floor.

Then Alphie, in a rage, was on him. She couldn't stop herself, even though she knew this was not the person she was. She was the pretty Rembrandt who'd cleaned up the Widows' cuts and bruises, who had let them sleep in her room when they were afraid of the darkness and the thunder and the crazy man bellowing in the street below. She was the one who long ago had tended to the chickens, the horses, the cats in the barn, the one who'd given extra milk to the runts. She was a good person, she believed, even though others had called her a monster. She just didn't know what to do with the fury inside her.

The soap-boy lay at her feet (unconscious? dead?), his eyes swollen and lewdly pink, like a newborn rat's. She remembered how Anthony had bludgeoned the man who attacked her that night on the waterfront—the drunk man who'd grabbed her by the hair, knocked over her stand. *Sempre libera.* They were fated and bound, like the lovers in an opera—and that's what the Signora couldn't bear.

The soap-boy's head was twisted to the side; his cheek was beginning to blue. Alphie lifted her foot and toed away the red trickle of spit on his chin. *Who's the ugly one now?*

Orchard rolled to her side and clutched her ribs, blood hissing from her teeth. Unsteadily, she rose to her feet, but still she hurried— unlatching the trunk, throwing back the lid. There was no way, Alphie thought, a grown person could fit inside. It was smaller than she remembered, maybe two feet by three. How desperate, how rash could their plan have been?

Still, Orchard grabbed a piece of newspaper from the trunk, crumpled and slimy with soap. She greased down her arms and her legs, slathered her face and her hair. She shook out her shoulders and folded up her limbs, then curled herself inside the open suitcase, like a baby bird in an egg.

"How is that possible?" Alphie whispered. "What happened to your bones?"

As Orchard rolled and slithered her body free, Alphie heard

the screams in the woods, the distant splashes of water, the terror of the bells. She peered through the doorway and saw, farther down the bank, women running into the river, tripping on their skirts, falling face-first into the black mud. The dogs chased after them, sinking their teeth into ankles and arms, shaking them and dragging them back to shore. Just beyond, a brigade of nurses prowled on horseback, lashes raised above their heads. They circled and shouted. Their whips cracked louder than guns. Alphie saw the madwomen's dresses break open. They fell to the ground, bleeding between the reeds. Above them the mosquitoes sang, ecstatic.

Quickly Orchard turned the soap-boy on his back and began to undress him—yanking off his shoes and bandanna, unbuttoning his shirt and trousers, sliding off his oily suspenders—until he lay there on the floor of the boathouse in only his underthings. Alphie lifted him with both arms and dragged him behind the boathouse, through the grass, leaving him in a gnatty thicket and covering his face with a useless handful of leaves.

Back inside Orchard waited for her. She was holding his clothes. She was holding his clothes out to Alphie.

Alphie felt her skin go fizzy, her hands begin to shake. She took a step back. "I can't," she heard herself say, even though she knew it was ridiculous. If the nurses should hunt them down, if they should find them here with the soap-boy bleeding and half-naked in the brush—here, with a pair of stolen scissors and an empty trunk, the conspirators who'd incited this riot—everything would be over. They'd be banished to the Violents for good.

Still, she found herself backing away. "I can't," she whispered again. "I can't."

A bell tolled over the water. She jumped. They both turned and saw, through the dusty window, a small boat bobbing across the current, drawing closer to the landing. The hounds were bounding farther down the shore, flapping their foamy chops. Horses galloped across the grass. She saw the nurses going from building to building: the pigeon cote, the abandoned dairy, the groundsman's shed, pulling women away by their hair.

The bell tolled again. Tears burned in Alphie's eyes and filled her mouth. It had been so long, and she'd fought so hard. She'd done everything she could to banish that other life of hers, a life never meant for her. She wept as she heard the scissors squeak open, as she felt the girl's breath against her ear. She thought of Anthony, of what his face would look like when she returned to him so changed. But this was the only chance she had anymore, and so she knelt down and shook out her hair.

She felt the scissors tense against her hair, then slice it away. It gathered, blond and lost, on the floor.

Standing up, her head felt light, her neck chilly. But she dressed. She pulled off her flannel dress and her filthy underclothes. She shook out the boy's pants, buttoned and cuffed them at the ankles. She pushed her feet into his plain brown shoes and brushed the dust from his bowler. She pulled on his plain cotton shirt, which smelled garlicky and damp, and shrugged on the well-thumbed suspenders. She tied the bandanna loose around her throat, careful to keep the tattoo covered. She rolled up the sleeves and rubbed the greasy wads of newspaper over her arms, until her skin was smeared with ink.

Orchard Broome stabbed a few holes in the trunk with her scissors, then twisted herself inside. Alphie snapped it shut and drew the buckles taut. She lifted it with more ease than she imagined.

She walked out to the landing, feeling the sun on her skin, the sting of brine on her lips. She licked them clean. Her fingers shook, but she unbuttoned the too-tight collar and let her Adam's apple flex. One button, and then another, enough to show the silky trail of hair down her chest. She ran a hand against her smooth cheek, shaved clean with the scissors in the nurses' chamber. It had been ages since she'd worn pants, since her ribs had stretched, since the pale skin of her chest had felt the warmth of the sun. Her mouth opened, blanched and bruised, her lungs shuddering but still drawing breath.

THE BOATMAN SAW A FIGURE on the landing. He squinted and shielded his eyes from the sun, which rose above the fog and turned everything white. There was a commotion on the grounds beyond—cracks and shouts, the thunder of horses. He would have mistaken it all for a picnic race if he hadn't known exactly where he was heading, and if he hadn't seen the women, wrangled and dog-bitten, bleeding on the shore. Christ, he thought—the fools were having another one of their fits.

"Just in time, eh?" he said as he slowed against the landing. "What malarkey." He looped the bowline around the horn, then looked up at his passenger. "Ready to go, chap?"

The young man nodded and lifted his trunk, turning his face toward Manhattan. "Yes," he said. "I've never been readier in my life."

SIXTEEN

ALPHIE WAS ABOUT TO STEP INTO THE BOAT WHEN ONE OF the nurses came clattering down the dock. "Wait!" she called, waving her arms. "Wait there!"

The boatman cursed under his breath. "What the hell's this?"

The old boards thudded underfoot as the nurse ran toward them. Alphie pulled down the brim of her hat and turned her face to the water. Her mouth went dry; her body began to tremble. She stared at the waves lapping against the stern, at the roiling chop beyond. She could jump now, just like those sad summer days in the Hudson, kicking out alone to the wooded islet where the mourning doves sang. Could she outswim them? Was she fast enough? The suitcase grew heavy in her hand. She pictured Orchard Broome sinking to the bottom of the river, coiled tight in her leather box, fish swimming through her hair.

"A few on the loose," the nurse said to the boatman, pinching her side. "Had any trouble?"

"Just pulled in."

"You don't mind if I have a look?"

"You don't believe me?"

The nurse glared at him. He sighed and grumbled, "As long as it's a fast one," then turned to Alphie. "Sorry, chap."

The nurse stepped into the boat and started clopping through the green scum of water. She threw back a canvas sheet and squinted at the knots of tackle. She nosed under the bench-seats, kicked back the lines. Wheezing, she turned to gaze back at the shore—the flash of horses in the thicket, the boathouse with its rust-red bell. Then she looked over at Alphie. "Boy, you didn't happen to see—"

But she didn't finish her sentence. Alphie had unbuttoned her trousers and stood pissing over the edge of the landing, into the water. The nurse shook her head in disgust and turned back to the boatman. "Protocol is all, y'see?" she said. "Just carrying out orders."

The boatman shrugged and reached to unloop the cable from the horn. Alphie shook off, buttoned up, and tipped her hat.

The nurse ignored her. "No more boats till we're finished here," she said, then turned on her heel and stalked away.

When the boat rocked away from the island, Alphie felt dizzy. She sat at the bow, tasting the chalky air, watching Manhattan draw closer. The sun rose over the riverbank behind them, warming her back through the thin shirt, turning the city ahead to glass. She kept her hat pulled down over her head, the trunk close to her side. She wanted to lean over and run her hand over the hole in the side, just to feel the touch of Orchard Broome's finger, a sign that she was alive. But she kept her eyes fixed straight ahead, her face turned stonily from the man at the helm.

Originally she'd had a different plan: she'd lose the baby before it was born. It happened all the time. A sickness, a fall. But as the months passed, she'd started to panic. She realized that a miscarriage wouldn't deter the Signora or win her sympathy. It would only feed her contempt. The Signora would call the doctor to the house obsessively, full of righteousness disguised as motherly concern. And how many times could Alphie avoid him? The Signora would take pleasure in the idea there was something wrong with Alphie and her body. The new woman: inferior, sickly. The wife Anthony had chosen himself: a failure. So Alphie had paid a visit to Mrs. Bloodworth, whom she'd heard about from one of the Widows. *Trustworthy,* she'd been told. *Discreet.*

And so it was done. Early one morning, with the Signora still sleeping and Anthony gone, Alphie arrived at Doyers Street wearing her plainest dress. Just as she was instructed, she walked through the green door of the apothecary shop and simply asked for a cup of tea. She was shown into a back room with Oriental screens, where a woman with pollen-dusted hands received her. Mrs. Bloodworth was both prickly and soothing, buttermilk and razor wire—Alphie wasn't sure how to behave around her. This was a woman who had seen stranger things than Alphie dared dream, and who only lit a pipe and smiled at her hawkishly with an interest that was genial but mercenary. Alphie smiled back, distracted by the sound of the clock on the wall, gurgling and clucking like a fat hen.

She told Mrs. Bloodworth simply that she couldn't bear children—a brief and hurried explanation—then pressed on: it didn't matter to her if the child was a boy or a girl, as long as it might have some of Anthony's coloring. She would prefer if the baby took after him in some way—it would be safer, after all—not like her own stalk-thin forebears, with their snot-yellow hair and overwet lips and bulbous, disbelieving eyes.

Mrs. Bloodworth considered her for a long moment. *And how did you come to find me here?* Alphie, short of breath, stammered the name of the Widow on the waterfront: *Why, it was Billie the Barber told me.* That's when Mrs. Bloodworth leaned in closer, her eyes lifting from Alphie's folded hands to her padded chest to her blushing face, taking slow inventory of her features. Alphie leapt from her chair—*I shouldn't have come*—but the woman reached out her hand and held gently to Alphie's wrist.

Don't you know I will help you? she said. *You are not the first of your kind who has come to this door.* Then, without another word, she rang for a tray of coffee and pulled a ledger from her desk.

Alphie stood there for a moment, her corset chafing her ribs. *You won't tell about me?*

Why would I? Mrs. Bloodworth raised her head and looked at her. *We both of us live by our secrets.*

The night of the delivery, alone in the carriage house, Alphie had prepared. Even though Anthony and the Signora had left for Poughkeepsie that afternoon—just as they'd planned—as the hours passed and the dark drew nearer, Alphie began to get nervous. For a moment she missed her days as a penny Rembrandt—mixing paints on her cardboard palette, seeing the fiery silhouettes of the coal ships on the river, smelling a gentlemen's expensive shaving soap as she leaned in to brush the gravel from his cheek. Still now, wherever she went—the butcher's, the cobbler's, even Mrs. Bloodworth's—she instinctively looked for a blue star on the door. *The north star.* It meant someone like her would be safe. But she wasn't one of those boys anymore—a fairy, and known as one, risking danger beyond the small constellation of havens that protected her. Now she was someone's wife, passing for good. She'd been in such a drive to get this matter resolved that she hadn't stopped to consider what it would be like to actually have a child. All she knew was that she wanted a different life, a better one. She never wanted to feel that terror again, the blackness exploding in the back of her brain when a drunkard would push her to the floor in a narrow room behind the shipyard, then rip the wig off her head and beat her because she'd made him do something wicked, something against God. But there were better times after she ran away and started working at her own stand—the freedom to walk the streets as she chose, learning the places where she'd be welcomed and safe, getting a tip from a blushing customer who stared, incredulous, at his face fixed up in the mirror.

That night she'd waited for the knock on the door downstairs. When it came, she crept down, clutching her padded stomach and gripping the banister, every nerve in her body alive. At the door she found a figure in a hooded cape, carrying a basket.

Quickly she'd led the young woman up the stairs. In the room, however, she froze up, uncertain what to do or say. So the girl set to work helping her. Together they turned down the bed and stripped the sheets to stain with blood. Alphie started to undress, to get rid of the pillow for good. She glimpsed the baby girl just once, over the edge of the basket.

It's a good thing you've done for me, Alphie whispered as Mrs. Bloodworth's girl helped her out of her dress.

The girl was quiet for a moment, her hands freeing the tiny seed buttons from their hooks. *You're lucky,* she said. *You have two spirits. Most in this life only have one.*

Those were the only words they'd spoken. As Alphie stepped out of her skirts and untied the pillow, she heard the door slam below, then footsteps rising. She and the girl looked at each other with confused stares, disbelieving, each waiting for the other to explain. There was a hesitation on the landing, a momentary creak of the wood, but then the steps continued, faster and determined—and she heard it clearer, the tick of those beads, the smell of licorice in the air—and the door, she hadn't locked it—

The boat pulled up to the dock. Her heart was pounding. She waited for the boatman to offer his hand, to help her out, but that was foolish now—she had to remember herself. As calmly as she could, she lifted the trunk and stepped onto the landing, making her way down the wharf. She wasn't used to moving in these clothes—she felt awkward, taking big, sloppy strides, one arm swinging as she tried to balance the trunk. She'd just passed the ticket bridge when she heard the stationmaster say, "Sir?"

She looked back and saw a trail of something on the planks

behind her, dark and wet. It dripped from the corner of the trunk, splatted on the toe of her shoe. She put a hand to the hole Orchard had punched in the side—something was leaking from it, and when she pulled her fingers away she saw they were sticky with blood.

"It's just soap," she heard herself say, wiping her hands on her trousers. "It goes soft in the heat."

The stationmaster waved over one of his men. "Please, sir, open the trunk."

The toady took a step toward her, not menacing, but with a routine firmness in his voice. She backed away, then broke into a run, tearing up the dock in the soap-boy's hard and poorly cobbled boots. Her shoulders ached and her fingers shook as she struggled to keep hold of the trunk. She pushed through the crowd of stevedores, through gusts of steam and spilling pallets, too scared to look back. Fifty yards away she ducked between two piano crates and sprang the latches on the trunk, then lifted Orchard Broome up by her soap-slick elbow. The girl wavered a little, queasy and pale. Without the mask, her mouth had started to bleed again. She couldn't spit—she had no tongue—so she hunched over and drooled into the street. Alphie pulled off her shirt and buttoned it over Orchard's damp flannel dress, so that no mark of the asylum could be seen. She unknotted the bandanna around her neck and helped her stanch the blood.

Then she looked back over her shoulder, but the wharf was so crowded—the faces bulging and blurred, the men black-eyed as scarecrows—that she couldn't pick out the stationmaster or his toady. She couldn't tell if anyone was even chasing them at all. Still, she and Orchard hurried across the avenue, dodging the slobber of cart-nags and the careless, thwicking whips of the drivers. They passed into the shadows of Fifty-fourth Street, wheezing and listing. The air grew close, the sky darker. Alphie grabbed at a cramp in her side. Her head ached, muddled by the steam whistles in the factories, the shrill tantrum of a grinding-wheel, the hansoms hiccupping over the cobbles. Somewhere she smelled dumplings frying in fat, and her stomach folded in on itself.

She had to get home before anything else happened—to see Anthony, to assure him that her love for him was absolute and she wouldn't disappear. She had to keep him safe from his mother, from himself. That was her job, wasn't it? That was her strength. Something tolled inside her—the memory of panic. The blush and gloom of the children at the Widows Walk—the men who scuttled there, craven and ashamed; the men who bounded proudly through the rooms, pot-bellied, bird-necked, sticky-fingered; happy for their meager slice of power, for the chance to say, *see what I can do to another. See how they turn to me, how they abide.*

They rounded a corner and saw two horses hitched outside a tavern. Alphie peered through the window—the grooms were drinking themselves to near death at a table in the back. Each contraction of her heart, each snap of blood in her wrists, each tender flicker behind her ears, all said the same thing: *Anthony.*

She unhitched the horses. "Can you ride?" she was about to ask Orchard, but the girl leaped onto the back of the horse and turned it expertly around. Alphie mounted hers, brisk and sure-footed, even though she hadn't done such a thing in years.

Together they drove out to the avenue. It had been a long time since she'd worn trousers, since she'd straddled a horse, since she felt the reins burn her bare palms and the muscles clench in her thighs and knees. She heard the clanging of the trolley bells. Here she was, bare-chested, gaining speed down Second Avenue.

They galloped past Forty-fourth Street—there, just a few miles away, on the banks of the Hudson, her feet had first touched the city sand. Years ago, just fourteen, she'd been ferried down the river by a fur-trapper in a canoe. The day her father turned her out, she'd walked for miles along the wooded bank, stunned and alone, the dollar loose in her pocket. She saw the trapper pushing off from a cove—he was taking his furs down to New York City to sell in the Tenderloin. *New York,* she dreamed. She gave him half of her dollar, for safe passage and a warm beer. She sat there among the coonskins and rabbit pelts while the valley glided past her, a pearled and craggy dream. The man didn't speak but made birdcalls to the sky. She felt light-headed as the oars pulled her away from her village and flung green muck on her knees. And here was her thought as she watched the rippling water: how good of her father, how generous, to spare a whole, hard-earned dollar. She remembered Sam's face and felt a fire in her stomach, a pulse in her groin. But what was it—loathing or desire? In the back of the store they'd been playing around, trying on some of the ready-made clothes. He'd put lipstick on her—a game, just fooling—then practiced a kiss. She could still taste the bittersweet paste in the corners of her mouth, feel the salty drag of his tongue against hers.

If she turned here and rode fifty miles up the Hudson, she'd find that old village, the home of little Alphie—known then as Alphonse Booth Jr., who worked as a shopboy for his father, sweeping and stocking, delivering eggs from the family coop every weekend. Alphonse, with hen bites on his pale legs, the smell of chicken shit on his shoes and clothes, steering the cart with its teetering crates down the lanes. Alphonse, who had let Sam Vetz kiss him and grope him in the back of the store. They'd wrestled and grabbed at each other, sick with some kind of longing that was both foreign and real—and then Mr. Booth had walked in.

Alphie steered the horse down into the Thirties, past the bakeries and the oyster barrels, past the stacks of corn and buckets of boot nails, the links of sausage big as oxen yokes and spotty with fat. The horses lurched and whinnied together, thrilled to be given the lead. Beside her the girl's look was hard and feral—she leaned forward in the saddle and gripped the horn, the soap-boy's shirt flapping around her small frame, her feet free from the stirrups and braced against the horse's flank.

There were times when Alphie hated herself for choosing a life in which she and Anthony had to lie, even when things felt truer than she'd ever known. Sometimes they still went down to the Shingle and Plank, to the places where people knew them, where other couples like themselves gathered, couples carrying on the same kind of ruse in their own houses. Gradually, though, Anthony began to leave her behind, drifting down to the water alone and not reappearing until dawn. Alphie would cry through the night, or pace the rooms, seething and furious, before falling asleep in the chair by the door. Those nights she almost hated him for making their life harder than it already was, and fleetingly she wondered if she could give it all up, if it was worth it. Wouldn't it be easier if she lived like a man, the way she'd been born, the way her parents expected her to be, the way Anthony lived now? Wouldn't it be easier for her to marry a plain, undemanding woman and father a few children and drift down once in a while to the waterfront to be the person she knew she was? Why couldn't she just do what came so easily to everyone else? But in the morning she'd rise and brush out her hair and lace up her corset and she'd feel whole again, like herself, and she looked in the mirror and knew who she was, knew that despite all of the dangers, a life of a different kind of deceit would kill her. How would it feel to know there were people who'd chosen to live as they felt, not as they appeared, and never looked back? Could she bear their happiness, as shunned as they were? Was she brave enough?

Was she?

This was her body, she knew, but not herself. Looking in the mirror every morning after she dressed, seeing in the flesh the way she felt inside—how could she ever give that up? She had to make a choice. This was hers. And she wasn't sorry.

She picked up speed, edging her way around wagons, weaving between pushcarts, watching the crowds in the street dodge and leap. Her back and torso were bare to the breeze, her skin sweating in the gray sun. Every week she used to pass this very butcher shop, where the fowl were slaughtered and hung from the awnings, their wings fanned out as if in flight. Sometimes she'd bring home a jar of blood—for puddings and sauces, she always told the shopboy—but then, late at night, she rubbed the blood into her monthly cloths to show the Signora. How she trembled there, as the Signora unrolled the cloth and turned it to the light—how she worried something else would be amiss: the silhouette of her dress, the smoothness of her cheek, the shape of her hands.

But for now there would be no crinoline skirts or twenty-buttoned boots, no pomegranate paste for her lips, no haircombs or bustles or gardenia perfume. She wanted them to be sorry. Bitterly sorry. And she would be there to see it on their faces.

SEVENTEEN

A FEW HOURS BEFORE DAWN SYLVAN WENT DOWN TO THE water. The fog was so thick he couldn't see much—just the hulls rising in the shipyard beyond, the scaffolding etched against the sky. Around him the docks were lit by a yellow pulse—a beacon from an island upriver.

He'd left Mrs. Izzo's at dusk. After a plate of ham and biscuits and a glass of honeyed milk, Odile had fallen asleep in the chair by the window, the baby in a basket beside her. For an hour she had stared at the little girl in wonder—brushing the fuzz of her hair, tracing the puckish tips of her ears. *I have a feeling,* she'd said, *that my sister would never have left her behind. This isn't her doing at all.*

She'd mentioned going to the police, but then thought better of it. An unwed mother, missing in the city; a baby abandoned in the slums—how many times had they heard that tale of woe before? How quickly would they act? She would go to the Jennysweeter herself, she decided—first thing in the morning, just as Lillian Edgar had said. As they finished their meal, she took out a piece of paper and smoothed it out across Mrs. Izzo's table—a list of theaters she'd copied from her mother's directory. She ran her finger down the names, but there was no Featherbone, nothing that even sounded similar. Her sister, she believed, had been familiar with a man who once worked there. But that could be anywhere in the city. And what—a hotel? A storefront? Saloon? She sighed and looked out the window, touching the bald spot behind her ear.

Sylvan sat quietly at the table, soaking his hands in a bucket of ice water, watching Mrs. Izzo change the bandage on Odile's knee. He couldn't help but feel a tick of sadness, or jealousy—that Odile would risk such a thing for her sister, that she loved her without question, that they shared something secret and their own—however reckless and troubled Isabelle was. He decided it for himself—he'd go that night, while Odile rested; he'd ask around and see what he could find.

He didn't wake her when he left, didn't even move to lift the edge of the afghan—there were biscuit crumbs, he saw, still on her fingers—he just whispered to Mrs. Izzo that he'd return in the morning, when his shift was over. She nodded—she was already back at her workbench, concertina spectacles perched on her nose, making intricate lace of a dead woman's hair.

He had made his way in the dying light, down to the taverns he used to haunt—those half-forgotten nights spent with Francesca, drinking until the stars sang and the pavement rippled—to the muddy cellar dives where he once hid like a frog, fingers gummed to the bar, knowing the ghost in the house awaited him. He asked a few of the old barkeeps—the wilier ones, the raconteurs, the top-hatted sachems with squeaky red faces—if they knew what the Featherbone was. And they liked these questions, the chance to prattle on their pulpit—they believed that the more they knew of the city, the more it belonged to them, native-born, not to the goat-hoofed immigrants. One fellow said he was sure the Bone was out by the shipyard, in back of the old whale skeleton, and not a place any right-blooded man would be seen.

Sylvan knew the kind of people who lurked around there at night, of course—grifters and dog-fighters; men on shore for the first night in months, out of their minds with sea-fever and drink. Whoever he was, this man Odile's sister had known, it was better if Sylvan saw to him first. He drank a beer, slept for a short spell in his own room on Ludlow Street, then made his way down to the water.

He moved through the slips where the taverns were loudest, between women in feathered dresses and packs of grizzled, hooting sailors, their faces streaked with coal dust and sweat. He heard the music and laughter from open saloons, but he kept to himself. Earlier he'd passed the stable where the night-soilers gathered before their shift. He had watched, from across the shadowed way, as the men had readied the slop-wagon, as No Bones stacked the buckets and Everjohn latched down the barrels. He'd listened to the beat of their shovels as they drifted away in the dark, the hymn they sang to strengthen their lungs. He'd turned the other way and kept walking. He couldn't bring himself to go back, not for another night of it: the smell of shit, the ghostly coating of lime-powder on his hands and his face, the way the other men turned their backs to him when they hosed out the wagon at shift's end. And then afterward: back to the cellar, to his carefully folded newspapers and rescued debris, a bottle of beer keeping cold in a hole in the floor, where the boards had given way to dirt. He couldn't.

Behind the shipyard he saw a shiver of light on the cobblestones—a perforated paper lantern, swinging from a post—and then, just beyond, an archway of bone. The whale skeleton, just as the old man had said. He remembered when the whale had washed ashore at the Battery a few years ago—they had set up a tent and charged people a quarter to see it, then sawed it up and boiled it down and sold off the blubber to the oil works. Now he walked under what remained: the ribs, curving up against the sky. The men who passed him in the dark, or who hung back between the bones, smoking cheroots, only dropped their eyes and looked away, their chins dug deep in their collars.

At the end of the path was a bare-shingled inn, sinking in a patch of sand. Young girls idled out on the terrace, leaning against the rail. He could see the glow of their wigs in the moonlight, as pale as clouds of mercury. They whistled huskily down as he slunk to the door. *Hello, sailor; hey, dandy, up here.* There was a blue star on the frame, he noticed, just as there'd been at the poppy box.

He jammed down his hat and buttoned his collar and stepped inside, through a sateen curtain, into a low-ceilinged room. Perfume and smoke, the liquor as black as ship's tar. Men sat at felt-lined tables, their faces turned from the light. He saw the glimmer of their watch chains, the wrinkle of their coats. Here and there a fat hand curled around a snifter—a clawed armrest—a young knee in a flounced skirt. In another room, someone played a lonely waltz on a harmonium.

Sylvan could feel the eyes dragging over him, picking through the oakum dust that lingered in the air, following him as he approached the bar, where a bald man mopped up a spill and ate a plate of pickled onions with a toothpick.

"I'm looking," Sylvan said in a low voice, "for a young man who worked here once."

The bartender stared at him, then speared another onion and dragged it, split, around the rim. "Upstairs," he said. "The Widows Walk. They'll take care of you."

EIGHTEEN

ODILE WOKE WHEN IT WAS STILL DARK OUT. SHE DIDN'T KNOW where she was at first—when she opened her eyes, she saw only a postcard from San Francisco, tacked to the headboard of the bed. White cliffs and palm trees. Women in lavender dresses, promenading by the sea. Then she smelled oyster brine in the air. For a moment she thought she was in a sea cave, festooned with kelp, but she realized it was only the braids that hung from the rafters, and she heard the hiss of the river beyond the walls. Quietly she rose and lifted the baby from her basket, whispered in the dark: *Tyger, Tyger, burning bright!* How many times had she recited the same thing for her sister in the middle of the night—when they were too nervous, too excited to sleep—when they lay awake with a candle lit and made shadow puppets on the wall?

Briefly she'd wondered if Belle, confused and alone, had tried to get rid of the baby—if she'd panicked and left her behind in a privy—if she believed that any fate, even death, was better than giving her up to someone else. But how could someone like Belle—always so strong-minded and loyal, a woman who'd tended to the children of the Frog and Toe, who'd taught them the same routines she and her sister once practiced in their own room at night—do something so desperate and cruel? She couldn't believe it. Belle was in trouble—she knew it by the tremble in her blood. Lines of that letter played around in her mind, like the haunting refrain of a song.

While Mrs. Izzo slept, she brewed herself a cup of coffee, bitter and black, and sat drinking it alone at the workbench. She took a swath of lace, the thickest and darkest, and made a veil for her hat. She would have to arrive at the apothecary shop as someone else: a girl in mourning, in trouble. Mrs. Bloodworth would know her face—it was her sister's face, although crooked to the side and slightly narrow. The mean little scrub-girl had seen her, too—a plucky naïf with a worn-out valise, chirruping at the yellow door. She began to think of a story: an immigrant girl, a chambermaid, lost in the city and needing help. Sitting there among the bobbins and needles, she felt as if she were back in the old theater, mending costumes before a show. She had stitched the golden flames to Belle's devil dress, the ruffles to Aldovar's gown, the sequins to Mr. Mackintosh's blindfold. She had a role, she reminded herself as she pinned the veil to her hat and laced the dagger in her boot. A performance of sorts. *Relax your face. Open your throat. Raise your chin like you have a secret that everyone wants to know.*

When Mrs. Izzo woke, she made Odile breakfast: a hunk of cheese, a cold egg, and a slice of ham. Odile thanked her, offered to pay something for the food and the bed, but Mrs. Izzo just shook her head. "I only want your word that you'll be back for the child. That Mr. Threadgill's thanked proper. That she's got a peaceful home to go to."

Odile unlatched her locket and set it down on the table, next to the cameos and brooches. "This is as good as my word, ma'am," she said. "It's yours."

It hurt her to leave the baby behind, even for a short while, but she was safe, at least—alive. There was some strange relief in that, wherever her sister had gone.

She drank the last of her coffee, looked out the window. She drew a crescent in the steam on the windowpane and peered through to the river-dumps beyond. *What immortal hand or eye could frame thy fearful symmetry?*

She remembered, when the tiger cubs were little, how she and Belle used to perch one on a stool in the ticket booth, then crouch red-faced below while a dithering patron opened her purse and asked for a pass and then screamed loud enough to shake the rafters. But there would be no more of that, she realized. No more of Mother and Belle's disquieting fights—Belle tearing at the curtains with her chalked-up hands, or bashing in a footlight with her heel—while Odile sat alone in the wings, plinking a mallet against her brace, trying to find a song of her own.

She'd never understood the poem before, not really—and she'd never said as much to Mother—but now it began to make some kind of sense. What god could dream up a creature so fierce? And what god could contain the thing he'd created, when she burned as bright as all the rages of heaven, and when she came to wield the very fire that had forged her?

A GOLDEN FOG HUNG LOW on the riverbank. As Odile walked down Cherry Street, she saw the black glitter of the water, the old row houses with their crooked shutters and maritime stars. In the air she could smell salt and fish, metallic water pooling between the cobbled bricks, a heel of rye left to harden and mold on the curbside. She passed buildings that seemed to have been lost: dwarfed in the shadows, on streets so narrow no traffic could pass.

Up on the Bowery the crowd grew dense. She looked at every passing face, hoping that one would be Belle's. But no one met her eye, and if they did they looked quickly away. *I'm a mourner,* she reminded herself. *Play the part.*

She reached the apothecary shop on Doyers Street, with its looming gold spectacles and dusty windowpanes. Above her the sky flamed red. The breeze lifted her hair, cooled her neck. A tired dray pulled a wagon down the lane—milk or ice or newspaper. She remembered drinking coffee on the beach with her sister, combing for shells under gray morning clouds, the boardwalk empty, the ocean like stone. For a moment she strained to hear the *ruff-ruff* of the stubborn surf along the shore, the nervous chitter of the trolley bell. But there was only the bump of wagon wheels along the ruts in the ground, the angry caw of squirrels on the roof.

She drew the veil over her face, stepped up to the green shop door and reached for the knob. She couldn't go home, she reminded herself. What had she left to return to without seeing this through?

She walked inside and a bell chimed above her, the most innocent of sounds. She glanced around at the rows of polished shelves, stocked with tonics and powders and pastes. Some of the labels had started to curl in the heat. She looked over to the counter, with its iron register and old scales, but the stool behind it was empty.

A few people idled beneath a fan that hung from the ceiling. She'd seen a fan like that once before, in the lobby of a seaside hotel. The blades whirred and squeaked. A young couple lingered drowsily in the breeze, studying tins of blemish cream. A sunburned man stood beside them, fanning himself with his hat and squinting at jars of soda powder. No one spoke. Odile looked back and forth, but they all seemed lost in a dull, overheated stupor.

She sidled up to the counter and waited, picking at the woodgrain. She studied the spidery knobs of ginger, the bottles of dandelion ale, the roots and herbs with confoundingly poetic labels: angelica, floating-heart, rabbit tobacco, meadow-rue.

A woman emerged from the back room. She wore a homespun

gray dress and a wilted-looking pinafore. "Help you?" she asked, drawing up to the counter.

She was young, Odile saw, not yet twenty, but already stooped—glum and wattled, the kind of woman whose gaze was both frank and bored, her tone unimpressed.

"Good morning," Odile stammered, the veil sticking to her lips. She puffed it away and cleared her throat. "I'm here for a cup of tea."

The woman didn't blink, didn't betray any emotion at all. "You have an ailment?" Her accent was Russian, educated—like the furriers' wives of Brighton Beach who played their violins in the tea garden on Sundays.

"It's a personal matter," Odile said.

The woman shook her head. "It's not possible today, I'm afraid." She plucked absently at her cuffs, which stood out from her plain and workmanlike dress: they were embroidered, pristine—a piece of distinction and pride.

Odile tried to picture Belle standing at this very counter, carrying her bag of poetry and swords, the baby growing bigger inside her. She studied the woman's face: her furrowed brow and downturned mouth, her hands busy sorting bills along the counter. She wondered if she might have been in a situation like Belle's, too, if she'd come here to give up her baby, to live in a strange room far from home, to spend her evenings in a parlor with nothing for company but an untuned piano.

"I've come very far," Odile said, feeling the burn behind her eyes as she drew up her tears. "Do you know what it is, to be homesick?"

And as she said it, she felt a tick in her throat. This was the longest she'd ever been away from home—a mere day—and already it felt as if the world had turned upside down, as if she were strapped to the Wheel but couldn't get off. She could walk away from this place right now, she knew—she could hail her way back to the docks, head home on the ferry, retreat to the lonely glow of the bungalow, forget everything she'd seen and leave Belle to tend to this alone. She'd never asked for Odile's help, anyway; she didn't even seem to want it. *You must believe, no matter what, that you are where you belong.* But what then? Before long all the players, everyone she knew, would scatter down the coast for the winter: to Atlantic City, the Florida fairgrounds, maybe even the grimy palaces of Cincinnati and Chicago. But what would she do? Where would she go? *Chin up!* her mother used to say as Odile stood blinking and dazed in the stage lights. *Cheat out to the crowd. There—show us your face. You have lightning bolts, for God's sake, and you're going to use them!*

"You have a seamstress in your family," Odile ventured. "Your mother, I suppose."

The woman looked up sharply.

"She made you these." Odile reached out and lifted the woman's hands, then rolled her wrists out so she could see the embroidery on the cuffs. From a distance it looked like a flowering bough—tendrils, buds—but up close she saw it was actually a line of music. She began humming it.

The woman, spooked, drew her hands away and pressed them to her sides.

"Prokofiev?" Odile asked. She remembered it from her lessons with the émigré professor, who had clapped his hands or thumped his cane as she plunked arrhythmically at the old piano by the hearth. Now she brought her hands down to the counter and played silently against the wood, her fingers running and skipping over each other, chasing up to the meadow-rue and down to the mint.

The woman grew pensive for a moment. She nodded along, then winced. "Your counting, ach!" she said. "You have to count. *Dah*-dah-dah, *dah*-dah."

Odile laughed. "My mother always said that, too."

The woman brushed and straightened her cuffs. She squinted at Odile, then hesitated. "Where are you from, did you say?"

"It doesn't matter, really. I can't go back."

The corner of the woman's mouth twitched. She reached over and pulled on a chain that hung near the register. Above them the ceiling fan sputtered to a stop. In the middle of the room the other shoppers scowled and shifted uncomfortably.

"Go on!" she called to them. "No buying, no staying!"

Slowly they skulked away. The door chimed as they dissolved into the white glare of the morning. When they were gone, the woman put her elbows on the counter and leaned forward.

"A woman's ailment, you mean."

"Yes." Odile found herself nodding. "Yes," she said. "That's exactly what it is."

She beckoned to Odile. "This way, then."

Odile followed her out the green shop door. The woman drew the sash and turned the lock, then looked back and forth down the street. She led Odile a few paces to the right, under a wayward thatch of ivy, through the yellow door—into the same low-lit foyer where Odile had ventured the day before, valise in hand: the same tiled floor and stacks of blankets, the quiet set of stairs.

"Stay here for a minute," the woman told her. "I will see, yeah?"

Odile only nodded, her heart pounding. *Be the part!* her mother had cried from the darkness of the theater, unseen among the empty seats. *Be it!*

The woman walked up the stairs and paused on the landing, where a young girl was on her hands and knees in the shadows, scrubbing the floor. "Mouse, see that she waits there, yeah?"

The brush paused for a moment, then continued, dunking and whishing. Odile stood there in the heat, straining to hear any conversation from the floors above. But there was just the sound of the young girl on the stairs—the clank of the bucket, the hiss of the brush, the creak of her elbows and knees as she worked her way down to the foyer. When she reached the bottom stair, she sat back on her heels and wiped the hair from her face. Odile recognized her—the scrub-girl, surly and bowlegged—the one who'd put the knock-out drops in her coffee.

Mouse.

In her pocket the envelope crinkled. That word—a name— written in her sister's hand.

There were footsteps on the stairs again, and the woman appeared. She nodded to Odile, her voice thick and authoritative. "Mrs. Bloodworth is ready for you."

NINETEEN

SYLVAN CLIMBED THE NARROW STAIRS, FEELING HIS WAY IN the dark. He heard whispers above, the scurry of little feet, the rasp of a wandering, half-remembered song. The walls were hung with old tapestries, which fluttered and swayed in the draft. Everything smelled like the damp of a ship, wet fur and raw potato.

He reached the top, the Widows' lair—nothing more than a small parlor, lit by a low kerosene lamp. He paused, letting his eyes adjust to the watery light, picking out shadowed figures along the floor. They lay scattered about, on piles of pillows and brown tasseled sheets. Some of them were curled up together on a blanket, sucking their thumbs, bleary as a litter of mice. They were all young, no older than fourteen or fifteen, with trembling lips and hooded eyes. They wore circles of blush on their cheeks, flounced skirts and fallen bouffants. But beneath their painted faces, their torsos—lean and green with bruises—were bare.

They weren't girls at all. They were boys, and they looked at him, numb.

For a moment he didn't know what to do—he wasn't sure what he was supposed to be looking for. All along he had pictured a man like he'd seen at the fights—ox-chested, gourd-nosed; a bellower, a brute. But these were just children, hairless and small, who turned their eyes away as he stepped onto the rug. Then from down the hall came the madam, knock-kneed in her petticoats, tutting a tune, tapping her nails along the papered wall. She studied Sylvan for a moment from behind her pince-nez, then smiled.

"What's your liking?" she asked, laying a hand on his arm.

The heat in the room was stifling, even with the open terrace doors. The stink of it—the spilled liquor; the moist pillows; the faint, yellowy flesh smell of sickness—his eyes began to water, and he lowered his voice. "I'm here about a man who once worked here?"

She drew a circle in the armband on his sleeve. "Of course," she said with a sigh, clucking her tongue. "Wasn't he the favorite, though?" She muttered something, then led him down the hall, back the way she'd come—to a room with only one small window, cut into the roof above. A wrinkle of moonlight lay on the floor like a dropped glove.

Sylvan took a step in, squinted to see. He smelled a touch of honeysuckle, sage, then spied a basket of nosegays on a table. A row of blond heads hovered in the dark, silent and bodyless. Wigs, setting on their wicker bulbs. Behind the table was a flicker of movement. A young man, seventeen or eighteen, emerged. He was holding a brush, looking up at the madam as she rapped on the jamb.

"William!" she barked. "Gent's here about the Rembrandt—wasn't you close to him?"

He nodded. His head was clean-shaven—lice, Sylvan guessed—showing off his pronounced ears and round, oversized spectacles, which pinched his nostrils nearly shut. He was dressed in a bengaline waistcoat and checkered pants—all handsomely mended, even though it seemed this man (sallow and soft-chinned, as mealy as an apple) had never been out of the room in his life.

"What's it you want?" William asked as the madam stalked

away and yelled something down to the onion-eating man at the bar.

"I'm looking for a fellow," Sylvan said. "I don't know him, but he worked here once. Friendly with a woman up on Doyers Street."

"Yes, yes, the Rembrandt." He seemed very tired. He pushed his fingers under his glasses and rubbed at the pouches beneath his eyes.

"You know who I mean?"

He nodded, sniffing his spectacles back up his nose, and picked at the bristles of the brush. "Such a shame."

"An acquaintance of Isabelle Church?"

"She ain't anyone I met, but he went and got himself a different life, so it's possible."

"Blond hair?" Sylvan said. "Slender? An acrobat of sorts?"

William smiled with one side of his mouth and began brushing out the wigs. "Don't they all look that way to you?"

Something turned in Sylvan's stomach. The boys, he realized, did have a certain air about them—fish-pale, hazy-eyed—but it might have just been the glow of their spun hair: those soft moons floating in the black cloud of the parlor. In here the wigs, drooping and tangled on their brittle, brown stands, looked different somehow—like the dug-up heads of aristocrats.

William took a pair of scissors from his coat and began to trim the frizzled curls. For a moment the only sound in the room was the whine and gnash of the blades, the squeak of his feet as he circled the bulbs.

Sylvan pressed on. "But he knew someone on Doyers Street?"

"Well, I don't say he *knew*. He was going to pay a visit there— the apothecary, as it were. He was in a predicament, as you can imagine. He wouldn't come around *here* no more—no, no, not with his gold charley!" The scissors flashed as he threw up his hands. "But lo, lo: here he washes up last spring—hides down by whale, catches me off to church. Says, *Billie, I'm in a spot.* Needs to find a baby! And who does he run to in the end, eh? But I'll do right for a good-hearted friend; I always do." He laughed, grim. "What a sap. I made him one of these, for his wedding day." He held up a nosegay. "Here, take it."

Sylvan smelled it and tucked it into his coat, remembering what Lillian Edgar had said about Mrs. Bloodworth. He pictured a woman on the river at night, throwing her silver net into the water, bringing up babies like fish. *Sold to a good family, you can only pray.* "And his wife, she wasn't very inclined to—or maybe she wouldn't—?"

"Wife!" William smiled at him piteously. "Oh, he ain't got no wife." He lifted a wig and set it down on his own head, grinning with all of his pebble-gray teeth. "Don't you see?"

Sylvan's blood began to thrum. *She don't look right*, the butcher's boy had said. *No—she don't seem right.*

"We were little ones together," William said. "Look—he fixed me here when I was hurt." He brushed back a curl, pointed to a burn on his cheek.

"Where can I find them?" Sylvan asked. "Where do they live?"

"Orchard and Broome, I hear it. They were all saying his charley got him a nice little house, with a nice little hearth, and hot cocoa and china plates and oranges whenever he wants. A real house!" His eyes grew damp. He brought up the brush and patted forlornly at his wig. "But I never thought that fellow so handsome myself."

"And who should I ask for? What name does he go by now?"

William looked up at him, bewildered. "What for? He won't be there."

"Why's that?"

"Don't you know?"

Sylvan shook his head.

"I only just heard it last night myself—so sudden and all."

"What?"

"Why, I thought that's why you was here." He pointed to the black band around Sylvan's arm. "The little Rembrandt—he's dead."

TWENTY

ODILE CLIMBED THE FLIGHTS OF STAIRS, HER HAND STICKY on the banister, her feet scuffing the boards. On the last landing the shopgirl opened the door, then scuttled back into the darkness.

Odile stood alone in an upswell of wind, staring at the scraps of sea fog that clung to the bridges, the ships at port, the glistening churn of horses on the riverbank, pulling an overturned scow to shore. Ahead of her the hothouse reflected the chimneys and the clouds, her own distorted face. Through the glass she saw a movement, pale and shapeless, like a fish in a greening bowl.

Mrs. Bloodworth.

She crossed over to the door, turned the latch and stepped inside. Her dress melted instantly to her skin; the veil puckered against her face. She smelled the sweet rot of flowers, a wet flintiness, and then something bitter and earthy, like vegetable root. She moved through the vapor, between hanging fronds, past tables overrun with plants. She saw baskets of snipped clover and feverfew, bulbs arranged like bonbons in a sweetshop window. Beds of orange poppies bloomed on the shelf—her mother had grown those in the garden once, a long time ago.

At the end of the hothouse stood a woman. She wore a cream-colored skirt and a plain shirtwaist, loosely buttoned, with her sleeves rolled to her elbows. Her head was lowered over a workbench, obscured by a drowsy bough of clematis, but Odile could still see her hands at work, slicing up a meaty green stalk with a razor. Her thumb moved in swift easy flicks, halving the stems and letting the liquid inside bleed into a jar.

"Mrs. Bloodworth?"

The woman looked up. She was tall and middle-aged, with the kind of hawkish face that stagehands loved to light—blue-green eyes that bulged above lean, sculpted cheeks. Her hair was gray at the temples and peak, her bare arms all freckles and sinew. Odile paused, unsure how to introduce herself, but the woman only wiped a hand on her apron and nodded.

"There's cold tea over there," she said. Her voice was burred and honeyed. She gestured with the razor. "On the table. Please."

Odile looked over and saw a glass pitcher, sweating in a slant of light, filled with melting chunks of ice and lemon halves. She remembered what Pigeon had said about the coffee. "Thank you, ma'am," she said, "but I'm well enough without."

"Then please—sit down."

Odile lowered herself onto a nearby stool, watching as Mrs. Bloodworth picked up a pair of shears and wiped them down with a rag. "What exactly is your situation?"

Odile cleared her throat. What would Belle have said? "I've left home."

The woman nodded and reached above her head, snipping a stem from the clematis. "Your family knows of your trouble?"

"No, ma'am."

"You're alone?"

"Very."

"Have you anywhere to go?"

Odile shook her head. "That's why I've come to you."

Mrs. Bloodworth plucked a leaf from the stem and chewed it for a moment, then spit a green wad of pulp into her hand. "Hmm." She lifted the shears again. *Snip, snip.* The branches came down in a basket. Odile stared at the blades, at the way they chirruped and bit, the way Mrs. Bloodworth dragged them across the front of her apron, wiping away the juice.

"And how did you come to find me?" she asked.

"Another girl"—Odile licked her lips—"she spoke of you."

Mrs. Bloodworth laid the shears back on the table. She smiled at Odile, not unkindly. "You may take your hat off, if you wish. It gets a bit humid in here, doesn't it?"

"I'd prefer not to."

She inclined her head. "If you're worried you might be spied on, that someone should know you're here, let me say plainly that you're very safe."

Odile looked up. "Am I?"

"You have my word," Mrs. Bloodworth said. "Where are your people from?"

"Gravesend, ma'am."

"Quite a ways. I mean your heritage."

Odile hesitated. She couldn't say the Scotch-Irish Willingbirds of Punxsutawney, or her great-grandmother's clan of Pennsylvania Dutch: Belle might well have said the same thing. She thought of her father, the sign-painter from Glastonbury. "Saxon, I believe." She nodded at the basket of clematis. "What's that for?"

"Oh—to brew." Mrs. Bloodworth touched one of the blossoms. "A little bark tea—good for cramping. And sadness."

Odile shifted in the heat, breathing deeply and evenly, using the muscles of her diaphragm, the way her mother had taught her. There were sheets of paper pinned to the corkboard above the table—she squinted to read them through the veil. It looked like the ingredients for some kind of witch's brew: *chewing's fescue, dame's rocket, bearded sprangletop, night-flowering catchfly.* She tried to imagine why Belle would have gone to such lengths—to come all the way to Manhattan, to a dangerous woman in the middle of the slums. Surely there was someone reputable and nurturing in Brooklyn? Odile would have helped her, without question—she would have kept her secret. If only Belle had asked.

"This is all very confidential, you understand?" Mrs. Bloodworth sat down on a castered stool and rolled closer to Odile. "People's reputations are at stake."

Odile swallowed. "Whose?"

"Well, for one—yours."

She clipped a flower from the clematis and pinned it to Odile's dress. It was big and scruffy and white, blown open in the sun. "The smell of this, I find, is so soothing. Especially when you're in distress."

Odile dipped her nose and breathed in the perfume. This had been her sister's world, from the sooty crook of Doyers Street to the children underground to an apothecary's botany. What was it she was missing? Belle, unwed and alone, had come here—to a Jenny-sweeter hidden in a hothouse fog. All without a word, even a hint, to Odile. But something had gone wrong—and here was this blithe, heron-necked woman, filling the bowl of her pipe, unhurried, as if everything else in the world were of no consequence. But Belle had sensed something—she'd written Odile, telling her in no uncertain terms to stay home. She'd been trying to protect her. From shame and scandal, from the dangers of the city—any number of things. From her own addled mind: melancholy, fantastical. From people out to do her harm.

Mrs. Bloodworth lit her pipe, then leaned back and examined Odile thoughtfully through the smoke. "No one came with you?" she asked, picking a bit of tobacco from her tongue. "No one followed you here?"

"No, ma'am."

"What's your name?"

"Threadgill."

"How old are you, Miss Threadgill?"

"Seventeen last October."

"And the father—does he know?"

"My father?"

Mrs. Bloodworth smiled patiently. "No, the child's."

Child. She wondered if Belle had actually told the father, if that was why she'd left so abruptly. It pained her to think there was a man that she herself might have passed every day on the street—an ordinary, no-face man, or someone she might even know well—there, selling waffles on the boardwalk, clapping wooden tongs in the air; or perhaps counting out her shabby dollars at the bank. Someone who had smiled and said hello, knowing exactly who she was and what she'd lost, but who had kept her willingly a fool. The father of that beautiful baby.

She shook her head. "He does not, ma'am."

"What are your relations with him now?"

Odile paused, unsure of how to answer.

"Has he tried to call on you?" Mrs. Bloodworth prompted. "Write to you? Does he know where you are now?"

"No, we've not spoken since the . . ." She gestured weakly in the air. She knew about sex, of course—she had from a young age. Mother never talked about it in any certain terms, although she'd always spoken plainly of their bodies. She'd given them menstrual belts and hot water bottles when their monthlies began, explained that they shouldn't take their clothes off in front of a man, not even in a dressing room. It stirred men's blood in *an animal way* and made their organs swell. (Odile had simply assumed she was talking about the heart.) The rest she'd heard about from Georgette and the other girls in the show—it made her squeamish at first, but then she began to see it everywhere, in every madcap, hootenanny revue. All those comics with their pull-whistles and cranks; all the dancing girls with powdered legs. But sex wasn't something she'd given much thought to in her own life—why would she? She'd never expected she'd get married or fall in love. She'd never considered a life beyond the one she had always lived: a house full of women, at work on the stage.

"Tell me what he looks like," Mrs. Bloodworth continued. "Or do you know?"

Odile bristled. "I'm not a whore, if that's what you mean."

Mrs. Bloodworth smiled. "You don't look it. You look cared for. You look like a loved girl."

"It was only once," she sputtered, embarrassed at her own imaginary coupling.

"Just a sketch," the woman said again, patiently. "His people, his origin, his temperament."

Odile tried to think of something credible and bland—a moment of hesitation that Mrs. Bloodworth mistook for bashfulness, or even shame. "Fair?" she suggested. "Dark? Stout, thin? A gentleman? A drunkard? Intelligent, crude, fluent in music? Anything you can offer will help me."

"Oh," she stammered. "He was just a boy, like any other. Dark hair. A beard."

"I know it's difficult to talk about."

Yes, it is, Odile thought. *But not in the way that you think.* "I'm not a bad person," she felt compelled to say.

"Of course not." Mrs. Bloodworth shook her head. "There are no bad women here. You understand that, don't you?"

"I suppose so."

"And how long ago was the event?" She took a draw on her pipe. "With this dark-haired boy like any other."

"A few months?"

"And how do you know that you're with child?"

"Because I know myself, I suppose."

She blew a line of smoke in the air. "You've missed your monthlies?"

Odile nodded: a brief, demure drop of the chin.

"Have you been examined by a doctor, a midwife, a friend—anyone at all?"

"No one. I simply walked out the door and left." She met Mrs. Bloodworth's gaze and felt something harden in her chest. Little Friendship Willingbird, hitchhiking through the hills of Pennsylvania in her dead brother's suit. Isabelle Church, sailing off to the city in a tumbledown boat, carrying her bag of swords. "Only a letter under the inkwell, to tell them not to come after me. I'd write."

Mrs. Bloodworth paused to refill her pipe. "Any cramping?" she asked, tamping down the tobacco with the handle of her shears. "Aches, nausea, spots of blood? Anything giving you trouble?"

Odile had no idea how to answer. What did pregnant women feel like? Sick, she figured. Swollen. Fatigued. What was it she used to say when she feigned sickness as a child? "Just a little fuzzy-feeling, I suppose."

"Have you had any bouts of melancholy or distress? Hallucinations? Macabre thoughts?"

Odile thought of the fanciful lines from her sister's letter: describing their mother as a mermaid. The tigers, undersea. Even Pigeon had talked of such magical beasts—mighty and finned, battling a suckered colossus. "Please," she said. Her throat grew watery and raw; her eyes began to burn. "I only want . . ."

"You want to move on with your life. I understand," Mrs. Bloodworth replied. "You want to return to the world unashamed, without consequence or disgrace. You want to wake from this dream and be able to resume your life. Yes?" She plucked a handkerchief from her apron and handed it Odile. "I understand."

Odile took it and drew it up under her veil. It smelled sweet and homey, like rosewater.

"You will be provided for while you're here," Mrs. Bloodworth went on. "But I must be strict on this point. You will not be allowed to leave the house during your confinement, or associate with any-one who might come to the door. I don't mean to be cruel, you see, only safe. If you must contact anyone, if only to maintain decorum or avoid suspicion, you mustn't relay one word about what happens under this roof. That's vital. We can never be too certain. Do you understand what I mean?"

"Yes." *Like a captive,* Odile thought. All those secrets, just as Miss Edgar had said. She wadded the handkerchief up in her hand, stared at the poppies on the shelf. Mrs. Bloodworth, supply-ing her flowers to the underground dens; mixing her nostrums and salves for unwed mothers, then selling off their babies to those who couldn't carry them, or who needed to cover up secrets of their own. She thought about the scrub-girl downstairs—sullen, fuzzy-lipped, eye-rolling Mouse. She must have known Belle, despite what she'd claimed yesterday. Odile smoothed her skirt and felt the envelope crackle in her pocket.

Mrs. Bloodworth stood up, the stool squeaking beneath her. "I'll have to examine you, all right?"

Odile looked up at her, startled. "I beg your pardon?"

"A normal procedure," the woman continued. "Just to see how you're faring. See when your term ends, what we can expect."

"Now?"

"It will be easy, I promise. Just a touch. Stand up."

"What about downstairs? You have a room somewhere, yes? Isn't there a proper way . . . some paper I should be . . . ?"

"Yes, just after this, I promise. No one can see you in here—you have my word." She drew closer, so close that Odile could smell her breath—leafy, a trace of tobacco and tea—through the veil.

"You wear a corset?" Mrs. Bloodworth asked.

"Just—just my knickers and a cami."

"Good, that's as it should be."

Odile swallowed hard, her fingers numb. There was nowhere to go in that little glass room; she was already backed against the table, tickled by vines, keeping company with old phosphate jars of snippers and razors and shears. Slowly she stood. She shook out her blouse and unbuttoned her skirt until the pleats of her knickers showed. She looked away as Mrs. Bloodworth's fingers, warm and tough, massaged her stomach and pushed gently around her navel. The veil, the fog, the tremulous threat of tears—she stood as still as possible, blinking in the swelter, waiting for it to be over. Perhaps Mrs. Bloodworth wouldn't be able to tell anything (she'd eaten so many sweets lately, after all—there were always bags of caramels and taffy backstage); perhaps she'd invite her down to the office to talk things over further—any place where she could find a trace of her sister, why she'd gone.

After a moment Mrs. Bloodworth stood back. "Miss Threadgill, I have something to tell you."

"Wh—what's that?"

"I don't believe you're pregnant at all."

Odile tried to look surprised, but she just felt breathless and sick. "No, no, that can't be—"

Mrs. Bloodworth broke into a smile and touched her shoulder. "Aren't you relieved? It's good news, right?"

Odile dropped her head, her ears hot. She pressed the veil to her face and began to cry.

"It's called a phantom womb," Mrs. Bloodworth was saying. "It might be your nerves."

Phantom womb.

"Have you been under particular stress lately? Perhaps something has shifted in your life? There's someone you've lost?"

The tears fell over on her cheeks, hot and stinging, thin as blood. She sat down on the stool and turned away.

"It's clearly a great burden you've been carrying, a great stress. Might I suggest a tonic for your nerves? We carry some in the shop if you'd like to stop on your way out."

Odile nodded at the glass wall. She felt the woman's hand rub her back.

"You are lucky that you came to me, that you didn't do anything rash."

The veil clung to Odile's face. She tasted the sour snot running from her nose; tears ached between her eyes. Mrs. Bloodworth's hands leafed gently through her hair. And then Odile felt it—the tip of the woman's finger, tracing the crescent behind her ear.

TWENTY-ONE

S OON ALPHIE NOTICED MEN WERE TRAILING THEM—MEN IN uniform, on horseback. She looked over her shoulder as discreetly as she could—they were following them down the congested lane, maybe forty yards back. A paddy wagon rounded the bend, and the other carts parted to make way. Orchard looked over at her, worried—by now the asylum would have alerted someone on the shore—and there she was in a blue flannel dress, riding a horse stolen from a saloon near the landing. And Alphie: wearing the soap-boy's clothes, her tattoo bared for all to see.

Alphie tried to spur her horse faster, turning the corner to lose them, but the swarm of coaches and pushcarts only grew thicker. The horses whinnied and balked. She looked over her shoulder, saw the shimmer of black through the heat. They wouldn't take her back to the asylum, of course. She'd be sent someplace even worse, the most brutal of men's workcamps. A tattoo was nothing—she'd heard male prisoners were branded on the face with hot pokers. A fairy there would be killed. And what she'd done—what she'd conspired to do: passing herself off as a married woman, buying a baby from a Jennysweeter's crib—was far graver than selling her body or drinking in a dress at the wrong bar. She would be put away forever.

She just had to get to Anthony. They could get on a train and take off, past Peekskill and Poughkeepsie, all the way to Montreal. She glanced back and saw the police horses weaving through the marketplace. The officers were faceless in the shadows of their caps; their nightsticks swung from their belts. She heard one of them whistle, jarring and shrill.

Orchard veered sharply to the right, guiding her horse between the fruit stands. Alphie jumped down from the saddle and started running, cutting through the living sea of the marketplace, squelching through horse shit, knocking past women with their baskets of laundry. She hadn't run like this in years—trousers flapping around her ankles, hard shoe-heels pulling open the skin on her feet, the bowler threatening to blow back from her head. A tough, she realized—that's what she looked like. The kind of boys she'd once been frightened of and fascinated by, knowing she didn't belong.

She'd paid Mrs. Bloodworth the fee weeks ago, in the back room of the apothecary shop. One hundred dollars—sweaty and rumpled, sewn into the lining of her coat. She'd laid the bills across the desk, then watched as the woman licked her thumb and counted them twice. For months Alphie and Anthony had skimped, saved, done what they could. Anthony sold off his good cuff links, the ones his stepfather used to wear to church. He even cut back on his mother's allowance—he told her that money had been scarce since the consumption swept through. They'd taken the bodies away in those wagons; there hadn't even been time for funerals. The Signora had been furious, indignant. She made a show of buying hard stale bread even though there was still enough money for olive loaves and onion rolls. Alphie did her best to stay out of her way, to find excuses to rest, unobserved, as her confinement drew nearer.

For a while at night—when Anthony stole down to the dens alone, when the Signora fell asleep with a knife beneath her pillow, waiting for the wolves—Alphie walked over the bridge to turn a couple of tricks. She felt guilty—she was married now, and this life was supposed to be behind her—but what else could she do? She couldn't make that kind of money with her paint-kit and lemon drops. She couldn't disappear for nights on end in the state she was in, waiting down by the waterfront for brawls to begin. This was quick, at least; nameless. It wasn't a betrayal, she believed; it was only a duty. It was for their life together, a life they'd worked so hard to preserve. She had to make some sacrifices, didn't she? Didn't everybody? So she went over the river where no one would know her, to the Brooklyn ports, to the thick-grown hedges by the shore, where men met faceless in the dark. She wore her old dress, too small for her now, and kept her eyes closed as she held it bunched around her waist, waiting for the act to be done. *It's a good thing,* she told herself as the sweat of a strange man tickled the back of her neck. This would be the last of it, she swore, and then things would be normal. But one night Anthony took the money she'd earned and spent it down in the dens—she felt sick and furious, betrayed. *Do you know what I did for that?* she cried the next morning. He just shrugged, gulped down some milk, and regarded her with cold, glassy eyes: *It's not like you minded it.* She broke down and cried—*I did it for both of us,* she sobbed, *for the baby. Please believe me. I'm sorry, I'm sorry.*

Anthony was supposed to take his mother away that day, on the four o'clock train to Poughkeepsie. They'd planned a visit to some cousins on his stepfather's side—people the Signora was wary of, but since they had a little money and were generous with family, she agreed to go. He and Alphie had talked about it, gone over it night after night as they readied for bed. He and the Signora would visit the family without her—she was confined, of course, and couldn't travel—and they'd return early in the week. Alphie expected she'd have a few days at least. She'd given Mrs. Bloodworth the directions, the list of things to be mindful of. *Avoid the main house—too visible from the street. Come through the back gate, to the carriage house door where he keeps his shop. I will be there alone. If someone should happen to stop you for any reason, just say you've been sent to fetch the undertaker. No one will think twice.* The baby would be delivered after ten, while the neighbors were sleeping off their days of hot and lonely work, while the toughs gambled and fought in corner taverns until they were black-eyed and hoarse.

Don't worry, Mrs. Bloodworth promised her. *Our girl is discreet—and fast.*

But the Signora hadn't boarded the four o'clock train to Poughkeepsie. She'd been home all along. Now, as Alphie pushed through the sweaty crowds on the street, as she looked over her shoulder at the glimmer of the police wagon—stalled for a moment by an overturned cart—she began to panic. What about Anthony? Had he gone to Poughkeepsie as planned? Had he even made it to the station? Where the devil had her husband been that night? And why hadn't he told her that the plan had changed—that something was wrong— that the Signora was home?

She tried to remember exactly how they'd said good-bye—she'd been nervous all day, distracted, packing Anthony's clothes while he played his accordion in the office below. After lunch he'd walked his suitcase through the yard to the main house, then returned to their rooms for a glass of cordial and a cigar. He'd patted her stomach absently as he smoked, the ash rolling down her dress. He told her he'd left money in the razor tin—it was hidden in the bottom drawer of her dressing table, behind the puffs and brushes. And she believed him. She tried to lie down and rest—there was a long night ahead, and her whole body hummed. She drifted in and out of sleep, her stomach churning against the pillow. She felt his hand ruffle softly through her hair, heard him set down his glass on the tray—then the click of the door, his light tread down the steps.

The baby, she remembered now. The baby had cried that night, hungry and wet, while she and Orchard Broome turned down the bedsheets and emptied the jar of blood. It wailed even louder—an animal shriek—as Alphie lay half-conscious among the teeth, a sharp pain in her groin, an echo in her ears. She struggled to open her eyes. She saw the Signora bend over the basket and lift the baby in her arms. She tried to say something, to lift her head, but the Signora just cradled the baby and turned away, shushing. Alphie felt her body tremble, her face go numb. Her eyes were still open but everything was dark. All she could hear was the creak of a chair and the Signora's voice—a lullaby, it seemed—quieter and quieter, a sound like water, singing like the sea.

TWENTY-TWO

ALL MRS. BLOODWORTH SAID WAS: "ODILE."

Odile stood up, stumbled back. "How do you know my name?"

Mrs. Bloodworth reached for her again, but Odile turned and ran, knocking over the pots and tool jars on the table, ripping through the fronds, slamming the hothouse door with such force she thought the glass would shatter. She rushed across the roof, back inside, locking the rickety door behind her—a latch and a chain. She was shaking and faint, but still she hurried, half-slipping, down the stairs.

On the bottom floor she heard noises coming from the kitchen. The clank of pans on a griddle, water glugging hollowly in a cup. She moved slowly down the hall, drawing the veil from her face, her nose filled with the smells of orange spice and boiled milk. She checked the dagger at her ankle, then peered around the doorway. The scrub-girl, Mouse, stood at the counter, peeling raw onions with her fingers, scowling and sniffling. There was no knife in her boot, Odile saw—it was out on the chopping block, a cheap toy thing made of wood. A whirligig lay beside it, at rest in a puddle of onion juice. As Mouse turned to drop the skins in the bin, Odile grabbed her.

"You know who I am!" she said, drawing the girl close and twisting her arm. "And so does Mrs. Bloodworth, so don't try and fool me."

Mouse grunted and pushed back, her nostrils flaring. "What did you tell her?"

"Where's my sister?"

"She—she can't know! I'll be in trouble!"

"Know about what? What did you do?"

Mouse wriggled and kicked, tried to pull away. Odile reached out and dragged her hand through the puddle of onion juice, then slicked the girl's face, down from her brows to her downy lip, smearing it into her eyes.

"What happened to my sister!"

Mouse hollered and threw back her head. "I was scared you knew!" She blinked frantically, eyes popping and red. "I thought that's why you was here!"

"Knew what?" Odile grabbed both of her wrists and gave her a shake. "Why did you put that bunko in my coffee? What happened?"

Tears chased down Mouse's cheeks. She pushed her face into her sleeve and moaned. "It was my fault."

"What was?" Odile squeezed her wrists, brought her closer. "What was your fault?"

Mouse rolled her head back and forth, her dark hair shaking loose, the water running faster from her mouth and her nose. "It was my job, you see—it's *always* my job. I'm the Hood."

"What do you mean?"

"I was supposed to take the baby that night." She sniffed. "I didn't think anything bad would happen. How could it? Everything was planned. It's always planned!"

"My sister's baby? Take her where?"

"To—to the new mother."

Odile thought of the privy behind the butcher shop; Belle's letter written in the night, despondent. "Something went wrong, do you understand? Tell me what you've done, and hurry."

"Mrs. B. can't know—she'll murder me!"

"Tell me *now* or I'll murder you myself."

"You're as mean as she is," Mouse growled, but went on. "Belle made me a deal—if I let her go in my place, she would find something out for me."

"All right, she took the baby to the mother herself. Then what happened?"

"I wish *I* knew. I wish she hadn't muddled the whole thing! I've been on pins! I didn't think anything bad would happen. I just wanted to know!"

"Know what? What was she going to find out for you?"

"The—the names of my parents."

"Your parents?" Odile let her go, stood back.

Mouse rubbed sulkily at her wrists, dragged the corner of her apron over her eyes, blew her nose. "Don't you understand?" she whispered. "I was one of those babies—the babies given up."

Odile looked at her standing there, hissing back tears, pulling and knotting the apron in her hand.

"She said she would look in Mrs. Bloodworth's ledger for me," Mouse went on, "the one with all the names, but she never did. She just *left*. She took the baby, and she never came home! I didn't know how to explain it to Mrs. B. when she was still gone in the morning. So I lied—I told her I'd done it and everything had gone fine. But that was two days ago now, and Belle still isn't home, and Mrs. B. is worried sick. She thinks maybe Belle just got sad and left us with no word, but before long she'll know something's wrong. And she'll know it's my fault. You can't tell her!"

"The ledger"—Odile's skin started to prickle—"where is it?"

Mouse stared at her now, eyes clearing. She licked at her teeth. "I'll show you," she said slowly, "but only if you promise you'll look in it for me."

"And it has all the names in it, everyone who ever came through here?"

She nodded. "But you *can't* tell Mrs. B."

"I won't if you won't. So show it to me—now."

Mouse led her through a pantry, past a tub-sink and a drying-horse and a rack of black cloaks. They moved down the hall, over a floor with a dingy runner. Odile peered into each room as they passed. In one she saw a small bed, neatly made, and magazine drawings pasted to the walls—cherubs and roses, holiday seascapes, Gibson girls in candy-pink dresses. A table was littered with handkerchiefs, combs, bobbins, and yarn. There was a sewing machine, an older model, with a baby's gown abandoned beneath the needle.

"That's where she stayed," Mouse said. "It's the best room. I always wanted it. But—" she frowned, then lowered her voice. "What if the parents come here and say she never made it? What if she took the baby herself and ran away? Mrs. Bloodworth will know I'm a liar. And then what—she'll send me down to the Frog and Toe, and I can't live there, I would *perish*."

She took a ring of keys from her pocket, shook one loose, then hesitated. "You'll really find it for me?"

"Of course," Odile said. "But you have to show me first."

At the end of the hall Mouse unlocked the door to Mrs. Bloodworth's office. Inside she fumbled with a candle—Odile heard the drag and hiss of a match. Then the wick caught, and the room seemed to open and glow. She saw a simple desk and wingback chair, bookshelves lined with old atlases and medical encyclopedias and what looked like a dusty flint of bone in a jar. Behind the desk stood a Chinese screen, inlaid with golden tigers.

Mouse jimmied open a drawer and pulled out a book—heavy and clothbound, frayed from years of thumbing. Odile lifted the cover. The whole thing fell open in the middle, where the spine had cracked. She leafed through, studying the snarl of penmanship in the candlelight, the columns of blotted burgundy ink. She couldn't decipher how it was organized—everything was annotated, abbreviated, cross-referenced—and the handwriting was so small it was almost impossible to read. She turned through the pages, hurriedly and damp-fingered, looking for her sister's name.

"Why would you make Belle do this for you?" she asked Mouse, who hovered by her side, leaning over the book and breathing loudly through her mouth. Odile's eyes began to water at the smell of the onion. "Why couldn't you just look for the names yourself, if you already knew it was here?"

"Oh." The girl whispered, then sniffed. "I can't read."

There was a knock and a bang from a floor above—Mrs. Bloodworth's voice, calling for Mouse. The sound of rattling, pounding; a loud thump.

"Hurry!" Mouse said.

Odile turned the pages, back and forth, looking for something, anything at all—a word, a name.

Then she saw it.

CHURCH.

She pressed her finger down and ran it, trembling, across the page. But it wasn't Belle's name that followed.

CHURCH, Friendship W.

She stared at the words, faded and blurred beneath the white of her fingertip. How could their mother have been there? She'd never given up a baby. Had she?

She scanned back and looked at the date: *September 30, 1875.* Almost twenty years ago.

ACQUIRED THEREIN:

CHILD 14
Sex: *Boy/androgyne*
Spec: *Brown eyes, hair; abnormal sex organs*

CHILD 21
Sex: *Girl*
Spec: *Brown eyes, hair; multiple appendages*

PAID

She put her hand to her throat. Aldovar and Georgette. Her mother had purchased them here, from Mrs. Bloodworth. Perhaps Belle had known about it.

Above she heard the door break open, footsteps fast on the stairs, Mrs. Bloodworth's voice, calling out.

"Am I there?" Mouse leaned over. "Hurry, tell me! Is it that one?"

Odile rummaged in her pocket for the envelope, then held it out to the girl. She could see it now: the stout frame and storky legs, the puckered mouth, the wobbly chin. "Your mother's name is Miss Lillian Edgar. She's a very kind woman and she plays at the Garden Theater in Greenwich Village."

Mouse reached for it, but Odile drew it back. "First tell me. Where was Belle taking the baby?"

Mouse looked quickly over her shoulder, then lowered her voice. "To the undertaker's wife," she said. "On Orchard and Broome."

TWENTY-THREE

SYLVAN STARED AT THE HOUSE ON BROOME STREET. IT WAS one of the few that still stood between the tenements, two stories of brick with a poorly shingled roof. The black curtains were drawn against the sun, and a wreath of flowers hung on the door, already limp in the noonday heat. The sight of it made him shiver. Even on this steamy summer day, no one was leaning from an open window or gathering on the stoop. The whole place was quiet, as if it were holding its breath.

A carriage waited at the curbside. It was polished so black he saw his own reflection in it, glowing like an apparition. It wasn't like the morgue wagons from last summer, with shrouded bodies piled on top of each other. He recognized the wedded stinks of flesh and medicine, the black gleam of the chassis in the fractured light. A funeral carriage.

Beside him another man, a neighbor carrying a bucket of eggshells and coffee grounds, paused on his way to the ash-barrels. He lingered next to Sylvan, sucking on a messily rolled cigarette, then barked at one of his children, who was playing around the wheels of the carriage. *"Smettila, ragazzo! Subito!"*

The boy had found something on the ground—an artichoke, thorny and stiff. He was so slight and bony, and the vegetable so majestically rotund, that at first he was overcome with excitement. He turned it around and around in his hands, quickly at first, then slower as his elation gave way to bewilderment. He tried to bite into it like an apple, then gnawed helplessly at the stem. When he started to cry—great, gasping, frustrated sobs—his father called him back again, and he came running. The artichoke tumbled away under the carriage and came to a rest in the dust.

Sylvan stared at it for a moment, round and gray as a lopped-off head. He thought of William on the Widows' Walk, brushing out the matted wigs—the ravenous fury in his eyes when he talked about *hot cocoa* and *oranges*.

Then he saw mourners passing around the carriage, ascending the steps to the door, murmuring to each other in Italian. One man carried a violin case, another a plate of melting chocolate. They would spend the day holding a vigil for the dead, he supposed—bringing food, taking turns comforting the bereaved, playing music to chase away the ghosts. There hadn't been as many wakes during the winter—there were too many dying, and too quickly. For a moment Sylvan felt a ripple of jealousy—this family could mourn the dead the way they wanted to, instead of watching two strangers drag a body away down the stairs.

Sylvan turned and asked the man in Italian, "What's happened next door?"

The man looked at him—curious at first, then disconcerted—a reaction Sylvan had come to expect, but which now only made him feel nervous.

"*Parto,*" the man replied. He flicked his cigarette into the dirt and grabbed his son by the shoulder, then steered him away down the street.

Childbirth.

TWENTY-FOUR

O DILE WENT AROUND THROUGH THE ALLEY, JUST AS MOUSE had said, and pushed open the gate. The yard was empty, the garden overgrown. The small carriage house was rambling and pitched, with a bank of peep-eyed windows that shone muddily in the sun. On the ground floor the doors stood open in the heat. She took a step forward and peered inside. It was the undertaker's shop, cluttered with tools—she could smell the sponge-burn of alcohol, the raw cedar of the caskets. On the cooling-board a cat looked up from its bath, bemused.

She found a door around the side and banged it open with her hip—there, a crooked flight of stairs, stretching up into darkness. She paused for a moment, then quietly reached down to her boot and drew the dagger from its sheath. It trembled in her outstretched hand, loosening the still, humid air around her. One step at a time she made her way up the stairs, the blade glinting in the murky light, bands of iridescence a-shiver on the walls. On the last stair she paused, the dagger pointed at the door. She strained to hear a voice, a sound, anything at all, but there was only the melody of a washday song drifting in from a tenement next door. She pushed on the door with the tip of the blade. It swung open, whining on its hinges.

Beyond were two small rooms. The first thing she saw was a cradle, empty. A big, sagging bed, the sheets stormy and tossed, a dented kettle on the floor and an upturned jar beside it. At her feet lay a pillow, sliced and gutted, the feathers blown across the room. The hooked rug was stained, littered with something that looked like rice.

She tucked the dagger back in her boot and started hunting through the rooms, looking for anything that might have been her sister's, any clue to tell her what might have happened when Belle had arrived that night with the baby. She threw open the armoire and sorted through the clothes—a beaded moiré blouse with leg-o'-mutton sleeves, custard-yellow poplin, a ratty old dressing gown—but nothing looked familiar. Everything was too dirty, too gamy-smelling and sad. She turned to the vanity, which was crowded with pots of color and cream. A paper valentine was tucked into the mirror frame. On the front, two rosy, disembodied hands held up a sentimental banner: *Faithful friends forever be.* Odile turned it around. The back was signed, *To my own "Violetta": Always Free.*

She sat down on the stool and started turning out the drawers. It reminded her of the dressing room at their old theater. Perhaps this woman, like Belle, had been on the stage, too. Was that their bond? Was that why Belle had brought the baby here herself? She rummaged through brushes and paints, tubes of ointment and blemish cream. Wart-remover, hand balms, powder. A bar of shaving soap. A tin of razors, empty. And then, something she recognized from Aldovar's dressing room, rolled up in the very back: a padded corset, with a leather cup at the groin. She studied it for a moment, disconcerted, then closed it away again.

Somewhere across the way people shouted and wailed. The tenement song blended with the clatter of traffic, and then—from farther away—the dirge of an old violin. Her eyes fell on a handkerchief, folded over like a dumpling on the vanity. She reached over. There was a weight to it, she felt—a shape. She unwrapped it and squinted into her palm. Twisted inside was something soft and blue, no bigger than a mouse.

She turned to the light. There, perched in her hand, offered up like a sweet. A tongue.

TWENTY-FIVE

LPHIE ARRIVED AT THE STEPS OF THE SIGNORA'S HOUSE. There was a mourning wreath, she saw, on the door. The parlor windows were open in the heat, and she smelled the familiar, rancid musk of carnations carried out on the breeze.

She looked over her shoulder, but no one had followed her—not yet. A few of the neighbors passed by, and she fell back into the street, quick to hide her face. She worried they would stop and gape, their brows wrinkled in disbelief, but they didn't even notice her. They moved briskly ahead, murmuring to themselves, their Italian too quiet and quick for her to make out. Three phlegmatic, fat-rumped women from the tenement next door—clad in black and linked together, drifting up the steps to the Signora's front door. Then she understood: even though she felt obscene and exposed, here on the street—in the body of a teenaged boy—she was simply invisible. Anonymous. Just another summertime laborer, standing shirtless and breathless in the sun, waiting to join up with friends for a cold beer and a rowdy jump in the river.

Shaking, she lifted her face to the house. The wreath, the flowers, the women in black in the dead summer heat, a violin playing a funeral song beyond. What had happened, and so quickly?

She remembered the blood spilled on the floor of her bedroom, and the doctor's words as she retched up the asylum swill: *Did you do harm to another?* Had she? Was it more than just a panicked nip as the Signora wrenched her up from the rug? (And why, of all things, would she have bitten the Signora right there on her hand, knowing what she'd suffered in the past?) She heard the wailing through the windows, and her skin went numb.

Anthony hadn't been there to stop the Signora that night. He hadn't come to Blackwell's to find her.

It was only a year ago that she'd stood here in her peach crinoline and best hat, her arm looped through his. A year ago she'd lifted her skirts and taken a breath and marched up these very steps to her fate. But now she ran, her body sore and broken but still teeming, and let herself into the parlor.

TWENTY-SIX

INSIDE THE HOUSE, SYLVAN MOVED QUIETLY AMONG THE STIFF, wilted gathering, listening to a feeble violinist scratch out a song. He'd spoken in Italian to the woman at the door—the same words of condolence that the Scarlattas had used when visiting their grieving neighbors. People arrived bearing plates of food and fresh-cut flowers. There was a table crowded with offerings: a whole muskmelon, chocolate torta and jugs of wine, lamb stew with a skin of orange grease.

He could see the casket from where he stood—a simple pinewood box. Underneath the heap of festoons—soggy carnations, cheaply dyed ribbon that bled out in the heat—he could smell the freshly sanded planks, see the glimmer of sap and crudely hammered nails. It reminded him of being a little boy, sleeping along the waterfront in boxes meant for the dead. He hung back near the parlor door, listening to the whispers in the hallway, the flustered patter of the white paper fans.

And poor Anton came in to find her dead.

She was always a nervous-looking thing, wasn't she? And his mother so good to her!

I won't speak ill, but there was always something crafty about her. And where are her people now, I wonder? Or does she have any?

An urchin, by the looks of it. I'm not surprised. Someone told me they'd seen her on the bridge once, going over to Brooklyn. And what would she be wanting there?

Poor girl. And the poor lamb with her. I heard the screams, but I didn't think . . . How could I have known? Didn't we all scream? I hardly remember, but the things I must have said!

He studied them out of the corner of his eye, looking for a sign of something suspicious or familiar. But these were very much women of the neighborhood—the kind he'd seen every day of his life. Their arms were thick, their faces drawn. They bore the scars and pock-marks of old illnesses, and the plain, unspoken sorrow of those who had buried many beloved of their own. There was a familiar, mor-bid relief in their eyes—the guilt and pride of having been spared. In the middle of the room were half a dozen women in beaded black shawls, crying louder than the rest. They were the *lacrimata*—the same women who'd come through the streets last winter, swinging their thuribles of incense, leaving trails in the snow. Their grief was an art; they were paid to mourn with such fervor and conviction.

On the divan behind the backgammon table sat the queen of the bereaved: a woman, plumed and veiled, who cooled herself with a black silk fan. A train of mourners snaked through the room, pecking at the knuckles of her limply offered hand, murmuring their sorrows, bowing their heads. Her veil was drawn back over the brim of her hat, so everyone could see that face—beautiful, Syl-van thought, though in a haughty, injured way. She held back her shoulders and bit down her lips, purred and demurred when the men called her a saint. After all, they intoned, she'd been the one to take in this waif, hadn't she? She'd been the one to sacrifice, and then to lose them both—*sigh, swish, whisper, kiss.* The line moved in rhythm around her.

What had happened here? He moved into line behind the others, bracing as he took a step forward toward the divan, and then another. The *lacrimata* dutifully wailed beside him—the more tears they shed, the more they earned—but this woman wasn't even dazed or red-nosed, although she clenched a handkerchief tightly. She was flint-eyed beneath the feathers of her hat, nodding along with the impotent tick of her fan. There was something angrily vacant about her face, something both prideful and dead.

Beside her sat a young man—listless, probably drunk, with pale skin and red hooded eyes. He said nothing to anyone, just stared into his lap, as if his hands were a stranger's that had miraculously attached themselves to his body. She talked for both of them, it seemed—the whispered platitudes, the properly cued sighs of remorse, the routine and empty mention of God. The man might have been her brother, Sylvan guessed, or maybe even her son. They had the same angular widow's peak, the same moody jut of the chin. With each word someone whispered into her ear, the woman slid her eyes over to look at the man, as if to see that he'd heard it too, but he didn't move. He didn't seem to notice her at all.

Something about his bleariness, his pout seemed familiar. As the line moved closer, as Sylvan slinked his way up toward the backgammon table, which was scattered with guttering candles and plates of half-eaten cake—as he saw her black-gloved hand lift and drop, lift and drop—he snuck a glance in the man's direction. The light was different—fuller and blue, bringing out the pores on his nose, the flick of his lashes as he gazed at his hands. He was sitting upright, combed and cologned, dressed in good Sunday black. But he knew him. It was the man from the opium den—the man who'd held his hand as they lay back on the cushions, who'd whispered nonsense to the whistle of the pipes. The man whose jacket he wore now.

Suddenly there was a commotion in the front hall—a door banging open, cries and murmurs, the confused shuffle of feet. The mourners parted and drew back. A young man staggered into the room. He wore no shirt, only trousers with suspenders and a pair of broken shoes. He was sweating, out of breath, stinking of mildew and horse. Everyone looked at him, then at each other.

He took a step toward the divan. He was ragged and wet-eyed, but that's not what made Sylvan stare. There, beneath his collarbone, was a single word, tattooed on his skin. *Leonetti*.

TWENTY-SEVEN

THROUGH THE ROOST OF FEATHERED HATS, BETWEEN THE ruffles of taffeta and paper fans, into the sweltering, overstuffed parlor with its smell of tooth powder and ricotta fritters and browning carnations—Alphie pushed ahead, toward the sound of sobbing. She saw a casket on the dining table, strewn with garlands, and ancient wailers in their black beaded shawls. They were swooning and kissing their prayer cards, crying so hard she thought they might pitch forward and collapse. Who were they weeping for, she wondered, and with such ardor? As she moved forward into the room, people muttered and fell back, picking up their skirts, chirring into handkerchiefs. The wailers stopped when they saw her approach. Their eyes grew large; their tongues went still. Alphie shoved past them toward the casket—toward the two figures seated on the chesterfield beyond—even as a hush fell over the room, even as the mourners turned like a murder of molting crows, confused and alarmed, to face her.

There was Anthony, alive. He was sitting beside the Signora, staring dumbly at his hands. He looked terrible—as if he hadn't slept or eaten in days—gazing down at his palms as if they were eaten through with maggots. He'd been down in the dens again, she could tell. His eyes were swollen and bloodshot, his fingernails black. He seemed to be held upright only by the crackle of his freshly starched suit.

"Anthony?"

He didn't look up. He just opened and closed his fists, then turned over his hands and stared at his knuckles. Beside him the Signora, in her finest mourning dress—a confection of frothy silks and French lace—turned away from her flock and raised her eyes to Alphie's.

The bruise thudded in the back of Alphie's head. *"Buon giorno,* Mamma."

The Signora stayed very still, her fan ticking but her eyes dead black. The cleft in her ear darkened with a wave of blood. The mourners stared at Alphie, awed and stricken, as if she were an animal escaped from a cage at the zoo. Then just as quickly they looked away—at their milky coffee and squared handkerchiefs, at the cluster of boots on the rug. As if by turning to stone and averting their eyes, they could somehow make her disappear. But Alphie just stood there, sweating and panting, waiting for Anthony to raise his head. This was the nightmare that she'd woken up from, night after night, year after year. Here, her body: a betrayal, exposed. Here, a crowd gathered around her, their faces grim and aghast. But it wasn't laughter or cruelty she was met with. Only silence.

"Anthony?" she whispered, her voice breaking. "What is all this?"

He reached over to the table for a glass of cordial, took a drink, then lifted his eyes to hers. She braced herself for it—the recognition, the relief. But he only stared at her blankly, then looked away.

"Anton," she said again.

"Who is he?" a child asked somewhere across the room. "Who is that man?"

"Nessuno," Anthony whispered, staring down into his glass. *"Nessuno."*

The Signora drew her lips into a thin, trembling smile. She took a step forward and slipped. She tumbled to the floor, but no one moved to help her; they could only stare as she lay sprawled on the rug with her hat askew and her fan ripped in half, gawping like a caught fish. Anthony didn't turn to help her to her feet—he didn't seem to hear her at all. He just took a sip of his cordial and stared at the wall.

The blood began to whir in Alphie's ears. She thought of the baby rattle Anthony had made himself, the shimmer of teeth as they fell to the floor and caught in her hair. *Il mostro!* She thought of little blue children laid out on his cooling-board, in dark rooms all across the city, and his pincers twisting their teeth free. She thought of how he shook out his pocket when he returned home, and how his mother would sweeten his coffee with bourbon and grab her golden box from the mantel. She would demand music—*Fisarmonica, fisarmonica!*—a merry song to chase away the night that pawed at the windows, furring the glass. Anthony would play his accordion then, and even through the sweetest music, Alphie could hear the whisper of grit in its lungs. Who were the wolves the Signora believed prowled beyond her door? Who were the beasts—shadowy, fanged— that her son had to prove he could vanquish?

Now someone was at her side. It was the parson, the scurvied man with puffy white gums. "Sir," he said, taking Alphie by the arm. "I'm sorry, sir—do you know this man?"

She turned to look at them—there, the Signora's blustery circle of friends in their bombazine and pearls; there, the neighbors, picking wormishly at their cakes; there, the wailers, a chorus of lachrymose toads. The candles had almost burned away; the air smelled of smoking wicks. She saw among the crowd the handsome black band that she'd knitted for Anthony, but on the arm of another man. She stared at it. How had he come by such a thing, unless her husband had made a gift of it? She looked over at the pair of them—Anthony, his eyes fixed firmly on the wall in front of him; the Signora, a woozy confusion of furbelows and perfume, white-faced on the rug.

What had happened? She stared at the coffin, laid out on the table. Cedar dust hung in the air—the sweet, peppery smell of death's shell. She remembered the bump of the carriage in the night, Orchard Broome's body beside her. She remembered the sawdust in her hair, the sawdust on her tongue—the taste of that cedar, thick in her throat.

"Sir?" the parson said again.

"Of course he knows me," Alphie said, turning back. "Why, you're the one who married us."

He stared at her for a long moment, his eyes watery and slightly a-bulge. The breath left his lungs in a long hiss.

"*E 'un uomo squilibrato!*" the Signora screamed. "*Squilibrato!*"

Alphie looked at Anthony again, but he seemed very far away—his elegant, dye-flecked fingers wrapped around his cordial glass, his eyes sunken and fixed on some immovable point. She stood there between them, worrying her tooth with her tongue. *I am the wolf he let in.* The tooth rocked back and forth in its coppery pocket, then slipped free. She tasted it rolling around in her mouth, a hot pearl of salt. She spit it out into her hand—it was small and nubbled and arrow-shaped, pink at the root.

The Signora gazed at her, shaking. There was something so sad in her eyes—Alphie didn't know what to think. She lifted the Signora's tiny, gloved hand as the others had done, and wrapped it around the tooth.

The parson shouted for someone to grab Alphie. The neighbors—who had been guided there only by dutiful manners and slyly rumbling stomachs—now stared at the specter in the room: *a blasphemer, a lunatic, bedeviled by drink. Where were the police?* Alphie pulled away and strode up to the casket. *Is it I who is mad?* she seethed, pushing the carnations to the floor.

Let's see who's mad. Let them all see.

She unlatched the lid and threw it back. But other than a sack of straw, the coffin was empty.

TWENTY-EIGHT

THE CARRIAGE HOUSE SMELLED TERRIBLE—THE SPILLED PER-
fume, the sweaty yellow sheets, the warm curl of meat growing
green in its handkerchief. Odile stared at it for a long moment.
A tongue too small to be an ox's or a lamb's, all rough-shorn and lean.
Slowly she wrapped it back up and shut it away in the drawer. On the
floor the rice glimmered in a patch of sun. She shuddered. Who were
these people? How could anyone stand to live here, with the smells
wafting up from the shop beneath—cedar, ammonia, flesh—and the
spiders scuttling over black stains on the rug?

Then there was a noise below—a door knocking open, someone
tripping up the stairs. Odile reached down and pulled the dagger
from her boot. She pointed it at the door.

She didn't know exactly what she expected to see—a neighbor
sent to fetch the undertaker. Mouse chasing her down. The lady of
the house herself—the painted wife in gamine clothes—returning
home with a leaky parcel from the butcher shop. But instead she saw
her own ghost appear at the top of the stairs. A young woman with a
bleeding mouth and a wild mass of hair.

Belle.

She stood alone in the doorway, sleek as a newborn foal, trembling on her skinny legs. She wore a man's shirt over a torn and dirty dress. On her feet were small, shapeless slippers, and her skin was greased with something that smelled fatty and butter-sweet, like soap. She didn't say anything, just took a step into the room.

Odile ran and threw her arms around her, pressed her nose into the crease of her neck. She smelled the grass in her hair, the pony-musk on her clothes. She felt her sister's heart beating fast, the tick of blood in her neck. Belle tensed for a moment, then fell against her shoulder. Odile drew a breath—she wanted to ask if she was all right, what had happened, what she needed, *let's go home*—but the words wouldn't come. She had a weird, fleeting thought that she wanted to *eat* her sister, like a sorceress in a storybook—gobble her down in her belly, keep her safe. But she just held on to her, an ache prickling in her nose, between her eyes, the dagger still damp in her hand.

When Belle leaned back, she saw it there between them—she saw her own eyes, stunned and red, staring back at her in the blade. She must have known where Odile had gotten it—she must have known she'd been down to the Frog and Toe. A look crossed her face—wonder, then shame, then a terrible distress. She made a sound Odile had never heard before, a low and doglike whine, rippling in the back of her throat. Odile started to cry herself—she couldn't help it. "I'm sorry," she sobbed, but even as the words came out, she wondered, *Why am I the one saying this?*

Belle just took her by the hand and dragged her, stumbling through the rooms—pulling the blankets off the bed, turning over the cradle, kicking aside the empty jar, the scattered rice—*teeth,* Odile saw, they were *teeth.* Belle threw open the armoire doors, pushed aside the mess of dresses, then turned around and reached for a basket on the floor. A blanket, a broken rattle. A loose flower, pulpy and black—nothing more.

Odile realized what she was looking for, of course—"The baby."

Belle turned to her, eyes wide, the sound growing louder in her throat.

"I've seen her. A man rescued her from . . . from . . ." She felt the tears start to come again—she pressed her hands to her eyes. She hoped she could find her way back to Mrs. Izzo's from here—somewhere by the river-dumps, the oyster house. "She's with a woman down by the water. I think I . . ."

Belle grabbed her by the arms. Up close Odile could see something was wrong with her mouth. It was too dark, a pit, as yawning and empty as an eel's. The only movement was the glisten of spit as she drew in a breath. She hadn't spoken a word, Odile realized—not once since she'd walked in the door.

Suddenly Odile was burning hot; the light snapped in her eyes. "Who did this to you?" She cupped her sister's chin—"Tell me!" But of course Belle couldn't say—*that was just it, wasn't it? She couldn't say!*—and Odile only felt a wave of blind, stupid frustration. Her own tongue prickled and swelled up like a sponge, pasting itself to the roof of her mouth.

Then: a noise beyond the door—footsteps on the stairs, a rasp. Odile looked over. She brought up the dagger, still sticky in her hand. A woman burst, breathless, into the room—Mrs. Bloodworth, still in her rumpled shirtwaist; still wearing her apron, smeared with green. She stepped over the sheets, the jar, the teeth. She looked around for a moment, her fingers pressed to her mouth, then hurried toward the girls.

"Good Lord!" she said. "Mouse told me—"

Belle only covered her face and began to sob.

Odile pushed herself in front of her sister. She took the dagger— the little, riddled old knife—and flung it through the air. Her wrist flicked, her elbow sprang. She felt a hitch in her back; a searing pain shot up her spine and fizzed through her neck. For a moment her whole arm went numb; her vision blurred. There was a quick, soundless gleam in the air, and everything went still.

Mrs. Bloodworth stopped in the middle of the room. She looked puzzled, surprised. She glanced down at the hilt, which stuck out sideways from her hip, like a hand crank on a barrel organ. The red began to bloom around it. She nodded slowly, calmly, as if she were agreeing with something someone had said. But the room was silent. Belle gasped and looked at Odile, then back at Mrs. Bloodworth, who stood there with her hand raised in the air, her eyes fixed on the hilt in wonder. For a moment it seemed as if she was about to reach down and give it a turn, to see what notes she might sing. Then she swayed and fell down to the floor.

Odile could feel the pulse of blood in her fingertips, a rushing in her ears. She seemed to lift out of her body and float in the air—there, looking down on the room from a great height: at Mrs. Bloodworth, shifting weakly in the dust; at Belle, not moving away from the woman, but running *toward* her, kneeling at her side. "Don't take it out," Mrs. Bloodworth was saying. "Quick, bring me that bottle"—her hand, outstretched to the credenza, the decanter on a tray—"and find something to stanch it with." Belle, hurrying to pour the cordial—rummaging through the trays of a tackle-box, turning up cotton scuds, a vial of iodine. She cut away Mrs. Bloodworth's skirt and fashioned a tourniquet from the remains of a pillow. Mrs. Bloodworth lay very still on her back, her hands clasped over her heart, her gray hair undone and fanned across the floor like a sandy tangle of seaweed. She stared up at the ceiling: she seemed to *see* Odile flying above her, weightless in the air. *How do you know me?* Odile whispered. *What is it I've done?* And then Odile saw herself leaning against the far wall, hunchbacked and panting, staring at her own reddened palm. *The floating eye!* She lifted higher and higher, through the ceiling of the carriage house, into the sky above the city. She could see into all of its darkening rooms: Mouse in a moth-eaten cloak, scurrying up to the doors of the theater; Lily Up-Your-Alley, illumined in the footlights, raising her head above a tray of macaroons. Sylvan, feeling his way through the swampy darkness, into a shallow pool of light, where young boys gleamed like oysters. She saw the baby, furred and red, in her roost at Mrs. Izzo's, and Mrs. Izzo singing a happy chantey, sipping her tea. And she saw her mother just ahead of her, riding a finned tiger through the air.

"I'm sorry," Odile whispered down through the clouds, even though she wasn't sure why she was saying it, or to whom. Then there was a noise—a whistle, shrill—and she was back in her own body, hard against the wall, breathing in the dust and rubbing at the spot behind her ear.

The whistle sounded again, this time louder. Across the room Belle lifted her head.

Odile turned to look out the window. There were figures in black swarming the yard—mourners, she thought at first. But then she noticed the glossy bills of their caps, the truncheons at their hips. A half dozen in all, scattering—she could hear them tromping through the workshop below, pushing open doors. There was a paddy wagon, a Black Maria, rounding the corner into the alley.

"The police?" she whispered.

Mrs. Bloodworth's breath came in short, rattling huffs. Belle looked frightened now—she ran to the armoire and began pulling off her rags. The man's shirt, the filthy slippers, the patchy flannel dress—as it fell to the floor, Odile saw the word *Asylum* printed across the back in grungy letters. Dear God—they were after *her*. She tried not to think, just hurried over and dumped out the drawers of the credenza. She found a pair of stockings, a fake silk scarf, a pair of old shoes by the door. Her sister, half-naked, now wriggled into a yellow dress—there was a tattoo beneath her throat, Odile saw: *Orchard Broome*. Her fingers shook at the sight of it, but still, she helped to fasten the buttons, lace the boots, tie back her sister's hair. She would ask her later—she would ask her everything.

Mrs. Bloodworth lay very still on the rug. Belle tried to lift her by the arm, but the woman blanched and stiffened, shook her head. "Not me. I have nothing to tell them."

There was a ruckus in the shop beneath—something fell and broke. A few curses followed, then an ornery rebuke. Odile's ears began to itch.

"Odile!"

She turned around—Mrs. Bloodworth was looking at her.

"Take her somewhere safe."

"W—what?"

"Take your sister out of here, any way you can, understand?"

"I—"

"Do as I say, and now."

Odile glanced around the room. They couldn't go out the way they'd come in—not with the policemen hunting through the yard, with the box of the Black Maria waiting in the alley. She turned to the peep-eyed windows and cranked open a casement. The breeze was warm with woodsmoke and frying oil. The carriage house was pressed between two tenements—she saw a fire escape in the yard next door, just above the neighbors' privies.

Belle reached for Mrs. Bloodworth again, but the woman shook her off. "You need to go with your sister."

Belle made a plaintive sound. At the bottom of the stairs someone kicked open the door.

"Go on!"

Odile didn't look back. She pushed herself through the small window and out to the eaves, then reached back to help her sister. She took Belle's hand and eased her through, freeing her skirt where it caught on the sill. They stood together on the roof, sweating and shivering—then they ran across the shingles to the farthest edge, which overlooked the yard next door. They jumped down onto the roof of the neighbors' privies, the wood shuddering beneath their feet. They hurried on, trampling over the untrue boards, under lines of sodden laundry, coughing back the terrible smell, while someone bellowed, alarmed, in a stall below.

At the end of the row, they hoisted themselves up to the fire escape. The metal burned their hands as they clambered over the side, but they ran—past children waving dry tobacco leaves, past nipping dogs and vines of yellow tomatoes, past pink-eyed women hanging out the wash, all the way up the clanging stairs to the roof. Odile's lungs opened as they reached the top—she looked out over the roofs of the city, a great ocean of brick and stone, stretching to the horizon. They fled between chimneys, scattering birds, breathing in the brine and smoke from the river.

Behind them they heard police whistles, the whinnies of a horse. Belle stopped on the edge of the roof and looked back. From where they stood they could see Mrs. Bloodworth being taken out on a stretcher. For a moment Odile thought that she turned her eyes to the roof—that she saw the girls standing there, watching her as she was carried away; that perhaps she even nodded her head: *go*—but it might have just been a trick of the light, the way the shadows played over her face. They watched as she was hoisted into the back of the paddy wagon, as a man leaned against the heavy door and brought down the latch, as he yelled to the driver, "Hospital!" The whip snapped, the horses lurched, and the carriage rolled away down the street.

A hot wind tore across the roof; gulls wheeled in the sky. Odile looked silently on. Whatever had happened, whatever was done, Belle leaned into her now, held fast to her hand—as if her sister were the only thing in the world that could keep her from flying away.

TWENTY-NINE

SYLVAN CHASED THE MAN OUT INTO THE STREET. HE FOL-
lowed the knobs of his naked shoulders, his dented and blown-
about hat. Back in the parlor, with the coffin flung open for
everyone to see, the woman on the floor had simply started to cry.
The man with the cordial had sat very still, even as bits of straw
floated through the air and fluttered down into his glass. No one said
anything; no one explained. The tattooed man simply turned his
back and walked out the door.

Now Sylvan ran after him in the marketplace. The Rembrandt
was lissome and fast; he slipped through the crowd ahead, past the funeral carriage and the fishmonger's, past the stands of gutted mackerel
in quick-melting ice. Sylvan saw him lift his hat in the air and run his
hands through his coarse-chopped hair. Through the press of people,
around the scattering hens, he kept his eyes fixed on the man's suspenders, the black Y against his pale skin. Finally, by the bread sellers,
where the air was thick with flour-dust, he caught up to him.

"Mr. Leonetti—"

The man turned around and looked at him coldly. His eyes
were swollen, his delicate skin burned pink.

"You worked at the Featherbone," Sylvan continued, catching his breath.

The Rembrandt took a step away.

"You were down in the poppy box—"

He drew the air in sharply through his teeth. "Once or twice, to find my husband. And how do you know him?"

"I don't."

"Then how did you come by his jacket?" He plucked at the armband, now pilled, and frowned back what Sylvan suspected were tears. "One of his gifts?"

"No." Sylvan shook his head. "I stole it. When he was asleep in the den."

The man's jaw clenched. He nodded, then looked away. "I see."

"I was actually looking for you."

"For me?" he said, surprised.

"About the baby—"

The man stared at him—stricken, bewildered. Sylvan faltered for a moment, then went on. He told him what he'd found: the baby, in a privy near the poppy box; the young man—his gold charley—delirious in the den. He said he'd been down to the Widows' Walk that very morning, and the wig-keeper told him the young Rembrandt was dead.

"But how can I believe you?" the man kept saying, his voice growing faint. "How can I believe anything you say?"

Sylvan lifted the nosegay from his coat. The Rembrandt tried to blink away his tears, but they spilled over down his cheeks, turning to pearls in the flour-dust.

"You don't know what happened?" Sylvan said. "You don't know about any of this?"

The man shook his head, stunned. He rubbed his eyes with the back of his hand, leaving a smear of ink on his face. "You promise me she's safe."

Sylvan nodded. "I only need to find her mother—Miss Isabelle Church."

"I don't know who that is," the man said, glancing back over his shoulder. "It was just a girl who brought her to me." He looked around the marketplace, then lifted his face to the sky. "So peculiar."

Sylvan turned to follow his gaze. There, standing at the edge of the rooftop, was Odile, at the side of another woman.

THIRTY

A MURMURATION OF STARLINGS CHASED AROUND THE smokestacks and lifted to the sky. The sisters looked out across the city—the billowing chimneys, the carts and horses, the black-clad people wandering in a daze from the house near the corner. Odile saw a half-naked man in a bowler hat hurrying away between the stalls, a few policemen lingering by the ice wagon, catching the drip in their hats and drinking it down. And then she heard someone call her name. She looked down—Sylvan was standing there between the pastry carts, waving up to her.

Odile touched her sister's arm. She mumbled something breathless—there he was, the man she'd met, the one who'd rescued the baby. He could take them to the oyster house, the dead tree, the braids of hair. The baby was there—she was safe with a good woman, a weaver.

And then Belle was running—over to the far edge of the roof, down an old fire ladder, half-rusted and swinging away from the bricks. Odile followed, slower, still mindful of her back, the pulsing cut on her knee. Belle dropped the last ten feet to the ground, arms wheeling through the air, sending a woman passing by into a fit of screams.

Odile hurried to keep up, but her sister ran ahead, disappearing into the crowd. "Wait!" Odile called. She pushed against the swarm of the marketplace, ducked beneath the swinging wares. She looked for the brim of Sylvan's hat, the crinkled sheen of his beard, the wild flap of her sister's clothes. "Move!" she heard herself say, shoving past vendors with their bundles of garlic, their swatches of wallpaper and leather shoe tongues. She turned around in the throng, but there was no sign of her sister anywhere.

The wind picked up, hot and stinging, blowing about the flour from the bread stands, the shower of sparks from a knife-grinder's wheel. Odile stumbled through the haze, blinking back grit. She called her sister's name. She wove between carts to the dithering song of a zither and flute; she heard the snap of awnings, the clanging of pots. And then she saw—through the dust, just beyond the pastry carts—the faint silhouette of her sister, running after the man in the bowler hat. But he was as slippery as a minnow and vanished into the swelling crowd.

Then someone grabbed Odile's arm—Sylvan. He was sweating, flushed, his blue eye bloodshot and his dark eye watering. She was about to ask what had happened, how he'd found her there, but he only pulled her toward him. For a moment her head went fuzzy—she had the startled thought that he was going to kiss her, right there in the middle of the market square—but he was looking past her, his jaw clenched.

She turned around to see. By the ice wagon the policemen were watching them through the lifting dust, craning their necks, pinching the water from their moustaches. They muttered to each other and sucked their teeth, twisted their hats back on their heads.

Belle was looking at them, too—worried now, drawing the collar higher up her neck. Sylvan started walking—he beckoned to them with a nod of his head. Odile took her sister's hand and followed. To-gether they weaved away down the street, through the rising clamor and smoke.

Odile was too scared to look back. They moved quicker and quicker, turned onto the Bowery (*the Growlery,* she thought again, picturing her father at his workbench, smelling once again the stage paint and oil and varnished wood). A sob bubbled up in her chest, but she kept her eyes ahead, her hand joined with her sister's. At the corner where the huckster bellowed through a cardboard cone, where the lightning-struck girl pranced around with her singed hair and loopy eyes, she began to feel faint. Her back seized up; her bad knee buckled. She stumbled there on the sidewalk, right in front of the medicine trunk. The huckster pointed at her on the ground, rud-dily triumphant, rapping his bamboo cane: "Don't you see, my dear faithful ladies and gents, a girl stricken right here at our feet—a girl who could be your daughter, beset by a malady that could arise in your very house! Weak blood! Delicate nerves! A lugubrious dispo-sition!" He held up his bottle to the gathered crowd, then reached down to Odile, who struggled to get to her feet. "THIS—*this* is an answered prayer, right before your eyes—guided to us by an almighty hand, knowing what physic we can minister."

But even as he said it, Sylvan collared him and shoved him off his box, punched him once in the gut so he gasped for breath. His as-sistant just sat down on the trunk and lit a cigarette, patted her hair, made eyes at the shoeshine boy on the corner.

Belle helped Odile to her feet; Sylvan lifted her and carried her away through the crowd. She could feel the wound split open in her knee, a hot crackle in her back—her spine seemed to contract like a telescope as they hurried over the bricks. She had an image of her old brace, the one she'd flung from the pier, now washing ashore in the night, crab-walking through the sand under a veil of kelp—a sea-monster bride, returning to her: *Croc! Oh, Croc!* She felt the brush of her sister's hand, the heat of Sylvan's breath. Upside down she saw a line of swinging pretzels, the paling light of Cherry Street, the pear tree in the rag alley where Mrs. Izzo lived.

Then Belle, racing down the alley—Sylvan yelling ahead: *The stairs, the left!*, and Mrs. Izzo shuffling out on the landing to see the commotion, the baby in her arms.

Sylvan, lowering Odile to the ground, helping to steady her—*Please, Mr. Threadgill, I'm fine*—

And Belle just ahead, running and tripping up the stairs—her hands, brindled with ink, reaching out to the baby—

Odile slumped down on the bottom step, sweat dripping from her hair. She drew a hard breath—her lungs felt pleated, beaded with sand. She was aware of a shadow above her, growing wider than the sun. She felt Sylvan's fingers move across her shoulder, slink up into her hair. He pressed gently against the crook in her neck, where a knot had formed. Something fizzed in the base of her skull. She turned to look back—at her sister on the highest stair, lifting the baby's face to hers.

The tickle in her knee. The twitch of her back. Hot stars of light in her eyes. She kept thinking of the dagger, flung—how she still felt its heat in the palm of her hand.

She had seen it done. Wherever they glittered in the afterlife—flying among the high rafters of heaven, swimming with her mother in an undersea cave—she hoped the tigers had known it, and roared.

WHEN THEY WERE WASHED UP and rested, Sylvan took the sisters to the pier on the river, where the Brighton Beach steamboat made its landing.

Odile dug sixty cents from her pocket and bought the tickets: two purple stubs that left her fingers fuzzy and stained. She handed one to Belle. They stood together in a slant of sunlight, under a poster that touted the wonders of the modern fleet: *They cannot burn! They cannot sink!*

Around them the pier was thronged with people—women with white parasols and picnic baskets; coxcombs in straw hats and shined shoes, their buttonholes pegged with chrysanthemums. In a few hours they would all be delighting in their stroll down the board-walk, clinging to each other in the cars of the Hee-Haw, gathering on the benches of Guilfoyle's theater. These were the faces, blank and pudding-soft, that shone beyond the footlights, watching her aloft on the Wheel.

Sylvan bought a newspaper and stood at the rail, quietly turning the pages. There was a band playing on the esplanade below: the merry tweedle of a clarinet, the harrumph of a tuba. Pennants snapped along the pier. Odile stared out to the Statue of Liberty, a warm smudge on the harbor, to the billowing ships coming in. The archway above the landing read, THIS WAY TO THE ISLE OF DREAMS!

She sat down with Belle in the shade beneath the timetable. Belle leaned back, lanky and loose in her yellow dress, while chalk dust lifted from the board and swirled around them in the breeze. In her arms the baby sneezed.

"You can have Mother's room," Odile began. "And you won't have to see anybody, not right away. We don't have to tell them you're back, at least until you're ready. We'll think up a story, all right? We'll find one that suits you."

Belle raised her head and nodded obliquely.

Odile had seen her sister quiet before, sometimes for days— mute with fury, sore and brooding, punishing everyone around her with an aloof disdain. But now her silence didn't seem uneasy or tense. She looked wistful, even serene, staring out at the water while the breeze stirred her hair. Still, Odile found herself chattering, anxious to make up for the silence. Belle and the baby should see the doctor first, she said. They would buy a bassinet. They would re-paper the room, shake out the rug. Belle could even work at Guilfoyle's for the time being, if she wanted—at least backstage, where they always needed help with stubborn costumes and tardy cues—and then maybe, just maybe, they could start a theater of their own together, once they'd saved enough. Perhaps they could create an imaginary husband for her—a sailor at sea. A tightrope walker who'd fallen from a great height, with no net to save him. Her mind raced; her tongue grew dry, and suddenly she was conscious of it: too conscious, how it slaked the roof of her mouth, how it ticked along her teeth, as brisk as the lever of a telegraph; how it slid, fat and eely, along her lips as she paused to wet them, unsure of what Belle wanted to hear.

For a moment she didn't want to go home. She didn't want to go back to Guilfoyle's. She didn't want him to stare at her sister, so changed. Lascivious, inquisitive, snickering things under his breath like *Dumb Belle! Haha!—get it?*—then swiftly ordering a stack of pamphlets that heralded the arrival of *Rubberwoman, Tongueless Wonder from the Orient!* "I promise," she said, taking her sister's hand, "I'll look after you. It's your life to resume without consequence, to live as you please."

Belle bobbed her head, and a long silence stretched between them. Odile realized it was the same thing Mrs. Bloodworth had said to her in the hothouse.

"Will you tell me what happened?"

Belle spelled a word across the palm of her hand: *Someday.*

"You'll tell me everything, right?"

She nodded. Her mouth ticked up, the glimmer of a smile.

Then from up the river they saw it—the steamboat coming in to dock. The painted paddle-boxes, the piping stacks—the *Coney Island Queen*, drifting grandly through the harbor. On the pier people began to queue, holding their hats to their heads.

The baby started to cry. Belle stood up and took a slow turn by the ticket booth, patting and soothing her while seagulls chased crumbs across the ground.

Sylvan tucked the newspaper under his arm and studied the boat, scratching the rough ends of his beard. "What if something happens to it?" he asked Odile. "Can you swim?"

"Sylvan! Of course I can swim."

"Are you sure?"

"Nothing's going to happen," she said as he dusted the chalk from her shoulders. She pointed to the banner above them. "See? Invincible."

HE READ THE WORDS slowly to himself and over again, but still felt a twinge of despair. How could something like that boat—piled with so many woozy people, with a deck so low to the sea, possibly stay right? Then, just over Odile's shoulder, he saw Belle returning to them, flushed. She moved the baby to her hip, brushed a strand of hair from her eyes. She held out a third ticket to Sylvan.

"No, no—" he said, but she pressed it into his hand.

Odile reddened, then looked quickly away. "It's her way of thanking you. You should take it."

He stared at it, a small scrap of paper curled up in his palm. He'd never been off the island before—not once in his life—unless it was a long time ago, with the white-kerchiefed woman who had cried in her hands.

"It's not all tinsel and sea-slime," Odile was saying. "Everyone thinks that, but it's lovely, it's more. And if you hate it, you can come right back tonight. But we should celebrate, at least. Have a good meal. And perhaps"—she looked to her sister—"Belle will even play us a song."

The two of them stood side by side, leaning into each other, their faces expectant, so alike. "Thank you," he said. He gazed down at the baby, now kicking in her mother's arms, her eyes open and turned to the sky. He didn't know what to do—he'd already planned his good-bye. The whole walk there he'd prepared himself, going over it in his mind: deciding on the particular cast of his eyes, his blithe but level words, even the pressure he would give to Odile's hand if they chose to shake. Now he felt disoriented, and the energy he'd worked up for that moment—as tight as a knot in his stomach—faltered and began to unravel. He didn't want to part, not so awkwardly, but drawing out the day and knowing it would only happen later seemed even worse. He'd never really said good-bye to anyone, he realized; he wasn't well rehearsed. He could turn and walk home; he could go back to Ludlow Street and find another match, a better purse, and hope that Mr. Everjohn would give him back his shovel. The loosened knot spun out in his gut—the ticket grew clammy in his hand, the blood rumbled like the ocean in his ears—and then he met the girls' eyes and said all right, yes. He'd go.

THEY BOARDED THE STEAMBOAT, *The Coney Island Queen.* Three tiers of sanded decks and fresh white paint and scuppers as dainty as eyelets. A floating petticoat, Odile thought. She followed Sylvan and Belle up to the highest deck, where they stood at a bend in the rail, watching the muslin sea. Everywhere people chittered and laughed, giddy as crickets, their faces turned up to the sun. They were happy fools—ready for their clambake, their valentine parade—sailing to the seashore under a cloudless wash of blue.

Her sister stood close at her side. Odile had missed the familiar press of her shoulder, goading but affectionate; the way Belle canted her head slightly to the left to meet hers, as if they were huddled in together, sharing a secret. They watched as a lost kite skittered through the air above them, with a tail made from a lady's checkered stocking. The baby reached up as if she saw it, too. Belle leaned back, shielding her eyes from the sun. The kite jumped through a rumple of steam, over the docks and the yellowing trees. The leg fluttered and kicked, dancing a jig over the rooftops of the city.

Odile smiled and laughed. Then Belle took her by the arm and kissed her on the cheek, fiercely, her eyes wet with tears. Odile felt the water bud on her own lashes, but it might have just been the sunlight on the deck, or the way the sails on the harbor glinted like tiny stars. The horn sounded, and everyone jumped, then laughed, including Sylvan, who put a hand to his heart. He started to chuckle—low and raffish, a bashful shake of his head. Odile started to laugh too, which only made him laugh harder, which in turn made her laugh so breathlessly that she began to cry, water spilling over onto her cheeks. Light-headed, she looked over to catch her sister's eye, but Belle wasn't there.

Odile blinked and stood on her tiptoes, craning her neck to see farther down the deck. There, beyond a group of older women, she saw the flash of her sister's hair, the ruffle of the baby's bonnet. She called out her name, but Belle kept walking.

Odile followed her, pushing her way through the crowd, but she lost her by the time she reached the stairs. She turned right, then left—maybe Belle had just ambled away to soothe the baby, or nurse her in the ladies' quarters, wherever those happened to be. Still, Odile circled the deck, two full revolutions, looking for the custard-yellow dress, the high and freckled chin. But the faces were all those of strangers. Then, leaning over the rail, she saw Belle on a deck below—walking against the tide of last-minute boarders who were edging their way onto the boat. Odile called after her, but Belle shouldered on, her head bent over her daughter. She made her way down the gangplank to the pier. Odile saw the purple ticket stub flutter down to the water.

"Belle!" The horn blew as she leaned over the railing. "Hurry!"

The wet chains rattled and clanked; the wheels began to turn.

Belle only stood there, watching as the plank was raised and unhitched, as the steam billowed from the stacks overhead.

Odile gazed down three decks to the water, black and foaming
under the sputter of the wheel. She could jump. She could risk it—
the cold shock, the pain splintering down her back, the pull and drag
of the paddle wheels, drawing her under. She wedged her foot up
on the rail, felt her skirts flutter around her ankles—but Sylvan was
quick behind her, his arms around her waist, lifting her back.

The horn sounded again; the paddle wheels churned. Odile
called her sister's name, but it was lost in the wind. Belle raised her
head to the light. There was something in her eyes: a wry sadness, a
dogged smile. It reminded Odile of something—of being high up in
the rafters and looking down at the Church of Marvels stage—at the
Shape Shifter, standing alone in the spotlight.

Belle raised her hand above her head. She crooked her finger.

The wheels turned faster; a pipe organ played; the smokestacks
left a pair of trails burned into the sky. All around them the crowds
buzzed and laughed, a garden of sunhats blooming at the rail. On
the shore beneath the pennants, her sister grew smaller—a fiery yellow dot, alone in a circle of light, her hand raised above her head.
The *Queen* made a wide, waltzing turn into the harbor. The engine
chuffed louder and louder. Then—a gust of steam, a passing ship—
and Belle was gone.

Odile wavered for a moment, blinking back her tears. In the
wake she saw ragpickers and fishermen—all skimming the harbor
with homemade nets, picking through the lost and the jettisoned. She
turned to Sylvan, who only shook his head in wonder. They stared
back at the city, a torrent of light.

Something passed through her then, a feeling she couldn't dis-
tinguish, but she'd felt it before—one summer day years ago, when
she was still a little girl in a metal brace. She hadn't been allowed
to swim, but her sister took her into the ocean anyway, when their

mother's back was turned. Belle, small but tough, hoisted Odile up on her back and carried her down to the surf. Odile kept her legs and arms wrapped around her sister, shrieking and laughing as Belle marched into the water—feet, then ankles, knees and hips—the waves rolling over them, lifting them up. They kept going, farther and farther out, until the sandbank fell away. Odile closed her eyes as they dropped—she held her breath, clung tighter to Belle. The water surged over her shoulders, tickled her chin—a mouthful of salt—but they didn't go under. Belle kicked and kept swimming. *You don't weigh anything!* she marveled. *Maybe I'm a strongman!* Odile laughed, her cheek against Belle's sunburned scalp. They swam past the breakers, their bodies slippery and locked. *Faster!* Odile cried. *Faster!* Belle paddled through the dappled water, frog-kicking and spitting back foam, until their mother—alone on the shore—called them back. Odile knew there would be a soft blanket to dry her, a lunch of seltzer and waffles from the stand on the boardwalk. *Come in now!* Their mother's voice, drifting out over the waves: *Come in now, girls!* But they didn't stop. *Faster, faster!* Together they dove underwater and came up for air. *A two-headed mermaid!*

Now she gazed back to Manhattan as the dark water carried them away—the huge sky above, the pale glimmer of stars, the ship-masts in the haze. She reached over and took Sylvan's hand. *They cannot burn! They cannot sink!*

And the city itself: an island of light. All of those windows, all of those rooms—lit now by candles and electric bulbs, hearthfires and stoves. Deep in its burrows were a thousand hands to kindle the torch: the flick of a match, the turn of a lamp, the spark of a switch; embers rising from chimneys to join the sun. The great hive glowed in its smoke. The world was lit by fire.

THIRTY-ONE

ALPHIE LIFTED THE BOWLER OFF HER HEAD AND RAN A HAND through her chopped, sweaty hair. She asked a passing man on the street for a smoke. When he stopped, she saw that it was Mr. Moro, the olive-vendor, rolling his pushcart home, but he didn't recognize her—not here, with her naked face and man's clothes, her sweaty chest and scabbed tattoo. He just nodded, distracted, and handed her a cigarette without a word. She thanked him as he continued on—*grazie, signor*—and for a moment she smelled the salty oil sloshing around the olive jars and was hungry. She lit the cigarette, inhaled the smoke, and stared up at the sky. The moon hung low in the pale light, just above the bridge. Salt and sand blew in from the sea. For the first time in a long time she wasn't sure what to do.

She kept walking. She had nothing on her—no money, no clothes, no box of powder and paint. She could do a little bit of bartending, perhaps, at any tavern with a blue star on the door, at least until she got her Rembrandt stand up and running again. She could live week by week at her old boardinghouse, eat supper in a saloon of her own choosing, with no one to please but herself. Her stomach cramped at the thought of it. Roasted chicken and crispy potatoes. Egg-drop soup. Rarebit on sweet brown bread. Beer.

She made her way down Orchard Street, toward the water. She passed the shipyard with its scaffolds and ladders and pots of tar, the whale skeleton rising from the earth. She passed the rickety wooden building where she'd tricked those first few months away from home, where she'd lived on black liquor and raw potato skins. She looked up to the terrace and saw the Widows at the rail—waiting out the heat in their tangled blond wigs, whistling down to the sailors and smiths. The littlest one smiled, dazed and grim, at Alphie, rubbing at the blue circles under his eyes.

A few blocks down she saw the door to the Shingle and Plank. Inside it was dim and cool, a relief after the heat of the streets, smelling like Irish beer and sour-bread. Here she knew every knot along the bar, every lewd drawing and lonely initial carved into the wood; she could see shapes in the darkest corners of the room. She had once navigated the paths between the tables as if they were the streets of her own little city. But now the bartender looked at her oddly, perched on a stool by herself. Alphie could see that he recognized her somehow, but he couldn't place her. She thought of the little Rembrandt he remembered: walking in with her folded stand, smelling like cologne and lemon drops, all the men buying her drinks while she smiled agreeably and looked past them, waiting for a glimpse of Anthony.

What a sight she must be now, after the care she'd taken. Her hair cut short, her skin clammy, an ugly scrawl beneath her throat. Would anyone think to find her here? Would they know where to look? She'd have to hide out for a while, she realized, keep away from the places where they knew her as Mrs. Leonetti, the undertaker's wife. She could not be seen with Anthony again.

Perhaps she'd move west, to the ports on the Hudson, just to be safe. She knew there was a shop nearby, above the cobbler's, where an old vaudeville star named Carlotta discreetly made dresses for men's bodies. She'd go there and order something new. But later. Now she ordered a pint of beer, prayed she could pay tomorrow, and put her head down on the bar.

It was Dolly, the songbird who lived in a room above, who recognized her.

"Not Alphie Rembrandt?"

Alphie raised her head. She felt ashamed of the way Dolly looked at her, tentative and scared, as if she were something that had washed ashore from a wreck.

"I almost didn't know you!" Dolly said, a hand fluttering up to her cheek. "You've gone back to—"

"No, I haven't." Alphie drank her beer too quickly and coughed. "But I'm a sight, I know."

"What happened to your gallant knight, your grand opera singer?"

"They all found me out."

"He's not with you then?"

"No."

"Well, we always knew he was the wrong sort," Dolly sniffed. "What did you want with the likes of him anyway, prancing around up there like he's straight as a preacher's prick? Sometimes it's too risky, trying to cross all the way like that."

"You're right," Alphie said. "He didn't love me."

"I think he did, little bird. He must have, to marry you."

"I don't know anymore," Alphie said. "I think he was just trying to hurt someone else."

Dolly ordered another round of beer and reached out to brush Alphie's arm. "Hey, I heard from Robbie that The Chandelier is looking for pretty female impersonators for their new revue. You've got a sweet, lovely alto, you know. I think you could try for it."

"No," Alphie said, hearing the edge in her own voice. "But thank you."

"Of course," Dolly said, blushing. "I only feel sorry you have no home to go to now."

Alphie didn't know what to say. She had wanted to feel safe and normal in a world that made her feel like she was wrongly made at every turn. She wanted to prove she was just as much a woman as anyone else. She'd seen Anthony's troubles as some kind of wrong she could right, as a place for her to be needed. She believed their pain was the same. She had given herself over to making his life better, believing that if she did, she'd somehow atone for her own. But he needed her far more than he loved her. And she'd mistaken her devotion for something more heroic—an unassailable moral purity; a high-mindedness above even sex. But she saw now it was little more than vanity and desperation, a desire to be known.

She could guess now what had happened that night. She'd seen Anthony's face at the funeral, heard it from the man on the street—he'd been down in the poppy box. How foolish could she have been? He had likely been gone all afternoon, drifting from den to bar and back again, lost track of the time. And when he finally returned home—well past the four o'clock train—the Signora had already found out the worst. Her own husband, rather than coming to her aid and defense, rather than protecting her—had chosen instead to protect himself. Now she remembered the lights of Bellevue Hospital, the swish of money exchanging hands; a brief glimpse of the wardens, vole-eyed and taciturn, folding the bills in their crisp paper bibs. An ambulance, already crowded with women, was bound for the moonlit wharf. He had left the person he loved, signed her away to the island to rot—to be discovered there for what she was, and then to be punished forever; a work-camp slave, a life of rock-breaking and maggot-meat—never to see Broome Street again.

FOR A MOMENT she imagined what her life might have been like if nothing had gone wrong that day—if he and his mother had gotten on the train, if the Jennysweeter's girl had delivered the baby without incident. But she knew what would have followed: a life even lonelier, waiting up for Anthony night after night, raising a child by herself while he drifted and drank—*but it's my fault if he's that way, isn't it?*—and then having that child (that sweet little girl!) fall under the obsessive tyranny of his mother.

The Signora—reaching for the baby in her basket that night. The Signora, singing a lullaby and rocking her as she cried. Alphie couldn't be sure what had happened, but this was how she pictured it.

The Signora, in a dream of love, had doted on that baby. For two days she had giggled and cooed. The bite on her hand glimmered, blacked to a scab, but she didn't even see it. Not even as she spooned the cooling milk from a saucepan; as she brushed the baby's hair. A baby girl: the daughter she'd dreamed of having. She called her *la mia piccola pipistrella!* My little bat. Even her voice was different, a little-girl laugh, and her cheeks were cream-pink roses. But when Anthony tried to speak, she turned and walked right past him, as if he weren't even there.

Anthony, alone—hot muggy mornings out in the yard, sanding the casket, retching in the weeds. The sawdust clinging to the hairs on his arms, while inside his mother sang to the baby.

He bought the wreaths and the garlands. He visited the *lacrimata* in their quarters behind the convent, where the nuns had been buried standing up, habits shriveled against their bones. *I will see to it,* he had said. He had done everything his mother asked of him, penitent, ashamed—and still he waited for her wrath.

But it never came. She'd made him a ghost. There was only the baby, new in her arms, red as a shelled bean and wearing his old baby bonnet. He tucked a blanket of gauze in her cradle when his mother's back was turned—it was the gauze he used to stuff the mouths of the dead, to give shape to their faces; to plug nostrils and rectums, to keep the leaks away. Even so, the baby slept happy and pure, untroubled by dreams. A life pristine. His mother's prize, the victor's.

What did he think, when he took her away that night, his old familiar walk to the den? That he would get revenge? That he would never again be reminded of the life he'd lost? Or that somehow, in death, the baby would be saved? Alphie would never know. But she knew that even now he would be looking over his shoulder, turning in his sleep, no matter who lay by his side. For wherever he went, something would follow, pawing and hungry, singing a witch-song to the moon.

All the wolves, they waited true. The wolves, they had their way.

AFTER ANOTHER ROUND of beer Alphie followed Dolly upstairs to her room. Dolly gave her a peck on the cheek, laid out a dress, and left Alphie alone to change. Slowly, methodically, Alphie brushed out the skirts. She bent over a bowl of water and washed away the Mother's Milk, the ink and sweat, the stink of horses and the dirt of the soap-boy's clothes. She peered in the dusty little mirror that hung on the wall. Her hair was a horror, with its hasty chops and stubborn cowlick. She brushed it out of her face and sighed. It would have to do for now.

As she dropped her eyes, she caught sight of it for the first time, backward in the mirror. His name, written on her body. She touched the skin where it blistered and peeled. She had believed so devotedly in him; she felt as though she couldn't live without him. She was certain that a life alone was a life failed. As a child she'd longed to be spirited away—to a world of beauty, a world apart. She dreamed of being transformed. But that world was not the Widows' Walk or the waterfront; it was not Anthony and his cooling-board and his carriage-house home. It was one she had carried with her all along: it was her own heart, and it still beat.

You have two spirits, Orchard Broome had said to her. *Most in this life only have one.* She supposed she must have imagined it that way over the years, but she'd always thought of them as two beasty shadows wrestling inside her, fighting for possession of her body and mind. But now she pictured it differently. The spirits weren't shadows, restless and ill. Instead, they were high up on trapezes, colorful as birds, reaching for each other's hands as they flew through the air.

She leaned toward the mirror and mopped the water from her chin. She powdered her face and buttoned up her dress. She pictured the spirits swinging higher—they were ruffled and plumed, one a woman and one a man. She penciled the kohl around her eyes, oiled and brushed her hair. She put on a spritz of Dolly's perfume. She saw them soaring and careening, closer and closer, their arms outstretched, radiant, bright.

She stepped back from the mirror, lifted her chin.

They held out their hands in the stunning lights. And when they touched, there in midair, she was whole.

THIRTY-TWO

T HEY'D RISEN EARLY TOGETHER, DUG THE PIT BEFORE DAWN.
First, Odile in the dark, drawing a square through the sand.
Then Sylvan, breaking up the sand with a shovel, lifting and
turning, digging down into the beach. He felt his lungs open in the
damp, salty air, the tickle of beachgrass around his toes. Above him
the stars held fast; the sky was as gray as the sea.

They walked down the shore and collected driftwood. They
carried the bundles back on their shoulders and stacked them at the
bottom of the pit. Together they laid down the slats of an old whiskey barrel, and Sylvan took a match to a twist of paper. He fed the
kindling, lay back in the sand, and watched the sparks chase up to
the sky. Odile knelt beside him in her topcoat and bathing gown,
picking through shells. When the fire was high, they cooked their
breakfast—salty gammon, potatoes on a stick, and fresh ears of corn,
charred and popping-sweet. They ate together on the tiger quilt,
watching the sun rise over the water, listening to the surf, feeling the
warmth of the fire at their backs.

The first meal he fixed her was a sorry one. The day they'd
arrived, Odile had been very quiet, faraway. They'd walked in si-

lence from the Brighton Beach landing to her house, where she sat
for a spell by the window, staring out at the striped turrets and onion
domes. He made her a plate of whatever he found in the pantry—
pickled yams, a slice of bread, some anchovies and a glob of mus-
tard. She ate it anyway, without complaint, and he read her the day's
paper, every story he could find: about a bicycle race on Manhattan Beach, a missing jewel thief in Texas, the marriage of a Sunday
school teacher to an elevator man at an ice cream factory. She listened and smiled but didn't speak. She didn't ask him to leave, and
he didn't feel inclined to go. So he stayed the next day, and the next,
waiting for her to give him word, or a ticket. But she hadn't done it,
and he hadn't asked.

He slept through the nights in Belle's old bed, wearing gloves
filled with cream, which Mr. Mackintosh said would be good for
his hands. For the first few nights Odile had stayed in her mother's
room, but she couldn't sleep—he could hear her up in the middle
of the night, restless, turning. Then she padded back down the hall
and fell, sighing, into her own little bed. She slept deeply, woke late.
Sometimes she would climb in next to him, and he would hold her
as she fell asleep, kissing the back of her neck, her hands clenched in
his. And when he woke, he found his hands were animate, tender—
they were healing.

He wondered how they spoke of him back home—Dogboy, vanished into air—if they ever sang about his fights, told tales of where
he'd gone. Would they imagine him walking by the old Church of
Marvels—a circle of bricks in the sand, overrun with marigold? Or
buttering toast in a bungalow, reading about the price of cheviot
suits? Sylvan would never meet Mrs. Church, but he felt for sure that
he knew her, for he walked among her things, drank ginger tea with
honey from her chipped china cups, read her books of poems and
plays, all marked in her curious, exclamatory hand. And when he
saw Odile in the easy chair beside him, laughing at the new color

cartoons in the Sunday paper, or reading a letter from Belle in the kitchen, balancing on one leg while the coffee boiled—*it's good for my back!* she said when she caught him smiling—he knew that she was tough. It had to be the hardest thing, even if he'd never known it himself—to accept that the ones you loved would find their own way home. And already her friends were starting to make plans for the winter: Mack hopping on a caravan through the Dakotas, Leland heading to a circus in Montreal. They talked about it often, gathered at the beer hall—Guilfoyle was ready to shut down early, go scouting in California. *What about you?* Sylvan asked Odile as they drank coffee one morning on the porch. *Where will you go?* She sat down on the brass elephant—*Right here.*

As the sun rose higher over the beach, Odile stood up from the blanket and took off her coat. "You're not coming in?" she said.

Sylvan hugged his knees to his chest. "I'm fine here," he said. "You go."

He watched as she made her way down to the water—her feet bare, her limbs glittery with sand, her hair wild around her shoulders. She walked slowly at first, then faster and faster, until she broke into a run. She splashed high-kneed into the ocean and dove under the waves.

He waited to see her emerge—the sheen of her hair, the crest of her shoulder, the pale flutter of her hands. She was swimming farther out—he saw her feet kick up through the foam. They hovered there for a moment—she waved her toes at him—then fell back into the water.

Slowly he stood and dusted the sand from his pants. He started to walk, hands in his pockets, wending his way down to the surf. He paused at the water's edge, then put one foot in. It was colder than he thought. The foam swirled around his heel and ate away at the sand.

He wobbled and continued. Through the strands of bubbled kelp, the sandcrabs, the bits of broken shells, the stones as smooth as sucked candy. He moved forward, the water hitting his shins and splashing up under his trousers, cold and sharp. He put his hands against the waves, felt the pressure of the tide. His feet found their way through the sand, to the place where the seabed dropped away. The water rose slowly to his hips, soaking his shirt to his stomach. Farther out Odile broke the surface. The light hit her face, and she smiled.

He drew the air deep into his lungs, until they were full, and fell back in the water. There was a sudden slap of cold, the light dazzling the surface. He kicked his legs, moved his arms. The sea surrounded him. He would swim.

EPILOGUE

M Y NAME IS NOT ORCHARD BROOME. IN FACT, I'M NO LONGER known as Belle. I will never be able to speak my real name, the name I was born with, if I had ever been given one at all. Here on the waterfront I am called simply Mrs. Church, and I've grown quite fond of it.

When I arrived all those months ago in Manhattan, Mrs. Bloodworth welcomed me into her home without question. She, too, was grieving my mother's death, which she'd read about first in the newspaper, and for this it was hard to forgive myself—I didn't write her with the news. I didn't write anyone after it happened, not even Mother's family back in Punxsutawney, whom I'd never met and only thought of as a gaggle of scowling, thick-jawed maiden aunts. I couldn't live at Coney Island anymore, not after the fire, not after walking through the ruins of my mother's theater, not with my secret growing bigger inside of me every day. And so I came to Mrs. Bloodworth's, repentant and searching, wondering what I was meant for.

I dreaded the baby's arrival. I dreaded seeing it outside of my body. When I grew idle or anxious I kneaded my belly, searching for a sign of something wrong. I woke from nightmares in my little room on Doyers Street, clawing blindly at the air, while down the hall other women sighed and turned in their sleep. In my dreams the baby sprouted legs and arms and wrapped itself around me like an octopus. I dreamed it was born with a face full of suckling mouths. I dreamed it was born with pincers, with talons, with fangs. I dreamed it came out of my body in pieces: a leg here, an arm there, a slippery head no bigger than a grapefruit. I dreamed it came out of my body slapping wetly to the floor, a gilled mermaid, a translucent eel, a jellied creature of the sea.

She was born on a hot July night—there in the birthing room behind the kitchen, on a bed that smelled like mice. The window was open in the heat, and through it I could see gulls flocking in the yard. Were they watching me? Were they coming to take her away? I heard them caw and flap. The baby answered. She split me and I screamed. Then there were shadows standing over me, bringing cool cloths and sips of rum, and then Mrs. Bloodworth slipped her larded hands between my legs and drew the baby out. I fell back into the pillows, crying. Did she have feathers, I wondered—a bill, webbed feet? I waited for someone to gasp or shout. I turned my head and saw Mrs. Bloodworth holding the baby in the lamplight, wiping her little nose with a handkerchief, then her mouth, her eyes. A tiny girl, briny and squalling and slick. She drew breath into her lungs and called out to the world. I was astonished, delirious—I thought there must be a mistake. She was perfect.

I nursed her those first few weeks, upstairs in my room. I visited her down the hall in the nursery, held her little mittened hand in mine while she slept. She looked like him, I thought—her father's daughter, with his rosy cheeks and thick hair and curious, reflective eyes. I had written my sister a letter, believing that I might die, that I would meet the end alone on the birthing bed, but my daughter and I were both healthy, alive. She would be going to another family, a good one with a little bit of money—merchants, perhaps—though I didn't know their names. This was always the arrangement—I was never to meet them or contact them; I would never see my daughter again. But I would leave Mrs. Bloodworth's with my good name standing, my life to live unblemished. So on a given night I would say good-bye, and Mouse would deliver her to her new home.

It's a hard thing to explain—I was unmarried. I had lost the people I loved. I was adrift in a city full of loneliness and spite; I had no home that made sense to me anymore. I was practically a child myself. I couldn't raise her, cursed and alone as I was, I believed— but I wanted to know that she was loved. I wanted her to grow up far from the shadow of the burned theater, from the things that haunted me then and follow me still. And I trusted Mrs. Bloodworth. I owed her my life. But still, I dreamed about these people, this ghostly couple who would raise my child. Were they good enough? Would she be safe, adored? Or would she be no better off than the children who lived, abandoned, down in the Frog and Toe? The children who never found homes of their own? I just wanted to know, so that I might imagine her as she grew. Through the years I could think back to whatever little house they lived in—the hearth with its cuckoo clock or cranberry garlands, its overstuffed pillows and claret-red rugs, and know: yes—there she is, warm in her nightgown—yes: there she is playing with her doll by the fire—now reading, now laughing, now dipping a cookie into her milk, now falling asleep with her grey-hound pup, now a young woman tending to a child herself. When I arrived at their door that night, they wouldn't even know I was the one who had birthed her. I just wanted to see where she would live. I wanted to look her new mother in the eyes—both of us silent, grateful, fulfilled, yet strangers—and take my proper leave.

So I made a deal with Mouse. I'd find the names of her parents in Mrs. Bloodworth's ledger if she let me be the Hood, just that one time. I was fast, I assured her. It would be dark, the dead of night, and I wouldn't breathe a word to anyone. It was a straightforward exchange, wasn't it?—I'd deliver the child and disappear. And I knew how badly she wanted those names—since I'd arrived she'd talked of little else.

Still, she was nervous. *It's just . . . it's not what you think,* she whispered as we stood shoulder-to-shoulder at the range, boiling the bottles and scrubbing the pots. *The mother's a . . . well, a fairy.*

A—what? I said lamely, thinking I'd misheard.

I overheard it when I brought them their coffee. I couldn't help it! She's a he: a passer, get it? Oh, hell's bells, I shouldn't have told you, should I?

Honestly, I didn't know what to think. My first thought was of my mother, living in disguise for months as a young girl, sleeping side by side with soldiers in the bivouac at night. What cunning and strength, to not get caught. I thought of Aldovar, brushing out his single braid, painting in his beauty mark, our gloved hands holding each other's in the gaslight. They would do whatever it took to survive. Is that what made Mrs. Bloodworth choose this couple for my baby? And if she found them worthy and sound, then I trusted her—I had to. But I wanted to know, too. I wanted to say good-bye. I wanted to see it done.

So I looked up the name of Mouse's parents in the ledger. After Mrs. Bloodworth took me into her confidence—after she told me the whole story, from the very beginning—I had looked up other names, too—early in the morning, when she was busy in the hothouse. Georgette, I found, was the daughter of French immigrants who were convinced that her deformity was proof of an Old World curse. Aldovar was born to a wealthy Jewish family on Lexington Avenue, a name I recognized from a department store. They'd left Aldovar with Mrs. Bloodworth and adopted instead a healthy, unnamed slum boy with Ashkenazy blood. I thought about arriving on their marble stair, pulling the thick braided rope, hearing the toll of the finely tuned bell. I wanted to tell them that their flesh nested in mine, that their blood ran with my own. *I loved your son,* I wanted to say. *He is dead now, but part of you still lives. Do you understand? You are still alive.*

It haunted me, that morning Aldovar and I met on the pier. It was dawn, chilly and gray; the seagulls stared at us from the railing. We had words, I regret to say, and I went home anguished and hurt and full of dread. It was the last time we spoke. Hours later he walked into the burning theater.

We had been friends our whole lives, since we were children, but as we grew up things began to change. Between shows I would see him flying kites out over the beach. We always smiled at each other, sly and taunting, and afterward I felt a flash in my gut, a honey-eyed burn that was gone as quickly as it came. Walking ahead to the theater, where the Church of Marvels banner snapped in the wind, I thought about how the rope twisted around his long fingers, how he drew his hands through the air like a bandleader, how the kites circled and soared. Waiting backstage, I daydreamed about his lopsided smile, his shy, twitching dimple and dark-lashed eyes. One stormy afternoon in October, he ran after me with an umbrella when I was caught hatless in the rain. He told me he was heading home to make some coffee and dry the kites (just past the sharpshooter booth and up those steps, in the leaky brick building behind the Mirror Maze: I'd been up there a hundred times before). But something was different that day. And I, pretending that I didn't know what was happening even though I did, followed him back to the boardinghouse.

It was only that one time. A tangle of kicked, sweaty sheets, and neither of us shy about it. As he bit into my neck, I heard the pop of toy guns in the arcade below, the rain coming down on the roof. Afterward we lay next to each other and shared an apple crisp, listening to the thunder above, the glassy warble of a street-organ waiting out the storm in a doorway below. As we watched the sun break over the beach, his hand, gritty with sugar, crept over the sheet and held mine.

He was a man, like any other, only as a child his circumcision had gone awry. Still, there was nobody I could tell about it, not even Odile—we had told each other everything all our lives, but I couldn't bear for her to be jealous or confused or disappointed in me—she, who'd looked up to me our entire life. But briefly, privately, I had dreamed of a future with Aldovar—of seeing him make kites for our children, of starring with him in an aerial show on the beach. I imagined the two of us in goggles and tailcoats, waving from a hot-air balloon as it lifted up over the boardwalk, as a brass band played a salute from the stands. I pictured my mother at the edge of the water, her head turned up in wonder, growing smaller and smaller as we drifted into the sky, until she was only a dot in a fur coat, standing alone in the sand.

But that life was not to be. It was gone forever, ash.

So that night on Doyers Street I put on the cloak and drew up the hood. I stepped into the overshoes and pinned the white flower to my breast. I went out into the night, down the dark narrow lanes, the basket at my side. We'd given the baby a nip of sherry to help her sleep. A blue blanket concealed her. I could smell the sweetness on her breath, the powder on her skin. I didn't know then that I was leaving Doyers Street for good. I didn't know that after that night I would never speak again.

Mouse told me there would be no trouble with the family—and if there was, I should leave. We were just couriers after all, not bloodhounds. She'd passed their house a few times before, with Mrs. Bloodworth in her carriage, just so she knew where to go. Mouse was not worried that the exchange itself would be muddled—only that Mrs. Bloodworth would somehow discover our ruse and punish her with extra chores: more laundry perhaps, extra diapers.

But when I got to the place Mouse had described—Orchard and Broome—I got turned around. I couldn't figure out where to go. It was night, you see, a neighborhood I didn't know well—I was never out at such an hour, and certainly not by myself. I walked back and forth in front of the small house, the one tucked between the tenements. I noticed a woman standing at the window. She'd been keeping watch—she wore a hat, a coat, and I saw a suitcase ready on the sill beside her. As if she were expecting someone. I took a step forward. But it was the wrong window, I realized—I was meant to go around back, through the alley, to the carriage house behind. My heart pounded—I walked away from the streetlight as quickly as I could and stumbled down to the mews.

When I knocked on the carriage-house door, Alphie answered. She was so young—so striking, really, with her golden hair and fair skin and delicate bones. Without a word—just a smile, a swell of relief and happiness that nearly broke my heart—she led me up those crooked stairs. There was a jar of blood on the dressing table, I noticed—to set the stage, to make it real. She shook out a nightgown. I helped her undress. There was an open bag—her husband's—with pincers and needles, a small knife, a roll of gauze. An undertaker, Mouse had said. Alphie took the knife and carefully cut the ties on the pillow, pulled it free from her stomach. Then a door slammed shut below, and she turned to me, and I knew from the look on her face that this was not the plan.

I heard footsteps and a sound I couldn't place: *tick-tick-tick*. The woman I'd seen in the window—the neighbor, I thought at the time—threw open the door and saw us there: me in my hooded cloak, the baby still sleeping in her basket, and Alphie, stark naked and holding the pillow at her side. The woman's eyes went black. I'd never seen anything like it. Her pupils grew to fill them, like a broken nib of ink.

She went after Alphie, wild with horror. Alphie screamed (and would anyone worry, I wondered, about a lone woman furiously screaming in the house of a baby about to be born?). I tried to push myself in front of Alphie as she scrambled back into her dress, but in my haste I knocked the blood-jar to the floor, and I slipped in the wet. From where I lay I saw the Signora bring a rattle down on Alphie's head with a sickening thud. It broke, and she reached for a kettle. I was amazed at the strength of that woman, the animal fear in her black, unseeing eyes.

I took the basket. I ran toward the door, the baby wailing. But the woman was quick behind me, knocked me down. She took the pincers and the knife, the ones from the bag; she pulled at my tongue while I hit her in the stomach and struggled for breath. She sliced it right out. She held it up to the light, flopping there in the tongs, while I lay on the floor, bleeding and bleeding, faint with shock. For a moment she looked confused and sick. And then she saw the basket— my little baby, crying in the night. She dropped everything—she reached for her—

The pain was unbearable; my consciousness went. A few things remain of the night: a man's face, a ruffle in the darkness. A wad of gauze stuffed into my mouth. The rock of the carriage, my blood on my hands. Being helped by a warden onto a cot. *They've attacked each other,* the man said, counting out the money. *You will see what I mean—they are not sound of mind at all.* The wardens didn't ask questions, just put us in an ambulance bound for the boat. We were passed off to others—the Matron, the nurses—and they all regarded us with the same mixture of impatience and disdain.

In the examination room the doctor iced whatever remained of my tongue and wrapped up my jaw. For a day I slept in the infirmary, waking every hour to the nurses washing out my mouth, changing the gauze. When I was better oriented, they handed me a pencil but I only stared blankly at the paper. I refused to write my name, my story, for whom would I imperil then? Mrs. Bloodworth? The scared unwed mothers who came to her for help? The desperate ones, like Alphie, with nowhere else to turn? So I refused. I was sick with pain and shock. So I played dumb, and I figured they would let me go.

But the mutes, unclaimed and terrified as I was, and with no identi-
fication, were kept until someone came for them. And no one could
know I was there.

The morning on the pier, when I first told Aldovar about
the baby, he said it was impossible. He did not believe me. I felt
frightened—he, my dearest friend, my confidant, whom I had trusted
since we were children, only looked at me blankly, dismissively. I'm
not sure what was harder for him: to accept the fact I was carrying a
child at all, or that the child was his—that he was capable of this, that
it was only him I'd been close to. *It's simply not possible,* he insisted.
He said I couldn't marry a man who was not really a man. His hands
trembled as he tried to light a cigarette in the wind. For if they knew
the baby was his, he rationalized, would they still think he was half-
woman? Would anyone really believe us?

I was stunned, frightened. I'd never heard him talk this way
before—not to me, not to anyone. When I came back from the pier,
I snapped at my sister, who was hiding in the pantry, only trying to
amuse me. I refused to go through with my routine. My mother took
me into the dressing room to talk. I stood, terrified, in front of her,
as she closed the door and sat down by the mirror. How could this
woman ever love me again, I wondered? I had ruined everything. I
was worse than a freak, and yet I still thought of myself as an innocent. I hadn't known. I hadn't. I was only curious.

She turned her eyes on me and waited. For a moment I was
numb. There was nowhere else to turn, no one else to help me. So I
told her everything. And she listened. She was worried, I could tell,
but she sat there and listened and held my hand. She told me that she
loved me.

I wish this was how it ended.

But then we argued. I grew more and more furious. In my temper I knocked the things off her dressing table—the paints, the pins,
the books with her photographs—and then, by accident, a kerosene

lamp. This is what I can never tell Odile, why I can't go back to Coney Island. The lamp wobbled and fell. I leapt toward it, but I was too late. It shattered, and the flames started up the edge of the curtain. Mother tried to tamp it out, but it jumped to the gabardine coat she'd hung on the door, then the upholstered chair. She told me to run and pump some water, quickly, and to see that my sister was safely outside. I ran and couldn't find a bucket, couldn't find Odile—and then I turned and saw the smoke, the flames through the windows, the wood red-black and crackling. I tried to get in through the stage door, but the heat was too much. The doorknob alone seared the palm of my hand.

Watching the theater burn, calling for my sister, choking on ash, reaching up to my face and feeling my eyebrows gone—I was confused and numb, but I was sure Mother had made it out. What hadn't she survived before? I waited and waited, sitting there on the curb, watching as the brigades arrived with their steam-pump engines (I will never forget the hiss of those valves in my ear, the sweat of the blinkered horses). It took two hours to put out the fire, and by then the theater was gone.

The dead were piled slowly on the boardwalk. Odile was the one who found her. Odile was the one who came to tell me she was gone. And all I could do was sit there, on a bench overlooking the indifferent sea, and nod, as if I'd known all along that it must be so.

To walk through the ruins afterward, to see the shrouded people who had died, to know it had been my hand—how could I ever go back? Sometimes I think I can hear the audience, I can see my mother, I can eat ice cream with my sister and brush the tigers' coats. Sometimes I believe Aldovar is still there on the beach waiting for me, his kites aloft in the air. I will never feel the breeze on a hot summer day without thinking of him. I will never pass the open door of a theater without wanting to step inside, just to see if my mother is there. I know I will never hide with Odile in the curtains of the old stage again. We will never buy sweet pastries from the man in the brown apron. We will never build forts with Aldovar and Georgette in the boardinghouse parlor, or play checkers on over-turned crates, bartering peanut shells and curling slivers of soap. Once I followed Aldovar up those steps under the umbrella, every-thing changed.

So I will let Odile think it was the shame of being unwed that drove me away, the confusion of being fallen and alone. I cannot tell her how the fire started and I cannot tell her why. I had expected Mother, upon hearing the news, to punish me in some way—call me harlot or jezebel, tell me I'd ruined the family, her good name—but she just shook her head tearfully. *This could hurt you, my dear—the labor might be dangerous. You might be risking your own life.*

Of all the things she could have said to me that day, nothing would have surprised me more. Of course childbirth was dangerous. But my body was such an instrument, so pliant and durable in my mind, capable of nearly anything—I hadn't yet worried about the pain.

She hesitated. I had never seen my mother doubt herself, never seen her stumble or pause to search for the right word. But I could tell she was wrestling with something. She had a hard time meeting my eye. I only looked at her levelly and said, *What do you mean?*

There were footsteps out in the hall. Mother held up her finger—*one minute*—and opened the door, called out to Odile. *Come in for a moment, will you?* But I didn't hear Odile answer—she just kept walking. Mother stood for a moment in the doorway. I saw her shoulders drop, heard her sigh, and then she turned slowly back to me, shutting the door behind her.

She took a seat in front of me, folded her hands. *You and your sister,* she said slowly, *you almost didn't live.*

I'd never heard the story of our birth—we had asked, of course, but she'd always shushed our questions and turned away. Now I began to wonder why.

Your birthmarks—, she said, and a feeling of dread began to overtake me. She tried again. *The day you were found—*

I looked her in the eyes and suddenly I knew. We weren't hers at all.

This is the story she told me. Seventeen years ago, on a foggy autumn morning in Manhattan, a woman named Mrs. Bloodworth found a suitcase on her doorstep. Puzzled, she looked up and down the street, but saw no one. There was no tag on the handle, no note of any kind. She was about to turn away, but then she heard a sound coming from inside, a faint rustling, like a bird in its nest. She knelt down and opened it. Inside were twin girls, newborns wrapped in newspaper. They were joined together at the head.

She took them inside, up the stairs to the nursery, which had been empty all summer. She threw the dusty sheets off the furniture and laid the girls in a crib. They were sallow and frail, heavy-lidded, but alive. She washed them with a warm sponge, fed them, swaddled them together and prayed they would live.

She wrote to my mother. The year before, Friendship had adopted two abandoned children for her burgeoning sideshow—a girl with four legs and an androgynous boy. If the twins survived, Mrs. Bloodworth thought they might find a home on the stages of Coney Island. Friendship wrote back and said she would come as soon as she could—she was busy opening a revue this week, but perhaps next?

Mrs. Bloodworth waited and nursed them, but the girls weren't getting any stronger. The smaller one was bent and curled beneath her sister, growing listless and weak by the hour. Her spine was twisted and soft, her body hunched unnaturally. As she bowed farther and farther to the side, her sister howled and kicked and stretched to fit her, her body like a pull of rubber.

Mrs. Bloodworth didn't know what to do. To save them, they had to be separated, and she'd never performed anything like that in her life, although she had seen some things in the war she would never forget. As a young nurse she had amputated men's arms and legs. She had tweezed bullets from their shoulders and swaddled their burns. She had set jawbones back into faces, sewn brains back into skulls. And so she lit her lamps and boiled her water. She cleaned her kit. She laid the children on the kitchen table beside a bottle of ether and said a prayer, then another—one for each child: two prayers that could keep each other company on the way to heaven. It was just a fine integument that joined the girls' head together—a flint of bone—but the veins were delicate, braided, snarled. She couldn't let her hands slip, her fingers shake. So she took a swig of rum and worked into the night, by the light of the oil lamp. She stayed up for two days and nights tending to them. Afterward, their heads limp and gauzed, the babies lay apart in a single crib. They took their milk slowly. They slept so deeply. Their color began to return. But if they weren't touching they cried—and so Mrs. Bloodworth kept them side by side, each soothed by the warmth from her sister. When Friendship arrived, Mrs. Bloodworth apologized—the girls would never again be the rarity she'd promised; she was sorry her friend had gotten her hopes up, that she'd come all this way. But when Friendship leaned over the crib and saw us—both looking back at her, Mrs. Bloodworth's neat stitching behind our ears—she couldn't walk away. Something changed within her, she said. That's when she knew we were hers. We were strong.

But we aren't yours, I seethed. *You lied my whole life!*

In my heart you are *mine,* Mother said tearfully. *I didn't want you to find out like this—I just want you to be safe. Who can know if you carry the same thing in your own body?*

I was stunned and betrayed. I didn't know what to believe. And so we argued.

After the funeral, while Odile pored over the account books at the kitchen table, I went quietly through the boxes in Mother's room—theater tickets, playbills, penny souvenirs from London and San Francisco, her old scrapbooks full of clippings. In a smaller box I found letters from this woman, Mrs. Bloodworth, all posted from an address on Doyers Street. I didn't know what to expect when I read them—something cold, perhaps, without color or life. But it was clear, from Mrs. Bloodworth's questions and musings, that Mother had written about me and Odile many times over the years, and very fondly, too. There were references to our exploits and mishaps— Odile flinging her brace from the pier with a savage whoop; a tender poem from Aldovar that Mother had found among my things (though she didn't embarrass me by mentioning it to my face, ever). I didn't tell Odile—I couldn't bear to show her the letters, not during her grief—but after the funeral I made the decision. I would go to see Mrs. Bloodworth myself. I wrote her a letter and packed my bags. When I arrived I would ask her: *Is my mother's story true? Did this all really happen? Where do I even belong?* And when she took me in, she told me that yes, this was our story, mine and Odile's, and that no matter what had happened before or since, my mother had always loved us. She offered to help me through my confinement—she would nurse me and shelter me, be vigilant for anything amiss. She would find a home for my baby, however it was born.

When Odile knocked on Mrs. Bloodworth's door that day, how could she have guessed that she'd crossed that very threshold before, joined with me in the woman's arms?

Sometimes as I sat in Mrs. Bloodworth's kitchen, warming my hands around a mug of tea—those early, gray summer mornings when I couldn't sleep, too shaken by my dreams—I imagined my other mother and father. I liked to think of them as handsome, well-mannered, with lovely names and matching furniture—I wondered if they were lonely, if they thought about me, regretted me, wondered where I was. Mouse was concerned with the same thing—had she ever passed her own father on the street? Would her mother come looking for her, even after thirteen years? We would sit there while the sun rose and warmed the table, dreaming up lives we'd never had. And because we hadn't lived them, and hadn't been disappointed by them, we believed they were somehow better—and ourselves better and braver within them.

But my blood parents were nameless to me and likely dead. They were no more than a curiosity, I came to realize—a puzzle and a sport in my times of distress, a diversion, a mirror fantasy at a sideshow. They had left us on a doorstep—too terrified, too confused, perhaps too ignorant to take care of us. Did they think it was an act of mercy, I wondered, or were they disgusted, ashamed? I will never know. But I grant them this—seventeen years after they abandoned me, they gave me an idea for escape, and for that I am grateful.

So here I am now. I live on a quiet street. I work in a small theater on the west side of town, for the Miss Chandelier revue. Alphie helped me find work there. But I'm no longer onstage. I'm doing something I love even more. I run lights. I pad the boys' breasts. I look down from the booth every night and take notes. It's a good show, rousing and rascally and full of lively music, and I'm proud of it; the boys are a blessing, and so is the crew. Besides, I never loved being a performer. I didn't love the rush the way that Mother did. I did it because it was expected of me—and perhaps, I regret to say, because I felt the need to make up for Odile's infirmity. I felt, for Mother's sake, that I had to have the strength and talent of two people. And her disappointment could be brutal, crushing, and her passion absolute. So here I take the reins. No more nights of sanding swords and mending costumes and sucking on ginger-bulbs to soothe my calamitous throat. No one here expects me to be a star. No man in a stovepipe hat hawks my talents to drunk passersby on the boardwalk. No one even has to know my tale.

Mrs. Bloodworth still lives on Doyers Street. Once in a while I pass by the shop—I'll spy her through the window, floating like an eye beyond the golden spectacles, leaning on a cane. It is safer for us to keep our distance, at least for now. But the shop goes on; the dens still thrive. Sometimes I'll go down and see Alphie on the waterfront. I have a few drinks with her and a kind British gentleman. I sit with them late into the night at a sidewalk café, watching the lights over the water. Alphie always brings me a bag of lemon drops. The gentleman tells stories of the sea. I've begun, slowly, to talk with my hands. I keep a small diary in my coat, alongside a penny pencil—the way Aldovar once did—so that even if I cannot speak, I am never without my voice.

And every day my daughter grows stronger. Every day she sees something new—she smiles, points, holds an ordinary spoon in her hands as if it's the most fascinating thing. Now she even walks. She plays in the wings, wanders onto the stage, brings her cookies to the boys while they try to land a number. I've named her Orchard Broome. I carry the words on me forever, so why not make them into something worthy? Her name on my body, my blood in hers. My daughter, whom I once dreaded and feared for, and now cannot possibly live without—this story is for her.

Here is what I understand now, what my mother used to tell me all those years ago—I have witnessed the sublime in the mundane, the things you see every day and fail to understand. Now I believe in the tiger in the grass. Because in truth, this story begins much earlier—before I boarded the ferry to Manhattan, before I knocked over the lamp, before I followed Aldovar up those steps on that rainy afternoon—before my sister and I were born to an unknown woman in the depths of the city.

It's a curious thing, the little incidents that lead to a life like this one. For when I knocked on Mrs. Bloodworth's door—when I stepped inside and shook her hand—I realized that I'd seen her before.

It was years ago, a Sunday afternoon—a cold, rainy day in the spring. I was being punished—I had cut off the toe of a boy on the beach; I had failed to show up at the theater as I'd promised. So I was housebound, sulky, forced to do chores while my mother entertained in the parlor. I scrubbed the kitchen floor, scoured the oven until my hands were cramped and raw. I lined up the shards of a plate I had broken and glued them back together. Meanwhile Mother laughed on the other side of the door. I was angry that the world without me was happy. Even Odile was gone, down at the boardinghouse with Aldovar and Georgette, playing cards and having fun—I suffered the injustice with no small amount of tears.

So there I was, bored and peevish, eavesdropping in the kitchen. I was told not to come out, to finish my work, but I couldn't help it—I peered through the door. Mother was sitting by the fire with a guest, a woman I didn't recognize. She was regal, tall, with a soft voice that I couldn't decipher—I could only hear mother's, lilting and droll. I had no idea what she could be doing here in our bungalow, drinking cheap coffee and laughing with my mother, who was stretched out in her easy chair, still in her stage makeup, smiling with all of her teeth. It seemed they talked forever, until dusk settled and I was sure everyone had forgotten me—waiting alone in the gloomy kitchen, scrounging around for the last pickled egg, keeping watch for Odile through the window. Then I heard footsteps in the parlor— Mother said "Good night," and closed the front door. Through the window I watched the woman disappear down the lane. I stared at the silhouette of her hat, black and sweeping against the golden sky.

In the kitchen afterward, as she was rinsing out the coffee cups, I asked Mother, "How do you know that woman?" This was clearly a woman from Manhattan, refined and well-dressed. An actress? I guessed. An opera singer?

"We're old friends," my mother explained to me. "I met her when I was about your age."

I couldn't think of any friends she still might have had, not after all these years—she'd left Punxsutawney, after all. She had traveled the world. She'd lived here most of her life and never looked back.

I watched her as she took out a cloth and dried the cups and set them back in the cupboard. I waited for her to continue, but she paused, halting over the dishrack. I reached out and touched her arm and saw, with surprise, that she hesitated, that her eyes had misted over. I had never seen my mother cry, not once in my life, not even when my father—her erstwhile husband, the man who had given us his name—left us for good and sailed back to a dreary sheep town in England, never to be heard from again. I suppose she knew by then that she could do it herself.

As I believed Odile could, too.

"It was back during the war," my mother told me.

She turned and lifted the edge of her skirt. She pointed to the scar that ran from her hip to her thigh, the wormy lavender line where a bullet had been dug from her skin. "Virginia Bloodworth sewed that up with a fiddle string," she said. "And for that I owe her my life."

LESLIE PARRY is a graduate of the Iowa Writers' Workshop. Her stories have appeared in *The Virginia Quarterly Review, The Missouri Review, The Cincinnati Review,* and *The PEN/O. Henry Prize Stories,* among other publications. She was recently a resident at Yaddo and the Kerouac House. Her writing has also received a National Magazine Award nomination and an honorable mention in *The Best American Short Stories.* She lives in Chicago.